The Good Death

S D Sykes

HODDER

First published in Great Britain in 2021 by Hodder & Stoughton
An Hachette UK company

This paperback edition published in 2022

1

A CIP catalogue record for this title is available from the British Library

Paperback ISBN 978 1 473 68023 4
eBook ISBN 978 1 473 68022 7

Typeset in Perpetua Std by Hewer Text UK Ltd, Edinburgh
Printed and bound in Great Britain by Clays Ltd, Elcograf S.p.A.

Hodder & Stoughton policy is to use papers that are natural, renewable
and recyclable products and made from wood grown in sustainable
forests. The logging and manufacturing processes are expected to
conform to the environmental regulations of the country of origin.

Hodder & Stoughton Ltd
Carmelite House
50 Victoria Embankment
London EC4Y 0DZ

www.hodder.co.uk

Praise for S D Sykes:

'The series gets better and better. It's building a very credible medieval world view while keeping the reader turning the pages at a gallop. And Oswald is such an appealing character, growing richer and deeper with every book, as the beastliness of his family becomes more and more evident. I loved the concept of a good death, too'
Andrew Taylor, author of *Ashes of London*

'The author's inventiveness and gift for description serves to deepen an already nuanced lead. Sykes solidifies her standing as a preeminent historical whodunit writer'
Publishers Weekly

'Sykes is a master at combining historical setting with mystery'
The Times

'The whodunnit aspect is neatly done, the family secrets and waspish relationships are intriguing, and humour and originality are abundant'
Daily Mail

'There's a nice, cliché-free sharpness to Sykes' writing . . . that suggests a medieval Raymond Chandler at work, and there are no phony celebrations of the peasantry or earth-mothers thrusting herbal concoctions down grateful throats. Plenty of action and interesting characters, without intervention of the libertarian modern conscience that so often wrecks the medieval historical novel'

About the author

S D Sykes lives in Kent with her husband. She is a graduate from Manchester University and has an MA in Writing from Sheffield Hallam. She attended the novel writing course at literary agents Curtis Brown where she was inspired to finish her first novel. She has also written for radio and has developed screenplays with Arts Council funding. *The Good Death* is the fifth novel to feature Oswald de Lacy, following *Plague Land*, *The Butcher Bird*, *City of Masks*, and *The Bone Fire*.

Also by S D Sykes

Plague Land
The Butcher Bird
City of Masks
The Bone Fire

For my sister, Kathy

Cuckoo Song

Sumer is icumen in,
Lhude sing cuccu!
Groweth sed, and bloweth med,
And springeth the wude nu —
Sing cuccu!

Awe bleteth after lomb,
Lhouth after calve cu;
Bulluc sterteth, bucke verteth,
Murie sing cuccu!

Cuccu, cuccu, well singes thu, cuccu;
Ne swike thu naver nu;
Sing cuccu, nu, sing cuccu,
Sing cuccu, sing cuccu, nu!

Summer has arrived,
Sing loudly, cuckoo!
The seed is growing, and the meadow is blooming,
And the wood springs anew,
Sing, cuckoo!

The ewe is bleating for her lamb,
The cow is lowing for her calf;
The bullock is prancing, the buck is farting,
Sing merrily, cuckoo!

Cuckoo, cuckoo, how well you sing, cuckoo,
Don't ever stop now.
Sing, cuckoo, now, sing cuckoo,
Sing, cuckoo; sing cuckoo, now!

Thirteenth-century poem

Prologue

Kent, June 1349

It was the first hot day of summer, and I had been sent to the forest to find Sundew. Brother Peter had told me where to look – in the quaking bog near to the river, where this rare flower hid amongst the Water Mint and the Creeping Jenny. According to Peter, the Sundew attracted flies to its leaves with a sweet-smelling gum. Once stuck there, the unfortunate creatures could not escape their fate – to be wrapped in the leaf and then ingested. It sounded like a strange plant to me, and it certainly grew in a strange enough place – in an open mire that was now steaming in the midday heat.

I had been told to return to the monastery with a full basket of leaves, as they were needed urgently to treat one of our oldest monks – a brother with an abscess on his leg that wouldn't heal. My tutor Brother Peter believed that the Sundew leaves would draw out the inflammation and ease the risk of the poison spreading throughout the patient's body – though I wondered if this were the only use Peter intended for this plant. I had also heard that it could be cooked up as a sedative. And sedation was most certainly needed in this case, for the old monk's constant groaning was so loud that it had disturbed the Abbot – a man whose patience was notoriously short. I knew that the Abbot had personally told Peter to solve the problem, even if it meant inducing the old monk into an almost permanent sleep.

As I tramped across the boggy ground that day, I must admit that I was feeling a little sorry for myself. The role of collecting herbs and plants in the forest had always belonged to a monk called Brother Merek. But then, about six weeks earlier, Merek had suddenly disappeared from the monastery, and somehow all of his chores had become mine. I half-wondered, as I made my way around the orange water of the bog, whether I might come across Merek's dead body between the moss and lousewort, since his last known whereabouts were somewhere in this area. Though this thought was just my own fanciful imagination, because it was much more likely that Merek had run away with a woman. At least that's what some of the brothers were saying.

As it turned out it wasn't Merek who I found that day. It was somebody else. But I'll soon come on to that.

After filling my basket with the leaves and stalks of the Sundew plant, I retreated to the trees beyond the bog, looking for some-where to wash my hands. The Sundew was as sticky as Peter had warned, and I needed to remove the gum and unpleasant scent from my skin. Not wanting to use the dirty water in the bog, I wandered a little way between the trees, where the soil was firmer and drier, soon finding a shallow stream. It was here, as I let my hands dangle in the cold water that I heard a noise behind me — a rustling and snapping of twigs. When I turned around, I saw a small face looking out at me from between the stems of a hazel bush. I recognised her immediately. It was Agnes Wheeler, a girl who sometimes came to the monastery to take away our clothes and sheets for washing and mending.

'What's the matter Agnes?' I called out. 'What are you doing here?'

But these simple words only terrified her. That's what I remember most. Her face was pale and panicked. Her eyes were flitting about in fear. I called out again offering my assistance, but this time she darted out from the bush and ran away from me, soon disappearing between the trees.

I only wanted to help her. That's why I chased the girl, even though I shouldn't have done it. The nearer I got to her, the faster she ran, until she came to the river. I thought she would stop here as it was a natural barrier. But instead she carried on, wading into the fast waters without looking back.

I shouted from the bank. 'Agnes. Stop! It's dangerous in there.'

She turned to speak to me at last, and I could see that her hair was tangled and her clothes were torn. 'Keep away,' she hissed. 'Keep away from me, priest!'

'But it's me, Agnes. Brother Oswald from Kintham Abbey,' I said, not understanding her reaction. I was only a few years older than Agnes and we had always been on good terms. I held out my hand and started to wade out, but this was my worst mistake of all. To escape me, she stepped out too far, where the water was deeper and the flow was faster. Within a flash she was washed away – her hands flailing as she vanished beneath the rapid, plunging flow.

I didn't know what to do. Try to swim after her, or run along the banks and try to fish her out. I chose the second option, as I wasn't a strong swimmer and my woollen habit was already heavy with water. I dragged myself out of the river, and found a path along the banks, hoping to catch sight of Agnes again. All the time, I was praying that she might have grabbed an overhead branch or clambered to safety at a shallow turn. But that's not what happened.

I eventually found Agnes, washed up in a pool, where the waters now lapped gently at the reeds, exhausted after their furious descent from the higher ground. It was here that I dragged her from the river and laid her out in the mud, trying to drain the water from her lungs. Her limp, silent body showed no signs of life however, no matter how hard I tried to shake the air back into her. She was dead, and it was my fault. I hadn't meant to kill her, but I had.

Chapter One

Mother pulled the sheet over her whiskery chin and looked at me in horror. 'God's bones, Oswald,' she said. 'What a dreadful story.'

'I know,' I replied. 'Not a day has passed when I haven't regretted my actions. Not a day has passed when I haven't wished I could return to save Agnes's life.'

Mother thought about this for a moment, before she muttered something under her breath and then closed her eyes. I thought she was feigning sleep at first, but soon she began to snore, proving that she hadn't been thoroughly horrified – not in a sufficient amount to prevent sleep. In her hand she clutched a letter – a fold of yellowing parchment with a broken wax seal at its centre. As her chest rose and fell, this letter slipped from her hand and rested momentarily on the bedspread, giving me the idea to grab it from her possession and throw it into the fire. This would have solved a lot of problems, and I might have done it, except that Mother half-opened an eye and the opportunity passed.

'Would you like me to carry on?' I asked, pulling my guilty hand away. The light was poor, since the heavy worsted curtains were drawn on three sides of the bed – but I could still see that

Mother's face was gaunt, the loose skin hanging from her bones as if she were already dead.

'I don't know what's the matter with you, Oswald,' she muttered. 'Coming up with stories like that.'

'I'm sorry,' I said. 'I thought you wanted to know the truth about the letter before you died.'

She opened her eyes fully, and swivelled her head towards me like an owl. 'I'm not dying,' she said. 'Everybody's wrong about that. I'll be dancing at the next Lammas Day Feast. Don't you worry.'

'Well, I sincerely hope that's true,' I replied, as a knock sounded at the door.

I answered it, finding that our visitor was my mother's physician, Thomas Crouch – a thin-faced, uninspiring man who was proudly brandishing his jar of leeches. 'May I attend to Lady Somershill now?' he asked, trying to peer over my shoulder. 'It is time for your mother's bloodletting.'

I might have refused him entry, had Mother not already heard his voice. 'Let him in, Oswald,' she called. 'Let him in. Crouch is the very man to cure me. He has the finest leeches in Kent, you know. They can extract the foulest of corruptions.'

I bowed my head and stood aside to allow Crouch to pass, not wanting to look too closely as he stood beside Mother's bed and lifted the lid from his jar. To this day I remain unconvinced about the efficacy of bloodletting, particularly with the assistance of leeches. I am a rare detractor from this popular treatment, however. If a person believes that attaching bloodsuckers to their flesh will provide some benefit, then who am I to disagree?

Mother was certainly an enthusiast. And if her claims about these particular leeches were true, then they would have a colossal task ahead of them. For there was a deep and embedded seam of corruption to draw from Mother's body.

'I'll come back later,' I said, 'when you're feeling more sanguine.'

'Don't bother,' she answered. 'I'll be down for supper.'

But Mother was not down for supper. The leeches had drained more than the corruption from her body, and we were informed by Crouch that she was too exhausted to even take a bowl of broth that evening. The next morning, she would only admit a priest and her lady's maid to her chamber, prompting us all to believe that her death was imminent. The carpenter was called upon to finish her coffin. Her grave was dug beside the chapel and letters were written, but not yet sent, to distant relatives.

Whilst the commotion and drama of a looming family death was sweeping through the house, I'm ashamed to say that I spent my time wondering how I might now retrieve the fateful letter whilst it was still in Mother's possession. I knew it would be difficult to steal, since Mother had placed it under the neckline of her chemise for security — as if she had anticipated a theft. Even so, I made sure to sit outside the door of her bedchamber, ensuring that I would be the first person to hear the news of her death, able to quickly grab the letter before anybody else found it.

Luckily I had no companions at this station, as my sister Clemence was far more interested in sorting out Mother's jewellery than keeping this vigil. But, as it turned out, it was all an unnecessary panic. Mother did not die that day. Nor the next. And by the third day, she was back to her usual self — issuing instructions that the children of the household should stop running about in the courtyard, that she should be served sweeter food at more regular intervals, and that my presence at her bedside was required immediately.

I re-entered the room, thankful that her maid had thought to crush some rosemary and lavender in a mortar. By this point Mother had been locked inside those four walls for many weeks, and was beginning to exude the sour odour of a stable that needs mucking out. That said, her appearance was much fresher than her perfume. In fact, she was in fine spirits – sitting upright in the bed, with her hair neatly combed under a veil and an embroidered shawl draped over her shoulders. I noticed immediately that she was holding the letter in her right hand.

'Please, Oswald, sit down,' she instructed, as she pointed to the stool beside the bed. 'Now that I'm feeling better, I'd like you to carry on with your story.'

'Are you sure?' I replied, duly taking my place beside her. 'You've been very unwell, and my story upset you the last time we spoke.'

She gave a short, dismissive laugh and then waved the folded letter under my nose. 'I don't think I have a choice, do you?'

I shrugged. 'Perhaps you could just give me the letter?' I suggested optimistically. 'I could throw it into the fire, and we need never think about it again.'

Mother ignored this idea. 'This is your handwriting, isn't it?' she said, pointing at the wording on the front fold of the letter.

'Yes,' I sighed. 'It is.' How vividly I remembered writing this letter, even though I hadn't seen the thing for over twenty years. Not that I had ever forgotten about its existence, of course. Indeed, when I'd first been recalled to Somershill from the monastery, I had spent many days searching for this same letter in my father's library. He and my two older brothers had only just died of plague, bestowing the role of Lord Somershill onto my shoulders at the tender age of eighteen. Yet, despite the fact that I was now the keeper of over a thousand acres and the master of a grand house, complete with hunting forests, cellars and a stable of fine horses, I had cared for little except finding this letter. In truth, I had needed to find it and destroy it, before it destroyed me. But, after many weeks of fruitless searching, I had finally given up – satisfying myself that the letter had been lost or thrown away, never suspecting that it had lain hidden amongst my mother's possessions for all these years. Never suspecting that she would discover it when she was setting her worldly affairs in order before she died.

Mother cleared her throat. 'So you agree there are questions to be answered?' she said.

I hesitated. 'Yes.'

She let a smile creep across her face, taking some pleasure in my discomfort. 'Would you call it a confession, Oswald?' she asked, her eyes now glinting with mischief.

I looked away, not wanting to agree. But she was right. This was a confession. If I did not tell this story to my mother before she died, then I would be haunted by its shadow forever. 'Very well,' I said. 'Let us call it a confession.' I paused and took her hand, finding it cold to the touch. 'But some parts of this story will be very difficult for you to hear,' I said.

'I'm sure I'll survive,' she said smugly.

'There are worse episodes than the girl drowning in the river,' I said. 'I want you to understand that before I begin.'

'Don't talk to me like a child, Oswald,' she replied. 'I know my own mind. If I say that I wish to hear this story, then that's exactly what I want.'

'Even if this causes you pain?'

'What do you mean?' she said. 'Why would any of this cause pain to me?'

'You'll see.'

She thought for a moment, before she heaved a long sigh and leant back against the bolster. Her eyes had lost their newly found spirit, and suddenly she looked crumpled and diminished, like a deflated bladder ball.

'I wish that I had not found this letter, Oswald,' she whispered. 'I truly do. I was about to throw it into the fire, alongside the other bits and pieces that need to go before I die. But then I recognised your handwriting, and I made the mistake of reading the damned thing.' She lifted the fold of parchment and deposited it back in its safe place, between her breast and the chemise. 'How can I have a good death, Oswald, if I do not know the truth about this letter?' she asked me. 'How can I journey to the next world and shorten my time in Purgatory, if I have not heard my son's confession? What hope is there for me, if I have not forgiven you fully in my heart? You know that the priest will ask me this question, before I receive the Last Sacraments? Have I forgiven those who have harmed me? What do you expect me to do? Lie to the man?'

'No. Of course not,' I said. 'But If I tell you the truth, please don't be angry that you've heard it.'

She hesitated. 'How can I be angry?' she replied. 'Unless your confession is not true.'

'It will be true, Mother,' I said. 'Believe me.'

'Very well then,' she answered. 'Please continue, Oswald.' She closed her eyes. 'You were on a riverbank, I believe. The girl was dead.'

Chapter Two

Kent, June 1349

I tried to lift Agnes's body, but she was difficult to manoeuvre – her limbs loose and heavy, her head falling from side to side with the weight of a net sinker. Even though I had dealt with dead bodies in the infirmary on many occasions before, I always had the help of a lay brother. I had never had to struggle myself with the wayward pliancy of a corpse in the first minutes of death. The way it flops and dangles and cannot be controlled.

I gave up after a while and laid her body back onto the ground, unable to look away from her drowned features, and seeing a very different girl to the Agnes I'd known from her visits to Kintham Abbey. Her face was blank and serene – as if she could never have uttered those words to me. *Keep away from me, priest*. Why had she spoken that way? Why had she not been able to distinguish between friend and foe? I felt my stomach roll, knowing that I should have realised that Agnes wanted to be left alone. If I had been more cautious, then the girl would still be alive.

I rubbed a tear from the corner of my eye and compelled myself to look closer, soon seeing the reason for Agnes's terror. Her clothes were bloodstained and roughly torn – injuries that could not have been caused by drowning. It was clear to me now that she had been attacked before we met. There were bruises on her arms, and there were banded, red marks at her wrists and ankles. I had seen such wounds in the past – on the prisoners who were dragged straight from the Royal Court to the gallows. They were the ugly, raw abrasions that can only be burnt into the skin by the rough fibres of a rope.

I pushed Agnes's matted, wet hair away from her forehead to reveal a fragile and delicately beautiful face that was almost childlike. I had an idea what had happened to her, though I chose not to raise her skirts to confirm my suspicion. And what would I have been looking for, anyway? Instead, I pushed Agnes gently onto her side, to see if there were injuries elsewhere on her body. And sure enough, once I had poked my fingers through the gaping rip in the back of her tunic, I could see a series of scratches on her skin – each deep and vertical, starting at her shoulder and ending at the small of her back.

I closed the tunic, pulling one side of the rip across the other, feeling sickened at first before experiencing another emotion – the sudden urge to run away. Nobody knew that I had been here. Nobody knew that I'd met Agnes and then mistakenly chased her into the river. Running away seemed like the right solution, and yet, even as I stood up, I knew that this was an act of pure cowardice. I could not leave Agnes's body here, at the mercy of the foxes and the crows.

My next thought was to bury her, but I could not dig out a grave with my bare hands – not a pit deep enough to lay her body to rest. And anyway, if I were to bury her, then I would have no proof that she had been attacked. Her injuries were important pieces of evidence – pointers that might help to identify the person who had previously assaulted her. There was only one option – to face up to the consequences of my mistake and return Agnes to her home village of Stonebrook. Once she was there, the Constable could examine her body before she was buried in a Christian grave.

I made reasonable progress with this plan, once I'd established that it was easier to lift Agnes's body over my shoulder and not in my arms. I still had to rest at regular intervals, however, where I suffered the same, terrible temptation – that I should hide her body in some undergrowth and then run away. It was an urge that I eventually managed to conquer, though I took no pride in this. The memory of that day still haunts me. Trudging through the forest with a dead girl draped over my shoulder like a wet shawl – her arms and legs swinging against my habit. The smell of her sodden, woollen clothes mixed with the stink of my sweat.

It was late afternoon when I finally stumbled into the small village of Stonebrook – a settlement of timber-framed houses and barns, arranged along a single street that ended at a muddy green. It was an unremarkable sort of place – the type of village you might find at the bottom of any country lane in Kent. Its only exceptional feature was the wall of trees that surrounded the outlying fields, bearing down on the place like an army of occupation and giving Stonebrook an oppressive, enclosed feel.

A crowd had gathered about me by the time that I reached the village green, where I rested Agnes's body onto a grassy bank and called for somebody to rouse her family and the local Constable. Stonebrook was located in lands that were owned by my monastery, so the villagers were used to seeing monks from Kintham about the place – though not one who had arrived with a dead girl across his shoulder. Needless to say, I was met with a mixture of astonishment and horror, as the villagers jostled against one another to get a look at Agnes's miserable, stiffening body. The women huddled together and held their hands to their mouths in shock. The men simply stared on in silence.

Eventually word of Agnes's death reached her only family – her mother, a poor widow named Beatrice Wheeler, who now pushed her way through the crowd and then grasped at her daughter's body, shaking the girl repeatedly as if this might bring her back to life. I didn't intervene, but when Beatrice had finally convinced herself that nothing would wake Agnes, I gently touched her shoulder. She looked up at me with eyes that were dazed and bewildered. 'Is it true, what they're saying?' she said. 'You found her?'

I nodded. 'Yes,' I said. 'It was me.'

'Where?'

'In the forest,' I answered. 'Near to the mire.'

'The mire?' The woman's mouth hung open, before her face tightened into a frown. 'But I don't understand,' she said. 'What was Agnes doing by the mire?' She shook her head repeatedly. 'Why would she go there? It doesn't make sense.'

'How long has Agnes been missing?' I asked. It was a simple question, but Beatrice Wheeler stared back at me as if she didn't understand what I was saying. I tried again, realising that she was frozen in shock. 'When did you last see Agnes?'

She finally nodded at this, as if the words had just been translated to her from a foreign language. 'Five days ago,' she said. 'Agnes left home on Thursday and never came back.'

'Where was she going?'

Once again her reaction to my question was delayed. 'To market,' she said. 'Agnes was taking some cheese to sell.'

'And you have no idea where she's been since then?'

She shook her head. 'I've been out searching for her,' the woman mumbled as she passed her hand through her daughter's damp, tangled hair, and then patted her sodden tunic. 'What's happened to Agnes?' she whispered, looking up at me with reddened eyes. 'I don't understand. Why is she wet?'

I took a deep breath. 'She drowned,' I said.

'Drowned?' she replied, now screwing her face back into the frown. 'In the mire?'

'No. It was the river.'

'But I thought you said that you found her by the mire?'

I was saved from having to answer this difficult question, by the arrival of the village Constable, John Roach, who scythed his way through the crowd like a reaping hook. Though we had never spoken before, I had seen Roach on many occasions previously at Kintham, when he came to make his monthly reports on the conduct of the villagers to the Abbot. Roach was a tall, conceited man with a shock of thick, white hair that rested on the top of his head like a sheepskin mat.

'What's going on?' he said, his voice booming across the heads of the smaller men and women. 'Why are you all gathered up in this rabble?'

A woman piped up from the crowd. 'It's Agnes Wheeler,' she said. 'The girl is dead.'

Roach drew in his chin and looked at the woman with disdain. 'What are you talking about?'

'See for yourself,' she answered, pointing at Agnes's body. 'Looks dead to me.'

Roach stepped forward to make his inspection, unable to disguise his initial disgust at Agnes's corpse, before gingerly prodding at her cold skin with the end of his finger. For a man responsible for dealing with crime in this village, Roach seemed curiously squeamish about death.

It was time for me to speak up. I could delay it no longer. 'I was the one who found her body,' I said, tapping him on the shoulder.

John Roach turned his head to face mine. We were the same height, meaning that he was unable to look down at me – a fact that seemed to cause him a certain level of consternation. 'And who are you?' he demanded to know.

I took a deep breath. 'My name is Brother Oswald,' I replied. 'I'm a novice at Kintham Abbey and son of Henry de Lacy.' I added this last piece of information in the hope that the mention of my family name would unsettle him a little. The de Lacy lands abutted those of the monastery, and my father was known to be rich and powerful.

'And what have you got to do with this?' he replied with much the same tone as he had previously used with the village woman.

Clearly my familial connections had not impressed him in the least.

'I met Agnes by the mire,' I answered.

He raised his eyebrows, causing his thick white fringe to tickle at his eyes. 'You met her?' he said, pushing the hair from his face. 'I thought you said that you found her body. So, which is it?' The crowd about us fell silent. They wanted to know the answer to this question as much as Roach did.

'Well, yes,' I answered. 'You see, she was alive when I met her.'

Roach folded his arms. 'Well, she's not alive now, is she? So, what happened to her?'

My heart began to pound, thrumming its beat in my eardrums. 'It was a chance meeting,' I said, suddenly realising how weak my story sounded. 'I was in the forest, collecting Sundew. It's a plant we use for—'

'Thank you,' Roach cut in. 'We know the uses for Sundew. I asked you why this girl is dead.'

I looked away, feeling panicked and wanting to rest my eyes anywhere but in the orbit of Roach's fierce gaze. For a moment I alighted upon a new face in the crowd – a woman who was watching me with a pair of the palest blue eyes. She was much taller and better dressed than any of the other women of the village, and appeared to stand in a space all of her own, as if she had the power to part the waves. Our eyes locked for a moment and she gave me an encouraging smile.

I wiped my forehead and turned back to Roach. 'I was washing my hands in a stream, when I found Agnes hiding in some bushes.' I paused. 'I called out to her and asked if she needed my help.'

'And what did she say?'

I hesitated, when I should have been more definite. I was telling the truth and had nothing to hide. 'She just shied away from me.' I said, before taking a moment to choose my next words. 'She seemed disturbed.'

'Disturbed?' he said. 'How was she disturbed?'

'Agnes didn't recognise me,' I replied. 'Even though we've met many times before at Kintham.' When Roach didn't make a reply to this, I continued. 'I tried to help her,' I said, clearing my throat in time to thwart the sob that had been stubbornly brewing. 'But she misunderstood me.'

'Why's that?' asked Roach.

'She seemed to think that I meant her some harm,' I said.

He raised an eyebrow. 'And did you?'

'No, of course not,' I replied indignantly. 'Agnes had been attacked by somebody before we met,' I continued. 'She was not of sound mind.'

'How do you know that?'

'Look at her body, Master Roach. See her injuries for yourself.'

'I will make all of the necessary examinations later,' said Roach. 'But you still haven't explained why Agnes was alive when you met her, and now she is dead.'

'Agnes ran away when I tried to help her,' I replied, looking about to see all the faces in the crowd staring back at me intently. 'She wasn't looking where she was going,' I croaked.

'Speak up,' said Roach. 'We can't hear you.'

'I tried to save her, I really did,' I continued, raising my voice but speaking far too quickly as a consequence. 'But Agnes ran into the river before I could stop her. I called out to her and told her to come back to the safety of the river bank, but it was too late. She was swept away by the strong currents.' I paused for a moment to catch my breath. 'I shouted at Agnes. Telling her to grasp a branch, or work her way towards the bank. But she couldn't hear me. By the time that I caught up with her downstream, she had drowned,' I said. 'I did everything that I could to save her.'

I felt exhausted and cornered, unable to think of anything else to say, but when I looked up, I was met by a wall of silent faces. My story had horrified the gathered crowd and they looked back at me with a mixture of scorn and suspicion. I cast my eyes across to the tall woman again, hoping to receive another friendly, encouraging smile, but even she avoided my gaze.

I was finally saved by a group of young women who pushed their way to the front of the crowd like a gang of wrestlers at a charter fair. At the head of this phalanx was Aldith Brewer, a young woman I recognised from the manorial court, where she often appeared to pay her childwyte fines to the Abbey. By the size of her belly, it seemed she would soon be back in front of the Abbot, for her latest bastard was surely due to be born at any day.

Aldith glanced at Agnes's body, before turning to point an accusing finger at Roach. 'I told you to go looking for her, didn't I? And now she's dead.'

Roach puffed out his chest like a cockerel. 'Oh yes,' he replied contemptuously. 'And what's this got to do with you?'

Aldith folded her arms across her belly. This pair were clearly old adversaries. 'I told you Agnes was in danger, didn't I?' she said. 'Just like my sister was. Just like all of those other women who never came back.'

'What others?' I asked, trying to intervene. Aldith either didn't hear my question, or deliberately chose to ignore me. 'How do we know those women aren't dead as well?' she asked Roach. 'Beaten and ill-used like poor Agnes here?'

Roach groaned. 'How many times do I have to say this same thing to you, Aldith Brewer? They're not dead. They left Stonebrook of their own accord.'

'That's not true,' said Aldith, 'and you know it. My sister Mary only went out to collect firewood, and she never came back. You should have gone looking for her that same day. But you couldn't be bothered.' The women about Aldith nodded and muttered in support. 'You wouldn't listen, would you? Mary meant nothing to you. Just because she was poor.'

'Your sister ran off,' replied Roach, as his cheeks started to redden. 'Everybody knew what she was like.'

'And what was that, then?' asked Aldith.

'Wilful and flighty.'

'She was not!'

'Yes, she was,' replied Roach. 'You just don't want to accept the truth.' The redness in his cheeks had deepened to form angry purple patches. 'That she took herself off to London.'

'You always say that,' replied Aldith. 'But it's not true. Mary was taken by somebody. Just like all those other missing women. You should have searched for them, John Roach. You should have done your duty.'

'Search for them?' Roach threw back his head in laughter. 'I'll tell you where to find your sister. With all the others who ran away. Working in the bankside stews of Southwark. Spreading their legs for a farthing.'

'That is enough, Roach!' I shouted, not able to listen to this any longer. 'There is a dead girl in our midst. Not to mention her grieving mother.'

Roach was shocked by my outburst and took a moment to compose himself. 'Well, who's fault is that, then?' he answered, turning to face me.

'It sounds to me as if you should have searched for these other missing women,' I replied. 'You bear some blame here.'

Roach stepped towards me, and had the audacity to put a heavy hand on my shoulder. 'So it's my mistake, is it? I like the cheek of that,' he said. 'You chase a girl into a river, and some-how I'm to blame?' I tried to pull away, but his grip was strong and I couldn't escape. 'It sounds to me like there's more to this story,' he leant forward to whisper into my ear. 'Did Agnes catch your fancy, Brother Oswald?' he said. 'Is that why you frightened her? Is that why she ran from you?'

'No,' I replied. 'Of course not.'

I was trying to escape his grasp when Aldith came to my rescue again, elbowing her way between the two of us. 'Leave him alone,' she said. 'At least Brother Oswald tried to help Agnes. That's more than you've ever done.'

Roach glowered. 'I thought I told you to be quiet.'

His threats had no effect on Aldith. She was commendably unafraid of the man. 'Brother Oswald's from the Abbey,' she continued. 'So if he says that he tried to help Agnes, then I believe him. We all should.'

Roach balled his fist. 'What would you know about abbeys, you dirty little trollop? You don't even attend mass at the parish church.'

'Least I'm not a liar and a hypocrite, like you,' Aldith replied, now squaring up to Roach – despite being much smaller than her opponent, not to mention heavily pregnant. 'Happy to court us at night, and then call us to court in the morning.'

'Shut up!' he hissed.

'Do you know what we call you, John Roach?' she said. 'The Cock Roach.' She turned to the other women in her gang and laughed. 'What's it we say?' she called out. 'Lock your doors. The Cock Roach is coming!'

Roach swung his arm at her face but Aldith swerved as deftly as a fist-fighter, prompting jeers from the other women that only served to infuriate the man further.

'Get here you little strumpet!' he shouted. 'I'd rather slake my lust with the cheapest Winchester goose, than bed the likes of you!' As he attempted to pounce on Aldith, fists bunched and arms spinning, the other women bundled in to form a defensive circle about their leader. I went to pull Roach away, but received a thump on the side of my jaw for my efforts. I fell back in pain, as the tall woman with the pale blue eyes finally stepped in and was able to bring this brawl to a swift conclusion. She pushed her way past the women and laid a hand on John Roach's arm, causing him to freeze immediately at her touch.

'Stop this, Master Roach,' she said, her voice confident and clear, and missing all of the drawl of the local accent. 'What a disgraceful spectacle.'

Roach dusted himself down. 'She started it,' he muttered, pointing at Aldith.

The tall woman ignored this remark and turned to me. 'Brother Oswald. I apologise that you have had to witness such behaviour.'

'Spirits are running high,' I replied, rubbing my jaw.

'Even so. You should have been shown more gratitude. Particularly as you made such an effort to return this poor girl's body to her home.'

'Thank you,' I said sheepishly – acutely aware that I didn't deserve any thanks, let alone an apology.

The woman bestowed another of those warm smiles upon me. 'You say that Agnes Wheeler was already injured when you found her?' she said.

'That's right,' I answered.

'Did she tell you who had attacked her?'

I shook my head.

'Did she say anything to you at all?'

I thought for a moment, considering whether or not to reveal Agnes's last words to me – *Keep away from me, priest*. Given my current circumstances and the potential for these words to be misunderstood, I shook my head and told a fib – saying that Agnes had remained silent.

The tall woman gave a sigh. 'What a shame,' she replied. 'We might have learnt more.' With this she turned back to Roach, with a sweep of her skirts. 'We should raise the Hue and Cry, Master Roach. You must search the forest for the man who attacked Agnes.'

'That's what we asked him to do last time,' said Aldith, with some umbrage that somebody else was taking charge. 'But Roach wouldn't do it, would he? Said he was too busy.'

The tall woman bowed her head respectfully to Aldith in response. 'I'm sorry to hear that,' she said calmly. 'In that case, we must not make the same mistake again. We cannot risk losing any more women.'

Aldith poked her nose in the air, but thought better of responding.

Roach, however, was unable to hold his tongue. 'Now just wait a moment,' he said. 'There's nothing to say that those women are—'

He wasn't allowed to finish his sentence. 'Master Roach,' exclaimed the tall woman. 'Agnes Wheeler was attacked in the forest. What more reason do you need to mount a Hue and Cry?' Roach opened his mouth to make a second objection, but she cut across him. 'Brother Oswald will tell you where to look,' she said. 'Won't you?' she added, casting her eyes back to mine. I nodded keenly in response.

'But—' he said, trying his very best to make one last objection.

'A Hue and Cry,' she announced with an air of finality. 'Search the forest with a band of men. Agnes's attacker must still be out there somewhere.'

Roach admitted defeat at last, unable to stand his ground against the power and authority of this woman. He puffed out his chest, pushed the mop of white hair from his face and then muttered a surly agreement.

As he shoved his way back through from the crowd, the women jostled and jeered at his retreating back. 'Cockroach, Cockroach,' they called, until he was finally out of sight.

Chapter Three

The crowd slowly drifted away, giving my new friend the opportunity to introduce herself. 'I don't believe that we've met before,' she said, inclining her head to mine. 'My name is Maud Woodstock. Perhaps you know my father, Roger?'

I nodded, since I knew the family name well, though I'd never met the famous Maud Woodstock in person. At least I now understood the reason for John Roach's grudging deference towards her, as Roger Woodstock was the richest farmer in the manor of Kintham, renting over two hundred acres from the Abbey and amassing more wealth than many local noblemen. He had been an industrious but difficult man until being struck down by an apoplexy more than two years earlier – meaning that Maud, his only surviving child, had been forced to take over his farm. I'd heard that Woodstock could no longer walk, talk or even feed himself, though he had remained alive, which was testament to the quality of his daughter's care, since most patients with this same affliction do not last longer than a month. I had often heard the Abbot complaining about having to deal with Maud rather than her father, particularly as she had gained a reputation for being high-handed and obstinate. But I paid no heed to the Abbot's opinion. The man had little regard for women – tending to dismiss them all as dull and stupid, especially the interesting and intelligent ones.

'Thank you for speaking up on my behalf,' I said.

'You're very welcome,' she replied, with another bow of her head. 'I've known your father and brothers in Somershill for many years. We often work together.' I nodded faintly, as I knew very little of my family's business dealings, having spent most of my life in the monastery. She must have detected this, as she quickly added, 'I sometimes join forces with William and Richard to trade fleeces in London. We achieve better prices by collaborating.'

We took a moment to step to one side as two men carried Agnes's body away from the green towards the distant cottages. One man held her under her arms. The other man held on to her feet. Unfortunately Agnes now looked like a drunken customer being removed from an inn by a couple of brothel bullies. The girl's mother, Beatrice Wheeler, staggered along at the tail end of this sad procession, being comforted by a group of three women.

Maud cleared her throat and turned back to look at me. 'But there are worse things than being undercut by a crooked London merchant, aren't there?' she said. When I didn't answer, she added, 'What a terrible experience this has been for you.'

I wiped my face clear of sweat. 'Far worse for Agnes,' I replied, once again feeling the strong urge to sob. It had become an involuntary compulsion, like shivering or an attack of hiccups.

'You mustn't blame yourself,' said Maud. 'It wasn't your fault that the poor girl died.'

'Yes, it was.'

She patted my arm softly. 'You were only trying to help Agnes,' she replied. 'Your intentions were good. There's no reason for you to feel any guilt.'

As her hands touched my sleeve I couldn't help but notice how handsome they were. They belonged to a noblewoman – smooth and white, without the callouses and red patches of hands that have worked the soil, washed clothes or tended to animals. For a moment I was transfixed by their beauty, before I experienced another sensation. How strange it was to feel the touch of a woman, after so many years of male company. Even though her hand was laid on the thick, woollen cloth of my habit, it felt as if she had caressed my skin. This feeling was both unwelcome and enormously thrilling.

Maud and I waited together on the green until Roach returned with a group of about six men for the promised Hue and Cry. This number was the minimum requirement for any such search, so it hardly displayed any efforts on Roach's behalf. If this deficiency were not bad enough, the men Roach had picked were a tired, dispirited bunch – not the baying mob that I might have expected to ride into the forest and search for Agnes's attacker.

Even so, I did my best to inspire their anger and sense of outrage at her death. After describing the many injuries that I'd seen on Agnes's body, I then identified the spot near to the mire, where I'd first seen her hiding. It was possible that this was near to the place where she'd been attacked, so I felt it was worth mentioning. My words had little effect on these men, however. They rode away with sullen, indifferent shrugs, as if they'd been asked to round up a missing goat or a disobedient dog. I watched them leave, holding out little hope that they would find anything. This supposed Hue and Cry was little more than a perfunctory exercise, carried out by Roach to satisfy Maud's command.

Maud had the kindness to stay with me for a little longer, but once the last rider had disappeared into the woodland at the edge of the village, she curtsied and excused herself, saying that she needed to attend to her sick father.

Now completely alone, I found myself wondering if I should return to the monastery, before deciding to stay. It wouldn't reflect well on me if I deserted Stonebrook before the Hue and Cry returned, and so I found a bench at the other side of the green, where there was a little shade. Every so often, I could see people looking at me from the main street of Stonebrook. Their glances were quickly averted, but I was being watched closely nonetheless. The attention was unnerving, so I resorted to studying the weave of my habit with great interest. This diversion worked well enough, until I found a stain of Agnes's blood, which only made me feel worse. In the end, I focused on an arbitrary spot in the near distance, and tried my very best not to make eye contact with anybody.

I don't know how long I sat there, as time stretches and bends when a person is waiting for something to happen. A moment can seem to last for hours. Eventually I was approached by a short and stout man – one of the fellows who had lifted Agnes's body from the green. He came to me with the news that the dead girl's mother wanted to speak to me again. The poor woman was in a wretched state, but I cannot lie. The prospect of another cross-examination about the circumstances of Agnes's death was most unwelcome. On the other hand, I could hardly blame the woman for requesting this interview. There was little more that I could reveal, but she deserved the opportunity to ask.

Beatrice Wheeler lived in a small cottage, situated in some rough land behind the larger houses that lined the main street of Stonebrook. It was a poor sort of place. At first glance, I had assumed it was a stable, for there were no windows and the thatched roof was slipping down over the door, like an overgrown fringe. I only realised that this was a place of human habitation when I heard female voices coming from inside, as they tried to comfort Beatrice's loud sobbing. Hearing her distress, I was tempted to turn back, except that I'd been followed to the door by the stout man – who now stood behind me with his arms crossed. I therefore had no choice but to open the rickety door and step across the threshold to come face to face with the same three women who I'd seen accompanying Beatrice across the green. Now they crowded around her bed, forming a protective wall in front of the woman. Though they looked at me with cold and reproachful eyes, I held their gaze, since I could not bear the alternative view. Just to my right Agnes's body was laid out on a table, with a linen sheet covering her small, battered body.

'Who's there?' came Beatrice's voice from behind the brown tunics and grey kirtles.

'It's the young priest,' whispered a girl who had removed her veil to reveal a head of hair that was so brightly auburn it was almost pink, like the colour of raw salmon. Even in this meagre light, it was luminous.

I spoke up. 'I understand that Mistress Wheeler wanted to see me,' I said. 'But I can come back later, if it pleases her.'

I stepped back in the hope of being excused, only for Beatrice to poke her arm and then her head through the skirts. 'No. I will see you now,' she said.

The women parted a little. 'Are you sure this is a good idea, Beatrice?' said her oldest companion – a woman who was wearing a white apron covered in filthy handprints. 'It may upset you.' The woman threw me a hostile look and then leant down to whisper into Beatrice's ear. 'After what he did.'

Beatrice sat up in her bed. 'I must see him,' she said firmly, pushing the woman aside. 'Leave us to speak alone.'

Her companions exchanged glances with one another, before they reluctantly filed out of the cottage, only to gather outside. We could see their feet huddled together through the large gap beneath the door.

Beatrice beckoned me to come closer and to take a seat on a stool beside the bed. I did as she asked and then waited for her to speak, only to find that she remained completely silent. Instead of saying anything, she just stared at me. Her red, tear-stained eyes not moving from my face.

'I'm so sorry about Agnes,' I said, not knowing how else to start this conversation.

If I thought this would break her torpor, then I was wrong, as she continued to stare until she finally spoke in a thin whisper. 'There's something that I want to tell you,' she said.

I hesitated, trying to conceal my instinctive wariness. For some reason I already knew that I didn't want to hear what she had to say. 'Oh yes?'

'Agnes was William's daughter,' she told me, blurting out the words.

I knew a number of Williams. Probably more than ten. After all, it is one of the most common Christian names in England. 'I'm sorry, Mistress Wheeler,' I mumbled. 'But which William are you talking about?'

She puffed out a short laugh at this. 'Your brother William.'

'I don't think that we have a Brother William at Kintham.'

'I'm not talking about a monk at your monastery,' she said. 'I'm talking about your brother. William de Lacy.'

My mouth fell open at this disclosure. 'I'm sorry,' I mumbled. 'I don't understand. Are you saying that Agnes was William's daughter?'

'Yes.'

I was nearly lost for words. 'Are you sure?'

'Of course I'm sure,' she hissed. 'And we were both sixteen. So I knew what I was doing, if that's what's troubling you? William didn't force me.'

'Does William know about this?' I asked, as a terrible realisation dawned on me. If this woman's story were true, then I had caused the death of my own niece.

'No,' she replied.

'But perhaps you should have told him?'

She managed a snort of laughter at this. 'Your brother is the son of Lord Somershill. And who am I? The daughter of a villein. The man who looked after your family's hounds.' She shook her head and sighed. 'When I found out that I was carrying a child, it was easier for me to keep quiet and marry Ned Wheeler,' she said. 'Nobody ever guessed that Agnes was William's daughter.'

'So why are you telling me now?'

'Because I want you to tell William that she's dead. I regret keeping it a secret. He should know what's happened.' As I struggled to find an answer to this proposal, she inclined her head to mine and whispered, 'My poor Agnes looked so much like your brother. Every day I could see William's likeness in her lovely face.' She paused. 'I often wondered if you would notice it, Brother Oswald? Especially as Agnes came to the monastery so often.'

Sweat was beading on my forehead. 'I'm sorry,' I replied. 'I never noticed a resemblance.'

Beatrice didn't like this answer. In an instant she'd thrown back the blanket and swung her feet to the floor. 'Come with me,' she said, stumbling over to the table where Agnes's body lay beneath its sheet. I followed reluctantly, keeping my eyes to the floor as Beatrice pulled back the linen pall that covered her daughter's face.

'Don't look away,' she said. 'This is Agnes. Your brother's child.' She grasped my right hand and thrust it against Agnes's cheek, so that my fingertips rested against her cold flesh. I wanted to pull away and yet I couldn't. 'Look at her, Brother Oswald.'

'I can't—'

'Look at her,' she repeated. 'Can you not see your brother's likeness?'

I forced myself to look down again at Agnes's tiny face for the last time, for she would be buried in the next few hours. I would tell you that the girl appeared to be at peace – but there was little human about her any longer. Her features were shrunken and artificial.

Beatrice squeezed my hand tightly, as if this would encourage me to agree with her. 'I want you to write to William,' she said. 'To tell him about Agnes.' She squeezed again. 'You owe it to me.'

I tried to pull my hand away, but her grip was tight. 'I'm not sure,' I said. 'Perhaps it would be better if you wrote it yourself?'

'No,' she answered. 'I can't read or write. You have to do it for me.'

I went to protest, but the words stuck on my tongue and wouldn't escape. I didn't want to write such a letter. In fact the idea was almost horrifying. William was twelve years my senior, and the proud owner of a volatile and cruel temper. I had spent my childhood at Somershill trying to avoid his attentions at all costs, not least because he had delighted in tormenting me.

Beatrice sensed my reluctance. 'Agnes was your brother's child. You said yourself that I should have told him.'

'Yes, but—'

'Will you do it?' she asked, glaring into my face. 'Yes or no?'

'I don't know.'

'Write to him, Brother Oswald,' she said, squeezing my hand again. 'Promise me that you'll do it.'

I mumbled some kind of answer and then pulled my hand from hers, before I blundered out into the daylight, knocking into the gaggle of women who were still huddled by the door. The girl with the red hair went to speak to me, so I quickly straightened up and strode away, hoping to put as much space between myself and Beatrice's cottage as possible.

I had nearly reached the street when the girl caught up with me and called out my name. I didn't want to speak to her, but she darted in front of me, and I had no choice but to stop.

'We don't blame you for what happened to Agnes, Brother Oswald,' she said. 'At least I don't.'

'Thank you,' I replied, trying to set off again, only to find that she darted in front of me for a second time.

'But was Agnes very frightened?' she asked. 'That's what worries me.'

'She wasn't herself,' I answered, hoping that the girl would take the hint and leave me alone.

'Did she suffer?' she asked, looking up into my eyes. 'I hate to think of Agnes suffering.'

Of course Agnes had suffered! What a foolish question. The girl had escaped a brutal attacker, only to be driven into the waters of a swollen river by a well-meaning fool. She could not have had a worse end to her life. I went to tell this girl as much when I spotted a familiar face on the other side of the green, striding towards me with his usual determination – his arms swinging in time with his legs, the sun reflecting from the dome of his bald head.

I was so pleased to see Brother Peter, that I nearly ran into his arms – only holding back at the last moment when I realised that this feeling wasn't mutual.

'By God, Oswald. Is this story true?' he said, grasping me by the shoulders. He looked strained and jumpy, as if he needed a drink. 'You found an injured girl in the forest and then chased her into a river?'

'It was Agnes Wheeler,' I answered softly, aware that the girl with red hair was creeping closer, no doubt with the intention of eavesdropping on our conversation. 'She was terrified,' I added. 'Somebody had attacked her.'

'I only sent you out to find some herbs,' he replied, dropping his hands from my shoulders and rolling his eyes in exasperation. 'When you didn't return, I thought you'd disappeared. Just like Brother Merek.'

I was about to answer when Peter suddenly turned on our red-haired spy. By this point the girl had crept up behind us and was practically touching my habit. 'This is nothing to do with you, Rose Brunham,' he boomed. 'Get out of here. Go on!' For a moment the girl stood her ground, locking her eyes insolently with Peter's until she finally retreated, wandering slowly back to Beatrice Wheeler's cottage – no doubt to immediately repeat our conversation to the other women.

Once we were certain that she was out of earshot, Peter turned back to me. 'How, in the name of Christ and all the saints, did you get yourself involved in such trouble?'

'I was only trying to help Agnes,' I answered. 'But she wouldn't listen to me. It was as if she didn't know me.' I felt the tears welling now and I was unable to stop them.

Peter's sympathy extended to another roll of his eyes. 'You have no idea of the danger that you put yourself in, Oswald. Turning up in a village like this, carrying the body of a dead girl.'

'I couldn't just leave Agnes in the forest, could I?'

'But you should have come to me first,' he said. 'I could have helped you, Oswald.' When I didn't answer, he grasped my arm, and pulled me forward. 'Come on. Let's get you out of here. Before you cause any more trouble.'

'But I need to wait for the Hue and Cry to return,' I replied. 'I want to see if they found anything.'

'Let the Constable deal with it,' said Peter. 'You've done enough today.'

'But—'

'We need to get back to the monastery,' he snapped. 'The Abbot wants to urgently speak to everybody.'

'What about?'

Peter heaved a sigh. 'There are worse troubles in the world than this, Oswald,' he said darkly. 'Believe me.'

Peter tipped my elbow and led me to the other side of the village green, where I was relieved to find that he'd arrived with a spare pony. After this, we rode for the monastery – not that my departure from Stonebrook passed completely without event. A number of villagers tried to speak to me as we trotted along the main street, only for Peter to loudly warn them all to go home and mind their own business.

As we rode past a grand, four-bay hall that dwarfed all the other homes in this street, Maud Woodstock came to her door to watch me leave. Our eyes met for a moment, before she nodded her head to mine and gave me another of those beautiful and reassuring smiles. I was about to return the gesture, when I saw that Peter was glaring at me, his face stern and disapproving.

'Eyes ahead, Oswald,' he barked. 'Eyes ahead.'

Chapter Four

'So this girl was William's child?' said Mother, drawing her hands across her face to pull the skin taut. The effect was disconcerting. For a moment, I saw something of Mother's youthful beauty, until she relaxed her hands and released her jowls from their hiding place.

'That's right,' I answered.

'Oh dear,' she whispered. 'Not another one.'

'You knew about this?' I said.

'I heard rumours and gossip,' she replied. 'As a woman does, in a house like this. And, of course, William's wife used to make complaints about his behaviour all the time,' she added. 'I used to hear the pair of them arguing about his brood of bastards.'

'Brood?'

She sighed. 'Yes. There were quite a few of these children, I believe. But it was so long ago, Oswald.'

'Did you know any of them?'

'No, no. I think they all died in the Plague, along with William's wife and legitimate children.' She cleared her throat. 'At least that's what I was told. I didn't ask too many questions, as I'm sure you'll understand.'

'What about Agnes Wheeler? Did you know about her? Or her mother, Beatrice?'

Mother raised her eyes to the ceiling in thought. 'Wheeler? Um . . . Wheeler?' she echoed. 'There aren't any Wheelers in Somershill. But I do remember a Beatrice some years ago,' she said vaguely. 'She was the daughter of our fewterer, Thomas Westlake. The girl used to come up to the house with her father, when he was readying the hounds for a hunt.' She puffed a laugh. 'It must have been her, I suppose. Especially as the foolish girl was always making sheep's eyes at William.' Mother gave another puff. 'And let's face it. A man of William's appetite rarely turns down a free meal.'

I couldn't help but groan at this comment.

'Oh Oswald,' she snapped in response. 'Stop being so prudish. Not all men are as devoted to their wives as you seem to be.' Her eyes brightened. 'It might do you some good to be more like your brother William for once. Why not father a few bastards about the estate? Seeing as your own wife is yet to bear you a child, let alone a son.'

I cleared my throat, determined not to rise to this provocation. 'I have a son, thank you, Mother. I don't need another.'

'Yes, but Hugh is at Oxford. And we all know the dangers of being a student in that city, don't we? Remember the riot on St Scholastica's Day? Many young noblemen lost their lives. Slaughtered by ignorant townsfolk. Just because a student complained about some wine in a tavern.'

'That was fifteen years ago, Mother,' I replied. 'Oxford is very peaceful now and Hugh is in no danger whatsoever.'

'A man needs more than one heir, Oswald. Look at your own circumstances. You had two older brothers, and yet they both suddenly died.' She sucked in her cheeks. 'With only one son, the de Lacy name hangs by the thinnest of threads. It could be cut in a moment. Never forget that. Your first wife was able to bear you a son . . . though the poor woman died in the process.

But your second wife seems to be barren. You do not even have a daughter with the woman.'

'Thank you, Mother,' I replied, clapping my hands together to indicate that this topic was finished. 'I'll remember those wise words. But, in the meantime, would you like me to carry on with my story?' I said. 'I can spare a little longer.'

Mother regarded me sourly. Though I had been Lord Somershill for twenty years now, Mother still outranked me. At least in her own mind. It was her prerogative to start and end a conversation, and not mine. 'No, thank you,' she said. 'I've heard quite enough today. Come back in the morning.'

That night I ate supper in the solar with my wife Filomena, my sister Clemence and her son Henry. It was an awkward occasion, especially as Henry was seated next to Filomena, and was refusing to speak in anything but a succession of mumbles. Though my nephew was twenty years old and now as tall as a tree, Henry still had the capacity to behave like an awkward child, particularly in Filomena's presence.

I knew the reason for this behaviour, of course, as my beautiful Venetian wife often provoked such a reaction in young men, causing them to blush and fidget whenever they saw her. It seemed that Henry's fixation was growing more chronic by the day, however. His eyes endlessly followed Filomena about the room – until she looked at him, that is – at which point he would cast his gaze to the floor, as if he couldn't stand the sight of her. If they were seated together at the dinner table then Henry found himself almost unable to speak. Just to make matters worse, Clemence, seemingly ignorant of the true cause of her son's bashfulness, would always attempt to use these opportunities to bring her son out of his shell.

'What is your opinion on that theory, Henry?' Clemence might say. Or: 'You used to know that boy, didn't you?' Or: 'What do you think we should do, Henry? You have a good eye for these matters.' As a younger boy, Henry had always reacted to his mother's barrage of questions by stuttering an answer. As he became older, he had developed a mastery of the insouciant shrug, knowing that this embarrassed his mother in company.

That particular evening Clemence was attempting to drag some information from Henry about a young woman called Matilda de Graveney – a girl whom Clemence considered to be a potential match for her son. Henry clearly didn't want to talk on this subject, especially in front of Filomena, but Clemence didn't read the signs and persisted, like a judge cross-questioning a witness in court. It didn't help matters that Filomena kept throwing Henry sympathetic and encouraging smiles, in the hope that this would ease his embarrassment and persuade him to talk. My wife meant well, but these morsels of her attention were causing a level of anxiety in the young man that was almost painful to observe.

'Does Matilda like hawking?' Clemence asked Henry, as she spooned some egg custard into her mouth. Henry replied with the usual rise and fall of his shoulders, a tactic that did not deter my sister. Clemence continued. 'You really should invite Matilda and her sisters to Versey Castle. It would give you the opportunity to show them our estate and advance your suit. And, of course, we have some of the best hunting forests in Kent, so she is bound to be impressed.'

This was an exaggeration, but I wasn't in the mood to contradict my sister. If Clemence wanted to embroider the merits of Versey – the estate she had gained through her marriage – then I was minded to keep quiet. Such boasting stopped her from complaining that Somershill had come to me, based solely on my sex, even though she was my older sibling.

Clemence pointed her spoon at Henry. 'You really should get on with it, you know. I've heard that Hugh Swanland has been courting Matilda.'

'They are betrothed,' replied Henry with a groan.

'Not formally,' said Clemence. 'Her aunt told me that Matilda's family might be open to a superior suitor. And Matilda has no brothers, you know. So there would be a lot for us to gain from such a union. The de Graveneys have all of the land to the north of the Darent.'

At this Henry stood up and stalked out of the room, before stomping loudly down the steps to the Great Hall.

'Where are you going?' Clemence called after him. 'Come and finish your custard, Henry. It's good for you. It will balance your bile.'

'God's bones, Clemence,' I said, once Henry was out of earshot. 'You're sounding more and more like Mother. Soon you'll be telling him to eat more fish to improve his seed.'

Clemence responded with a fierce flash of her dark eyes, before placing the spoon next to her bowl and composing herself. 'Talking of Mother. How is she?' She paused to purse her lips. 'I would visit more often, but you've been hogging all of her time.'

'Nonsense,' I replied, knowing the exact way to counter this. 'You are welcome to visit Mother at any time.' I pointed towards the passageway that led from this solar into the private bedchambers. 'She is only a few feet away.'

Sensing an argument was brewing between myself and Clemence, Filomena quickly rose to her feet and made her excuses, claiming that it was time to join our guests in the Great Hall. My wife dusted down her dress, gave me a sweet smile and followed Henry down the stairs.

Clemence glanced at Filomena's fitted green kirtle with a peeved expression and then pointedly smoothed her own loose skirts across her knees. In recent years, my older sister had taken to dressing like a nun – in a plain black tunic and a long veil, with a string of rosary beads hanging from her belt. Clemence might have been a widow, but there was no reason for her to dress with such drab austerity. I could never tell whether this clothing was an attempt at genuine spirituality, or simply an affectation? In any case, I made sure not to ask.

'Filomena is in a hurry to get downstairs,' remarked Clemence, using that judgmental tone that she reserved for my wife.

'She doesn't like it when we quarrel,' I replied.

My sister grunted a laugh. 'I think her eagerness has more to do with our guest,' she said. 'Sir John has promised to tell everybody a new tale tonight.' She sniffed derisively. 'Something about the beast of Damascus, I believe.' She rearranged the thick fold of cloth that hung about her chin. 'Where on earth did you find that man, Oswald?' she said with a sigh. 'He's dreadful.'

'Sir John is an old friend,' I said. 'We've known each other for years.'

Clemence raised an eyebrow. Did she know that this was a lie?

'I enjoy his company,' I added, feeling the need to defend my guest.

'But did you have to invite the man to stay here until the spring, Oswald?' asked Clemence. 'I find his stories highly improbable.'

'Sir John is lifting our spirits,' I replied. 'I'm pleased he is here.'

'But he eats like a horse,' she said. 'It must be costing a great deal to feed him. And when he sucks bones at the table, it is enough to make me feel sick.'

'It's a custom he picked up when sailing, I believe. I've barely noticed it.' Which was not true, but I couldn't tell my sister that I found Sir John's manners equally disturbing. She was looking for any excuse to criticise the man.

Clemence frowned. 'Where did you say that you met him?' she asked me. 'I can't say that I've ever heard his name before.'

I mumbled something about London, not wanting to reveal the true story behind my friendship with Sir John for fear of ridicule. I couldn't admit to my sister that I'd only met the man for the first time in the summer and subsequently invited him to Somershill on a whim. That this invitation had been a gesture intended to prove to my wife that I had friends, after Filomena had accused me of being a recluse. That I had quickly regretted this reckless invitation, when Sir John had accepted immediately, leaving me to wonder why his diary was so free?

Luckily this arrangement had turned out well for both of us. Sir John, seemingly impoverished after a life of travelling, was happy to earn his keep by entertaining the household each night with lurid descriptions of his many adventures. In return, I had achieved a far superior result than proving my wife wrong, I had succeeded in delighting her. Filomena now had the company that she craved – a guest to alleviate the boredom of the long winter nights in a rural manor house. Somebody with more conversation than the price of fleeces, the lineage of a ram or the condition of local ditches.

Sir John kept my wife entertained and that was good enough for me. 'You wanted to speak about Mother, I believe?' I said, quickly changing the subject.

Clemence cleared her throat. 'What is there to say, Oswald? Each time I go into her bedchamber, Mother pretends to be asleep. I sit and pray with her, but only until her snoring becomes too bothersome.' My sister paused for a moment and felt at the beads of her rosary. 'I'm sure that she does it on purpose.'

Excessive praying was another of Clemence's recently acquired affectations, often conducted in public, with the expectation that others would participate, or at least have the courtesy to remain silent. It was a habit that Mother had struggled to respect when in good health, so it was hardly surprising that she could not tolerate it now, on her deathbed.

'Why not return home to Versey?' I suggested. 'I can call you here very quickly, if Mother's condition worsens. It is less than a day's ride from Somershill.'

Clemence thought this over, trying to determine whether or not I had some secret motive. 'No, no. I must stay here. I want to ensure that Mother has a good death,' she replied. 'She must repent of her sins before she quits this earth.'

'The priest is always close at hand,' I told her. 'He can administer the Last Sacraments at a moment's notice.'

Clemence gave me a sidelong glance. 'And are Mother's affairs in order?'

I couldn't help but sigh at this question, for this was the true reason that my sister had stationed herself at Somershill and would not leave until Mother's body was buried beside the family chapel. 'Yes, Clemence,' I replied. 'I have not interfered with Mother's will since we last spoke on this subject.' I put my hand to my chin and pretended to be thinking. 'Now . . . when was that? Oh yes,' I said with a flourish. 'It was yesterday, wasn't it?' I patted the ends of my fingers onto the back of her hand. 'You mustn't worry,' I said mockingly. 'Mother has not changed her mind. You still inherit all of her jewellery.'

Clemence withdrew her hand sharply in obvious offence, but couldn't hide a sly and satisfied smile at the mention of her inheritance, even though she was seldom seen wearing any jewellery, other than a simple crucifix. Indeed, all of Mother's polished gemstones, gilded brooches and enamelled rings would go unnoticed beneath Clemence's copious folds of black clothing. Filomena was the member of our family who liked to wear jewellery, but unfortunately my wife was not to be bequeathed a single copper pendant nor an iron hairpin.

'I'm not worried about the will,' Clemence lied. 'I only ask about Mother's preparedness for death, because it's important that she's severed all links to the material world,' she added. 'Otherwise her time in Purgatory will be long, no matter how much I pray for her.'

'Mother has forsaken all her worldly goods,' I said. 'Don't worry.'

'I am relieved to hear that,' said Clemence. 'But what about forgiveness, Oswald? You know that Mother must pardon all those who have harmed her. Otherwise she will suffer eternal damnation.'

How could I tell my sister the truth? That I was spending hours at my mother's bedside, seeking her forgiveness for a matter that must never, ever come to Clemence's attention.

'We're working on Mother's forgiveness,' I said. 'As you know, it has not always been one of Mother's best qualities.'

Clemence cocked her head to one side. 'Well, I disagree. I think she's forgiven a great deal over the years,' she said darkly, before rising to her feet. 'Particularly when it concerns you.'

The next morning, I took up my post again at Mother's side, after the maid had fed her a watery porridge and a cup of nettle ale. Mother was wearing a mantle that was richly embroidered with silk threads and amber beads – so she had not forsaken all of her worldly goods. Not yet, at least.

We talked for a while about the weather and the family, once she had bidden me to pull back the drapes about her bed. Mother's physician, the disagreeable Crouch, had ordered the maid to keep these drapes closed all day, but what harm was there in some daylight and fresh air? Mother was dying, so there was no need for her to end her days in this dark suffocation. And anyway, I needed Mother to remain as alert as possible in the time we had left. I could not accept forgiveness from a defeated woman. Mother needed to pardon me whilst fully in charge of her senses.

Once she was relaxed and attentive, I began again.

Chapter Five

Kent, June 1349

We had known plague was coming. Who didn't? We had all read the letter from the Bishop of Winchester, written the previous autumn, in which he described the dangers that were approaching from the Continent. We knew about the foulness of the disease, the speed at which it spread and the difficulties we would experience in dealing with the dead. But, somehow, in June 1349, the Plague had not yet reached our small corner of Kent. Instead it had marched its way to London and forgotten to stop.

The brothers of Kintham Abbey felt blessed and vindicated by this exemption, as if we had been the people of Israel in the Book of Exodus, painting our doors with the blood of a male goat and waiting for the Lord God to pass over our house. They believed that our deliverance was due to the holy shield we had created about the lands of our Benedictine monastery – deploying protective measures as prescribed by the Archbishop himself. Indeed, we had received a long and thorough list of instructions from the man. We were to recite the fifteen psalms of degrees every Wednesday and Sunday in the choir. We were to make a solemn weekly procession about the walls of the monastery – with bare feet and heads bowed, as we devoutly said the Lord's

Prayer and the Hail Mary, lamenting our sins and calling for
Heavenly deliverance. We were to station the statue of Saint
Sebastian in the narthex of the abbey, in the hope that this saint
of intercession would speak to God on our behalf.

So far these acts of penitence had appeared to protect us. Or
so the other brothers firmly believed. I kept my opinion on this
matter to myself, however. Kintham was a minor abbey
surrounded by unimportant villages devoted to a mixture of
forestry and sheep-farming. The villagers hadn't, as yet, attended
the annual fleece fairs, so the movement in and out of the parish
had been limited. It seemed to me that we had been saved by our
remoteness and unimportance.

When Peter and I finally returned from Stonebrook it was already
evening – but instead of heading to the refectory for our supper,
we hurried straight to the Chapter House to attend the Abbot's
mystery meeting. The brothers usually only went into this room
for the Chapter Mass each morning after breakfast, so there was a
buzz of anticipation about the cloisters and passageways. We all
knew that something was afoot, since the Abbot never did anything
out of the ordinary – not unless it was absolutely necessary.

We filed into this octagonal hall and sat in our allocated places
on the benches about the walls – the novices and lay brothers
near to the door, the older and more important monks nearer to
the Abbot. Peter, not wanting to leave me on my own after my
experiences in Stonebrook, asked another novice to budge along
the bench, and took a seat next to mine. I will admit that I was
pleased to have the benefit of his supportive presence beside me,
as I felt exhausted and insubstantial after Agnes's death – ready
to slip off the bench at a moment's notice.

I remember looking across the hall at the Abbot's face that
night, seeing his features illuminated by the bank of candlelight,
while the rest of us sunk into the shadows. I could tell, by looking at the man's pinched lips and furrowed brow, that he was

annoyed to be here. At this time of night the Abbot was usually teaching Syriac to some poor unfortunate oblate.

Thankfully, I'd never been subjected to the Abbot's enthusiasm for ancient languages, nor been a victim of his nightly prowls, as I had shared a cell with Brother Peter since I was seven, rather than sleeping with the other novices and oblates in the eastern cloister. This was a privilege secured by my family's status, and made at their request. Perhaps they had heard rumours about the Abbot and had wanted to keep me safe from his roving eye? In any case, Peter had been unofficially engaged as my guardian within Kintham, and he had always taken his duties very seriously. We slept in the same room at night and worked together in the infirmary during the day. It was Peter, rather than the novice master Brother Thomas, who had been responsible for most of my education at Kintham. I was Peter's pupil and he was my tutor. Sometimes I tired of his assiduous care, since he could be over-protective and hard to please, but mostly I was thankful for his friendship. I don't think I could have stomached life at the monastery without him.

The Abbot began the meeting that night with a prayer, followed by some meaningless preamble about God's grace, which only served to raise the anticipation among the brothers. At last he came to the point.

'I have learnt, today, that plague has reached Fallowsden,' he announced. When this caused a murmur, he raised his hands to silence us all. 'Listen, please.' He cleared his throat. 'I am told that some of the Abbey's tenants, a man and his three daughters, have died of the affliction. As this village is within our estate, we must accept that plague is now at our door.'

The babbled muttering returned, which the Abbot silenced this time by banging his walking stick upon the floor. It was not permitted to speak in the Chapter House, not unless the Abbot specifically asked you a question.

He continued. 'As a result of this sad news, I've decided that we must end all visits to this village. In fact, I have ordered the forest gates to Fallowsden be closed, and none of the villagers allowed to leave.'

'But what about the poor souls who are stuck there? What are they to do?' The voice belonged to Brother James. The oldest monk in the abbey. Probably the only man who might have dared to speak out in these circumstances. 'Are we to abandon them to a death without the sacraments? Is this the act of a true Christian?'

The murmuring started again, and only stopped when the Abbot banged his stick upon the stone floor for a second time. The silver tip created a harsh and resounding echo about the cold walls. 'Perhaps you would like to move to Fallowsden, Brother James?' suggested the Abbot. 'That way you may serve these people yourself.'

Brother James frowned at this. 'I'm a very old man, Father Abbot,' he protested. 'I would only be a burden to these people. I can hardly see my hand in front of my face. Might not a younger man go?' He looked about the room, squinting into the shadows in the hope that somebody would come forward.

The muttering rose yet again, combined this time with a little nervous laughter at James's suggestion and subsequent excuse for not going himself. In any case, it was soon evident that nobody wanted to volunteer to take up this position.

The Abbot struck the floor again. 'Very well,' he said. 'It is God's decision that the village must be isolated. I have spent most of this day in prayer and meditation and God himself has told me how to proceed. We will not visit Fallowsden, nor will we suffer any of their number to come amongst us.'

It was the cellarer, Brother Wilfred's turn to speak out. 'But I wonder if we have enough provisions, Father Abbot?' he asked. 'Most of our wheat flour comes from that village. And our supplies are already low until the next harvest.'

'It is your job to find alternatives,' replied the Abbot. 'I expect you to plan our meals with your usual exactitude.' Brother Wilfred pulled a face which did not go unmissed by the Abbot. 'We are about to endure the evils of Pestilence,' he warned. 'You have all heard the stories yourself, and read the letters we have received from the Archbishop and from the King. We have been blessed, thus far, in being spared from these sufferings. But now it seems that plague has arrived, and so it is our Christian duty to keep ourselves safe. If we invite sickness into this monastery, then we risk the very future of our brotherhood. We are already a shrinking band, with fewer oblates and novices coming to us each year. With a spate of deaths, we may find ourselves subsumed under the auspices of a larger Abbey. And then, who will tend with due care to the spiritual needs of our villages? For the sake of those poor souls, we must keep ourselves safe.'

This was something of a long speech from the Abbot, who usually kept away from any flourishes of oratory at these meetings, preferring instead to rush through proceedings, after the reading of a chapter from the Rule of St Benedict. In fact, he seemed to have exhausted himself.

'Are we allowed to visit Stonebrook?' inquired another monk. It was Brother Louis, the sacrist. 'There is no plague in that village. Perhaps we may purchase flour at their mill instead?'

'The older monks may visit Stonebrook,' said the Abbot. 'But only if it is absolutely necessary. From now on all the novices and oblates are confined to the monastery.'

At the name of Stonebrook I started to shake, as if all of the emotions that I'd been holding back all day attempted to escape in one overpowering surge.

Brother Peter laid a hand upon my shoulder and whispered into my ear. 'Take control of yourself, Oswald. People will see.'

It was a little late for this warning, however. Brother Cuthbert, a short-tempered and fastidious monk, turned around from the bench in front of us. 'Is the boy unwell?' he asked Peter in a loud whisper.

'No,' said Peter. 'Brother Oswald is just a little tired, that's all.'

Cuthbert narrowed his eyes. 'Has he been near to Fallowsden recently?'

Peter sat up straight. He could be intimidating when required. 'Of course not,' he said. 'The boy hasn't been anywhere near that village.'

Brother Cuthbert turned back to face the Abbot. 'I hope you're telling the truth, Peter,' he said. 'Because I'm told that the Plague starts with a shivering fever.'

'Brother Oswald does not have the Plague,' said Peter, leaning forward to hiss into Cuthbert's ear. 'Don't you dare to make such a suggestion.'

'Says you,' said Brother Cuthbert, turning around once again to throw me one of his condescending glances. 'How are we to know the boy isn't sick?'

'Because I say so,' said Peter. 'I'm the infirmarer of this monastery. And he is in my care.'

Brother Cuthbert laughed in response. 'We all know of the extra care and attention you bestow upon that boy, Peter. Some of us wonder if this is entirely proper?'

Peter put his hand onto Cuthbert's shoulder and let his fingers dig into the black wool of his habit. 'Keep your sordid insinuations to yourself,' he said.

'Or what?' said Cuthbert, trying to shake off Peter's hand.

The exchange had come to the Abbot's attention. 'What is going on over there?' he shouted, peering across the heads of the other monks. 'There is supposed to be silence in this Chapter House.'

Peter released Brother Cuthbert's shoulder and bowed his head. 'My apologies, Father Abbot,' he called out. 'Brother Cuthbert was complimenting your leadership in these trying times.'

The Abbot huffed at this answer, unmoved by this clumsy flattery. 'Thank you, Brother Peter,' came his reply. 'These are, indeed, trying times, so we must all pray for God's guidance.' With this, the Abbot rose to his feet, muttered the words of a Hail Mary and then left the room to its confusion.

That night, Peter gave me a draught of lavender and chamomile, and wrapped my body in a thick blanket. I had stopped shaking, though I still felt cold and nauseous.

'Don't be frightened about the Plague,' said Peter, as he placed a candle next to my bed. 'We'll be safe inside the monastery.'

I turned over – not wanting to look at his face. 'I'm not worried about plague,' I said.

'Is it the girl, then?' asked Peter, with a sigh. 'Is that what all this shaking and agitation is about?'

'Don't mock me,' I replied. 'You didn't watch her drown.'

'I'm not mocking you,' said Peter, as he sat down next to me on the bed – the frame creaking at his additional weight.

'Agnes wouldn't let me help her,' I said. 'She just spat some words at me, as if we'd never met before.'

'What words?'

I hesitated before answering. '*Keep away from me, priest.*'

Peter took a deep breath. 'Those were her exact words?'

'Yes.'

He thought for a while. 'Did you mention this to anybody in Stonebrook?' he asked me.

I hesitated again. 'No. I was afraid that they might misunderstand.'

'Well, thank the Lord for that,' he replied. 'At least you showed some sense in the end. These people can be so ignorant, Oswald. So easily inflamed.' He paused. 'You wouldn't believe the things I've been told in Confession. It is no wonder that the Abbey can never get a priest to stay in Stonebrook for long. Take that red-haired girl, for instance. Rose Brunham. A true beggar's mistress.'

I turned back over to face Peter. 'What's wrong with her?'

He ignored this question. 'Or the tales I've heard about Maud Woodstock,' he continued. 'Unbelievable.'

'I liked her.'

Peter puffed a laugh. 'Oh yes. I saw you smiling at Mistress Woodstock when we left the village, Oswald.' He leant forward to stare me in the eye. 'She might have a pretty face, but be warned. The woman is a she-wolf. A termagant.'

'I disagree,' I replied, making sure not to look away. 'Maud Woodstock has courage. John Roach only raised the Hue and Cry at her insistence.'

Peter drew back and laughed again. 'That sounds like her,' he said. 'Always telling people what to do.'

'Roach didn't care that Agnes had been attacked, Brother Peter,' I retorted, irritated by his criticism of Maud. 'That's why she became involved. Did you know that there are five women missing already from Stonebrook? And Roach has never looked for one of them.'

Peter shrugged this away. 'There could be any number of reasons why those women have disappeared,' he said, lifting his leather flask to his lips and taking a long sip of the contents. For a moment I caught the strong perfume of mead as the nutmeg, cinnamon and honey invaded my nostrils.

'Are you going to say that they ran away to London as well?' I said. 'Because that's John Roach's theory.'

Peter put the flask down. 'I'm not discussing this with you tonight, Oswald,' he said. 'You're too tired and emotional.' He stood up to walk away, but I put my hand out and grabbed his arm.

'There's something else I need to tell you,' I said.

Peter looked back at me wearily. 'Can't it wait until the morning?' he asked. 'I think we've both had enough for one day.'

'No, it can't,' I said, pushing back the blanket, and sitting up. 'I found out something else about Agnes Wheeler today,' I told Peter, finding that my heart was beating faster even at the mention of her name. 'I should have told you earlier. But I couldn't find the words.'

'Oh yes?'

I hesitated, still uncertain that I wanted to tell Peter this story. 'My brother William was Agnes's father,' I admitted.

'What?' Peter immediately stiffened. 'Who told you that?'

'Her mother, Beatrice Wheeler. I was called to the family cottage, after Agnes's body was laid out. Beatrice told me herself.'

Peter pulled at the mole on his neck. 'Well, I've never heard that story before,' he said. 'Not even in the Confessional.'

'That's because Beatrice has kept it secret for years,' I replied. 'Even from William himself.'

Peter grunted a laugh. 'Well, if that's the case, then I very much doubt that the story is true.'

'Why would Beatrice Wheeler lie about something like that?'

Peter groaned and shook his head. 'Because the woman wants some money from you, Oswald. That's why. She wants you to feel even more guilty about Agnes than you do already.'

'She didn't ask for any money.'

Peter gave another puff of scornful laughter. 'She will do. Don't you worry,' he said, before patting me on the shoulder in that condescending manner that really irritated me. 'I just told you what the people of Stonebrook are like, Oswald. They lie without shame.'

I pushed his hand away. 'I think Beatrice Wheeler was telling the truth.'

'You don't know that.'

'She asked me to write to William and tell him about Agnes. Why would she ask me to do that, if her story were a lie?'

'Well, I hope you refused,' he said, now looking exasperated. When I didn't answer, he continued. 'God's bones, Oswald! Whatever next?' Peter started to pace the room. 'Are you completely senseless?' he added. 'You, of all people, know what William's temper is like.'

'But what if Agnes is his daughter?' I whispered.

Peter approached again and now made the point of looming over me. 'And how do you think William would receive this news?' he asked me, lowering his head to breathe fumes into my face. 'Tell me that?'

'I don't know,' I stammered.

'Exactly,' he replied. 'And what would you write?' I shrugged, trying to turn my nostrils away from the stink of his breath. 'Dear William, I'm writing to tell you that you have a bastard daughter in Stonebrook. You probably don't remember fathering this child . . . but just in case you do, I'm sorry to say that I accidentally killed her today.'

I shrank further away, unable to answer.

Sensing that he had upset me, Peter put his hand upon my shoulder again and softened his voice. 'Oswald. Please listen to me. You must not write to William. It would only anger him unnecessarily. This woman's story is almost certainly a lie.'

'But what if it isn't?' I said, looking up into his face and feeling tears budding in the corners of each eye. 'Not only have I killed an innocent girl. She is also my own flesh and blood.'

As tears rolled down my cheeks, Peter took a seat beside me again. 'Come on, Oswald,' he said, patting my hand lightly. 'Don't be upset.'

'I can't forgive myself,' I sobbed.

'But you didn't kill her,' he answered, now locking me in an embrace. It was firm and comforting and so very welcome. 'The girl's death was an accident,' he said. 'You know that, and so does everybody else.'

'I'm not sure some of the villagers would agree,' I said, now weeping like a child.

'Who cares what they think?'

'You should have seen their faces, Brother Peter,' I said. 'They didn't openly accuse me, but I knew what they were thinking.'

Peter kissed the top of my head. 'Oh Oswald,' he sighed. 'What am I to do with you?' When my tears had soaked into his habit and I could cry no more, he settled me back into bed and pulled the blanket over my shoulder. 'Go back to sleep now,' he whispered as he stroked the hair from my forehead. 'Let this be forgotten. I won't wake you tonight for Matins or Prime. Rest your eyes until the morning.'

'The other brothers will ask where I am,' I said.

'I'll tell them that you have a headache.'

'They'll say I'm carrying plague again.'

'No, they won't,' he whispered as he blew out the candle. 'If I say you have a headache, then you have a headache.' He opened the door softly. 'Now go to sleep.'

I tried to rest, as Peter had advised, hoping that the darkness of the cell would help – but continuous, uninterrupted sleep eluded me for that night and the following two. Unfortunately this bout of insomnia gave me such a pallor that the other brothers became convinced that I'd contracted the Plague. It didn't matter how many times Peter said that I was simply suffering from a headache, a summer cold or even a mild case of the Flux, the rumour soon took hold.

I learnt, subsequently, that some of the brothers had wanted to banish me from Kintham immediately, though their voices were silenced by Peter, who would not tolerate a word said against me. If I were truly suffering from plague, as they had asserted, then where were the throbbing buboes and fierce fever that were said to afflict the sick? Peter stood his ground against my detractors, but in the end the Abbot stepped in, instructing Peter to house me in the isolation cell in the gardens, where I was to stay until it could be proven, beyond doubt, that I was not infectious.

I found some solace at last in this isolation, not least because it was a break from the endless, tiresome routines of monastic life.

Peter visited regularly, bringing decoctions and tisanes he said would calm my nerves – though typically these contained more brandy than herbs. His own nerves might have been cured by brandy, wine, ale or mead – in fact, Peter was a dedicated and steady drinker, never without some medicinal tonic in his leather flask – but brandy did not soothe my spirits. It did not prevent my mind from going over and over the events of Agnes's death and contemplating the terrible prospect that I had killed my own niece.

I tried to accept Peter's assertion that none of this was my fault, but I couldn't even close my eyes at night without seeing Agnes's body – laid out on the crude wooden table in her mother's dark cottage. She still wore the blank expression that had previously disturbed me, but now that I studied this memory, I could perceive something different in the girl's features. I tried not to see it, but it was there each time I closed my eyes. It was my brother William's face – his long brown lashes fringing a pair of proud, almond-shaped eyes. The slightly arrogant pout of his full lips. The ears that poked out from beneath his hair. It was clearer each time I closed my eyes and saw Agnes's face. She was his daughter.

Peter had soundly warned me against writing to William, but I knew that it would be far worse for me if my brother heard this story about Agnes from somebody else. Beatrice Wheeler might not have been able to read or write, but I feared that she would find some other way of telling William, especially if she suspected that I hadn't kept my mumbled promise.

With this in mind, I decided that I would write to my brother at Somershill without telling Peter. Kintham was not yet completely cut off from the outside world – it was only the oblates and novices who were confined to the grounds. I knew that I would be able to persuade one of the lay brothers to deliver a letter to Somershill on my behalf. These men were recruited from the poorest families in neighbouring villages, to labour in

the fields and gardens of the monastery in return for accommo-
dation, food and the most basic of educations. They did not take
the holy orders, and they had no personal wealth, so it was well
known that they were often open to inducements. In fact, I used
my supply of spare brandy to persuade one of them – Brother
John, a man regularly hauled before the Abbot for petty offences
– to bring me a square of parchment, a pot of ink and a quill
from the scriptorium. And then I set about writing my letter of
confession to William.

I started that letter three times. Each time I washed away the
ink and began again. Peter was right. How do you inform a
person that his daughter is dead, when this girl's existence was
unknown to him in the first place? How do you explain your
own part in her death, without sounding like you are making
pathetic excuses? How do you tell him that this girl was attacked
and probably raped before you found her, and that her mind was
so disturbed that she waded into a dangerous river rather than
accept your help? It was impossible. My hand shook with appre-
hension each time I dipped the tip of my pen into the black ink.
If I had been weighed down by guilt before, I now found it
crushing.

In the end, I gave up. I wiped down the parchment for one last
time, removing all my attempts at this letter. There was only one
way forward for me. I could not write to William with this news,
but equally I could not hide away in this monastery and do nothing. I would tell William about his daughter – but not before I
had discovered the truth. Not before I had found Agnes's attacker
and brought the man to justice.

Chapter Six

I began the next morning, whilst I still enjoyed the advantages of the isolation cell, where I was not bound by any of the restrictions imposed on the other novices. I set off after breakfast – once I was sure that Peter had returned to the infirmary – pulling on my cloak and creeping away through the vegetable gardens towards the forest. It was a walk of six or seven miles to Stonebrook, so I didn't dawdle. The day was clement, and the paths were dry.

I reached the village by mid-morning, holding back at the forest edge to observe Stonebrook before entering. I felt apprehensive about returning here after my last visit, wondering how I might be received – but I was troubled by another concern as well. According to Peter, there had been no cases of plague beyond Fallowsden – but I was still cautious about mixing with new people.

As I watched from the safety of the trees, I could see the villagers going about their usual lives – a gang of children were playing with long sticks and leather balls in the street. A man was leading a cow across the green, its sagging udder swinging between a pair of bandy legs. A group of women were laughing together as they washed their sheets in the clear waters of the brook. If this village was beset with plague, then it certainly wasn't causing any disturbance.

Deciding that it was safe enough to leave my hiding place, I slipped past the humble village church, soon passing a newly occupied grave that was marked by a mound of tilled soil adorned with flowers and a short crucifix. The grave bore no name, but I knew immediately that it belonged to Agnes Wheeler. For a moment I felt compelled to stop and say something to Agnes, but I moved on quickly after realising that my presence had attracted the attention of some small boys. I had noticed them earlier, removing stones from the soil in an adjacent field, but now they had abandoned their work and were peeping over the wall at me. When the smallest boy launched a stone in my direction, I quickly headed for the main street of Stonebrook, and then made sure to march along the centre of this road, rather than skulk along in the shadows. I had been noticed already, so there was little point in trying to hide.

As I continued along this roughly made road, I half-expected Beatrice Wheeler to catch up with me, demanding to know if I had written to my brother yet? Thankfully the woman was nowhere to be seen, though I kept an eye out for her appearance. When I quickly glanced over to her cottage, squeezed between the hay barns and granaries, I noted that her single door was firmly shut. This was a relief, so I pulled up my hood and kept walking, sensing that I still had an audience. At either side of my peripheral vision, I could see village women standing at the doorways of their untidy, lopsided homes and watching my progress along the road. Some rested a baby on their hip. Others had their sleeves rolled up while they took a break from some chore or other in order to get a good look at me. They were not hostile, but neither were they welcoming. But who could blame them for this cool reception? The last time I came to Stonebrook, I had arrived with the body of a dead girl.

I bowed my head every so often and offered them God's blessing, hoping to display all of the humility expected of a Benedictine, until I finally reached my destination – the large, oak-framed home of Maud Woodstock. I quickly knocked and waited, making sure to affect a studious admiration of the fanciful hinge straps across the door, rather than turn around to look at the gang of children, dogs and general busybodies that had collected behind me. When nobody answered, I knocked again until Maud herself opened the door and invited me inside.

She greeted me with one of her smiles, but she also looked flustered – apologising for having taken her time to answer with the explanation that she and her maid had been attending to her father, as the old man had just fallen out of bed. As I stepped over the threshold, I heard some soft, low moaning coming from somewhere on the upper floor of the house, which prompted me to ask Maud if she needed any help with her father. She thanked me for this offer, but then assured me that the old man was now back in his bed, and had been given a soothing tonic. As her face relaxed into another smile, I was struck again by this woman's singular beauty. The strong, symmetrical features and those eyes – so intensely light and blue.

She beckoned for me to follow her inside, before leading me along a wide passageway that was surfaced with stone slabs rather than the usual beaten earth of the typical village home. We passed a kitchen and buttery to our right, and then entered a large central hall to our left – a cavernous two-storey room, furnished with a fine oak table, a selection of chairs and benches, and an elaborate wrought-iron brazier. Maud stopped in the middle of the room until I had said something flattering about the impressive dimensions and elegant tapestries, before we stepped through another door into a parlour – a room that was much smaller and friendlier than the hall, and where Maud clearly spent most of her time.

She quickly moved her embroidery from a box chair and indicated that I should take this seat, before she left to rouse her servant – an articulated twig of a girl who soon appeared with a pitcher of small beer, and a slice of custard pie. Once the food was laid out before me on a small table, the servant girl scamp-ered away as if I might be about to bite her. I wanted to ignore the food, since I had come here to talk about Agnes and the other missing women – but it looked so delicious compared to the miserable fare at Kintham. The temptation was too strong and I couldn't help but bolt down the custard pie like a starving dog, aware that Maud was watching me closely as I ate.

'Don't they feed you at the monastery, Brother Oswald?' she asked, taking a seat next to mine.

'Not like this,' I replied honestly, feeling my melancholia lift for the first time in days. The healing power of good food is astonishing.

'I make the custard pie myself,' said Maud. 'With saffron and cream. My mother gave me the recipe before she died.' She paused for a moment and let her lips curl into a smile. 'I have an ox pie in the kitchen as well. Cooked to another family recipe. Would you care to try it?'

I shook my head. 'No, thank you,' I said quickly, although the idea of this pie was very appealing. 'I'm not allowed to eat the meat of a four-footed beast. Not unless I'm unwell.'

'And are you unwell?' she asked, pretending to look serious. 'You do look a little pale, if I'm honest. I'm sure that some meat would warm your blood?'

'No, thank you,' I replied, realising that I was being teased. 'How is Beatrice Wheeler?' I said, making an effort to change the subject. 'I've been worried about her.'

Maud's face fell. 'She's still in mourning, I'm afraid,' she said, the mischief gone from her eyes. 'I've taken her some bread and cheese in recent days. It's only simple food, but it's gone some way to restoring her spirits.'

'Perhaps I should go and see her?' I suggested, though the idea of such a visit filled me with dread.

Maud winced a little at this suggestion. 'No. I wouldn't do that, Brother Oswald,' she said quickly. 'The woman is still in distress.' She forced a smile, and briefly touched my arm. 'Why don't you leave such a visit for a few weeks? I'm sure that Beatrice would be pleased to see you in the future. But only once she has found more peace.'

'Oh,' I said, taking her meaning. 'I see.'

'Don't worry,' replied Maud. 'She isn't angry with you. She's just sad about her daughter. I hope you understand?'

We sat in an awkward silence for a while. My hands fidgeted, whereas Maud placed hers demurely into her lap, one set of long fingers resting over the other. In a different woman, this gesture might have seemed meek or even deferential, but not in Maud's case. I had met forceful women in the past – not least in my own family – but I had rarely come across a woman who radiated this quiet, self-assured power. It was unnerving. I felt my cheeks colour and my heart beat faster, so I moved my fidgeting fingers to clutch at the wooden crucifix that hung from my neck and let my fingertips glide over its smooth surface. It was a self-comforting action that I hoped would ward away the unwelcome, embarrassing thoughts that were beginning to intrude into my mind. There was no doubt about this. Maud Woodstock was the most beautiful woman I had ever met and I felt disturbingly excited to be sitting alone with her.

Brother Thomas, the novice master, had prepared his pupils for situations such as this. His recommendation, I now remembered, was to poke a finger into the flame of a candle when overcome with lust. According to Thomas, the pain of burning skin was a violent but effective method of warding off the seductive lure of a woman. In the absence of any candles, I could only rely on the wooden crucifix for help – though this holy object was failing miserably to stop my eyes from wandering to the mounds of Maud's breasts – so tantalisingly visible under the cloth of her fitted tunic.

I looked away when she gave a polite cough. Had she read my mind? I sincerely hoped not. 'So, Oswald,' she said, before pausing. 'May I use that name? It seems so cumbersome to keep calling you Brother Oswald.' She paused to smile again at me.

'Yes, of course,' I replied, now clutching my crucifix so tightly that my knuckles had gone white.

'Thank you, Oswald,' she said, standing up to pour me some more ale from the pitcher. 'In that case, you may call me Maud,' she said, as she filled my cup. 'Thank you for coming to see me, but I assume this isn't a social visit?'

'Yes, that's right,' I said, once I'd released the crucifix and quickly downed the ale – hoping this drink would do a better job of calming my nerves. Unfortunately it only caused me to blurt out my intentions, in a rather childlike fashion. 'I want to find the man who attacked Agnes,' I announced, wiping the froth of the ale from my lips. 'And I'm concerned about the other missing women, of course,' I added, immediately aware that they sounded like an afterthought. 'I believe their disappearances are connected.'

'I see,' said Maud, taking a seat, but continuing to watch me intently.

'You were very kind to me when I last came here,' I said. 'I appreciated your intervention with John Roach.' I paused for a moment. 'I wanted to ask for your help again.'

'You know that the Hue and Cry discovered nothing?' she said. 'Though Master Roach claims they spent hours searching the forest.'

I nodded. 'I've heard that,' I replied. 'Though I didn't expect any different,' I added. 'Roach didn't seem very interested.'

Maud raised her eyebrows and gave a small sigh. 'You're right, Oswald,' she said. 'Unfortunately he's not interested at all. Even though these disappearances have blighted women's lives in Stonebrook for many months.' She paused to rearrange her hands in her lap. 'Do you realise that many of the women will no longer travel the forest paths alone? We are prisoners in our own homes.' Her face tightened momentarily into a frown and her cheeks reddened. 'As if a woman's life were not suffocating enough already.'

I could tell that she was annoyed with herself for displaying this flare of emotion, as she took a moment to relax by glancing out of the window. While she looked away, I was able to study her profile. Her thick blonde hair was pulled back from her face in the net of a crespine, revealing features that were stronger and larger than the average woman's. Perhaps it was fairer to describe her as handsome, rather than beautiful.

'Have you felt frightened yourself?' I asked. Somehow this seemed an unlikely idea, as I couldn't imagine Maud Woodstock being frightened of anything. And yet the flush returned to her cheeks.

'Sometimes,' she said, looking back at me, as she washed away this new show of emotion with a forced smile. 'Though I'm lucky enough, Oswald. I never have to travel alone. But fear will take over our lives if we're not careful. Some of the women are already saying there's a monster in the forest.' She fixed me with her gaze – her eyes large and so disconcertingly blue. 'I'm afraid that the people of this village can be very foolish at times. If it's not demons and devils, then it's omens and curses.' She suddenly laughed loudly. 'Curses indeed,' she said. 'I hope you don't believe in such nonsense?'

I shook my head. From an early age, I had refused to believe in anything that couldn't be seen, heard, or otherwise proved to exist. Of course, this had been a difficult opinion to hold in a monastery, so I had kept it to myself. Brother Peter was the only person who had ever guessed at this fault line in my faith, but he rarely pressed me on the subject. He didn't want to hear the answer.

'No. I certainly don't believe in curses,' I said. 'Nor ghosts or demons. I never have done.'

She suddenly clutched my hand in response to this statement. Her touch burnt at my skin – reminding me again, in blunt and undiluted terms, of the pleasures I was about to eschew by becoming a monk. It was only months before I was due to take my vows and commit myself to a life of celibacy. 'Thank you, Oswald,' she said. 'I'm glad you feel the same.'

I froze until she removed her hand, surreptitiously wiping my nervous sweat onto the cloth of my habit.

She composed her hands into her lap again, aware that she had embarrassed me. 'So, tell me, Oswald. How is it that I can help you?'

'I wanted to find out more about the women who've disappeared,' I said, trying to concentrate again. 'To see if there's anything that links them.'

Maud leant back on her chair and appeared to be thinking as she bit her lip. I'm ashamed to say this was another gesture that I found myself studying with too much attention. 'I suppose they were all young. Under twenty.'

'What were their names?'

'I only knew their Christian names,' she admitted. 'But let me ask Johanna. She knew these women better than I.' Maud rose to her feet, stepped gracefully across the parlour to call her maid from the doorway. We soon heard the girl's feet trundling down the wooden stairs, before she dashed into the room at full speed. When Johanna saw that I was still there, she stopped dead and cast her eyes to the floor, as if the sight of me might turn her to stone.

Maud didn't acknowledge this strange behaviour. 'The girls from Stonebrook who are missing,' she said. 'Can you tell Brother Oswald their names please, Johanna?'

The girl hesitated.

'Come on, Johanna,' said Maud. 'You knew them well, I believe?'

The girl trembled, mumbling their names to me, as if she had been asked to list the horsemen of the Apocalypse. I asked her to repeat these names three times so that I could commit them to memory. 'Mary Ancoats, Mary Chandler, Winifred de Terre, Mary Brewer and Jocelin Baker.' The list bore out a certain truth. If you wander into any village in Kent, then at least half of the women are called Mary.

'Can you tell me how they disappeared?' I asked. This question appeared to flummox the girl.

'Let me answer that,' said Maud, before turning to her servant. 'Run along now, Johanna. Father needs washing and turning in bed.'

Johanna retreated at speed from the room, leaving Maud to share another smile with me. 'I'm sorry, Oswald,' she said, once the girl was out of earshot. 'Poor Johanna can be afraid of her own shadow sometimes. But don't let it alarm you.'

Maud returned to her chair, and began to tap the ends of her fingers together. I was half-afraid and half-hopeful that she would take my hand again, but she was lost in thought. 'I believe the first two girls were on their way to market in Burrswood when they went missing,' she said. 'I'm afraid that I can't remember which ones, though.'

'Were they travelling together?'

'No, no. It was on two separate occasions. The second disappearance was about one month after the first.

'And the others?'

'I believe that two of them were collecting firewood in the forest,' she said. 'And the last one was visiting an aunt in Crowbridge.'

'And they were also travelling alone?'

Maud nodded. 'That's right.'

This didn't surprise me. A man who attacks women is unlikely to pick upon more than one victim at a time. 'How often were the disappearances?' I asked.

Maud puckered her lips. 'I suppose they have been fairly constant,' she said. 'About a month or so between each one.'

This was more revealing to me. It seemed that the man had developed a habit. Meaning, of course, that he would act again.

'Have there been disappearances from other villages nearby?' I asked.

'No,' she said quickly, before qualifying her answer. 'Well. Not that I know of, Oswald. But then again, we don't hear a lot from outside Stonebrook, as nobody is straying far from home these days. With the threat of plague, we barely see anybody outside of this parish.'

I wondered if she knew about the family who had died in Fallowsden, and then decided against mentioning this. There was enough darkness to this conversation already without talk of plague. 'Is there anything you can tell me about the women themselves?' I asked hopefully.

This prompted a bashful smile. 'I'm sorry, Oswald. This is a small village, but I didn't know any of them very well.' She dipped her head for a moment, and seemed almost embarrassed. 'I'm not a haughty woman. Please don't think that. But equally, I have to keep my distance.' She looked up again. 'I have two hundred acres to manage in the place of my father, and therefore I cannot be too familiar with the other villagers. They would not respect my wishes, if I were to sit about the brook, gossiping with the other women as we washed our sheets.' She sat up straight. 'I have to maintain my standards. I hope you understand that?'

I looked about this room again, noting Maud Woodstock's standards. I saw a carved oak coffer, fastened with iron bands. A dresser full of pewter plates. A glass decanter of spiced wine. Cushions made from green damask. A worsted carpet on the floor. All were of the best quality. This was not to mention the smell of the freshly baked ox pie that was now drifting through the air with tantalising appeal. Not the usual sulphurous stink of boiling cabbage that haunted the average village home.

'Of course,' I said. 'You cannot be their friends. I understand.'

'I sound so stupidly proud and conceited, don't I?' she replied. 'But it's difficult to be respected, Oswald. Especially when you are a woman doing a man's job.'

'I've heard that you do it very well.'

She bowed her head in response. 'Thank you,' she said. 'I try my best. But it has meant making many sacrifices. Sometimes I feel very lonely and isolated from the rest of the village.' She heaved a sigh. 'Sometimes I wish my life had taken a different course, and that I could have married.'

I didn't know how to respond to this, so we sat in silence for a while – though the atmosphere wasn't awkward. Instead it was intimate. I felt flattered that Maud had revealed something of herself to me, as she didn't seem the type to do so readily. It prompted me to make a confession of my own. To reveal a secret that I had not intended to share with her. 'There's something else I wanted to tell you,' I said.

'Oh yes?' she replied, looking up from her brief reverie.

I hesitated for a moment. 'Agnes did speak to me,' I said. 'When I found her in the forest. Just before she died.'

Maud sat back. 'I see. Why didn't you say so before?'

'I'm sorry,' I replied. 'I should have done. But it was too difficult for me to repeat in front of everybody. And . . .' I hesitated again. 'And I was worried that they would misunderstand.'

Maud leant towards me and rested her chin on her hand. 'Go on, Oswald,' she said. 'Please. Tell me what she said.'

'It was just before she threw herself into the river.' I looked away feeling suddenly embarrassed, unable to hold Maud's intense gaze. 'She said, *Keep away from me, priest*.'

Maud narrowed her eyes. 'Why do you think that she said this to you?'

'It was more the way she said it,' I replied. 'Agnes was terrified. Almost as if she'd mistaken me for somebody else.'

'You mean the man who attacked her?'

'I do.'

Maud paused. 'Then there's something I should tell you,' she said. 'It might be relevant, now that you've shared this information with me.' She cleared her throat. 'There was a monk from

Kintham who kept visiting the village until recently. A lay brother, I believe, given his clothing.' She hesitated again, unsure about her next words. 'To be honest, there was something about him that I didn't like.'

'What was his name?' I asked.

'Brother Merek.'

I coughed in surprise. Should I tell Maud that Merek was also missing, having allegedly run away with a woman? I quickly decided against it. 'Why didn't you like him?' I asked instead.

Maud hesitated again. 'It was probably nothing, Oswald. Perhaps I shouldn't even have mentioned it.' She gave a sigh. 'It's just that he spent far too much time with the women. Particularly the poorest girls in the village. I used to see him hanging around with them at the edge of the forest. Or bringing them small gifts.' She paused to frown. 'I thought he was too friendly and generous, and . . .' She looked at her hands as if the next admission embarrassed her. 'I've seen it before, Oswald,' she whispered. 'Men who work very hard to build a relationship of trust with a woman. Only to then manipulate and exploit her.'

'Do you know if Brother Merek befriended Agnes? Or any of the girls who are now missing?' I asked.

'Yes. I believe that he did,' she said. 'Though he tried to keep out of my way, so I can't be entirely sure.' She paused again. 'I was about to make a complaint to the Abbot, and ask for him to be removed. But then he stopped coming. About six weeks ago,' she added. 'I don't know why. Perhaps somebody else complained before I had the chance?'

Of course, I knew exactly why Merek had stopped coming to Stonebrook, but once again I stopped short of sharing this information with Maud. The story was too incendiary in the current circumstances – not to mention the fact that the brothers had been forbidden to speak about Merek outside of the monastery. According to the Abbot, his disappearance was a potential

embarrassment to Kintham — especially if he had genuinely
absconded with a woman. And so I thanked Maud, assuring her
that her concerns about Merek were probably something and
nothing, before telling her that I needed to get back to Kintham
Abbey for Nones. I wanted Peter's advice before acting on this
new piece of information. I should have sought out my tutor's
help when Agnes died, and I wouldn't make that mistake again.

Maud offered me another slice of the custard pie before I left,
or even a secret slice of the ox pie that was increasingly filling
this chamber with its delicious, savoury smell. But it was time to
leave. Otherwise I might never have found the heart to go —
especially as Maud grasped my hand in hers again and earnestly
thanked me for taking an interest in the lives of these women.

With her touch still warming my skin, I made my way back to
the monastery, my feet feeling heavier with each step. I should
have been thinking about Brother Merek and his unexplained
visits to Stonebrook. I should have been thinking about the missing girls and making sure that I committed their names to
memory. But instead, I was thinking about Maud Woodstock.
The mounds of her breasts and the intensity of those beautiful
blue eyes.

Chapter Seven

Mother sat up and rearranged her pillows, pummelling the bolster with surprising energy and giving me the impression that she wasn't quite as ill as we had all imagined. Then again, she had retired to her bedchamber each winter for the past three years, with the announcement that she was preparing for death, only to make a miraculous recovery by the following March.

'You always were a fool when it came to women, Oswald,' she said, flopping back against the bolster, her face now losing some of its colour. 'This story doesn't surprise me in the least.'

'I was very young,' I said in my defence. 'I didn't know what I was doing.'

She pulled the linen sheet over her chin, as if it were a shroud. 'Yes, but you don't get any better, do you, Oswald? That's the trouble.'

'What do you mean by that?' I said, rising to my feet. I had become distracted by a noise outside in the courtyard below. Two of the kitchen boys were shouting at one another, and it sounded as if a fight were brewing.

'Are you listening to me, Oswald?' Mother asked, as I looked out of the window.

'What was that?' I said absentmindedly.

'I said, You don't get any better, do you?'

'At what?'

'At dealing with women, of course.'

I ignored this comment, as the fight had intensified. One of the boys was clutching a cat to his chest, while the other boy tried to grab the creature. My old steward Gilbert was sitting on a stool to one side of this spectacle, and whittling a chestnut branch into a pointed rod as he scowled in their direction. Gilbert was said to be nearly eighty, though nobody, including Gilbert himself, was sure about his age. Ever since I could remember, he had been ancient. In fact, he should have retired to the village long ago, to be cared for by his daughters and grandchildren. Instead he remained at Somershill, as much a feature of the house as the curtain wall and the north-west tower. Unable to part himself from our company, he was usually to be found in some corner, cleaning a roasting spit or sharpening a knife. This was the sort of quiet, undemanding work that suited his age, but Gilbert could still summon the energy of his younger years when the need arose. I watched as he sprang to his feet and approached the boys – whipping the chestnut branch through the air and threatening to thrash the pair for their behaviour. As usual, his idea of peaceably breaking up a fight was more violent than the altercation itself.

I decided it was time to intervene, so I quickly crossed the room, heading for the door when Mother dealt her blow. It was accurate and deadly, aimed at the heart. 'So, you don't want to know what your wife has been up to, then?' she asked me.

I let my hand fall from the latch, but didn't turn around. 'What do you mean by that?' I said.

She paused. 'Perhaps I shouldn't say?'

'Shouldn't say what?'

I could hear Filomena's voice in my head, urging me to leave the room and ignore this provocation. Don't take the bait, she was saying. Don't fall for her tricks. But I was weak. Too easily hooked. 'What's your point, Mother?' I asked, turning around to face her.

Mother couldn't resist the shortest of victory smiles, though she quickly lifted her hand to her mouth and smothered her delight with a yawn. 'Filomena is very close to Sir John, wouldn't you say? I've seen them laughing and whispering in the courtyard.'

'What were you doing out of bed?' I replied. 'You've been told to stay there.'

This accusation threw her, but my small triumph was not to last for long.

'A woman must stretch her legs on a daily basis,' she said. 'Particularly if she's to maintain some dignity. I refuse to sit in bed and urinate into a pot.'

'Then take care to stay away from the window,' I said.

'I wasn't spying, Oswald,' she replied. 'If that's what you're suggesting. It's just that I couldn't help but see what's been going on.'

'You need have no concerns about my wife and our guest,' I said firmly. 'Sir John is staying here for the winter at my invitation.'

Mother gave a huff. 'So you say.'

'Sir John is my friend,' I insisted. 'Filomena is as fond of him as I am. He likes to entertain the household with his tales. That is all.'

Mother closed her eyes. 'I hope you're right, Oswald,' she said. 'I would hate to see you taken advantage of again. By another woman.'

I lifted the latch and quickly stepped into the passageway before I said something that I would subsequently regret. I was about to close the door when she called me back.

'Oswald!'

'What is it?' I said tersely.

'You will come back later, won't you? I want to hear more of your story.'

I closed the door and didn't answer.

I didn't return later to Mother's bedside. I suppose it was my idea of punishment – the removal of my company in revenge for her mischievous story. But she won in the end, for I spent a miserable afternoon, worrying about something that had never occurred to me before – a romance between Filomena and our house guest, Sir John.

That evening I watched the pair closely as we sat about the fire – noting how greatly Sir John entertained my wife with the stories of his travels. Noting how she chose his company over everybody else's. Spotting an incident where she touched his arm lightly and then let her hand linger on his sleeve. I had never even considered this man as anything other than amusing company before, but now I was watching his behaviour like a hawk. And I wasn't the only person showing an interest. When I looked about the fireside, I also saw Henry keeping their relationship under observation with a pair of watchful, jealous eyes.

And what of our love rival himself? It wasn't as if Sir John was a handsome man. His face was dominated by two bulges at his forehead that looked like the podia for a pair of horns. His mouth was wide and thin, and his complexion was an odd shade of pinkish brown – where the strong sun of the Mediterranean had weathered his skin into a patchy leather. It was his personality that was captivating, however. When Sir John began to tell a tale, this strange arrangement of features was immediately transformed into a different face completely. At this point, it was barely possible to keep one's eyes from him.

That particular evening, he had promised to tell us about travelling to Sinai to visit the monastery of Saint Catherine. Usually his tales began with some mention of Venice, my wife's home city and the place where we had met one another in 1357, after my first wife had died in childbirth. Venice was the port of embarkation for every one of Sir John's journeys about the Mediterranean sea – whether he had travelled to Jerusalem, Egypt or Tartary, and so it had never surprised me previously that he began each of his accounts with a preamble about the many fascinations of that incredible city.

But now, following Mother's insinuations, I began to wonder if this scene-setting were Sir John's genuine motivation, or whether he mentioned Venice so often to please my wife? It was clear to all that Filomena was enchanted by his descriptions of Venice, to the point of closing her eyes and sighing with delight upon hearing about the Piazzetta or the Molo. I could see that Sir John enjoyed Filomena's response, so, rather churlishly, I asked him to quickly move on to the monastery visit when he mentioned Venice that evening, claiming that I was feeling tired and needed an early night.

John graciously complied, since he was always keen to keep his audience happy and never be seen to dominate the conversation (though he often did, at everybody's insistence), but I could tell that Filomena was disappointed by my intervention. If we could never return to Venice in person, then at least she could travel there in her mind.

When we retired to bed that night, Filomena turned her back to me and pretended to be asleep when I touched her shoulder.

'What's the matter?' I whispered, as if I didn't know.

'Nothing,' she replied resentfully.

'Is it because I asked Sir John to get to the point?'

'No.'

'It is, isn't it?' When she didn't answer, I foolishly added, 'I thought his story was rather boring.'

'Boring?' she echoed, turning over to face me. 'I can tell you what boring means, Oswald,' she said with a mocking laugh. 'It is winter in this castle.'

'You have my company.'

Filomena puffed her disdain. 'You are constantly at your mother's side, Oswald. I never see you.'

'Mother's dying,' I said. 'What do you expect me to do?'

I thought this comment might have won the argument, but Filomena merely brushed it aside. 'It wouldn't be so bad for me, if you hadn't sent Hugh and Sandro away. And left me with nobody but Sir John.'

I groaned inwardly, as this was the same argument that we'd
had so many times before. 'Hugh had to leave for Oxford. He's a
nobleman and must be educated.'

'But what about Sandro,' she retorted. 'He was just a servant.
You could have kept him here.'

'Sandro begged to go to London, Filomena. It wasn't fair to
keep him at Somershill any longer.'

'He shouldn't have asked to leave,' she grumbled. 'It was so
ungrateful, after all you did for him.'

'Sandro gave me years of loyal service.'

'Loyal service?' she puffed. 'Who was Sandro before you
found him? Nothing but a ragged orphan living on the streets of
Venice.' She harrumphed. 'You should have left him there to
starve!'

'You don't mean that, Filomena,' I said.

She sighed. 'No,' she said at length. 'Of course I don't.' Even
though it was dark, I could hear that she was holding back the
tears. 'I just miss Sandro so much, Oswald. He was my last tie to
Venice.'

I kissed her lips and promised that we would go up to London
to visit Sandro in the spring, as soon as the days lengthened. This
seemed to please her and she soon fell asleep, but I found it
harder to settle. All of this nonsense about Sir John was Mother's
doing. She had planted the seeds of enmity, but I had stupidly
allowed them to grow. There was no reason to be jealous of Sir
John. He was simply indulging Filomena's love for her home
city.

And so, I made up my mind. I would not react to any more
such tales – no matter how goading they might be. Tomorrow I
would return to Mother's side and continue my own story without such interruptions. I would make my confession, and we
would part with our account in balance. I would seek her forgiveness, and she would grant it. The letter would be mine, and then
I could destroy it forever.

Chapter Eight

After leaving Maud Woodstock's house, I returned immediately to Kintham, slipping back into my isolation cell without being seen. Nobody seemed to have noticed my absence, but I wondered how much longer I would be able to enjoy this privilege. In truth, I was not looking forward to returning to the rigidities of monastic life, after the freedom of recent days.

Peter appeared not long after my return, clutching a small hessian bag that contained my evening meal – a slice of stale bread and a square of cheese so small and hard that we might have scored holes into each face and used it as a dice. Seeing this offering, I thought again about the meaty pie that I had refused at Maud's house, and my enthusiasm for this way of life diminished just a little bit further.

'This is the best I could do,' said Peter, seeing my reaction to his parcel. 'The kitchens are saving supplies for the feast of Pentecost.'

I thanked him for bringing it anyway, and then placed the bag under my bed. I would save it until the middle of the night, when a hungry person will eat anything – even such unpalatable morsels as these.

Peter looked at me quizzically. 'I thought you'd want to eat immediately,' he said. 'You haven't had anything since breakfast.'

'I'm not hungry,' I replied.

'Are you still unwell, then?' he asked, taking a seat on the bed next to me – groaning as he bent his knees and lowered his backside onto the thin mattress.

'No.'

He looked me up and down, and then retrieved his leather flask from his scrip, taking a long sip of the brandy, before he licked his lips with a satisfying sigh.

Now that Peter had started drinking, I decided that it was a good time to confess to my outing. His mood sometimes softened with a drink – at least to begin with anyway. 'I went to Stonebrook today,' I said in an offhanded way, as if visiting this village were a regular arrangement. 'I was given some food there.'

Peter drew back in consternation. 'What did you say?'

'I said that I went to Stonebrook.'

'But you were supposed to stay in the monastery, Oswald.' His cheeks instantly reddened. 'What on earth were you doing there?'

'I wanted to speak to the villagers,' I admitted. 'About Agnes Wheeler.'

Peter's mouth fell open for a moment. It seemed that my gamble about his mood had failed. In fact, Peter looked angrier than ever as he rose to his feet and paced up and down the room – his face screwed into a grimace and his hand gripping the neck of his leather flask.

'You are such a fool, Oswald,' he hissed. 'I cannot believe you would flout the Abbot's rules with such boldness. Did you not hear what he told us in the Chapter House? There is plague in Fallowsden. A deadly, uncontrollable plague.'

'I saw nothing of it in Stonebrook,' I answered. 'Life was continuing as usual.'

'Then you are even more stupid than I thought,' he said, coming to a standstill in front of me. 'Plague creeps up silently. It does not announce its arrival with the call of a bladder pipe. For all you know, the miasmas from Fallowsden could have already blown over to Stonebrook.'

'Well, they haven't,' I replied. 'Nobody is ill there. Nobody at all.' After this confrontation we stared at one another until Peter finally drew back and muttered something under his breath about ignorant young men.

'I learnt something of interest to my investigation today,' I ventured, once certain that Peter's temper had abated a little. 'So I'm pleased that I went.'

Peter gave a scornful laugh at this. 'Your investigation?' he repeated. 'Whatever next? Who are you, then? The bishop's summoner? I've never heard of such haughty presumption.'

'Nobody else is interested in finding out the truth about Agnes and the other missing women, Brother Peter,' I said sharply. 'If I don't investigate, then who will?'

Peter went to answer, but stopped himself. Instead he heaved a long sigh and took a seat next to me on the bed again. 'Look, Oswald,' he said softly. 'It's extremely tragic that this poor girl died, but it wasn't your fault. There is nothing that you can do to bring her back.'

'I can try to find the truth,' I replied. 'Surely I owe Agnes that much?'

He shook his head at this. 'You must listen to me,' he said. 'I know that you mean well, but you are a novice on the verge of taking your vows. You must put your own feelings of guilt about this girl to one side and concentrate on your own future.'

'But I thought you'd be pleased that I cared. I thought that you admired those men and women who sought out the truth? That's what you've always taught me.'

'Not when you put yourself in danger with such reckless acts,' he said. 'Not when plague is stirring. You must see that?'

He tried to put a hand onto my arm, but I shrugged him away. 'Leave me alone,' I said, turning my shoulder to him. 'I don't want to talk to you. You've disappointed me, Peter.'

The tactic worked perfectly. 'So, come on then,' he said wearily. 'What is it? This interesting piece of information? You may as well tell me?'

I hesitated, knowing that Peter would find fault with my story as soon as he heard it. 'I was told that Brother Merek was a frequent visitor to Stonebrook before he disappeared,' I said. 'Apparently he made a point of befriending the poorer women. Including the ones who are now missing.'

Peter didn't answer this. He just stared at me.

'Don't you think that's interesting?' I asked. Although I had half-expected this reaction, it still irritated me.

'Not really,' he replied. 'We're Benedictines, Oswald. We're supposed to care for the poor.'

'Yes. But not in that way.'

'What way do you mean?'

'You know exactly what I mean, Brother Peter,' I replied. 'His friendship was unwelcome.'

Peter knitted his brow into a frown. 'Who told you that?' he asked. 'Was it that girl with the red hair? Rose Brunham? Because I've told you before about her . . . she is a notorious liar. You really shouldn't believe anything that she has to say.'

'No,' I said. 'It wasn't her.'

Peter cast his eyes over my face, trying to judge if I were telling the truth. 'So, who was it, then?' He gave a laugh. 'I suppose it was Maud Woodstock, wasn't it? With her striking eyes and proud manners. Oh yes,' he sneered. 'The attentions of a mere lay brother such as Brother Merek would certainly be most unwelcome to the likes of her.'

'It doesn't matter who told me,' I snapped. 'Only that I believe it's true.'

Peter took a long gulp of brandy and then wiped his mouth

with the back of his hand. 'So, come on then. What's your theory about Merek?' he asked, leaning towards me and raising his eyebrows. His indignation had turned to amusement, which, if anything, I found even more riling. 'You've obviously got one.'

I refused to answer.

Peter tutted and puffed his lips. 'Then let me tell you,' he said, poking a finger into my thigh. 'You don't believe that Brother Merek was attacked by bandits and murdered. Even though that's the obvious explanation for his disappearance, given that nobody has heard from the poor man for over six weeks.' He poked at my leg again. 'You think that Brother Merek is hiding out somewhere in the forests of Kintham, picking off poor girls from the village of Stonebrook and murdering them for his own, depraved amusement.'

I was briefly lost for words. 'It could be true,' I said at length. 'Remember what Agnes said to me before she ran into the river. *Keep away from me, priest.*'

'Of course it's not true,' said Peter, throwing up his arms in indignation. 'Merek was the most devout of lay brothers. A genuine man of God. He would never commit such outrageous sins.'

'Then why was he spending so much time with the women of Stonebrook?' I said. 'It seems very suspicious to me.'

Peter growled at me. 'Your theory is offensive and ridiculous, Oswald,' he said. 'I never want to hear it again.'

'But how can you ignore this?' I said. 'There must be a link between Merek and the missing women.'

'Why?'

'Because, because . . .' I stuttered.

Peter shook his head vigorously. 'You see. You can't even explain it yourself. You've based your whole ridiculous theory on a coincidence, Oswald. Nothing more. It is a typical error of youth. You've taken two separate disappearances and conflated them to create your own fantasy.'

'I have not imagined this,' I snapped. 'Don't say that.'

'Can you remember the teachings of William of Ockham, Oswald?' he asked me.

I shrugged in response.

'Oh come on,' he said. 'I know that Brother Thomas has encouraged you to read Ockham's work, even though you barely attend any of his classes.' He leant towards me, and I could see that his eyes were red and that his skin was dry and flaking. His breath smelt worse than ever at this proximity. 'Remember what Ockham said. The explanation requiring the fewest assumptions is the most likely to be correct.'

'Meaning what?' I said.

'Meaning that your unlikely story is most unlikely to be true.'

I tried to argue further, but the bell for Vespers rang out in the far distance. Peter stood up without thinking, for a monk must obey the horarium. His life is ruled by the tolling of bells.

'Come along, Oswald,' said Peter, stiffening his shoulders and heading for the door. 'You've spent too long in this cell.' He looked me up and down. 'You are well enough to return to your duties now. And, in any case, I cannot leave you here alone any longer to flout the rules.'

'So you're not going to help me?' I said.

'With what?' he asked.

'My investigation into Brother Merek, of course.'

He stopped by the door. 'Oswald,' he said solemnly. 'Please listen to me, because I won't say this again. There is absolutely nothing to investigate.'

Chapter Nine

I caused a stir when I appeared at Vespers that evening – though the other monks were supposed to be singing their canticles, rather than turning around to stare at me. When Peter noticed their reaction, he made a point of holding my arm as we walked up to the altar together. If the infirmarer of Kintham would touch me so willingly, then they could feel reassured that I didn't pose any risk.

After a day or so, my reappearance finally lost its novelty and I could travel about the cloisters without being remarked upon. And anyway, any curiosity and gossip about the state of my health was soon supplanted by a new topic of conversation. A white stag had been seen in the woodland about the monastery, treading through the undergrowth at a safe distance from the walls, but still close enough to be seen. According to many of the brothers, the stag was a sure sign that Christ himself was watching over Kintham in these troubling times. Whatever the stag signified – whether its presence were divine or natural – this was seen as uplifting news. Something to occupy the brothers' thoughts and prayers, rather than the gathering clouds of plague.

I used this time to continue my investigation into Merek, despite Peter's attempts to warn me off. There was more than coincidence at play here. The disappearance of the women and the disappearance of Brother Merek were connected. I just needed to find out how.

I had known Merek a little, since he had also worked under Brother Peter's supervision – though he had tended to keep himself to himself. In truth, I had always found the man to be rather awkward and sullen, rather than the honourable man of God whom Peter had described to me. I needed to find out what the other brothers thought of Merek, so I managed to persuade (or should I say induce) Brother John, to tell me more about Merek's earlier history at Kintham – before he had come to us in the infirmary. I must say John's account of Merek did little to change my opinion of the man.

According to John, Merek had started by working in the scriptorium when he first came to the Abbey as a lay brother – though his unsteady hand had soon vexed the provisioner to the point of exasperation. Merek was only supposed to be stretching and chalking the parchment in readiness for the scribes, but he had still managed to damage the precious skins. No matter how many of Merek's mistakes were blamed upon Titivillus, the demon said to haunt scriptoria and cause the monks to spoil their holy work, Merek could not be allowed to wreck such expensive materials indefinitely. After being dismissed from this role, Merek had then been sent to the cellarer, the kitchener, and the sacrist – displaying no aptitude in any of these areas, until he had been passed on, at last, to Peter.

From this point onwards I could continue Merek's story myself, – though the man didn't last long at the infirmary, as his clumsy fingers were unable to cut a clean incision, nor neatly sew a gaping wound. It was in the herb garden where Merek finally found his vocation. Thanks to Merek's skills in cultivation, there were soon rows of healthy lavender, sage and dill, alongside the fennel, garlic and comfrey. The bays, previously stunted and diseased, had been replanted and had grown into tall trees with abundant, glossy leaves. There was even an apricot tree clinging to a wall and producing fruit in most years, as long as there wasn't a late frost.

But there was more than an aptitude for gardening to Merek's talents. He was also an expert at foraging in the forests – finding those herbs that cannot, or will not, grow, in a garden. The Wood Betony to purify the blood. The Mullein for voiding the chest of phlegm. The Shepherd's Rod to cleanse the liver. For this reason, Merek had often been given permission to leave the monastery for many days at a time . . . but now I began to wonder if these long excursions had been entirely motivated by the search for herbs?

Of course, Brother Merek had not been alone in seeking time outside of the Abbey, as the cloistered life could induce a suffocating melancholia in some of the brothers. Hearing confessions, or tending to the sick in the nearest village were popular excuses for an occasional escape. In addition, some brothers would regularly volunteer to make pilgrimages – anything that might release them from the monastery for a number of weeks. But Merek's absences were more systematic than this. It seemed that he had managed to contrive a regular excuse to leave the monastery – which was suspicious in itself . . . but still not enough to specifically link him to the crimes.

I still needed to know more about the man. And so, when Peter was busy letting the Abbot's blood one afternoon – a treatment that the Abbot was now requesting at regular intervals – I made my way over to Merek's old cell, in the hope of finding something in his room. Anything that might shed some more light onto his character. I couldn't say exactly what I was looking for – but, in the absence of any other ideas, I felt it was worth a try.

Brother Merek had been fortunate to have been allocated his own bedchamber, since the lay brothers were not usually granted such a privilege. But there had been a good reason for this favour. Merek's loud and resonant snoring had been highly disturbing to his fellow brothers – so this room, with its thick walls and out-of-the-way location beyond the Abbot's kitchen, guaranteed that the other monks had been able to sleep. This cell had not yet been re-occupied since his disappearance, as the Abbey was far from full. The Abbot had been correct when he warned that our numbers were dwindling. Nevertheless, the room had been cleaned in anticipation of the next occupant, whomever that might be.

The cell itself was dark, with a north-facing window and walls that were lime-washed and free of any decoration. There was still a straw mattress on a simple bedstead, with a pillow and a roughly woven blanket that was tucked over the mattress, ready for use. I lifted this blanket to find a yellowing linen sheet beneath that gave off a fusty odour, as the bed had not been properly aired for many days.

Looking about the room, I saw that somebody had roughly piled Merek's belongings in the corner, waiting for these items to be distributed or thrown away. There was a pair of knitted socks, some rough leather gloves, a collection of snail shells and a knife with a horn handle. These items all rested upon a plain psalter that was bound in leather.

A Benedictine is supposed to eschew all worldly goods, but this rule had not stopped most of us from accumulating possessions – small trinkets and souvenirs from our old lives. I still owned a few clay marbles and a small sling that I'd been given by Gilbert before leaving Somershill at the age of seven. I hid these keepsakes in a bag beneath my bed and pulled them out every so often, when I needed a reminder of the outside world. Such possessions were tolerated, as long as they were kept discreetly and did not openly offend our vows of poverty.

I took each of Merek's belongings from the pile in turn, surprised to find that the snail shells had been painted with linseed oil to reveal their subtle beauty. I held one of these shells up to the light for a moment to admire the colours before I returned to my search. The gloves, socks and knife were a little more revealing to my investigation. Each item was useful and of good quality, so I wondered why Merek had left them behind? It was a niggling difficulty with my theory that he was now eking out a living in the woods. If Merek had been planning such a primitive life, then why had he not taken these items with him? I let my mind ponder on this question for a while, without coming to any particular conclusion.

I then opened Merek's psalter. It was clearly a work in his own hand – perhaps an exercise he had completed when working in the scriptorium? The lettering was almost childlike, and the text was illuminated with the roughest of marginalia – curling vines and creatures that might, or might not, have been rabbits. It was difficult to tell. This was no great work of art, more of a practical exercise in the use of a pen. And yet this psalter looked as if it had been treasured.

I quickly flicked through – passing the psalms, calendar and the litany of the saints, until I came to some blank pages at the back of this small book. Sometimes such pages are used to write a personal note or thought, so I hoped that Merek might have obliged me with an anecdote or message – some evidence that would inextricably link him to Agnes and the missing girls. It was an optimistic idea at best, but I still found myself disappointed to discover that the page was completely bare, without even so much as the indentation of a scribble that had been subsequently washed away.

I might have replaced the psalter onto the pile, had not something caught my eye when leafing back through the book to see if there were a hidden page, or a loose sheet of parchment waiting to fall out. Yet again, I was in search of that elusive piece of evidence. And I did find something. Though not where I had expected.

The book fell open at the calendar, suggesting that this part of the psalter had been more regularly opened than other pages. This intrigued me enough to run my finger down the list of saints' days, finding ten strange words squashed together in pairs at the end of five separate lines. These words were written in a character set that I did not recognise. It was certainly not Greek or Syriac. And the ink was different to the rest of the psalter. Unlike the oak-gall ink used by the brothers in the scriptorium, with its rich, dark-brown pigment, these words appeared to have been written in a crude medium. Probably from a mixture of charcoal and water, given the faint and transient nature of the lettering.

My suspicions were immediately raised. Not only were these words easy to wipe from the parchment, should the need arise – they had also been deliberately hidden in a part of this book that was not designed for personal notes. I soon understood what I was looking at. It was a code. I guessed at a simple substitution cipher – the type of code that I had sometimes used with a fellow oblate when younger, to pass a note expressing our opinions about the size of the Abbot's nose, the novice master's bad breath or even a cruel observation about another boy in our class.

Were these coded words in Brother Merek's psalter something similar? A joke perhaps? Something that had amused him in a solitary hour? Perhaps they meant nothing at all . . . and yet I didn't think so. It was the way that they were squeezed in amongst the saints' days, when they could easily have been written at the back of the psalter. There was something secretive about them, subversive even.

I dropped the psalter into my bag and turned to leave the cell when I found myself face to face with Brother James. The old monk had crept silently to the threshold where he now occupied the doorway, meaning that I could not pass.

'Brother James,' I said in surprise. 'I didn't see you there.'

'Ah, so it is you,' he replied. 'Young Oswald. I thought so. I recognised the sound of your feet.' I had made an effort to come here as quietly as possible, but I had forgotten that Kintham was patrolled by the likes of Brother James – prowling vigilantes, always on the lookout for sin. This old man might have been nearly blind, but he had the ears of an owl. 'What are you doing here?' he asked me.

I hesitated, realising that I should have prepared an excuse. 'I . . . I was looking for something,' I stammered.

'In Brother Merek's cell?'

'Yes.'

'What was it, then?' He stared at me with a pair of milky eyes, and I wondered if he could see me after all?

'I lent Brother Merek a comb before he disappeared,' I said quickly, my mind now working a little faster. 'And I wondered if it was still here?'

'A comb?' he said. The idea seemed to offend him.

'Yes. It was a gift from my mother. It's carved from ivory and I've always treasured it. I thought that I'd lost it, but then I remembered that Merek had asked to borrow it.' I pointed to the pile of Merek's possessions in the corner, though James would not have been able to see it. 'I thought I might find the comb here, in his cell.'

'Did you find it?' he asked.

'No. Unfortunately not,' I said. 'So I shall just have to keep looking.'

I then stepped forward, in the hope that James might move himself out of my way. Instead, he kept his feet firmly planted on the threshold and I was unable to pass.

'You should not become attached to worldly goods, young Oswald,' he said, his tone accusatory.

'Yes, you're right, Brother James,' I replied. 'It's just that it has a personal value to me.'

His eyes narrowed. 'It sounds to me as if you were rather too proud of this comb. Too delighted in its hollow beauty.' He sucked his lips over his gums, making an unpleasant, smacking sound. 'Carved from ivory indeed? What foolery. And equally, your mother should not have given you such a covetable object. Was she hoping to provoke petty jealousies amongst the brothers?' He wagged a bony finger in my face. 'We must think of such dangers when we live in a community. We are each responsible for one another's souls.'

'Thank you, Brother James,' I replied. 'I hadn't thought of that.'

Again I hoped he might move, but again he remained rooted to the spot, tutting to himself. 'Mind you. I'm not surprised that Brother Merek has stolen such an object from you,' he said.

'It wasn't stolen,' I replied.

'Where is it, then?' he snapped. 'Merek asked to borrow this comb and then left the monastery. It sounds very much like stealing to me. The man was vain and untrustworthy.'

'I always thought that he was the most devout of lay brothers,' I said, repeating Peter's description of Merek to judge Brother James's reaction. 'A man of God.'

Brother James sucked his lips against his teeth again. 'Then you have a lot to learn about life,' he said. 'Brother Merek was never devout. And I should know. I taught him myself in the scriptorium for long enough. But he could not stretch the thickest sheet of vellum without causing a tear.' He paused. 'And do you know why? He spent too long staring out of the windows. That was his problem.'

'Staring at what?' I asked.

'At the servants, of course,' replied James. 'The women.' He puffed the air from his cheeks. 'The Abbot makes sure to employ the plainest, most demure of women to come to Kintham, as he doesn't want to provoke the brothers into lustful thoughts.' He wagged the finger again. 'But, even so, I knew that Merek was spying upon these servants, despite their plainness. Looking at the way they walked to and from the kitchens. Staring at their breasts or their behinds. He was flagrant in his lechery. Absolutely flagrant.'

'Are you sure about this, Brother James?' I asked.

'What do you mean?' he said, offended at this question.

I mustered my courage. 'I just wondered if you might be mistaken about Merek's lechery?'

'Why would I be mistaken?' he said.

'Because your eyesight is poor,' I answered timorously. 'I wondered how you might have seen Merek staring out of a window?'

He was displeased with this observation – flaring his nostrils to display his affront. 'You really are a stupid boy, aren't you?' he said, poking a finger into my chest. 'When a man's eyesight is weakened, his other senses grow in strength. For example,' he said. 'I may not be able to see your face properly, Brother Oswald. But I know you're feeling nervous because you have just lied to me.'

'I haven't lied to you,' I said, far too defensively.

He took a moment to consider this. 'So you say. But your stance is timid, and you've been sweating. I can smell the odour on your skin.' At this point I was disturbed to find that he leant forward to sniff me. 'They say that a horse can smell fear,' he continued. 'Well, so can I.' He then cupped a hand to his ear. 'And you should also know that my hearing is extraordinary. With such skills of perception, I am not duly troubled by my poor eyesight. In many situations, I am able to perceive more than a man with perfect vision. And do you know why? Because that man makes the mistake of relying solely upon his eyes, when his ears, nose and sense of space might tell him more.'

'I'm sorry,' I replied. 'I shouldn't have doubted your story about Brother Merek.'

He huffed disdainfully. 'You may take this from me, young Oswald. Brother Merek's humours were too dry and hot to be a monk. Too passionate. He could not keep to his vows, and that's the truth of it.' He waved a twisted hand. 'I do not believe that Merek was accosted by robbers, which is the story I hear over and over again, especially from your tutor Brother Peter. Merek has found himself a woman in one of the villages and has eloped with the foolish wench. No doubt he is in London now, or some other town where he believes he might mingle into a crowd to disguise his identity.' He leant towards me, fixing me with those unnerving, opaque orbs. 'We will not see him here again, Brother Oswald,' he said ominously. 'You can be sure of that.'

Chapter Ten

Once Brother James had finally stood aside to let me pass, I sped back to my own cell and closed the door – before quickly pulling Merek's psalter from my scrip to look again at the code he had hidden in the calendar. Could these curious, secretive symbols be relevant to my investigation, or were they just a few meaningless scribbles? Whichever the case, I needed to decipher the code as soon as possible – so I copied the symbols into my own day book, before returning the psalter to Merek's cell. I didn't want Peter to find it in my possession.

After this I started to play around with the code, trying to apply the basic principles of cipher substitution that I'd learnt from studying Bede's *Reckoning of Time*. I assigned different letters of the alphabet to each symbol to see if I could find some meaning across the five groupings. The puzzle was so absorbing, that I didn't notice when Brother Peter entered our cell, only sensing his presence at the last moment, when a shadow fell across the table. I instinctively turned the page of my day book before he could see what I was doing, finding myself looking at a poem that I'd been writing for most of the previous year.

Peter and I had not spoken very often since our William of Ockham conversation, as I had been minded to ignore him. I was still annoyed with Peter for refusing to help me with my investigation, and he knew it.

'What are you doing with yourself in here?' he asked brightly, hoping to engage me in a conversation.

'Nothing much,' I replied, not looking up from the poem.

'I thought you were working in the gardens today,' he said. 'The thyme needs clipping.'

I deliberately mumbled an answer to this, as I knew it would irritate him. I could hear him clear his throat, as if he were about to say something – before he changed his mind and took a seat on his bed. He then delved noisily into his scrip to retrieve his leather flask. Like every dedicated drinker, Peter always carried a supply of liquor with him, wherever he went.

'Brother Eric is jaundiced again,' he told me, after taking a gulp of the brandy. 'He's so yellow that it looks as if we've washed him in a tub of dyer's broom.'

'Is that so?' I answered, still not looking up from the page of poetry.

'I've treated him with a decoction of soapwort,' Peter continued. 'But he looks feebler than ever. I wonder if he will last out the week.'

'Poor man,' I said glibly, before scribbling a line of verse that neither scanned nor rhymed. They were just the first words that floated into my mind, and were even worse than my usual attempts at poetry. I continued to stare at the page, aware that Peter's eyes were boring a hole into the back of my head, but I didn't submit to this pressure. After a while, he accepted defeat. He stood up, replaced the flask into his scrip and flounced out of the room with a puff of frustration.

Over the next few days, I used every free moment to work again on the cipher, though I began to experience an increasing sense of frustration. Merek had never struck me as being particularly intelligent, so I felt irritated at not being able to solve his code with any more ease. I tried any number of letter to symbol substitutions, but was still unable to extract any sense from the words. To make matters worse, Brother Peter nearly caught me out on three occasions, bursting into the room unexpectedly, or trying to lure me into giving something away in a conversation.

His suspicions were definitely raised, but I was always able to feign an enthusiasm for writing poetry whenever he caught me working. Seeing as he had always encouraged me to write verse to express my feelings, he could hardly now complain at my new dedication to this pursuit. To his mind I spent far too long reading the works of Pope Pius and Aquinas, or studying the trajectory of Venus. An appreciation of the liberal arts was to be encouraged, so that my education would be more rounded.

By the third day, I had decided to abandon the code in a fit of dejection. There was no reason to think that these random symbols had anything to do with the missing girls. Perhaps Peter had been right all along? I had conflated similar incidents in a naive attempt to solve this mystery. There was nothing to prove that Merek was guilty of anything, other than disappearing without trace from the monastery.

It was just as I was about to wash away the workings in my day book, that one final idea occurred to me. After three days of staring at Merek's code and attempting to solve his method of substitution, I wondered if I were approaching the problem from the wrong angle? Perhaps I'd even over-complicated matters? Rather than starting with Merek's code and trying to randomly substitute each symbol for a letter of the alphabet, and subsequently working through the endless possibilities that this created, I took some words of my own – words that were relevant to my investigation – to see if they could be imposed upon the code. I had expected this to be another long and laborious process, but to my great surprise I found that my idea worked almost immediately.

However, in the thrill of this success, I had failed to notice that Brother Peter had crept into the room on one of his regular snooping missions. Within moments, he had pounced on me and grasped my day book from the table.

'This isn't poetry,' he said, looking through my workings. 'You've been lying to me again, Oswald.'

'No,' I replied. '*You've* been lying to me, Brother Peter.'

I regretted this accusation almost immediately – especially since Peter was drunk.

'Me lying?' he seethed. 'About what?'

'About Brother Merek,' I replied. 'He was no man of God. No devout monk. And now I can prove it.'

'Oh yes?' he asked. 'And how do you intend to do that?'

I grabbed my day book back from Peter and pointed to the top of the page, where Merek's five pairs of words were written in their strange cipher. 'See this,' I said. 'It's a code that I copied from Merek's psalter.'

Peter looked at me with a frown. 'What about it?'

'I've solved it.'

'And?'

'And these words are the names of the women missing from Stonebrook,' I said. 'Mary Ancoats. Mary Chandler. Winifred de Terre. Mary Brewer. Jocelin Baker.' I waved the page in Peter's face. 'Now do you believe me?'

Peter took a moment and then dropped his backside onto the bed, wiping his brow as his anger dispelled.

I continued. 'And it's not just this code that's damning. I spoke to Brother James about Merek, and he described a very different man to your portrayal. According to James, Merek was a lecher. A womaniser.'

Brother Peter shook his head, but did not look up to face me. 'That's not true,' he said. 'James is mistaken. Merek was a little odd, that's all. His interest in poor women was motivated by his concerns for their welfare. Nothing else.'

'I don't believe you.'

'Well, you should.'

'I think Merek was the man who attacked Agnes,' I said. 'That's why she spat those words at me before she died. She was so distraught with fear that she mistook me for him.'

Peter didn't look up, but continued to shake his head in denial.

His reaction annoyed me. 'Come on, Brother Peter. You cannot continue to blindly protest Merek's innocence,' I said. 'Not when there is all this evidence against him.'

'What evidence?' he hissed.

'Merek was known to loiter around the poor women in Stonebrook,' I replied. 'Brother James called him a lecher. And now I find the names of the missing women, secretly written in Merek's psalter.'

Brother Peter raised his eyes to mine with wearied exasperation. A look that he reserved almost solely for my benefit. 'I warned you to keep away from this, Oswald,' he said.

'Merek has written the names of the missing women in code,' I repeated. 'Why would he record their names like this if he wasn't involved?'

I studied Peter's face for a moment. There were heavy bags under his eyes and his cheeks were flushed. 'Oh Oswald,' he groaned, wiping the sweat from his forehead. 'You think you're so clever, don't you? But you couldn't be more wrong.'

Chapter Eleven

Somershill, November 1370

I tapped Mother on the shoulder to see if she were still awake, only to find that she didn't respond. I drew closer, panicking that she might have died while I was talking, before I detected her chest rising and falling. For a moment, I saw my letter, poking out from the neckline of her chemise. In an instant, I felt myself reach forward, wanting to pluck the letter from its hiding place – having to fight against the strong draw of this temptation.

I strode out of the bedchamber before I changed my mind, finding that Thomas Crouch was hanging around in the passage-way, wearing an expectant face and holding his jar of greedy leeches. I was already feeling unsettled, so his presence did nothing to improve my mood. Why could Mother not be left to die quietly without being decorated with these creatures? Crouch might have argued that her yellow bile needed dampening, but he risked draining her life spirit away.

Angered by this thought, I escorted Crouch to the gatehouse, and told him not to return to Somershill until he was called upon. He objected, of course, arguing that Mother's health was too fragile to be deprived of his redoubtable skills, but I insisted that he leave the house, find a room at a local tavern and not return before being expressly invited. I gave him this warning,

Should I find him hanging around Mother's room without my approval, then he would spend a night in my gaol house. This final threat was enough to secure his cooperation, and he was soon seen scampering away towards the village, clutching his bag of clothes and box of dubious remedies. I could only hope that he had not done too much damage already. I needed Mother to stay alive to hear the end of my story.

That evening, we were gathered at the supper table, eating one of my least favourite meals — one that was often served in the winter months — salted herrings and wheat bread. At least the herrings were not smoked, since the stink of that particular dish could linger throughout the house for many days.

Our resident entertainer Sir John was in an exuberant mood, having consumed too much of our Gascon wine for his own good. Usually his stories were sensible-enough recollections of his journeys. The style of boat he had sailed in. A description of the unfamiliar architecture and strange customs of some foreign land. Even an example of an unfamiliar language he had picked up from a sailor, an innkeeper or a lover. But that evening he told a tale that would stretch the credulity of the most gullible of listeners.

By all accounts, Sir John had sailed to a lonely island in the Mediterranean, only to find that this outcrop of rock was populated entirely by a race of giants. Men with a single eye that was situated in the centre of their chests. These men (he didn't mention any females) had, over the centuries, pulled up all of the many trees that once grew on this island, so that they might use the trunks to fight one another to the death. The winner subsequently eating the loser. This act of self-destruction had ended when the last of the trees had disappeared, leading the giants that remained to finally call a truce. Since that time, this strange race had survived instead by luring sailors to their shores with their sweet singing, (a story that was starting to sound suspiciously like the myth of the sirens). Once they had plundered the shipwrecks, they then ate the sailors – preserving those men that they couldn't manage at the first sitting in salt.

It was, of course, a preposterous story, but I seemed to be the only person about the table who wasn't thoroughly taken in. I'm afraid to say that Filomena had seemed particularly enthralled by the tale – cooing and gasping at every absurd detail. I should have laughed it off, but unfortunately Mother's theory about Sir John and my wife had once again worked its way under my skin like a stubborn splinter. Despite my best intentions, I couldn't help but feel my childish jealousy and suspicion return. So, when Filomena drew the drapes about our bed that night, I made the mistake of broaching the subject.

'What did you think of Sir John's tale about the giants?' I asked her.

'I thought it was wonderful, but also terrifying,' she answered, pulling the sheets over her chest. 'To think that there are such evil creatures in the world. Monsters who would kill men with such cruelty.'

'You don't believe it, do you?' I asked, making sure to add a contemptuous laugh.

'Of course,' she replied. 'Why not?'

'Oh come on, Filomena,' I said. 'You lived in Venice for many years. Did you ever hear of a sailor being lured onto an island by a singing, one-eyed giant?'

'The sea is large,' she said. 'Many men disappear when sailing. Maybe this is the reason?'

'So how did Sir John escape?' I asked. 'Why wasn't he lured to his death?'

Filomena fiddled with the sheets and rearranged the bolster. 'Weren't you listening, Oswald?' she said. 'Sir John and the other men stuffed their ears with strips of linen so that they couldn't hear the singing. They were clever enough not to fall into this trap.' I didn't remember this detail of the story, not least because

I had been studying Filomena's face while Sir John was speaking, rather than paying full attention to his far-fetched tale.

'It's nonsense,' I said. 'The man is making the whole thing up. You must be able to see that?'

'I don't agree. Sir John has travelled so much more widely than we have.' There was a distinct note of rebuke in her voice. 'We never go anywhere beyond this parish. So who are we to challenge his tale?'

'Sir John drank far too much of my wine tonight, and his imagination ran away with itself.' I laughed again, this time with genuine mirth. 'A man with a single eye in the middle of his chest? As if that could be true.'

I was subjected to a long silence in return for this comment. 'I thought Sir John was your friend, Oswald?' said Filomena at length. 'But now I see you don't like him very much.'

I shrugged. 'What makes you think that?'

'You pull faces when he's talking.'

'So do you,' I said.

'What sort of faces?'

I hesitated to answer, knowing that I would be straying into dangerous territory. 'It doesn't matter.'

Another long silence followed before she turned her back on me and muttered something in Venetian. A rebuke about jealous husbands.

I fell asleep in a bad mood, and woke in a worse one, resolving not to return to Mother's bedchamber for a while. In the meantime, Clemence took over this duty with enthusiasm. However, after two days of my sister's prayers and hectoring company, I received the message that Mother was begging for me to return.

I entered Mother's room to find Clemence had once again drawn the drapes about the bed, which was an unnecessary precaution, since the day outside was mild and the room itself was adequately warm. It made me wonder if Thomas Crouch had been re-admitted during my absence, since the removal of light and air was one of his favourite remedies. It is my own opinion that illness needs to be ventilated and showered with daylight, since an accumulation of heat and darkness can lead to lethargy and even melancholia. And so I drew back the drapes to throw some light across Mother's face, finding that she had a bloom to her cheeks, which gave me to believe that Crouch and his leeches hadn't been here after all. It was a consolation.

'There you are, Oswald,' said Mother, making an effort to sit up. 'I thought you'd abandoned me.'

I must admit that the idea had crossed my mind, and I considered telling her the reason for this – but then I risked being drawn into another conversation about Filomena and Sir John.

'You were very tired when I last visited,' I said. 'You fell asleep while I was speaking.'

'Nonsense,' she said. 'I heard every word.'

I decided to test her. 'Can you remember where we ended, then?'

'Of course I can remember, Oswald,' she snapped. 'I'm not a child.'

'Very well,' I said. 'I'll carry on. If you recall, I had deciphered some coded words written inside Brother Merek's psalter.'

She frowned for a moment – clearly not remembering this detail at all – before realising that she didn't want to make this admission. She quickly changed her expression to a thoughtful smile. 'Just run through that part of your story again,' she said. 'I think you missed out some important details.' Before I was able to gloat, she added. 'You do not consider your listener with enough care, Oswald. Your tale is more muddled than a stirred egg. Sometimes I don't know if I'm listening to the white or the yolk.'

'Perhaps you would prefer it if we talked about the weather?' I suggested. 'If not, Clemence has given me some prayers we could read together?'

This was threat enough. 'No prayers, thank you, Oswald,' she said quickly. 'Please summarise the last few points of your tale and then continue.'

'If you remember, Mother, the words I had decoded in Brother Merek's psalter were the names of the missing women. When I confronted Brother Peter about this, he became upset and claimed that I couldn't have been more wrong about Merek. That my theory was very mistaken.'

'What theory was that?' she asked lightly.

'My theory that Merek was befriending women from the village. Using his position as a monk to gain their trust, before he lured them to their deaths.'

Mother cleared her throat. A sure sign that she was about to lie. 'Yes, of course. I remember now.' She waved her hand at me. 'Well, carry on, Oswald. Carry on.'

Chapter Twelve

Kent, June 1349

Peter's complexion was permanently flushed – his cheeks laced with a web of small veins, whilst the end of his nose became a little more inflamed and pitted with each year. It was a drinker's face, of course, and one that I had become accustomed to seeing. But that afternoon his complexion had reddened so vividly, that I wondered if he was about to suffer a seizure of the heart.

'Are you unwell?' I asked him.

'This is your fault, Oswald,' he said. 'Making up these foolish lies about Merek. I've had enough of you.'

'Then how do you explain these names in his psalter?' I asked.

Peter hesitated, and then rubbed his hands through his hair. 'It's better that you don't know, Oswald. It really is.'

'Why?'

'Because . . .' He couldn't finish this sentence. Instead, he rose to his feet and headed for the small arched window of our cell. As he leant against the sill, the thin light fell onto one side of his head, picking out the contours of his careworn face. He spoke without looking back at me.

'There is a good reason why Merek wrote the names of those women in his psalter, Oswald,' he said. 'He was doing what you're doing. Trying to find out why they had disappeared.'

This took me by surprise. 'How do you know that?'

'Because he told me, of course,' said Peter, spinning around to look me in the face. 'I was his ally. His confidant.'

'Are you sure he was telling you the truth?'

'Don't be a fool, Oswald,' said Peter with a scowl. 'Merek befriended those women because he wanted to help them. It was the act of a true Christian.' He paused for a moment. 'You see. You're not the only one who cares. Merek's visits to Stonebrook had nothing to do with lustful thoughts or craving female company. Brother James was wrong about that.'

I felt confused and couldn't answer.'

Peter continued. 'Now can you understand why I found your accusations so offensive? Merek was only trying to help those women, and yet you seemed determined to believe the very worst of him.'

'So why didn't you tell me about this before?' I asked. 'And why have you stood in the way of my efforts to find answers, when you say that you helped Merek?'

'For a very simple reason. I was afraid for you, Oswald. Merek's investigation ended in his disappearance. For all we know, he's dead.'

'Do you think he's been murdered, then?' I asked. 'By the same man who's taken the women?'

Peter hesitated to answer. 'In all probability,' he replied before taking another long pause. 'Merek was getting too close to finding answers.'

'Did he tell you what he'd discovered?' I could tell that Peter didn't really want to answer this question. 'If you think that Merek was murdered, then you need to tell me what you know.' I insisted.

Peter pulled at the mole on his neck. 'I only know that Merek had spoken to one of the women in Stonebrook, and that she'd told him something important. She gave him a name, I believe.'

'And Merek didn't tell you this name?'

Peter shook his head. 'Unfortunately not. Merek promised to share this information with me, once he'd made a further investigation.' He paused. 'But then he disappeared, and it was too late.'

This news was frustrating, but not completely disheartening. 'So I just need to find this woman in Stonebrook,' I said. 'And see what she said to—'

Before I could finish my sentence, Peter had grabbed me by the wrist. 'No Oswald,' he said. 'Have you not heard me? It's too dangerous to continue. Merek was murdered when he persisted with this investigation. I will not allow you to suffer the same fate.'

'So we do nothing? We allow more women to disappear? We turn a blind eye and let this man continue?'

Peter was momentarily lost for words. 'No, that's not what I'm saying. You're deliberately misunderstanding me. But we must be cautious.'

'Why?'

Peter released my hand. 'Because there are worse dangers out there than a murderer, Oswald. There is a plague raging. That is why. This is no time for running around and looking for missing women.'

'There is no plague in Stonebrook,' I replied. 'So, there's no reason why I cannot carry on.'

Well then,' he said. 'You should listen to this.' He felt about his habit, slipping his hands beneath his belt to pull out a fold of parchment. 'It's from my friend Brother Robert, the infirmarer at Lowhampton Abbey,' he said, waving it in my face. 'I received it yesterday, and if this doesn't frighten you then nothing will.'

Peter unfolded the letter and squinted at the writing. 'The devastation of plague is monstrous,' he told me. 'Far worse than we've been led to believe. Robert says that they've lost nearly all their monks. And it is not a pleasant way to die, Oswald. It starts with a stiffness of the limbs and a fever, before great boils appear at the neck and armpits. But these swellings are not filled with the usual puss. Instead it is blackened blood! Robert has tried everything to save the lives of his brethren. He's even lanced these boils as a last resort. It releases the infection, only for the patient to die of shock.'

Peter heaved a long sigh, refolded the letter and placed it softly in his lap. 'This is the reality of the world outside these walls, Oswald,' he said. 'So, please listen to me. I will help you with this investigation myself, when the Plague has abated. If he still lives, then we will find this murderer and we will bring him to justice together. But in the meantime, we must stay here and we must stay safe.'

'Very well,' I said. 'I agree.'

Peter frowned at the speed of my response and then leant over to study my face. 'Are you telling me the truth, Oswald?' he asked. 'Because this is your last chance. If you defy me again, then I will lock you in the lunatic's cell and keep the key at my waist.'

I bowed my head solemnly and made this promise, though I had no intention of keeping it. Peter would forgive any of my transgressions in the end, despite his threats. I was completely secure in his love and affection. And as for his lecture on the dangers of plague – I thought it was an exaggeration, designed to frighten me into submission. Peter could not deter me from this investigation. My course had been set the moment that Agnes drowned.

Chapter Thirteen

Mother opened a single eye to fix me with a beady, unnerving stare. It was a look that I knew well, as I had been on the receiving end of such scrutiny since childhood. I was being examined and found wanting. 'You do surprise me with this story, Oswald,' she said finally.

'Why?'

'Well,' she said, now opening her other eye. 'Are you sure this is the absolute truth?'

I sat back and folded my arms in annoyance. Who was she to question my story? A woman whose own tales often bore little, if any, relationship to the truth. 'Why do you ask that?' I said calmly, trying not to give away my irritation.

'You had only just turned eighteen at the time of this tale,' she replied. 'And you were such a quiet little mouse back then. Do you remember? After your father and brothers died of plague, we could hardly get you to speak to the servants or even sit in your father's chair. Even though you were now Lord Somershill.'

'I'm not sure that's entirely true,' I countered.

She puffed her thin lips. 'Oh come along now, Oswald. You must recall those times?' She added a sigh. 'I know it was difficult for you. You had expected to become a monk, not a lord. But even so . . . you spent the first months hiding in your father's library. Messing around with his ledgers, so that you didn't have to be seen.' She gave a laugh. 'Goodness me, we could barely get you to come out for supper.'

'What's your point, Mother?' I asked tersely.

'It's very simple,' she replied. 'I remember the Oswald de Lacy who suddenly became Lord Somershill in 1349. He was a shy, awkward boy, who liked his own company, or that of his books. And yet, you now describe a completely different person. Some sort of crusading hero. A young man who took grave risks and disobeyed the rules to avenge the deaths of some village girls.' She puffed a laugh. 'I know that time is apt to play tricks on the memory, Oswald, but I can hardly believe we are talking about the same person.'

'I wasn't the same person,' I replied.

She paused to look at me. Her veil had fallen back from her forehead, to reveal a pinkish scalp that was feathered with wisps of white hair. I had never seen her look more ancient and desiccated. 'What do you mean by that?' she snapped.

'Let me finish this story, Mother. And then you will understand.'

Chapter Fourteen

Kent, June 1349

In the days following Peter's warning to me about the Plague, he found it difficult to keep a watchful eye on my whereabouts. The condition of the old monk with the abscess on his leg had taken a turn for the worse, as the poison had not been drawn out by the Sundew leaves, as Peter had hoped. Nor by a compress of comfrey, nor even a poultice of fuller's earth. It now seemed as if the inflammation and corruption were spreading up his leg, meaning that Peter would have to amputate or the old man would die. My tutor was an experienced barber surgeon – but I was too noble to be an apprentice to this profession, so I was not called upon to help. Cutting flesh and bone was not considered to be a suitable career for a man of my status. If noblemen worked in the area of medicine, they became physicians, not surgeons.

As a consequence, my duties about the infirmary were lightened, and I was left to my own devices, despite Peter's sporadic attempts to keep me under his supervision. The lay brothers working under Peter's stewardship didn't care about my whereabouts and equally, I was not missed by the novice master, Brother Thomas, as I rarely attended his classes anyway. All of this meant that I had the perfect opportunity to continue my investigation.

*   *   *

When the bell rang for Terce, I left via the gate in the vegetable garden and headed directly into woodland. After this, I made my way along the forest paths to Stonebrook, and soon found myself crossing the village green and heading up the main street towards Maud Woodstock's grand home.

My appearance didn't attract the attention of my previous visits, as the village seemed much quieter than before. No women came to the doors of their cottages to stare at me, and no shoeless children followed me up the street, trying to tug at my habit and beg for attention. I wondered if the villagers of Stonebrook had become more circumspect about visitors since the last time I turned up – aware that plague always arrives with a stranger. For my part, I was pleased to be left alone, as I picked my way along the dry ground beside the stream of muddy water that now ran down the centre of this street, flowing with some force after the overnight rain.

But my peace was not to last, however. When I felt a hand on my shoulder, I turned around to see John Roach standing behind me – the midday sun shining through his crop of white hair and creating an aura about his head, as if he had been blessed with a halo.

'What are you doing here, Brother Oswald?' he asked, eyeing me from head to toe.

I wondered if Roach were about to mention the restrictions on novices leaving the monastery, so I went to defend myself, before having the good sense to bite my tongue. If Roach had known about the Abbot's latest rule, then he would have mentioned it immediately. Pedants such as Roach are never more grateful than at the gift of a new law to enforce.

'I left a psalter with Mistress Woodstock,' I said. 'It's needed by the Abbey.' I stepped back, accidentally treading into the stream that I had been trying to avoid.

This amused Roach and he took a moment to regard my wet shoes, before returning his eyes to mine. 'Don't you have enough psalters?' he said. 'I thought Kintham was packed with them?'

I answered this with a bow of my head and a short, disdainful smile – the type that's often doled out to idiots. Its meaning was not lost on him. 'Well. I'll wish you good day,' I said, as I walked away, now marching through the stream, not caring what I stepped in.

Roach didn't follow. Instead he watched me closely until I knocked at the door to Maud's house. Our eyes met for a moment as Maud's thin maid Johanna answered the door, before he spun on his heel and marched away.

The girl seemed startled by my appearance, mumbled something inaudible and then ran away to find her mistress immediately. As I waited to be allowed entrance, I enjoyed the smell of cooking that was drifting into the street from Maud's kitchen – the eddying vapours of another meaty dish.

Johanna soon returned, and then led me through the central hall of the house into the cosy parlour, where Maud was seated at a table with her back to me, reading a ledger. She appeared to be deep in concentration, but put down her quill and stood to greet me when Johanna announced my arrival.

'Good day, Oswald,' she said with a smile. 'You're a welcome sight.' She waved her hand at the table. 'I've been working on this Roll of Expenses all morning, and I cannot make the costs match the items purchased.' She gave a short huff. 'I must say that I'm finding it very frustrating.'

She was wearing a gown of the lightest blue that day – a shade that picked out the exact shade of her eyes. It was the colour of a shallow sea at high tide. In fact, she looked so strikingly beautiful that my throat seized up for a moment and I found that I couldn't speak.

It was no wonder that she laughed at me. 'Dear me, Oswald,' she said. 'Have you been struck dumb by the angel Gabriel?'

I found my voice quickly, acutely aware of my foolishness. 'I'm sorry,' I said, before coughing to clear my throat. 'I rushed here from the monastery and it's a warm day.'

She laughed again, which only served to make me feel even more embarrassed. 'Then you must have some ale,' she announced. And before I could reply, she had recalled Johanna to the room and teased the girl for not having offered me a drink immediately. I couldn't help but notice that Johanna trembled at this mild rebuke.

Maud saw my reaction. 'You mustn't worry about Johanna,' she told me, when the girl had retired to the kitchen. 'I know she seems nervous, but she had a very sad beginning to her life.' She paused. 'I'm not sure if she will ever gain full confidence.'

'I see,' I replied, hoping she might elaborate.

Maud read my mind. 'I was visiting the Winchester wool fair when I first came across her,' she said. 'Poor Johanna was living like a stray dog in an alley. It wouldn't have been long before she was picked up by the local brothel keeper, so I brought her back here to Stonebrook. I wanted to train her as a lady's maid.' Maud raised her eyebrows and puffed her lips. 'I'm sorry to say that she has never quite settled. Sometimes Johanna will still cringe from her own reflection.'

'It was good of you to take her in,' I said.

Maud swayed her head from side to side, in polite rebuttal. 'It was the Christian way to behave, Oswald. And anyway, I have done well out of this arrangement. Johanna is very gentle with my father.' Maud glanced upwards towards the roof. 'You may hear him today, I'm afraid. We washed his bedsores this morning with vinegar, and he is never happy afterwards.'

I couldn't help but wince. 'Might not salted water have been a little less astringent?' I suggested.

'We have tried that,' she replied. 'But it's much less effective against the corruption. And Father complains just as much, whether we use salt or vinegar.'

At that moment, almost as if the man were listening to our conversation, a soft moaning came from the bedchamber on the floor above us, where Roger Woodstock was said to spend the whole of his life. There was a short pause before he groaned again, louder this time, followed by the clatter of footsteps on the wooden steps as Johanna rushed upstairs. We heard the girl trying to calm Woodstock, but the groaning became even louder.

Maud hesitated for a moment, before rising to her feet. 'Excuse me, Oswald,' she said, as she made for the door. 'I'll just see what's going on.'

'Would you like any help?' I offered.

'No, no,' she said firmly. 'There's no need.'

While Maud was absent, I heard footsteps running to and fro on the floorboards overhead, and then a loud, crashing bump followed by a low moaning. My curiosity got the better of me, so I went to the door of the parlour and opened it a little, hoping to hear more. The groaning stopped, just as suddenly as it had begun, but then there was a shuffling, dragging noise followed by hissed whispers.

When I heard Maud returning down the stairs, I quickly closed the door and retreated to my seat. She reappeared soon after, looking a little flushed.

'Is everything all right?' I asked.

'Father fell out of bed again,' she answered.

'You should have called me.'

'That's very kind of you,' she replied. 'But Father wouldn't like it. I'm afraid that he's ashamed of his condition.' She heaved a sigh. 'We must allow him some dignity . . . though he can be very hard work at times.'

'Perhaps you should consider sending him to the infirmary?' I suggested.

Maud shook her head. 'There's no need,' she answered. 'We can cope with him here. A man should be allowed to die in his own home, don't you think?'

'But sometimes it's difficult to offer the right care in a small bed chamber, Maud,' I argued. 'And Brother Peter is very experienced in the treatment of apoplexies. And, you never know, your father might be more comfortable at the monastery? I have seen men with his same affliction begin to prosper and flourish when they have more company.'

'Thank you,' she replied sharply. 'I know you mean well with these suggestions, but I promised Father that I would look after him in his old age. And I will not renege on that promise. No matter how difficult he becomes.' She sat up straight and laid her beautiful hands softly into her lap. 'So, Oswald,' she said. 'Enough about Father. What can I do for you today?'

I felt a little blown off course, unable to immediately retrieve the speech that I'd prepared for this moment. 'There's something I needed to tell you,' I said finally.

Her face relaxed into a smile, all talk of her father's illness forgotten. 'This sounds intriguing.'

'It's about Brother Merek,' I said. 'I asked around at Kintham after hearing your concerns, and I wanted to let you know what I discovered.'

'I hope I wasn't speaking out of turn,' she replied, suddenly guarded. 'They were just my own thoughts. Nothing more.' She paused. 'Perhaps I shouldn't have mentioned them?'

'No. You were right to be suspicious about Merek,' I replied. 'And I should have been more honest with you at the time.'

'Oh yes?'

I hesitated, feeling awkward at making this disclosure. 'You see, the thing is . . . Merek has also disappeared. He's been missing from the Abbey for more than six weeks.'

Maud stared back at me in surprise, her forehead knotted into a frown. 'Oh,' she said. 'I see.'

'I'm sorry. I would have mentioned it before,' I replied. 'But we're forbidden to speak on the matter.'

'Why's that?'

'The Abbot wants to keep the story quiet.' I cleared my throat, feeling more awkward than ever. 'There are rumours that Merek has run away with a woman.' Maud's face immediately registered shock, so I quickly added, 'But it's not true.'

She narrowed her eyes. 'Are you sure about that?'

'Yes, absolutely. It's gossip, nothing more.' I paused. 'But there is a good reason why you saw Merek so often in Stonebrook. A good reason why he appeared to be befriending the poorest women.'

'Go on.'

'Merek was carrying out his own investigations into the disappearances.' I said. 'He didn't believe the story about those women running away to London either.'

Maud's frown only deepened as she tapped her fingers together. It seemed that she was far from convinced. 'How do you know all this, Oswald?' she asked me.

'Brother Peter told me,' I said. 'Merek confided in him before he disappeared.'

'Brother Peter,' she repeated. 'He's your tutor at the monastery, isn't he?'

'Yes, that's right.'

'So why didn't Peter tell you about Merek before?' she asked me. 'Especially after Agnes died.'

I hesitated. 'Because he doesn't want me to get involved. He thinks it's too dangerous.' When she threw me a quizzical stare, I added, 'Peter believes that Merek was murdered when he got too close to finding answers.' I looked down at my hands, which were now pale and sweaty. 'Peter doesn't want the same thing to happen to me, Maud.'

I looked up to see that she was studying me closely. I could now see tiny flecks of violet in the blue of her eyes – fragments of colour that were glistening like the iridescent streaks in a wet pebble. There was such unsettling beauty in her gaze that I found it very difficult to concentrate.

I'm sorry, Oswald,' she said finally. 'It seems that I was very wrong about Merek. I feel foolish now.'

'Please don't apologise,' I said. 'I'm pleased that you told me of your concerns. If nothing else, it forced Peter's hand. Otherwise he would never have revealed the truth to me about Merek.'

Maud turned her face towards the window for a moment and let the breeze blow over her face as she thought. The shutters were raised today because the weather outside was sultry and close, but there was still a thin current of air seeping its way into the room through this open void. Maud and her father might have been wealthy, but they could not yet afford glass in their windows.

She turned back to me. 'You say that Merek confided in Peter. And that he was close to finding the killer. So, did he tell Peter who he suspected?'

I shook my head. 'No. I'm sorry.'

She sighed. 'That's a pity.'

'But I do know that Merek discovered something important from speaking to one of the women in the village,' I said quickly. 'Apparently he believed that this information might lead him to the killer.' I paused. 'Unfortunately we can only assume that it did . . . since Merek's not been seen since.'

Maud rested her hand on my arm. 'Do we know who gave him this information?' she asked, her face full of anticipation.

'No,' I admitted, thwarting a sudden urge to take her hand in mine. 'Though it must have been one of the women you saw talking to Merek,' I added. 'That's why I've come here today. I wondered if you could give me their names? I will need to speak to each of them.'

Maud looked at me with a thoughtful expression. 'Of course,' she said. 'But I might have a better idea. Why don't I gather them here instead? We could question them together.' She paused for a moment. 'It would certainly save you time.'

I was taken aback by this offer and didn't answer immediately. Unfortunately Maud misread my hesitation as offence. 'I'm sorry, Oswald,' she said quickly, withdrawing her hand from my arm. 'I'm always doing this. Trying to take over.' She inclined her head to mine. 'I shouldn't interfere.'

'No, no,' I replied. 'Thank you. I think it's a very helpful idea.'

'You do?'

'Of course.'

Maud let the tips of her fingers brush against the skin on the back of my hand. 'You're a good man, Oswald de Lacy,' she said. 'A rarity.'

Before I could respond to this compliment, Maud had called Johanna into the room and asked the girl to round up certain women in the village. When Johanna asked if she should name a purpose for this gathering, Maud told her to be vague – although to be sure to mention that food and ale would be served. With such an incentive, the women were certain to accept.

With Johanna gone, Maud and I moved into the main hall, where we arranged two benches along either side of the long trestle table – agreeing that we would ask the women to sit here, whilst we would take two chairs at the head. Maud then lifted a large wooden crucifix from the wall and laid it across the middle of the table so that it would be visible from all of the seats.

When she noticed the look of surprise on my face, she said. 'This will help the women to concentrate, Oswald. To be honest and measured.'

'You think they need reminding of that?'

She gave a short laugh. 'Wait until you've talked to them, Oswald,' she replied. 'Then you'll see what I mean. The women of this village are very good at inventing stories.' She patted the crucifix. 'This will remind them to tell the truth.'

Chapter Fifteen

Johanna soon returned with a group of about fifteen women and girls, who filed into the hall and stared upwards to the roof trusses as if they had just entered the nave of York Minster. I was struck immediately by their height, or lack of it. In this village, more than any other I had ever visited, a person's size seemed to depend upon their wealth. In their brown and grey dresses they looked like a flock of hedge sparrows, whilst Maud moved amongst them, standing out like a colourful jay.

Once the women had dispensed with their wonder at this house, (a building which they had clearly never entered before), they gathered about their leader, Aldith Brewer, for safety. I noted that Aldith's belly was now so low, that I feared she might go into labour before we finished our discussion. I looked about at the other women in this group and I must say that I was relieved not to find Beatrice Wheeler's face among them.

'So then,' said Aldith, turning to Maud. 'What's this all about?' She folded her arms over her bump. 'We're all busy, you know. We haven't got time to sit around and chatter.'

This statement caused Maud to share a quick smile with me. The pressures on these women's time had not been so great that they weren't able to immediately accept this invitation. Clearly the mention of food had done its trick. 'Brother Oswald would like to speak to you all,' she said.

'What about?' replied Aldith. 'Is it plague? Because we all know about the family in Fallowsden.'

I went to reply, but Maud held up her hand to stop me. 'Please,' she said, smiling about the room. 'Take a seat along this table first, and let me offer you some bread and ale. Then we can talk.'

Aldith hesitated, not inclined to surrender immediately to Maud's will, whereas her cohorts had accepted the invitation without a second thought. At the mention of food the other women had rushed to the table and were now eagerly waiting for the meal to be served. Realising that she had lost this small battle, Aldith pushed aside two women to ensure that she took the best place at the table – at the centre of the bench where she could see everybody's faces.

'So,' Aldith announced, as if she had called this meeting herself. 'Let's eat first, and then we'll see what Brother Oswald has to say.' This declaration was met with a flurry of nods and small cheers, prompting Maud to glance at me again and share another amused smile.

As Johanna rushed from kitchen to table with a succession of loaves, wedges of hard cheese, bowls of green cheese and tall jugs of ale, the women eagerly filled their stomachs, as if they had never seen such a feast before. I waited until the laughter and the chattering had finally subsided and then I stood up, ready to speak. It was only then, as I looked down the table at the row of expectant faces, flushed after the excitement of their unexpected banquet, that I suddenly regretted having agreed to this meeting. For a moment, my nerve faltered, as I noticed a wave of furtive smirks and giggles hidden behind hands. One of the women even joked about trying to look under my habit.

Of course, I knew why I amused them. There's something uniquely comical about a boy at that age – with his slender frame, smooth skin and pincushion of whiskers sprouting from a spotty chin. He is still a press-mould of a man, yet to be fired in the kiln.

Maud spotted my nervousness and gave me one of her encouraging smiles. 'Thank you for coming,' I managed to say, making an effort to look directly into their faces. 'I wanted to ask you all some questions about the missing women.'

'They're not missing,' said Aldith, chewing on a hunk of bread. 'They're dead.'

'We don't know that for certain, Aldith,' came another voice. It belonged to a stout and muscular woman, who sported a pair of forearms that wouldn't have looked amiss on a wrestler. I had sometimes seen this woman in the fields outside the village, directing a ploughing team of four oxen with a whip. 'They could still be alive,' she said. 'I don't think we should give up hope.'

'Oh come on,' replied Aldith, spooning some cheese into her mouth. 'We spent days looking for each of them and we didn't find a thing.'

'I blame the manticore,' said a woman who was missing the majority of her teeth.

'The what?' laughed Aldith, scornfully. Out of the corner of my eye I could see Maud bristle, as this was exactly the type of wild story she had feared.

The toothless woman was not deterred. 'The manticore has the head of a man, the body of a lion and the tail of a scorpion,' she explained. 'It creeps up on a person and then stings them to death with its tail. I've seen it myself,' she added. 'Skulking in the woods. Looking for its dinner.'

'When's that, then?' said Aldith. 'After you've been in the tavern all day?'

This caused an outbreak of laughter that lasted until I loudly cleared my throat. 'I believe that some of you spoke previously to Brother Merek?' I said. 'I know that he was also trying to find answers to this mystery.'

'But he gave up, didn't he?' said Aldith, adding a sniff of contempt as she pulled a small piece of dough from her bread. 'We haven't seen him for weeks.'

'That's because Brother Merek is also missing,' I replied.

Aldith put down the bread. 'What? Is he dead as well, then?'

'We don't know,' I answered truthfully, having to shout to make myself heard over the subsequent uproar. 'But I believe that Merek discovered something important to his investigation by speaking to somebody in this room.' The women stopped talking and glanced darkly at one another. 'So please try to remember what you said to him.'

A girl at the end of the table spoke up. She had a small round face – the shape of a boiled pudding. 'I told Brother Merek that I'm fed up with being trapped in this village. I don't dare to go anywhere.'

'It's all right for you, Margaret Tucker,' said the girl sitting opposite her. 'You don't have to go to the market on your own. If I stayed here, then my family would starve.'

'I might not have to go to market,' replied the pudding-faced girl. 'But I still have to go into the forest by myself. To collect wood. Otherwise we'd never have a fire. So don't go thinking that you're the only one with troubles.'

Maud clapped her hands to break up this argument. 'No woman should be going anywhere by herself,' she announced. 'It's too dangerous.'

All heads turned to Maud. 'That's easier said than done,' said Aldith sharply. 'You've got a servant to do your bidding. None of us have that luxury.'

'That's true,' Maud replied calmly, refusing to be riled by Aldith's hostility. 'I do enjoy that privilege. But I'm still afraid of being attacked, should I venture out alone.'

'You needn't worry,' scoffed Aldith. 'This man's not going to pick on the likes of you, is he?'

'Who's to say that?' snapped Maud, staring at Aldith until the younger woman looked away. 'It seems to me that this man simply chooses victims who are travelling alone. If I were to wander into the woods without an escort, then I would also be in danger. I am no safer than you.' Maud paused for a moment and took a deep breath to regain her composure. 'All I'm saying is that we should organise ourselves to make this man's life difficult,' she contended. 'Let us starve him of opportunity, until he is forced to leave us alone.'

'And how will we do that?' asked Aldith, crossing her arms sulkily.

'Always find another woman to travel with,' said Maud. 'It's the only way to protect ourselves. I doubt this man will ever pick on a pair of women.'

'It's not always possible to find a partner,' argued Aldith, not ready to back down, though her constant antagonism was beginning to look childish and petulant. 'You don't know what our lives are like,' she said. 'It's not always easy to find another woman to do your bidding.'

'Then come to me in that case,' said Maud, looking up and down the table to make sure that she had everybody's attention. 'If you cannot find another companion, then I will accompany you myself.'

Maud's declaration was met with stunned silence at first, for this was quite an offer. The daughters of rich yeoman farmers do not usually travel about the forests and paths of England with poor villeins and cottars as company. The women took a moment to digest Maud's proposal, before they expressed their gratitude with cheers and clapping. Realising that she'd lost the argument, Aldith quickly claimed association, nay ownership, of Maud's generous idea, by raising a toast to Mistress Woodstock as their friend and protector. Following this, Maud was thanked specifically for the ale and bread – which, of course, prompted her to call for more. Soon Johanna arrived with another jug of ale and two loaves of bread – though I noted it was barley bread and small beer this time, and there was definitely no cheese.

Now that the mood was congenial again, I returned to my questioning. 'Please think back to your conversations with

Brother Merek,' I said. 'I'm interested in anything. No matter how unimportant it might seem.' When this question was met, yet again, with blank faces, I added, 'Think carefully. There must be something you know. Something that could help me?'

I was about to give up, when a young girl spoke. I had hardly noticed her before, since she'd been squashed between two larger women, like a line of mortar daubed between two pillar stones.

'My sister's got something to say,' she said, pushing her way past the bulk of her neighbours' tunics and pointing to another girl on the other side of the table. 'Haven't you, Rose?' Her sister was an equally thin creature who was perched on the end of the other bench like a newly fledged bird.

I leant forward to get a better look and realised it was Rose Brunham – the girl with salmon-coloured hair whom I'd met at Beatrice Wheeler's house. I hadn't recognised her before, since she was wearing a veil.

Rose scowled back across the table at her sister. 'No, I haven't,' she hissed. 'Shut up, Christina!'

'Tell them about Jocelin's bracelet,' said Christina. 'The one she was wearing when she disappeared. Explain why you've got it now.'

Aldith gasped. 'Is this true, Rose?' she said. 'Have you got Jocelin's bracelet?'

Rose dropped her eyes to her hands. 'I was given it,' she whispered, her shoulders sinking as she tried to disappear from view. 'Nothing wrong with that.'

'Who gave it to you?' I asked.

'Doesn't matter.'

'It was that Ranulf Sawyer,' carped Christina. 'The charcoal burner.'

The mention of this name caused another outcry. 'What's Sawyer doing back here?' groaned Aldith. 'I thought we'd seen him off a couple of years ago. He's supposed to be in Epping forest.'

Christina shook her head. She was enjoying this moment of victory over her sister. 'No. Sawyer's back, isn't he? 'Cause he's in love with Rose.' She turned on her sister. 'I keep telling you to stay away from him, don't I? But you won't listen. Even though he's a dirty pig.'

'He's a charcoal burner,' spat Rose. 'He's only dirty 'cause of the soot.'

'By the saints, Rose Brunham!' said the woman with muscular arms. 'Don't say that you're sweet on that man? You wait until I tell your mother about this. You'll get a beating.'

Rose put her hands to her face as the other women scolded her, roundly attacking the girl for consorting with this supposed scoundrel. I tried to ask more questions about Ranulf Sawyer, but was unable to make myself heard above the cacophony this time, no matter how many times I tried to get everybody's attention by clearing my throat.

It was Maud who finally restored order by picking up the crucifix from the centre of the table and brandishing it in Rose's face. 'You need to tell us the truth, Rose. On this holy cross. Why did Ranulf Sawyer give you Jocelin Baker's bracelet?'

The girl rubbed tears from her eyes. 'He found it,' came the mumbled response.

'Where did he find it?'

Rose cringed, the veil falling away slightly to reveal a flash of her red hair. 'Somewhere in the forest.' she replied. 'That's all he told me.'

Aldith rose to her feet – nearly losing her balance thanks to the size of her belly. 'It's Sawyer,' she announced. 'He's the man who's been taking the women.' She pointed at Rose. 'You should have told us he was back before now. It's obvious it's him.'

'Ranulf hasn't done anything,' sobbed Rose. 'He's not like that.'

'Oh come on, you stupid little fool,' replied Aldith. 'What do you know about men?' she said, taking a moment to pat her own belly.

'Who is this Ranulf Sawyer?' I asked.

'He's a filthy charcoal burner,' Aldith told me. 'Likes to sneak about the forest with his hood up, scaring the life out of people. Especially women.' She gave a scornful laugh. 'Thought we'd chased him out a couple of years ago,' she added. 'But now it turns out that he's crept back here.' Aldith put her hand onto her neighbour's shoulder to balance herself. 'I say that we get some of the men together and hunt Sawyer down,' she cried. 'Hang him up for what he's done.'

This idea was met with approval until Maud waved the crucifix again. 'Be quiet for a moment!' she said, waiting until the women finally settled. 'I know it seems obvious to blame this man,' she said. 'But let's not jump to conclusions. We have no real evidence against Sawyer.'

'It's got to be him,' said Aldith, irritated at Maud's opposition. 'The man had Jocelin's bracelet. What more evidence do you need?'

Maud fixed Aldith with another of her stares, until her younger opponent reluctantly returned her bottom to the bench. 'Sawyer is odd, I agree,' said Maud, as she calmly replaced the crucifix onto the table. 'But I dealt with him for many years before he left, and I always found him to be honest enough. As Rose has pointed out, it is his job that's unpleasant. Not the man himself.' Maud sat down again and placed her hands elegantly into her lap. 'We must not assume Sawyer is guilty,' she said. 'Just because he found a bracelet from one of the missing women.'

'That's right,' said Rose, encouraged by Maud's support. 'There isn't anything wrong with Ranulf. He didn't do nothing.'

'But he only says he found this bracelet,' insisted Aldith. 'How can we believe him? Who's to say that he didn't kill Jocelin and then steal the bracelet from her dead body?'

Maud considered this point for a moment. 'It's possible, of course. But I say that we must proceed with caution. Let's not string up this man, only to leave the real killer at large. Surely that would be the worst crime of all?'

Aldith was about to argue, when we were all distracted by a scuffle at the door. Within a moment, John Roach strode across the hall, followed by Maud's thin maid Johanna, who skipped along in his wake with a look of desperate apology on her face.

'I'm sorry, Mistress,' she whimpered at Maud. 'I tried to stop him. But he pushed his way in. He wouldn't listen to me.'

Maud stood up to face Roach. 'What are you doing here?' she asked, as Roach took up a position in the middle of the room, standing with his legs parted and his arms folded.

'I hear you're having a meeting,' he replied. 'About those runaways?'

'They didn't run away,' said Aldith. 'They've been murdered. By Ranulf Sawyer.'

Roach frowned. 'What?'

I spoke up. 'Sawyer's name has come up during our discussions. Nothing more.'

'Come up?' said Roach, now addressing me. 'How's that, then?'

'I was asking about the missing women,' I replied. 'It turns out that Sawyer found a bracelet in the forest. It had once belonged to Jocelin Baker.'

'I thought you were collecting a forgotten psalter, Brother Oswald?' he said. 'Not holding a meeting.' When I didn't answer, he unfolded his arms and started to wag a finger at me. 'I'm the Constable in this village. If you're discussing these women, then you ask me first.'

'Why would we do that?' I replied sharply, annoyed at the way he had spoken to me. 'You don't care about them.'

Roach balled his fists and stepped towards me. I think he was half-intending to punch me, when Maud stepped into his path. 'I must say that I think very poorly of a man who pushes his way into my house,' she said. 'So I'd like you to leave immediately.'

'I should have been invited,' answered Roach. 'What right do you have to exclude me?' He stood back nevertheless. Maud had intimidated him.

'It's my decision who enters my home,' said Maud. 'Mine alone.'

'But—'

'This is my house,' she thundered, her cheeks now flushed with anger. 'Do not dare to question me!'

Roach stepped back and then retreated towards the door. 'No more gatherings without my permission,' he blustered, in an attempt to save some face before he left. 'Next time you'll all be arrested. No matter where you're meeting.'

The women jeered as the front door slammed in the distance, with calls for the 'Cockroach' to scuttle away, but the mood of the room had changed. With Roach's departure, the last act of today's drama had been played out. There was nothing more to say, the ale and bread had been consumed, and Maud had positioned herself by the door in an obvious sign that the women were expected to leave.

Most headed for the door immediately, but Aldith remained seated, refusing to move before she'd spoken to me. 'So, Brother Oswald,' she said. 'What are you going to do about Sawyer, then?'

'I'll go and speak to him,' I said.

'Good. Because he's guilty.'

'We don't know that.'

'I think we do,' she contended. 'To my mind, there's no argument.'

'I agree with Mistress Woodstock,' I replied. 'We mustn't jump to conclusions about Ranulf Sawyer. Let me talk to him first. Let's see if he can explain how he found Jocelin's bracelet.'

Aldith eyed me for a moment, before she leant on the table and then clumsily lumbered to her feet. 'Your decision,' she said wearily. 'Just make sure that you don't disappear as well.'

Most of the women had filed out of the hall by now, but as Rose passed me, I grabbed the girl's arm and pulled her to one side for a private conversation. Her sister Christina tried to hang back to listen, but Maud had the sense to take Christina's arm and accompany her towards the front door.

Now there was just the two of us, Rose immediately launched into a stirring defence of Sawyer. 'Ranulf didn't do anything to Jocelin,' she said. 'He just found the bracelet on the path. He only gave it to me because he didn't need it. We're not courting or nothing like that.'

'Did you tell Brother Merek about this bracelet?' I said.

She dropped her eyes from mine. 'No,' she replied.

'Are you sure about that?' I asked. She shook her head vigorously in response. 'It's very important that I know the truth, Rose,' I said. 'Did you ever mention Sawyer's name to Brother Merek?'

'No, Brother Oswald,' she said, looking up at me in earnest. 'I've never said anything about Ranulf to anybody. You've seen what the people here are like. They won't give him a chance.'

I paused to study Rose's face, looking into those strange grey eyes that were fringed by the palest, sandy-coloured lashes. Her skin was so translucent that I could see the blue veins threading across her temples. 'Where is Sawyer now?' I said eventually.

'Burning charcoal.'

'Yes. But where is he burning charcoal?'

'Follow the forest path from Stonebrook until you reach the crossroads to Tonbridge,' she told me. 'Then walk through the trees towards the north-west, for about four hundred yards. Ranulf's pits are there, in a hollow.' She dabbed the corner of her eye with a birdlike finger. 'I won't get Ranulf into trouble, will I?'

'That depends,' I said. 'On what he has to say for himself.'

I walked Rose to the door and then returned to the hall to bid Maud farewell, only for her to insist that I eat something else before leaving. Now that the village women had departed, the hard cheese and best bread soon reappeared at the table.

'I wonder if we can trust Rose's story about this man,' I said, sinking my teeth into a thick slice of deliciously salty cheese. 'She had no intention of telling anybody about this bracelet, until she was forced to.'

Maud took a sip of ale from her cup. 'The trouble is, these girls have nothing, Oswald. You must remember that. I imagine Rose was afraid that this prized gift would be taken away from her.'

'And what about this Sawyer?' I asked. 'You say that you know him?'

'Yes,' replied Maud. 'He's harmless enough,' she added. 'At least that's always been my impression.' She paused. 'And anyway. I doubt he's involved in this mystery. Why would he abduct a woman and then give one of her belongings to another girl in the same village? It's too incriminating . . . unless the man is a complete fool.' She paused. 'But I know Sawyer, and he's not stupid. I think it's just a coincidence that he found this bracelet in the forest.'

'You're probably right,' I said, wiping the crumbs from my chin and rising to my feet. 'Even so. I need to speak to him,' I said.

She seemed surprised at this. 'Are you going now?'

I nodded my head. 'Yes. The gates of Kintham will be shut against plague soon, and then it might be months before I can leave again.'

'Shall I come with you?' she asked, also rising to her feet and now standing so close to me that I could almost feel her breath on my cheeks. For a moment, I wanted to lean forward to kiss her on those full and sweet lips. They were at exactly the right height, only inches away from my own mouth. The opportunity was there, and yet I didn't have the courage to act. What if she rejected me? . . . What if she didn't?

'Thank you, Maud, but I should go alone,' I said, trying to move away from her, but not quite succeeding.

'Take care then, Oswald,' she said, touching my cheek. 'Sawyer isn't a bad man. But he's gruff and uneducated. He might not take kindly to your questions.'

'Should I be afraid of him, then?'

'No, no,' she smiled. 'He just looks a little frightening. That's all.'

With this, she leant her face towards mine, before her sweet, warm lips touched my own – and for a moment I felt over-whelmed. The joy of kissing this beautiful, unattainable woman. The kiss was all I had ever imagined it might feel like, and yet even more thrilling. For a moment, I was overcome with a feel-ing that I could only just control, as I felt the urge to grab her breasts and press myself into her.

I forced myself to step back, giddy at the strength and power of this desire – aware that the evidence of my lust was now trying to poke its way through my habit. After a moment of silent awkwardness as I tried to rearrange my robe and tighten my belt, Maud took me by the hand and led me to the front door. 'Do you know where to go?' she asked me.

'Yes,' I said. 'Rose described the place where Sawyer lives.'

She opened the door. 'Take care, Oswald,' she said, standing aside so that I could leave.

'I'll come back to tell you what I find,' I promised.

'Thank you,' she said, blowing me a kiss. Within a moment the door had closed and suddenly I was out on the street again. Alone with the sensation of that kiss still stinging at my lips.

It was even quieter in the village now. Eerily so. The women from Maud's meeting had been reabsorbed into their homes and were nowhere to be seen. All I could hear was the mewl of a distant infant, or the calls of some men pulling eels from a fish trap by the water mill. If they noticed my passing, then they didn't raise their heads to watch me.

I was being watched by somebody, however. As I turned the corner, I found that John Roach was blocking my path ahead, mounted on a fine white palfrey.

'Where are you going?' he asked me rudely.

I bowed my head – still basking in my amorous glow and not feeling in the mood to argue with the man. 'I'm returning to Kintham,' I said brightly. 'Good afternoon to you.'

Roach waved at the path on the other side of the green. 'The monastery is that way,' he said.

I bowed again. Brother Peter had always taught me the power of politeness to unnerve an opponent. 'Thank you, Master Roach,' I said with the broadest of smiles. 'But I'm going to take this route instead. I find it more pleasing.'

He laughed at this. 'Do you indeed?'

'Good day to you,' I said, and just to annoy him further, I added, 'And may God bless you.'

I walked on, hearing him kick at the flanks of his horse as he rode behind me until we reached the edge of the village. But Roach didn't follow me as I entered the forest. Instead, he stopped his horse at the boundary, where the trees met the fields. And then he watched me leave – his eyes boring into my back, until I was finally out of sight.

Chapter Sixteen

The air was cooler once I entered the forest. Dappled light fell on the path from the gaps in the branches of the trees overhead – a knitted tangle of oak, sweet chestnut and maple. The scent of elderflower wafted headily through the air, now overpowering the perfume of the wild garlic and the last of the bluebells. For a while, I felt happier than I had done in weeks, before the feeling evaporated. After my encounter with Maud, I wondered how I could ever become a monk? How I could ever spend my whole life in celibacy?

I imagined myself in love with Maud already, and it was certainly a strong and overpowering emotion – though perhaps not the romantic perfection that I had read about in the poetry of the troubadours? In all honesty, this feeling was not so different from the desires that invaded my dreams most nights, and were vaguely present each time I saw one of the village girls in the monastery. The Abbot might have chosen the plainest girls to venture inside our four walls, on the basis that he was reducing temptation, but their plainness was not the point. His own tastes did not extend to an interest in the female sex, so he didn't realise that the mere presence of a woman, whether she were handsome or not, was enough to provoke lustful thoughts. Particularly in the novices.

My feelings of despondency were thankfully short-lived and soon I began to fantasise instead about leaving the monastery, choosing to forget, momentarily, how impossible this would be to achieve. I had been sent to Kintham Abbey by my family, with the intention that I would rise through the ranks to one day become the Abbot myself. I was the third living de Lacy son. A quiet, diffident boy who didn't particularly care for hunting, farming or fighting, so what other use was I to them? Better for all concerned, if I were shelved away in the monastery, like a dusty book. Reached for on those odd occasions when my ecclesiastical skills were required, such as family births, marriages and deaths.

Leaving Kintham was not an option, so I turned my mind towards the ways in which I might cope with my future life. Plenty of monks, particularly those of noble birth, were able to keep a mistress and live a semblance of life as a normal man. Some even fathered children – or so I had heard. This might have been an option, but I dismissed this idea immediately. I knew, even at the age of eighteen, that it would be difficult for me to live in such duplicity. I was not yet so jaded and disillusioned with the world, that I accepted such dishonesty as an unfortunate but acceptable fact of life. I only knew that I wanted to change my future. The trouble was, I had no idea how.

I must have been daydreaming like this, dawdling a little on the path, when the spell was broken by the sound of a horse braying somewhere behind me. I turned quickly, and for the briefest of moments, I saw the blur of a white horse and its rider quickly disappear into the trees. My first fear was bandits, because this was exactly the right sort of territory for such attacks – lonely and shaded – before I realised that my follower was John Roach. He had trailed me into the forest after watching me leave Stonebrook.

I quickened my pace until the path turned a corner, where I scrambled into the trees and waited to see if Roach would attempt to catch up with me. I must have stayed there for nearly half an hour, but nobody came past me on the path. I could only assume that Roach had given up the chase, after realising that he'd been seen. In any case, I couldn't waste any more time hiding in these trees. The longer I stayed away from Kintham, the more likely it was that Peter would discover my absence.

And so, I cautiously picked my way back through the under-growth and rejoined the track, following Rose's directions and heading for Sawyer's pits. I passed the crossroads, where one road led towards Tonbridge, then worked my way along the path that Rose had described, before reaching Sawyer's charcoal pits in the hollow of a small woodland clearing. The smell of the place hit me immediately — the smouldering, earthy stink of four charcoal piles, each of them covered in earth and moss, and each of them releasing their thin, blue tendrils of smoke into the air. Near to these piles was a hut — a ramshackle building, which strangely clung about the trunk of a tree like the ball of a wasp's nest.

A hooded man was seated on a wooden stump nearby, poking a stick around in a small fire beneath a blackened cauldron. It could only be Sawyer. Despite Maud's assertions that this man was harmless, I suddenly began to wonder if I had put myself in danger by coming here alone. Charcoal burners did not enjoy a reputation for civility — especially the ones like Sawyer with a licence to burn charcoal for the whole year. They might earn a good living by selling their charcoal to the furnaces near Tonbridge — where the iron rods were forged for the smiths and nailers of London — but these men were often treated as pariahs. It was a hard way of life that produced a hard sort of man.

I took a deep breath and emerged from the trees. 'Ranulf Sawyer?' I asked, as I approached him.

Sawyer rose to his feet slowly, eyeing me from beneath the hood of his cloak. He was an exceptionally tall man, with broad shoulders and large hands, and I felt intimidated immediately. Not only was his height extraordinary — so was his appearance. The soot from his work was not only embedded into the skin of his face and hands, it had also collected in the lines about his mouth and eyes in a dusty sediment. His blue eyes looked out from this blackened mask like two bright ellipses of light. The effect was almost demonic. 'Yes,' he said. 'Who's asking?'

'My name is Brother Oswald,' I said, trying to steady my voice. 'I've come from Kintham Abbey.'

He folded his arms, wrapping one large hand under the elbow of the other arm. 'My licence was granted by the Abbot,' he said. 'I'm allowed to be here.'

'It's nothing to do with your licence,' I said quickly. 'It's another matter.'

'Oh yes?'

'I wanted to ask you some questions about a bracelet. The one that you recently gave to Rose Brunham.'

He stared at me for a moment. 'What about it?' he asked brusquely.

'It belonged to a girl who's disappeared from Stonebrook,' I replied. 'Her name was Jocelin Baker.' I hesitated. 'I'd like to know why you had it?'

'What's it got to do with you?' He asked.

I felt my nerve deserting me. 'I'm trying to find out what happened to Jocelin,' I managed to say. 'She hasn't been seen since she last left Stonebrook. She was wearing the bracelet when she left.'

Sawyer stared at me from beneath his hood, before taking his seat again. It seemed he didn't want to answer my questions. Instead, he took a long wooden spoon and started to stir the stew inside the pot. Some onions and rabbit bones were floating about in a grey broth. 'You a friend of Brother Merek's, then?' he said finally.

'Why do you ask that?'

'Because he was here as well,' he said. 'Just the same as you. Asking just the same questions.'

I took a deep breath. Rose had lied to me. She must have told Merek about Sawyer after all – otherwise why had Merek come here? 'When did you see him?' I asked, now fearing that I had walked into exactly the same trap.

Sawyer continued to stir the stew, poking around at the bones distractedly. 'About six weeks ago, I suppose.'

'Six weeks?' I repeated, swallowing the tension in my throat.

Sawyer lifted back his hood a little and grinned at me. The white of his teeth glowing against his filthy skin. 'You want to see them as well, then?' he said. 'Is that it?'

'See what?' I asked.

'The bodies,' he said.

'Whose bodies?'

'The women, of course. The dead ones.'

'How do you know where they are?' I whispered, as I realised that Sawyer's cloak was not so different to a monk's habit. Is that why Agnes had been so afraid of my appearance? Was Sawyer the man she had mistaken me for?

'I see things in the forest,' he said ominously. 'When I'm look-ing for firewood. Secret things. Things that nobody wants to know about.'

My heart pounded in my ears. Though I wanted to run, my legs were heavy and my feet wouldn't move. 'Did you take Brother Merek to see these bodies?' I managed to say.

He was about to answer when he appeared to be distracted by something over my shoulder. Believing that he had seen some-body behind me, I turned instinctively, only for Sawyer to use this opportunity to dart away, soon disappearing between the trees.

I had fallen for the simplest of tricks, and I should have turned and retreated immediately, except that I did the opposite. I cannot explain why exactly, but suddenly I obeyed the oldest of urges – to chase escaping prey. I set off in pursuit of Sawyer, desperate to catch up with the man and discover why he was fleeing. Why he had offered to take me to see the bodies of the women. But I had only run a short way between the trees, when

I felt a thudding blow against the back of my head. The pain was sudden and overwhelming – before the world faded into a hazy, warped miasma that ended in darkness.

I don't know how long I lay amongst the leaves, but when I regained consciousness, the pain in my head was searing. It took me a few moments to remember who I was and why I was there – but when I realised that Sawyer was nowhere to be seen, I stumbled to my feet and headed into the depths of the forest, walking as fast as my strength would carry me. I finally came to a stop beneath some willow trees, when I was overcome with nausea and exhaustion. I was sick repeatedly before I forced myself to stagger just a little further. I had to get away from this place and find somewhere to hide. I had to get away from Sawyer. The man had tried to kill me.

Chapter Seventeen

Somershill, November 1370

Mother asked me to finish there, which surprised me at first, seeing as we had just reached the part of any story that she usually liked best – the point at which mystery meets violence. But, instead, she suddenly asked me to quit the room and call for her maid, warning me not to return until dusk at the earliest. In truth, I was more than happy to comply, since she'd been complaining earlier about her digestion, and I suspected this sudden instruction was somehow related to this problem.

I left in search of her maid, finding the girl flirting with my new valet in the great hall. This man was turning out to be the latest disappointment, in a long string of disappointments, as it had been so hard to find a replacement for my previous valet Sandro. Filomena wasn't the only person to miss the Venetian. This latest appointment was an older man, who was married with three children, and should have known better than to be chasing a young girl about the Great Hall like an aroused billy goat. My words were sharp to her, and even sharper to him. He wasn't suiting my requirements at all, and this new indiscretion prompted my resolve to replace him at the earliest opportunity.

Once I had told the girl to see to Mother's needs immediately, I went in search of company. Usually Filomena would be sitting in the solar at this time of day, reading a book or completing some piece of needlework. There would be the chatter and noise of visitors wandering about the hall, or the boom and thwack of Henry's arrows, as he practised his longbow skills out on the lawns. But there was no sign of Henry, nor anybody else for that matter. I couldn't even find my sister Clemence in the chapel, where she was usually keeping a prayer vigil in Mother's honour.

Finding myself alone, I meandered over to the stables and discovered, from one of the grooms, that my family had all taken a ride to Tonbridge, intending to shop at the market and then eat lunch at an inn. Even Clemence had joined them on this excursion, which was especially unusual, given her dislike for riding any distance. Hearing this news, I suddenly felt resentful, since nobody had made the effort to invite me along. They could easily have knocked at the door at least and told me where they were going. But then again, I had made it known that I would be sitting with Mother for most of the day, and didn't want to be disturbed – so I could hardly complain when everybody respected this instruction. Even so, I couldn't help but feel childishly slighted.

For a while, I kicked about the stables, grooming the horses and feeling rather sorry for myself, until I decided to ride to Tonbridge myself and join the others. The day was bright and dry, so the roads were passable – meaning that I could be there for lunch if I rode swiftly enough. By the time that I reached my destination, I found that most of the market stalls were already being dismantled for the day, and so I made my way directly to the Nag's Head. But, just as I turned the corner, two figures immediately caught my eye. It was Filomena and Sir John, who were standing outside the tavern, their heads closely drawn together in conversation. I stopped my horse and secretly watched them for a while, seeing that Sir John appeared to be telling Filomena an amusing story, as she continually threw her head back in laughter and then patted his arm. But I wasn't their only spy. From this vantage point, I could see that my nephew

Henry was also watching them from a dark corner. There was a look of bristling resentment written all over his face.

I had seen enough of this tableau – my wife and her two admirers – one a fanciful entertainer, the other a lovesick boy. My recently made resolution about not being provoked into jealousy suddenly vanished – so I kicked at the flanks of my horse and approached Filomena and Sir John, causing the pair to immediately step apart like two guilty children.

Filomena looked up at me in surprise. 'Oh, Oswald,' she said, 'I didn't know that you were joining us.' Was there a taint of disappointment in her voice? I thought there was.

'Mother was unwell,' I said. 'I've left her to sleep this afternoon.'

Sir John took my horse's reins as I dismounted. 'How pleasant to see you,' he said. 'I was just telling Lady Somershill about my meetings with the monks at St Catherine's monastery in the Sinai. How they live like hermits, eating only a diet of boiled roots and preserved dates.'

'And you find that funny?' I asked, turning sharply on him.

Sir John stiffened. 'No, Oswald,' he said, shaking his head. 'Why do you ask?'

'I saw you both laughing.'

Filomena threw me a peeved look. 'We were not laughing at the monks,' she said. 'Sir John was telling me about a donkey he met. It ate one of his shoes.'

I raised an eyebrow and headed for the door of the tavern without another word. It was a churlish act, but I was annoyed with them both. How dare they stand outside a tavern in Tonbridge and laugh!

Unfortunately, my petulance threw a cloud over the following meal – an occasion that should have been an enjoyable break from routine. After we had eaten our pies and finished our wine, Filomena rode back alongside me to Somershill, but refused to speak to me for the whole journey. This punishment by silence only caused me to feel more aggrieved than ever, determining that I would rid myself of Sir John before the man caused me any further irritation.

After our frosty meal at the tavern, Sir John had had the good sense to keep out of my way and ride at the back of our party with Henry and Clemence. But once we returned home, I took the man to one side and asked him bluntly. When was he planning to leave Somershill?

Sir John took offence at this question, though he managed to disguise his umbrage as confusion, claiming that he was under the impression that I had asked him to stay for the whole winter (which, to be fair, I had done). He was unable to argue, however, when I explained that this supposed invitation was a misunderstanding on his part. In any case, I told him that I was expecting a new arrival into the castle any day – a distant cousin who wanted to visit Mother before she died. His bed would soon be needed for this guest, so it was not possible for him to stay with us any longer. Sir John accepted defeat at this point, and told me that he would write to some relatives of his on the Isle of Sheppey, where he hoped to beg a bed until he could make his return to Flanders in the spring. I'm ashamed to say that I told him to get on with it.

I crawled into bed that night feeling both bad-tempered and foolish – angry that Filomena had encouraged the man, and foolish that I had given their relationship the opportunity to blossom. I had spent far too long recently with my mother, and not long enough with my wife. So, the next morning I decided that I would take a ride out with Filomena, both to enjoy her company, but also to keep her out of Sir John's way. I suggested that we could ride through the forest, or visit some of my wealthier tenants. It was that time of year when we discussed their rent and customary duties for the following twelve months, and Filomena's presence always made these conversations more agreeable. She was popular amongst my tenants in Somershill, since she always took such an interest in their lives and their families.

But, just as I had pulled on my leather riding mantle and asked the groom to saddle up my horse, I was summoned to Mother's bedchamber. The news was grave by all accounts. Mother could not keep a drink down. Not even a cup of cooled, boiled water.

I rushed to her chamber immediately, and I must say that she looked deathly when I entered the room, waving me over to her side and then pulling my ear to her mouth.

'Will you get that man out of here, please?' she whispered. 'I can't stand him any longer.'

I turned to see Mother's physician, Thomas Crouch, hiding in the shadows. His long black robes disappearing against the gloomy tapestries.

'What are you doing here again?' I asked the man. 'I told you to stay at the tavern until you were called upon.'

He stepped forward and gave a bow. 'I'm sorry, my Lord. I thought you had requested that I attend Lady Somershill?'

'No,' I said. 'I didn't send for you.'

Mother cut in. 'It was me, Oswald. I told the maid to search him out.'

'Why's that?'

Mother beckoned me over, wanting to whisper into my ear. 'I needed a purgative,' she whispered. 'My bowels have been impacted for days.' I went to answer this, but she didn't allow me to speak. 'But it went too far, Oswald. Too far. God alone knows what was in Crouch's tonic. I'd rather be bunged up than suffer this indignity. I haven't been off the pot all night.' She grasped my hand rather desperately. Her skin was cold and clammy. 'There's nothing more in there, Oswald. And that's the truth. And yet the fellow is trying to force another dose on me.'

'Perhaps it's doing you some good, then?' I said. 'You have been complaining of constipation after all.'

Mother waved this away. 'Just get rid of him, Oswald. The man is a saddle goose. I don't want to ever see his face again.'

For the second time that week, I escorted Thomas Crouch to the gatehouse, except this time I didn't ask him to wait at the tavern to be called upon again. Instead, I settled his bill and told him to leave Somershill for good. I knew enough about herbs and medicine to treat Mother myself, and my own remedies would surely be better than his mixture of leeches and loosening medicine.

After Crouch's departure, I returned to Mother's bedside, passing Filomena as she waited for me in the courtyard. She was wearing her best, fur-lined cloak and was mounted on her favourite jennet – a graceful, bay-coated horse that Filomena had named Lauretta. I told my wife that I wouldn't be long, as I just needed to settle Mother, but this plan was thwarted as soon as I returned to the bedchamber.

When I approached Mother's bedside, the old woman looked shrivelled again – her face wrinkled and wilted like a turnip that's spent too long in the store cupboard. I took her hand, and found that it was limp and fragile.

'Will you finish your story now, Oswald?' she whispered.

I wanted to tell her that I was spending the day with Filomena, but I couldn't do it. Not now. Instead I removed my cloak and took a seat beside her bed. 'Where was I?'

'That charcoal burner had hit you about the head,' she said. 'You were hiding in the forest.'

Chapter Eighteen

Kent, June 1349

Ilay beneath a holly bush, trying my best to stay awake in case Sawyer found me again. Thankfully I heard and saw nobody for the whole night, so at first light, I crept out from this secret dell and started to retrace my steps through the woods — ever mindful of making too much noise and drawing attention to myself. I even picked up a thick branch, ready to fight off the man, should he appear. This weapon would have been hopeless against a man of Sawyer's height and strength, but I found it reassuring nonetheless.

As it happened, my only adversary that morning was the headache that was still riveting its way through my forehead and disturbing my eyesight. As a result, I was disorientated and lost my way on numerous occasions, finally returning to Kintham by noon, when I could hear the bells ringing for Sext. I crept in through the side gate in the vegetable garden, pulled my hood over my bloodied hair and hoped that nobody would notice me — but I was not in luck. The lay brother, Brother John, stopped me immediately.

'Peter's been looking for you,' he told me, smothering a grin as he looked me up and down, amused at my dirty clothes. 'We're to send you directly to the Abbot's quarters, if we see you.'

My heart sank. 'Why's that?' I asked.

'They've been worried about you,' he replied. 'They thought you'd disappeared. Like Merek.'

I went to hurry away, but not before the man had grabbed my sleeve with his large, muddy hand. 'And you've got a visitor as well,' he said. 'So you might want to clean yourself up a bit?'

'A visitor?' I said, immediately concerned. 'Who is it?'

The man shrugged. 'I don't know,' he replied, releasing my arm as he turned his attention back to the peas. 'But you can't turn up looking like that,' he said, picking a swollen pod and throwing it into a woven basket. 'You look like you've just fallen out of the Tabard Inn.'

Brother Peter met me at the door to the Abbot's quarters with an embrace, but it was not warm. 'Where in God's name have you been, Oswald?' he growled into my ear. He immediately spotted the matted blood in my hair. 'And what's this?' he asked. 'What happened to you?'

Before I could explain, he quickly pulled the hood further down over my face. 'Come on. There isn't time for this. William is here to see you.' He took my arm and tried to propel me into the room.

'William?' I said, digging my heels in and refusing to move. 'My brother William?'

'Yes.'

'Does he know about Agnes?' I asked, feeling my heart begin to beat a little faster. 'Is that why he's here?'

'No,' said Peter. 'I don't think so.' He caught hold of my arm again and this time he forced me to move. 'So just listen to me. When we get in there, keep your hood up and agree with everything I say.'

A moment later I found myself in the Abbot's quarters — a part of the Abbey that I had been invited inside. It was a large and lavish chamber, glowing with all the red and gold ornamentation of an archbishop's palace. Though it was the middle of the day, wax candles blazed in bronze candlesticks, and the air was filled with the scent of cinnamon, cloves and rose water from a large pomander. My brother William was sitting at the centre of all this splendour at a long trestle table. The Abbott sat beside him, at an inferior position, whilst a feast was set before them both – boiled meats, baked fruits and pickled fish. It seemed that the kitchens had not stinted in their mission to assuage William's famous temper. No doubt he was not in the best of moods, having arrived at Kintham to discover that the monks had lost his younger brother.

When William smiled at me, I felt the urge to be sick. I saw Agnes's face in his features immediately.

'Here he is at last,' said Brother Peter brightly, clapping me soundly on the back. 'I said that Oswald would return to us safe and sound, didn't I? It seems he got himself lost.' Peter turned to me and glared. 'Did you find any of that Water Mint I asked you to look for?' I took his meaning immediately. 'The type that only grows in the forest?'

I went to answer, but Peter spoke over me. 'Never mind. I really shouldn't have sent you out of the monastery at a time like this. This is entirely my fault, Father Abbot. Oswald only left Kintham at my behest.' He placed his hand on my shoulder and squeezed his fingers, expecting my cooperation with this story.

The Abbot rose from his chair. He disliked entertaining guests in his personal quarters, and it was clear that he was eager for William to leave. 'I must say, Brother Peter,' he said, wiping some crumbs from his hands. 'It was very irresponsible of you to send the boy out now. Especially in the current circumstances. Especially when I have specifically forbidden the novices to leave Kintham.' He directed these comments towards my brother, to ensure that William appreciated his own blamelessness in this whole affair. I saw William respond with a knowing smile.

'I can't apologise enough, Father Abbot,' added Peter. 'I was totally at fault. Oswald was only acting on my instructions.'

William put down his cup of wine and took a moment to speak. 'At least he is safe now,' he said before he addressed me directly, pointing at my dirty clothes. 'Did you sleep in a ditch?' he asked. I looked down to see the mud and burrs that covered my habit. 'Or have you been for a roll in the hay?' he added, his eyes gleaming. 'Who knows what trouble you get into when they let you out of this place?'

I felt my throat tighten. What sort of trouble did William mean? Was he talking about Agnes? I looked into my brother's face and I just couldn't gauge his mood. Was he being mischievous or menacing?

But then again I had always had this problem. Since being a child in Somershill, I had never been able to tell if my older brothers William and Richard were about to play a silly trick on me, such as putting a spider in my sock, or a caterpillar in my soup. Or whether something more dangerous was afoot, such as tying me to the roasting spit and then lighting the fire, or burning the ends of my hair with a candle.

The Abbot padded towards the door, and started to fiddle with the latch. 'I cannot apologise enough about this incident, Lord de Lacy,' he said to William. 'But no harm has come to Oswald, so you may take him home now.'

'Take me home?' I said, in dismay.

William remained seated, ignoring the Abbot's cue to leave, and taking another gulp of wine. 'You're to return to Somershill, Oswald,' he told me, before refilling his cup from a decanter.

I was dumbfounded. 'But I don't want to go back to Somershill,' I said, once I'd eventually found my voice.

William paused. 'Sorry, Oswald. It's Father's orders.'

'But—'

'Come on, Little Brother,' said William, now picking up some bread and tearing it into pieces. 'We can't have a de Lacy locked away in this mouldy old monastery, can we? Not when the Plague is coming.' William nodded towards the Abbot, who was still loitering by the door, more eager than ever that we should leave. 'Who knows if any of this lot will survive?' he said. 'I'm told that Winchester Abbey has been cleared out.'

'I'm sure that our monastery will be a safe haven,' retorted the Abbot. 'Especially if our novices obey the rules,' he added pointedly.

I turned to Peter. 'But I don't want to leave now,' I whispered. 'There are things I need to do.' I narrowed my eyes and stared at Peter, hoping that he would take my meaning.

If he had any idea, then he deliberately ignored me. Peter cleared his throat, and spoke loudly. 'I think it would be much safer if you were to return to Somershill, Oswald.'

'You do?' I said in surprise. Peter usually took my side in a public argument, especially when we were in the company of my family. Our disagreements were only ever played out in private.

'Yes,' he replied. 'Your brother William is correct about the dangers of staying at the monastery. The contagion moves swiftly from one person to the next. We live in confined quarters, so we are more likely than most to suffer.'

The Abbot removed his hand from the latch. 'You haven't expressed this opinion before, Brother Peter,' he said nervously. 'You assured me that we would all be safe here.' I noticed a fleeting wave of panic cross the man's face.

Peter bowed his head. 'My apologies, Father Abbot. It is an opinion that I have only formed since I received a letter from a dear friend of mine. The infirmarer at Lowhampton Abbey.' Peter paused. 'I'm afraid that he has seen the devastation at first hand.'

The Abbot frowned. 'Are we to worry, then?' He rubbed his hands around his mouth. 'Perhaps we should all return to our family homes?'

'No, no,' replied Peter. 'We should be safe enough, but only if we retain our isolation.'

'Then let me stay here, with you,' I urged Peter, touching his arm to press my point. 'There's no reason for me to return to Somershill.'

'No,' said Brother Peter, glaring at me again. 'It's your father's decision that you go home. You must respect his will, Oswald.' This statement stuck in the craw, particularly as Peter had never displayed any respect for my father's wishes in the past – often expressing the opinion that Henry de Lacy was an avaricious bully who didn't deserve his title and position.

'Oh come on, Oswald,' said William, still seated at the Abbot's table and still drinking the man's wine. 'Don't be difficult about this. We could do with your company at Somershill. Somebody with some conversation and education at last.' He gave a jaundiced sigh. 'Richard is a bore. Father keeps repeating himself. And Mother pines for you.' He paused. 'You know that you've always been her favourite, Oswald. Remember how she used to love those pretty golden curls?'

I didn't reply to this comment, which only prompted William to laugh. 'Oh come on, Little Brother,' he joked. 'You can come back to your precious monastery after the Plague has blown over. Then you can take your vows and start working your way up the ladder. You know that we all expect you to take his place one day.' William nodded at the Abbot. 'Every noble family should have their own Abbot.' He winked at me. 'Isn't that right? Someone to plead their case to God.'

The Abbot was offended by William's comments, but was not able to respond with anything but a loud sniff. Such was the privilege of being a de Lacy. It opened doors and shut mouths.

'So it's decided,' said Peter, ending the awkward silence that followed William's last observation. 'Oswald will return to Somershill today. I will write to your father when it's safe for him to return.' Peter then tipped my elbow. 'Come along then, Oswald,' he said. 'Let's go and collect your things.'

With this, he pulled me out of the room, along the passageway and then pushed me into an alcove in the cloister before venting the full force of his anger. 'Where on earth did you go to last night? I spent hours wandering about the forests. Calling out your name,' he told me. 'Hours!'

'You came to look for me?'

'Of course I did, Oswald,' he said. 'I nearly suffered a catalepsy to the heart, thanks to you.'

'I'm sorry. I didn't mean to worry you.'

Two passing novices stopped to watch this altercation, before Peter spun around and told the pair to be on their way. He pulled back my hood. 'And why are you wounded? Did somebody attack you?'

'Yes,' I replied. 'A charcoal burner called Ranulf Sawyer. He tried to kill me.'

'What?'

'He's the man who's been taking women, Brother Peter.'

'How do you know that?'

'Because I followed in Merek's footsteps, that's why. I went to speak to the women of Stonebrook.'

Peter rolled his eyes. 'Even though I expressly forbade you to leave Kintham.'

'But I found out Sawyer's name,' I replied. 'So it was worth it.'

Peter shook his head in disbelief. 'And then you went to accost this man on your own, I suppose?' When I nodded at this, he added. 'What is the matter with you, Oswald?' he said. 'Have you no care for your own life?'

'I'm not sorry,' I said adamantly. 'Sawyer admitted his guilt.'

'He did?'

'Yes.' I paused for a moment. 'Well, he asked me if I wanted to see the bodies of the missing women?'

Peter started to pull at the mole on his neck. 'And did you see them?'

I hesitated. 'Well . . ., no,' I said.

'And why's that?'

'Because Sawyer ran off from me.'

'And you gave chase, I suppose?' There it was again. That trace of despair in his voice. 'You pursued a man who'd offered to show you his previous victims. Giving him every opportunity to add you to his collection of dead bodies.'

'I didn't think he would attack me,' I replied, waiting until the novices had passed by. This was their third revolution of the cloister, as they tried their very best to eavesdrop. 'Sawyer hit me on the back of my head,' I whispered. 'He thought he'd killed me, but I'd only passed out. When I came round, I was able to get away and hide.'

Peter put a hand to his forehead and wiped his brow. 'By the saints, Oswald. This story only gets worse.'

'And I think Sawyer killed Merek as well,' I said, determined not to be discouraged by Peter's reaction.

'Oh yes? And why's that?'

'Because Merek went to see Sawyer as well,' I replied. 'About six weeks ago. And then he was never seen again.'

Peter groaned. 'You could have died. You stupid, stupid fool.'

'But I didn't,' I said. 'So now we need to hunt down Sawyer with a few of the lay brothers.'

Peter stepped back in surprise. 'Absolutely not,' he said. 'You're returning to Somershill with William.'

'No. I can't,' I said. 'I need to find Sawyer. He's a rapist and a murderer.'

Peter grabbed my wrist and pulled me out of the alcove. 'You're going back to Somershill, Oswald,' he growled. 'And that's the end of the matter. I can't control you any longer. At least your father might be able to keep you out of trouble.'

'Let go of me, Peter,' I yelped as I tried to pull away. But Peter was so much stronger, and I couldn't escape his grasp. His eyes blazed with fury as he dragged me through Kintham until we reached our cell, whereupon he threw me through the door and slammed it behind us.

We stared at one another in silence, until he finally wiped his brow and took a deep breath. Now that his temper had died down, he walked over to pull back my hood. 'So this is where Sawyer hit you?'

I nodded.

Peter told me to sit on a stool while he visited the infirmary, returning with a bowl of salted water and a bunch of comfrey leaves. He then sponged the salted water through my matted, bloodied hair, washing the wound until it stung.

'Please don't make me go back to Somershill,' I said, looking up at Peter. 'Please. We need to find Sawyer.'

He pushed my head back down and continued to wash. 'You have to go home, Oswald, and that's the end of it,' he said, laying some wet comfrey leaves against my wound and pressing them into my scalp. 'There's nothing that I can do about it.'

'But what about Sawyer?' I asked, as the salted water dribbled down the back of my neck. 'We need to act quickly, or he'll get away.' Peter didn't answer this. 'Don't you care?' I asked.

'Of course I care.'

'Then don't make me return to Somershill.'

Peter pulled the leaves away. 'Listen, Oswald,' he said at length. 'I'll seek out Sawyer myself. Does that satisfy you?'

'But how? You don't know him.'

'Yes I do,' Peter replied. 'Sawyer's been burning charcoal in the Abbey's forests for years.'

I was facing defeat. There was no doubt about that. 'Will you go today?' I asked. 'It has to be today.'

'Yes, Oswald.'

'Take others with you, Peter,' I said. 'The man is dangerous.'

'Don't worry,' he replied. 'This wound is enough of a warning.'

'And if you can't find him in the forest, speak to Rose Brunham.'

'Why's that?'

'She's Sawyer's lover.' I said.

Peter sighed. 'I warned you about that girl, didn't I? I told you she was a beggar's mistress.' He said, now patting my wound with vinegar.

'And you will write to me at Somershill?' I asked, trying not to wince with the pain as the vinegar burnt at my skin. 'As soon as you've found him?'

'Yes.'

'Do you promise me?' I asked, turning around. I needed to look into his eyes to see his answer. I needed to know that Peter was telling me the truth.

'Yes, Oswald,' he said solemnly. 'Of course, I promise you.'

I packed my spare braies, tunics and winter boots into a hessian sack and joined William in the courtyard. I mounted my horse, said my farewells and I rode for Somershill with my brother William at my side. For many months now I had longed to escape the dismal walls of Kintham Abbey. To be freed of the relentless routines, the petty rivalries, the plain food and the hard beds. But now I wanted nothing more than to stay.

Chapter Nineteen

William and I rode in silence, following a couple of cursory conversations about the heat of the day and the comfort of our saddles. I hadn't wanted to talk to my brother, but equally I didn't find this lack of conversation comforting. I knew that I would soon need to tell William the truth about Agnes, especially now that Peter was about to apprehend her attacker. It couldn't wait much longer. A number of times I cleared my throat, ready to make my confession, only to find that my nerve deserted me at the last moment. I couldn't predict how William would react to such a story. Although we were both men now, and I was taller than my older brother, I still felt petrified of this solid, muscular man. It was just as if I were a child again and he were my much older brother.

And so we continued in silence, plodding along the narrow paths of the forest, with William leading the way. Since we were riding in single file, I couldn't help but focus on the back of my brother's head, finding my eyes continually drawn to the way in which William's hair curled at the nape of his neck. I'm sorry to say that it prompted a particularly vivid and unpleasant memory – one which I hadn't thought about for years, but which I now struggled to dismiss.

I had been seven and William had been maybe nineteen or twenty, and I was in trouble for accidentally releasing his favourite hound — a dog named Whitefoot. I'd known it was wrong when I untied his tether, but the poor creature had looked so miserable, secured against a post in the courtyard without any food or shelter. I remember thinking that Whitefoot could do with a run around the lawns. Of course, I hadn't expected the dog to run off and never return. When William found out that I was responsible for Whitefoot's disappearance, he had wanted to beat me, except that Mother had stepped in to prevent this from happening.

Not that I went without punishment, of course. The next day I came into the courtyard to find that William was dangling my favourite toy above the well and threatening to let go. It was just a hollow thing, made from thinly cast pewter — a small knight mounted on a horse — but I had treasured this toy dearly since Father had made a show of presenting him to me in front of the family, after returning from a trip to London. Now, as I begged William to hand back my precious knight, my brother only laughed and leant over the well. How clearly I remembered the shape of William's hair at the nape of his neck as he let my little knight fall into the water far below, where the toy landed with a distant, melancholic plop.

I cast the memory away. That was many years ago. And we were different people now. I had no reason to fear William . . . but even so, I was not yet ready to tell him about Agnes.

After an hour or so in the forest, we finally emerged onto the London to Rye road, where we found ourselves heading north against an unexpected sea of travellers. They were family groups, huddles of people who seemed to be carrying all of their worldly goods across their ponies' haunches, or strapped onto their own backs. Pans, longbows, flails, brooms, baskets and cages stuffed with chickens and ducks. Even goats led by leashes. These groups were accompanied by gaggles of exhausted children, and shadowed by thin dogs that had refused to be abandoned.

It wasn't hard to guess why these people were on the road. Not that this stopped William from confronting the man at the head of the first group, and demanding to know if he and his family had permission to be travelling? When this man gave a discourteous and evasive answer, William reminded him that a villein cannot simply desert his village because he feels like it. Even tenants must have the permission of their lord before they move away – even if they are escaping plague. The man eventually named his family and parish, before William agreed to let him and his brood of thin-faced children pass. My brother even issued a warning that he intended to report them to their master. But it was an empty threat.

We passed many other such groups in the next hour or so – people who collected at the turns in the road, like piles of dried leaves. William could not threaten to report all of them, so he stopped asking their names or where they usually lived. Instead, we cantered through each group, as William shouted for them to part and let us through.

Our progress north was steady enough, until we turned a corner to come face to face with the strangest of sights – a group of bare-chested men, moving towards us in a caterpillar, screaming their prayers to the sky as they walked. At every third or fourth step they struck at their naked backs with whips of knotted thongs. Sharp stones were embedded into each of these knots and were causing a criss-cross of ugly scarring and open wounds across their skin. We approached these men gingerly, as our horses were startled, but our attempts to quickly pass were thwarted, despite William's demands that they should stand aside. When these men saw my black habit and wooden crucifix they quickly surrounded me, chanting their prayers with more urgency as they grasped at my feet and hands with bloodied fingers.

This was enough for William. He took out his own horse whip and began to thrash at the air until they reluctantly moved back.

Now that we were free of their attentions, we made our escape, cantering away until we reached a safe distance. It was here, at the brow of the hill, that we finally stopped to look back at this spectacle, seeing that the men had now thrown themselves to their knees and were wailing like a gaggle of starving children.

'Who, in the name of God, were they?' said William.

'Flagellants,' I replied. 'They come from Flanders, I believe.'

'What's the matter with them?'

'They're praying for forgiveness,' I said. 'They hope to persuade God to spare the world from plague. The more they whip themselves, the greater our chances.' I watched as the men crawled back to their feet and rearranged themselves again into their previous formation. 'It's a shame they cannot see the irony in their actions,' I added.

William cocked his head. 'Oh yes?'

'As they wander about England, they're probably doing a better job at spreading plague, than preventing it.'

William regarded me solemnly for a moment, pinching his lips together, before his face softened into a smile. 'What witless fools,' he said, before he started to laugh. His amusement was muted at first, but soon he was leaning against his horse's neck and guffawing until his shoulders shook and tears streamed down his face. Laughter is contagious, and it wasn't long before I caught this infection. There is nothing funny about plague of course, and yet we had done little more than pass doleful groups of men, women and children all morning. Their misery hovering above us like a low cloud. How wonderful it felt to laugh, no matter how inappropriate.

When our amusement had finally run its course, William slapped me across the back and told me that I had a good de Lacy sense of humour. This was the first time, in my whole life, that William and I had ever shared a joke — and I enjoyed the experience. I felt, at long last, as if we were something akin to equals.

*   *   *

After this encounter, we decided to leave the main road and return to the forest paths, now heading in a north-west direction towards Somershill. Our horses were pleased of the shade under the trees after the open roads, and I was pleased not to be riding against a tide of people.

We continued in silence again for a while, until William suddenly spoke. 'So, Oswald,' he said as our horses now trudged along side by side like two elderly companions. 'I expect you're looking forward to seeing Somershill and your family again?'

I hadn't been back to Somershill for over two years, and I wasn't in the least bit excited to be returning – but I lied out of politeness. 'Yes,' I told William. 'It will be good to see the place again.'

William tilted his face towards mine and gave a smile. 'And what about your family?' he asked.

'I'm looking forward to seeing Mother.'

'And Father?'

'Yes. Of course,' I added quickly, though, in truth, I had no particular longing to see him. My father was a man who continually found fault with the world – usually angry about something or other whenever we met. That said, whatever injustice, slur or discourtesy had most recently infuriated him, these offences usually paled into insignificance when he caught a look at me. Particularly in recent years, I seemed to anger my father just by existing.

William must have read my mind. 'You can say what you like to me about Father, you know. There are no bonds of affection between the two of us.'

'I thought you were on good terms?' I said, tempted to add that I had always thought of William as Father's favourite.

'No, Oswald,' replied William. 'Our relationship has never been good.'

I went to answer, but the words stuck in my throat.

'You're surprised to hear this, aren't you?' he commented.

I nodded. 'Yes, William. I am.'

'Father has always been hard on me,' he replied. 'Very hard. But nobody ever knew.' He kept his eyes on the road ahead, unable to look in my direction. For the first time in my life, I saw William look uncomfortable. Vulnerable even. 'I was beaten more than you or Richard,' he told me. 'But it was always in the privacy of Father's library, so that nobody would know. I am his eldest surviving son.' William grunted a short laugh. 'One day I will be Lord Somershill, so Father could not risk belittling me in front of the household.'

I hardly knew what to say. 'I'm so sorry,' was all that I could manage.

William released one of his hands from the reins, to run his fingers through his hair. 'But now that Father is losing his mind, he doesn't care who hears his scorn for me. I am mocked from one side of the house to the other.'

'Losing his mind?'

'Yes,' replied William, turning his head to face mine. 'Prepare to be shocked, Oswald. Father is not the man you met at your last visit. He repeats himself endlessly. He forgets where he's put things. He often forgets names or places. Sometimes he becomes aggressive for no reason. Particularly with me.'

'He's always been a difficult man,' I suggested. 'Perhaps it's just that this has worsened with age.'

William shook his head. 'It's been a steep decline,' he said. 'The role of lord is clearly vexing his temper and intellect. He's made so many mistakes that it's becoming embarrassing. He should pass responsibility to me, now that I'm thirty. But I'm treated no better than a servant. Allowed to follow his orders, but give none of my own.'

This conversation made me feel uncomfortable, prompting that variety of disquiet that comes from the sensation of sand shifting beneath your feet. I had always thought of Father as the obdurate but dependable rock of our family, but now it seemed I could no longer rely upon that certainty.

'Have you tried discussing the matter with him?' I ventured. 'Father might agree to pass on more responsibility, if he knew how you felt?'

William sighed and kicked at his horse again. 'Come on, Oswald. Let's get home. Then you can see for yourself.'

We rode on for several miles, picking our way along seldom-used tracks that were edged with foxgloves – their purple spikes watching our progress like an audience of spindly onlookers. A wake of buzzards circled above our heads, piercing the still air with their plaintive calls. The air was filled with the mossy, verdant scent of the moisture that has been trapped under the canopy.

After a while, the trees thinned, and the forest gave way to fields and hedgerows, until we turned a corner to see the house of Somershill, standing proud beyond the crooked homes of the village, with its square elevations and crenellated walls. It was somewhere between a grand house and a castle. A home that could also be an intimidating fortress. But that day, as the sun caught the warm hues of the sandstone, Somershill looked welcoming, not hostile. Suddenly I felt pleased to be home.

Chapter Twenty

William and I trotted along the main street of the village of Somershill, to be greeted with a flurry of perfunctory bows and curtseys from the inhabitants, before these people immediately returned to their work. Their gestures of respect were involuntary reflexes – unthinking and instinctive reactions to a pair of noblemen riding past.

'Look at them all,' said William, a little disdainfully. 'Sometimes they remind me of sheep. They barely lift their mouths from the grass.' There was some truth to his observation, even if it were a little unkind. The people of Somershill seemed to be caught in this same trap as farmyard animals – fighting a never-ending cycle of feeding themselves and their children, with only the barest of opportunities to enjoy the thrill of living itself. It was a sobering thought, and reminded me to be pleased of my own wealth and position. I, at least, had the time to stare at the sky and listen to the birds.

Once we had reached the end of this short street, and had been greeted by each and every one of the residents, I realised that I'd seen none of the panic about plague that we'd witnessed on our journey. There were no carts being packed with pots and pans, nor animals and children being rounded up. There were no prayers being chanted, nor naked flesh being flogged. I might have mentioned this to William, but his good humour had dissipated the moment we entered the village, and he seemed determined to ride along this street with an ugly scowl upon his face.

We arrived at the house via the south-east gate, crossing the ditch that had once formed part of a moat, before heading for the stables. There was a strong smell in the air that day, as the warm weather had heated the foul contents of this ditch into a stinking miasma. After many years of neglect, the Somershill moat was now little more than a latrine, into which the servants threw all of the household waste and ordure.

I must have pulled a face at the smell, since William turned to me and smiled. 'Had you forgotten the delights of our moat, then?' he asked me.

'I'm used to the latrines at the monastery,' I replied. 'We use running water.'

'Father would never agree to the expense,' said William, as he dismounted from his horse. 'But we could easily dig some proper pits and cover the shit with some soil,' he added, passing the reins to the waiting groom. 'I have suggested this many times. But Father is happy to live in this stink, so what can we do?' William held out his hand to help me dismount. 'But don't worry, Oswald,' he said, leaning over to whisper into my ear. 'It's the first thing I'll sort out.'

I followed William towards the Great Hall, where he chose to enter the house via the main doors, rather than walking around to the back porch near the kitchens. This door, a colossal creation of oak panels with long iron hinge plates, was stiff and needed to be kicked open. It was an unnecessary way to announce our return, especially as we lacked an audience. The hall itself was empty, apart from a pair of servant girls who didn't bother to look up from their work as we entered – preferring to concentrate on scrubbing down the long table that reached across the dais. They continued to ignore us, as we crossed the floor, passed the smoking embers of the central fire, and then climbed the spiral stairs to the solar, where we found the family at last.

My brother Richard and my sister Clemence were sitting at the table, playing at Nine Men's Morris, and barely looked up from the board as we stepped in. Father was asleep in a chair and Mother was sitting beside the fire, fiddling with some embroidery. She dropped this cloth to the floor and came over to embrace me immediately, though she was quick to find fault with my complexion, my weight and my posture. Once I had been welcomed with a quick appraisal of all my physical shortcomings, she then disappeared to the kitchen to order a soup that was certain to cure all of my many deficiencies and imbalances.

Father opened his eyes and took a moment to revive, before he addressed William. 'You took your time, then,' he said, without bothering to acknowledge me.

William wandered over to the window seat and threw himself down on the cushions, crossing his arms and leaving his legs to sprawl across the room. He looked ready to sleep himself. 'It's a long way to Kintham Abbey, Father,' he said. 'And we had to avoid the main road for most of the journey. It was full with travellers.'

'Travellers,' said my sister Clemence, with her eyebrow arched. 'Where would people be travelling? There are no feast days until midsummer.'

William grunted a laugh. 'So you haven't heard about the plague, then?' he said mockingly.

Clemence pulled a sour face. 'Of course I know of plague,' she replied, placing a piece onto the board. 'I'm just surprised to hear that the sufferers are tramping around England with this affliction, that's all.'

'They don't have plague, Clemence,' retorted William with a groan, as if he were speaking to the village fool. 'They are fleeing it. Most of them are coming south from Southwark or Bromley.'

Clemence waited for Richard to place his piece and then made her own move. 'Well, I don't want them coming here,' she said, turning to address Father. 'We should close off the gates to the village, and stop anybody from arriving or leaving.'

'Nonsense. We'll do no such thing,' said Father, before rising to his feet and circling me, as if he were putting a price on my head at market. 'We just need to get on with our lives as usual,' he said. 'There are too many exaggerated tales about this illness. And I don't believe a word of them. Not a word.'

'Then why was I called home, Father?' I asked, deciding to speak at last.

'I have no idea,' he replied.

William rolled his eyes, before sitting up to catch Father's attention. 'You insisted I go to Kintham to fetch Oswald, Father. Remember? It was your express instruction. You were afraid that Oswald would die of plague if we left him there.'

Father shook his head at this, though without complete conviction, and I saw some of the contrariness that William had described to me earlier. His face was suddenly clouded with confusion, before he wrinkled his nose and shook his head, as if forcing himself to concentrate.

'These people should be on their home estates, working in the fields,' he announced. 'Not marching about the high roads of England. What will become of our farms if this is allowed to continue?' He gave a deep snort of discontent. 'No lord would allow his villagers to leave their land at this time of year. Particularly not in June.'

'Then perhaps their lords are dead?' said William, turning to look out the window.

Father bristled at this. 'Nonsense. The Pestilence only attacks the poor and weak.'

'I don't think that's true,' I said, speaking out again and not considering the consequences of openly disagreeing with Father.

'Oh yes?' he said, turning on me. 'I hear only of peasants dying. Thanks to their foul practices.'

I was tempted to say something about the rotting food and shit that was festering in the ditches of this very house, but I held my tongue on this topic. William looked at me and smiled, knowing exactly what I was thinking.

'Many monks have died at Winchester,' I said instead. 'Their practices are not foul.'

'Pah,' said Father. 'Monks, indeed. Nothing but scroungers. I'm talking about men and women of nobility. We have nothing to fear from this plague. Nothing at all.'

William quickly sat up and glared at me, urging me not to say anything else, but I felt riled. 'What about Joan of England?' I said. 'She died of plague. And she was the daughter of King Edward himself. You couldn't be any nobler.'

Father's eyes narrowed. 'But Joan was in France when she died. It is no wonder that she perished,' he added, balling his hands into fists. 'I am astounded that our king tried to marry his own kin into such people. What was he thinking?'

'Joan was only travelling through France,' I replied. 'She was due to marry Peter of Castile. He is Spanish, I believe.'

It was Clemence's turn to flash her eyes at me. A warning to stop antagonising the old man.

'I see that you are still a pedant, Oswald,' said Father, relaxing his fists and shaking his head. 'I see that the Benedictines of Kintham have not succeeded in teaching you any humility?' He paused to purse his lips. 'Well. Welcome home to you. May your stay here be short.' He paused. 'For all of our sakes.'

Following this he tapped Richard on the shoulder, informing my brother that they had some matters to attend to on the farm. Richard had remained silent during this whole conversation – which was his usual tactic for dealing with family politics. Say nothing and hope to avoid attention. Now that Richard had been noticed by Father, he stood without the merest modicum of enthusiasm. But then again, my brother preferred to spend his days hunting in the forest, rather than helping Father on the farm. I noted Richard was already wearing his leather boots and green tunic – ready to leave with his hounds at a moment's notice. He even picked up his hunting hat as he left the solar – a bycocket decorated with an array of embroidered peacock feathers. I could only hope, for Richard's sake, that this supposed farming chore was just an excuse for Father to leave. My brother would have been hopelessly overdressed for a visit to the pig sties or the cattle sheds.

Once the pair had headed off down the stairs, Father negotiating each step down to the Great Hall as if it were made of ice, Clemence turned to me and laughed wryly. 'You will regret infuriating Father, Oswald,' she told me, as she carefully replaced the pieces from the game into a small leather bag. 'He never forgets a slight.'

'What do you mean, Clemence?' said William. 'The man's memory is rusting over. He'll have forgotten this whole conversation by this evening.'

Clemence rose to her feet. 'Father is not as forgetful as you may think, William,' she said. 'Nor, indeed, as you would like him to be.'

'What do you mean by that?' snapped William.

'It means that Father is still the lord of this estate,' she said. 'Not you.' She then swept out of the room, following Father and Richard to the Great Hall, and prompting William to turn to me and smile.

'So, Oswald,' he said with a glint of mischief in his eye. 'Welcome back to Somershill.'

Chapter Twenty-one

I spent the following three days either avoiding my father, or trying my very best not to annoy him whenever we did meet. A few times I thought about returning to Kintham, since Father had clearly forgotten his desire to have me at Somershill – but when I mentioned this idea to William, my brother soundly warned me against leaving. Plague was now rumoured to be present in the lands between Somershill and Kintham, and it would be too dangerous for me to make this journey.

In some ways I was heartened by William's concern, but then again, this thoughtfulness only made me feel worse about Agnes. Sooner or later, I would have to confess to my part in his daughter's death – as unpleasant a task as this promised to be. I still felt that this conversation would be easier to conduct once I could soften the blow with news of Sawyer's arrest. The trouble was, I had yet to hear from Brother Peter, though he had solemnly promised to write to me. I had waited for three days already, and heard nothing from the man.

In the meantime, I distracted myself by wandering my old childhood haunts – climbing the remains of the curtain wall to look at the mantle of forest on the distant hills, or sitting in the cellars, behind the barrels of pickles and sacks of salt. This was a favourite hiding spot, though I was always forced to move on when the steward of Somershill appeared. Gilbert was never pleased to see me at the best of times — but if he found me in the cellars, then I was shooed away like a wandering chicken.

On the morning of my fourth day at Somershill, I decided to visit the family chapel, opening the door to this small stone building, only to find Gilbert coming in the opposite direction. The old man looked sheepish, as he was holding a loaf of bread and a lump of cheese covered in a bloom of woolly mould.

'Good morning,' I said, before pointing at the bread and cheese. 'What are you doing with those?'

'I found them in here, Master Oswald,' he said. 'They were hidden and then forgotten.'

The loaf of bread was large. The piece of cheese generous — strange items for a person to hide and forget about. 'Who's been doing that?' I said.

He looked over my shoulder to see if anybody was nearby. 'I'm not sure I should say.'

'Why's that?' I asked. 'Has somebody been stealing food from the kitchen?'

His eye twitched. 'There are no thieves here,' he said. 'You mustn't go round spreading rumours like that.'

'Then what is this food doing in the chapel?' I said, offended at his tone.

Gilbert bowed his head to me, as if apologising for his previous rudeness. 'I think it's your father,' he said with an awkward smile. 'I've seen him doing it.'

'Why would Father be hiding food in the chapel? He can eat whenever he wants.' Gilbert's story sounded fanciful, and yet I knew that this man was not the imaginative type.

'I'm not telling lies,' he replied. 'I've seen him doing it. Creeping out here at dawn with a bag of food. He doesn't know that I can see him. But I can.'

'Have you asked Father why he's hiding the food?'

Gilbert shook his head. 'No, Master Oswald. I haven't. I just look around the chapel each time he's been here. To see what I can find.' He presented me with the mouldy bread and cheese. 'Must have missed these two.' He paused and then looked up at me with wary eyes. 'Perhaps you could ask him what he's doing?' he suggested. 'Seeing as you're his son.'

I made a weak gesture that was somewhere between a shrug and a nod. 'Yes. Well, perhaps,' I said, before clearing my throat with more certainty. 'Though I'm sure there's a very reasonable explanation for all this. I expect that Father is leaving the food for somebody.'

Gilbert frowned. 'Except that nobody ever comes to fetch it.'

'Well, I'll ask him if the chance arises,' I said.

'Up to you,' he replied. 'But it would be good to know what ails your father. I haven't seen this sort of thing since your grandmother Alice was alive.'

'She hid food as well?' I asked. Alice de Lacy had died when I was very young, so I had no memory of the woman – other than the stories I had heard from Mother. None of which were complimentary, given that she had been my father's mother.

'Oh yes,' said Gilbert. 'All the time.' He grunted a laugh. 'Thought we were trying to poison her. Wouldn't eat a thing we served.'

'You think my father is suffering from the same affliction?' I asked.

Gilbert paused. Clearly the idea had crossed his mind. 'Well, I wouldn't like to say,' he answered. 'But it might help if somebody were to talk to him about it?' He raised a bushy eyebrow and stared at me, and for a moment, I felt as if this commitment were about to trip rashly off my tongue. But I stopped the impulse just in time. Was I about to ask my proud, volatile father – a man who already disliked me – if he were hiding food in the chapel, because he was under the delusion that somebody was trying to poison him? No. I was not. I would leave that conversation to William.

'Just keep this to yourself, please,' I snapped. 'My father's reasons are his own business.'

I searched out William straight away, thinking he might be in the solar, only to be told he was working on some manorial ledgers in Father's library. I descended the stairs again and headed across the Great Hall, ready to knock at the library door, when I heard raised voices coming from within the room. One belonged to Father. The other to William. I looked about the hall to make sure that nobody else was around, and then I put my ear to the door. The pair were arguing about a tenant who had failed to discharge his contractual duties on the demesne. Father wanted to evict the man, whereas William was suggesting a fine instead.

'It is not for you to decide,' said Father. His booming voice travelled easily through the wooden panels of the door. William's voice was harder to hear, unless I pressed my ear to the door jamb.

'You cannot ignore this man's failure to cut his hedges for months,' said William, 'and then suddenly evict him.'

'I'll do what I want,' said Father.

'Yes, but perhaps you should listen to me, Father?' said William. 'I have agreed a suitable settlement with the man. He will cut the hedges immediately, and then he will work for three extra days on the demesne fields at harvest time. Not only that. He'll pay an extra five shillings for his rent this year. I think we should be satisfied with this outcome.'

'Well, I'm not in the least bit satisfied,' said Father. 'The churl has disobeyed the terms of his tenancy.'

'Accept the offer, Father,' said William. 'You'll get more work out of this man. And more money.'

Father laughed. 'You really have been gulled, William. Haven't you? Five shillings isn't nearly enough. When will you grow a spine and stand up to these people? How on earth do you expect to be their lord when I'm gone? They'll trample all over you.'

A short sequence followed that I couldn't hear, before William's voice cut through again. He sounded exasperated. 'Listen to me, Father. Who will take on the tenancy if you throw this man and his family from the land?'

'It is good land,' argued Father. 'With dew ponds and woods. Plenty of tenants will be interested to take over.'

'No,' replied William. 'They won't. You're wrong about that.'

I drew back from the door as I suddenly sensed the presence of somebody behind me. I looked around to see it was my brother Richard, standing in the shadows and watching me. He held a pair of dead hares by their legs, their fur stained with blood. Our eyes met for a moment and I think it crossed his mind to ask me what I was doing, before he carried on towards the kitchen, deciding, as ever, to mind his own business.

I turned my own attentions back to the library, where William was now speaking again. 'Nobody will want that land, Father. Not when the Plague has passed. We both know how many men will die in the coming months. After that, the survivors will be able to pick and choose their plots. We'll be left with empty lands and even less income.'

'I don't agree,' said Father. 'All this talk of plague is nonsense. We haven't seen a single death on our estate. It's just fear-mongering from London. You shouldn't listen to a word of it.'

'But the deaths will come, Father,' said William. 'Don't you worry. The Plague will not pass Somershill by.'

Another passage of mumbled conversation followed, which ended when Father roared, 'You listen to me. I am Lord Somershill. Not you! And I say they are evicted. Now get out of here, and stop sticking your nose into my business.'

There were heavy footsteps across the floor, before William flung the door open and marched out, failing to notice that I was standing with my back against the wall. I stepped forward when my brother had passed out of sight, then looked through the open door into the library, where Father stared back at me with a vacant expression. For a moment, I don't think he recognised my face.

His eyes focused. 'What do you want?' he said aggressively.

I bowed my head and stepped away from the door. 'Sorry, Father,' I said. 'I was just passing by.'

'Well, go and pass by somewhere else,' he shouted. 'Your face gives me indigestion.' With this, he suddenly stood up from his desk, stumbled out of the library, before heading across the Great Hall towards the large entrance doors. Once there, he stopped and pressed his nose against the iron banding of the door and stood perfectly still, as if he had turned to stone.

I approached with caution. 'Can I help you, Father?' I asked softly.

He turned on me as if I had tried to burn him with a poker. 'Get away from me . . . um, um . . .' he said, as he tried desperately to remember my name. 'I don't need your help.'

'Where are you going, Father?' I asked.

'To the kitchen, of course,' he answered. 'What do you think I'm doing? I want some ale.'

I tapped his arm gently. 'The kitchens are over there,' I said, pointing across the hall to an exit on the other side of the room.

Father frowned, until he shook the muddled look away. 'I knew that,' he snapped. 'I was just checking that this door was locked.'

I tried a reassuring smile. 'Of course, Father,' I said, not wanting to belittle him any further. 'That's a good idea.'

He wasn't pleased by this small kindness. In fact, my words only succeeded in riling him. 'Stop idling around here, Oswald,' he said. 'You're always under my feet. Haven't you got any work to do?'

Before I could answer he spun on his heel and headed for the kitchens. I didn't try to follow.

Chapter Twenty-two

I had my chance to speak to William about Father that night – once the candle in our room had burnt out and the sounds of the castle had settled to the occasional creak. I was sleeping in the small room that my eldest brother normally shared with his wife and two young daughters, but they had been relocated to my mother's bed chamber during my stay. I had offered, repeatedly, to sleep on the floor of the solar, but Father insisted that I should be accommodated in William's room, and he would hear no objections. Needless to say, I was not spared the complaints of William's wife – a torrent of barbed comments about uncomfortable beds and Mother's snoring, but William himself had no objections to the arrangement. He told me that he was secretly pleased to have a few nights away from the woman, since she was forever getting up to use the piss pot in the middle of the night. I gathered that theirs was not a happy marriage – though I didn't pry. They could barely stand to look at one another, let alone have a cordial conversation.

William was restless that particular night, turning over repeatedly in bed, so I knew that he was still awake. The canopy was not drawn about his bedstead, as the day had been warm and the room was stuffy. I was sleeping in a truckle bed – a piece of furniture that had been built for a child, and didn't accommodate my long limbs. That said, it was better than sleeping on a straw mattress in the solar.

I cleared my throat. 'William,' I whispered through the darkness.

'What is it?' he asked, his voice drowsy. 'You're not going to force me to say some prayers, are you?'

'No,' I replied. 'Don't worry on that account.' I paused. 'I just wanted to talk to you about Father,' I hesitated. 'You're right. He isn't well.'

I could hear William sit up a little, though he didn't answer me.

'Father couldn't remember my name today,' I continued. 'And he didn't know how to find the kitchens.' I paused. 'And then I discovered that he's been hiding food in the chapel. He seems to think that somebody's trying to poison him.'

William smirked. 'There's an idea.' When I didn't laugh in response, he continued. 'I'm sorry, Oswald. Sometimes humour helps me to cope with Father's contrariness, but it's not funny. I agree.' He paused. 'At least you know the truth now.'

'I overheard you arguing with Father today,' I said. 'About evicting a tenant.'

'When was that?' His tone was suddenly guarded.

'In the library.'

'So you were listening at the door, were you?'

'I was looking for you,' I said quickly. 'I couldn't help but overhear the conversation.'

William lay back in his bed, causing the slats to creak and groan like the frame of an old ship. 'Then you understand what I'm fighting against. The more I offer to help Father, the more he rejects me. The man just won't listen.'

'What about Richard?' I asked. 'Perhaps he could persuade Father to relinquish some of his responsibilities? They seem close,' I said, remembering Father's invitation to Richard on my arrival day.

'He's of no help,' sighed William. 'Richard is a coward. He won't acknowledge Father's problems because it might affect his

own purse.' He gave a snort. 'What does Richard care about
Somershill, or the condition of Father's mind? He only wants to
ride about the forest, catching herons or digging out badgers.'

'And what about Mother?' I asked. 'Surely she's noticed
Father's affliction?'

The snort came again. This time with even greater disdain.
'She doesn't believe that there's anything wrong with Father.
Can you believe that? Every time that I discuss the matter
with her, she either shouts me down or quickly changes the
subject.' He gave a long sigh. 'Father is clearly losing his mind,
and yet nobody will admit to this problem, let alone talk
about it.'

'Well I know it's true,' I replied. 'I've seen it for myself. There
is a great change in Father's disposition since I last saw him.'

William paused for a moment and then reached down from
his bed to touch my shoulder. 'Thank you, Oswald,' he said.
'Your support means a lot to me. At last. A de Lacy who will face
up to the truth.'

An idea suddenly came to me. Was this the right time to speak
to William about Agnes? My brother had certainly softened
towards me over the last few days. You might even say that we
had formed the first bonds of friendship. Not only that, he had
just thanked me and complimented my judgment. It would be
easy to now tell my story, even if I wasn't able to mention
Sawyer's arrest. The room was dark and I couldn't see William's
face. This environment had all the warm and reassuring intimacy
of a confessional. This could only help my cause. And yet . . .

And yet the words were still so hard to find. I wanted to lie
back down in my own bed and leave this awkward conversation
for another day. I convinced myself that this was the right decision, and yet . . .

And yet, if not now – then when? Was my decision to wait for
news from Brother Peter just an excuse to delay the inevitable?
In the darkness, I could hear William's shallow, rhythmic

breathing as he started to drift back into sleep. Soon he would be snoring and this moment would be gone.

'William,' I whispered into the black.

'Yes. What is it now?'

'There's something else that I wanted to tell you.'

I could hear him rustling with the sheets. 'Oh yes.'

A silence followed, as I tried to think of the best way to tell this story. Should I start by telling William that he had a daughter with Beatrice Wheeler, before I admitted that I'd caused her death? Or should I start with the death, and then reveal the girl's parentage? There was hardly an easy way, and the more I thought about it, the more tongue-tied I became.

'What is it, Oswald?' said William, now fully awake and becoming mildly irritated. 'Come on. Out with it.'

I closed my eyelids and tried to concentrate. In my mind's eye, I could see Agnes wading into the swollen waters of the river. I called out desperately, warning her not to tread out any further, but she didn't listen to me. Instead, she let the river consume her, until her face was fully covered, with only her long hair visible as it fanned out in a delicate halo on the surface.

'What's the matter?' asked William, his tone now one of concern.

I snapped out of my reverie. 'I'm sorry,' I said, feeling my heart racing. 'It's . . . difficult.'

William reached a hand to my shoulder again. 'Then it's better said quickly.'

'It's just that . . .'

'It's just that what?'

I hesitated again, regretting having started this conversation. Now I had to say something.

'Come on, Oswald,' urged William. 'If something's troubling you, then you must tell me.'

I took a deep breath. I meant to tell William about Agnes. I really did, and yet it was a completely different story that fell from my lips. 'I don't want to stay at the monastery,' I blurted out. 'I don't want to be a monk.'

There was a long pause. 'Well, I don't think any man wants to be a monk, do they, Oswald?' he said at length. 'Not really. All that praying and fasting. Not to mention the celibacy. Who wants to live without a woman?'

'But some men are called to God's service,' I said. 'They choose willingly to devote their lives to the church.'

'I suppose so.'

'But I don't feel that way, William.' I cleared my throat to drown out a pesky sob. 'I don't think that I can take my vows.'

William sat up in bed. 'So, what's the problem, then, Little Brother? Is it the praying and fasting?' He paused. 'Or is it the celibacy?' When I didn't answer, he started to laugh again. 'By the saints. It *is* the celibacy, isn't it?'

'No,' I said quickly. Too quickly.

He didn't believe me. 'Have you met a girl in Stonebrook who takes your fancy, then?' he asked. 'Is that the problem?'

I shook my head, not trusting myself to speak.

He leant out over the bed, so that I could see the outline of his head through the gloom. 'Who is she?'

'It doesn't matter,' I said, wafting my night shirt. My tenseness was generating an additional level of heat, over and above the mounting stuffiness of the room.

'So she does exist, then,' said William. 'I knew it!' He paused before dropping his voice. 'You know that many monks have mistresses, don't you, Oswald? Why not bed this girl anyway? Nobody would blink an eye.'

'She's not a girl.'

'Oh.' He said, starting to laugh again. 'It's a boy, then? Is that what you're telling me?'

'No, no,' I answered, as the sweat started to run down my forehead in rivulets. 'I meant that she's a woman.'

'So she's older than you?' he said, now laughing even louder. 'Ha! You do like to make things hard for yourself, don't you, Oswald? It might be simpler to find a younger girl to begin with. They're more easily impressed.'

'I don't want to find a younger girl,' I retorted, now annoyed that I'd opened myself up to ridicule. 'Please. Let's not talk about this any more.'

William fell back against his pillow, and there was a moment of silence before he gave a great, resounding guffaw. It sounded so odd and dislocated in the darkness. 'By the saints,' he said. 'I know who you're in love with. It's Maud Woodstock, isn't it?'

'No,' I said, far too defensively.

He sat back in his bed. 'It *is* Maud Woodstock, isn't it? God's bones. Not you as well?'

'What do you mean by that?'

'You know that Richard was infatuated with that woman for many years?'

My nightshirt was now sticking to my skin and I felt nauseated. 'No. I didn't know that,' I mumbled.

'Richard used to mope about the house, writing her love letters . . . until Father put a stop to it.' He laughed again. 'At least Father had his wits about him in those days,' he said. 'Because you know what they call Maud Woodstock, don't you?'

'No.'

'Widow Woodstock.'

'How can Maud be a widow?' I replied. 'She's never been married.'

'Exactly, Oswald,' he said. 'And do you know why?'

'No.'

'Every man who was ever betrothed to that woman, ended up dead before the wedding day. Three times she was due to marry. Three times the fellow died.'

'How did they die?'

'I don't know,' he huffed. 'The Flux or an ague. Something like that. The villagers say she's cursed.'

'That's just a stupid story,' I said, now understanding Maud's sensitivity on that particular subject. 'Curses are nonsense.'

'Believe what you like,' said William. 'But no man will touch her now, Oswald. So I'd keep clear of her if I were you.' He dropped his voice to a whisper. 'Because if you manage to get yourself out of Kintham, then she'll try to take you for a husband in a flash.'

'Maud doesn't want to marry,' I protested. 'She's content looking after her father and running their farm.'

'Of course she wants to marry, Oswald,' said William. 'Every woman needs a husband in the end.'

A silence followed, while I felt thoroughly frustrated with myself. I had said too much and too little. William now knew about Maud and my desire to leave the monastery, and yet I had failed to say a word about Agnes. 'Don't mention this to anyone, William,' I begged. 'Please.'

I expected my brother to laugh, or continue to tease me, but he didn't. 'I can speak to Father, if you like?' he said, his voice suddenly softer and more understanding. 'About taking your vows, that is. Don't worry, I won't mention the widow Woodstock.' He paused and then heaved a long sigh. 'I'm not sure that Father will listen to me, Oswald,' he said. 'But there might be some other option than the church for you.'

'Such as?'

He paused again. 'I don't know,' he said honestly.

'No,' I said despondently, laying my head back down on the pillow. 'Neither do I.'

Chapter Twenty-three

Somershill, November 1370

Mother caught hold of my hand and grasped it tightly. 'I always thought you wanted to be a monk, Oswald,' she said. 'I always thought that we'd dragged you away from that monastery.'

I had to think carefully before answering. When the topic of my years at Kintham came up – as sometimes happened when I was talking to my circle of friends and acquaintances, I usually told the story about having once been a committed novice, happy at the thought of taking my vows at the age of eighteen and then becoming a monk for the rest of my life. It was only the sudden death of my father and older brothers that had changed this destiny. In fact, I'd told this story so often that I had started to believe it myself. In many ways I had clung to this fabricated reality, because it was such a straightforward tale, which usually satisfied the other party and was rarely followed up with any more questions. But my mother was dying, so what was the point of telling it again?

'No, Mother,' I said. 'I never liked the monastery. I never wanted to be a monk.'

'I'm not sure that's true.'

'It is completely true.'

My certainty on this topic had angered her, so she found another part of my story to attack. 'You know that there was nothing wrong with your father,' she said. 'I disagree entirely with your version of events, Oswald. You make him sound like a lunatic with all these stories about hiding food and forgetting names.'

'His mind was unsound towards the end of his life,' I said. 'You must agree with that.'

She waved a pale hand at me. 'No, no, I don't agree at all. It's very disrespectful to malign the dead in such a way. Particularly when they cannot answer for themselves. I hope you will not take such liberties with my character, when I am finally gone? I would like my successors to know the truth about me.'

I bowed my head. 'Don't worry, Mother,' I said. 'Rest assured. Your true character will be known to all future generations. I will make sure of that myself.'

She threw me a sideways glance, unsure how to read this promise, before deciding to take it as a compliment. 'That's good to hear,' she said. 'But keep to your word, Oswald.' She raised an eyebrow and chuckled. 'Or I will haunt you.' She withdrew a bony finger from beneath the sheets and waved it at me. 'I will rise from my grave and punish you for any untruths.'

This might have been a sobering thought. The idea that I would never escape her attentions, even after her death. It was lucky then that I had not the slightest belief in the afterlife. 'Would you like me to continue?' I asked.

She poked the hand back under the sheet and closed her eyes. 'No. Come back later,' she whispered. 'I need to sleep now.'

I crept from the room, looking back to see her body – lying on its back beneath a linen sheet. Her eyes were closed and her mouth was hanging open. In this pose, my mother looked every bit like a stone *gisant*, recumbent upon the top of her own tomb.

Her life was numbered now in days. The maid told me that she rarely ate a meal, other than a thin broth. Her urine was dark brown and her stools were small and hard, like rabbit's droppings. Sometimes she was so delirious with pain that she had to be given a draught of dwale to induce sleep. A potent mixture of vinegar, henbane, poppy seeds and hemlock – a concoction that was strong enough to kill a person with a weaker constitution. But not my mother. Somehow she still found the energy to continue.

I left the room and wandered down the stairs towards the Great Hall, finding that the main door was wide open to the elements. An icy wind was blowing in across the hall, so I strode over to close the doors, only to find that a party had gathered on the lawns outside to bid Sir John farewell. Seeing this, I cursed myself for bothering about the door, as I was now forced to witness this awkward parting. Seeing Sir John's glum face made me feel guilty about my fit of jealousy, but I had no choice but to shake his hand and wish him a safe journey.

Filomena glowered at me. 'I hope you're happy now,' she said, as Sir John plodded away into the distance, cutting a rather pathetic figure against the horizon. His horse was an aged, piebald palfrey, and the leather of his saddle was scuffed and worn. Sir John might have travelled the world collecting stories, but he had not succeeded in accumulating any wealth. Wearing a dirty riding mantle and perched between two saddlebags stuffed with clothes, he looked like a peddler heading off for market with the entirety of his stock hanging from the saddle.

'Sir John wanted to see his family in Sheppey,' I said. 'I think he was pleased to get away.'

Filomena sighed at this remark. 'The winter here will be so dull now,' she lamented.

'You have me,' I suggested.

She huffed at this. 'You spend the whole day in the room of a dying woman. And I only have the company of your sister Clemence and her fainthearted son.'

'Henry's not fainthearted,' I said in the boy's defence, aware that he was hanging around in the near distance and trying to listen to our conversation. 'He is just quiet, that's all.'

'Then why doesn't he stand up to his mother?' she asked. 'Clemence constantly scolds the boy. I wonder that he can stand it.' She added a disdainful laugh. 'You de Lacy men and your mothers,' she said. 'You are ruled by them.'

'There's no need for such insults,' I replied.

'I think there is,' she said. 'Your mother invents a story about me and Sir John and you believe her.'

'Sir John's departure has nothing to do with Mother,' I lied.

'Of course it does,' she said, her beautiful face now red with fury. 'You would prefer to believe her story, rather than mine. Your own wife. If there is anybody throwing insults here, then it is you.' She pointed into the distance, where Sir John continued to slowly plod away on his horse, looking back occasionally as if he might suddenly be called back. 'But it is not bad enough that I am insulted. You then punish an innocent man,' she said. 'You invite Sir John to stay for the season, and then you change your mind.' She pursed her lips and shook her head. 'You have played with him, Oswald. And it's not fair.'

I saw a tear in Filomena's eye, and I suddenly felt very irritated. 'Don't tell me that you feel sorry for him?' I said.

'Yes, I do,' she replied. 'Sir John wasn't ready to leave. You forced him out.'

I grasped Filomena's wrist. 'Are you in love with him?' I said, squeezing tightly. 'Is that it?'

She wriggled her wrist, trying to free herself. 'Get off me, Oswald.'

I don't know what came over me, because I squeezed a little harder. 'I said, Are you in love with him?'

'No!'

I released her wrist and stormed back towards the house, diving in through the main door and then falling against a wall to catch my breath. The anger quickly abated and then I felt sick and thoroughly ashamed of myself. I had never succumbed to such jealousy in the past, even though I was married to one of the most beautiful women in Kent. I had certainly never manhandled her in such a disgraceful way. I looked up as footsteps approached, hoping that Filomena had followed me inside. Unfortunately it was Clemence. It seemed that she had witnessed my altercation with Filomena.

'What's going on, Oswald?' she said. 'What a show to put on in front of the household.'

'It's none of your business, Clemence,' I said, running my fingers through my hair and trying to speak calmly.

'You should pay more attention to your wife,' she said. 'No wonder she is feeling aggrieved.'

'Please don't get involved,' I said, trying to pass her.

Clemence blocked my path – the flowing skirts of her black gown giving an added width. 'You spend too long with Mother,' she said. 'When you should devote more time to your wife.'

'Mother is dying,' I said. 'I need to be with her.'

'But what on earth are you doing in there all the time?' she replied. 'Reading Mother the Old Testament?'

'Just let me pass,' I replied, making a second attempt to circumvent my sister.

'Are you making a confession,' she asked, putting her hand out to grasp my arm this time.

'No,' I snapped. 'What makes you think that?'

'Mother told me that you're feeling guilty about something.'

I could feel my stomach instantly turn. 'What's she been saying to you?' I demanded to know.

Clemence's eyes narrowed. 'What's going on, Oswald?' she asked. 'Why are you being so defensive?'

'I'm not being defensive,' I snapped. 'I am simply spending time with my mother before she dies. I can't see why that offends you or Filomena.' I then stalked away before Clemence could ask another question.

*   *   *

That evening, I returned to Mother's bedside once she had eaten a boiled egg and a slice of baked quince. Apparently it was what she fancied, and now that we had dispensed with Crouch's services she could eat what she liked. This strange meal had revived her sufficiently for me to feel able to ask my questions.

'Have you told Clemence about the letter?' I asked, taking a seat beside her bed.

'No,' she answered. 'What makes you think that?'

'It was something she said.'

'Your sister comes in here sometimes, Oswald,' she said. 'Trying to find out what we're talking about. Asking lots of questions.' A mischievous smile crept across her face. 'Of course, I don't tell her anything. But it doesn't stop her from asking. You know how inquisitive she is.' I could tell that Mother was enjoying this power over my sister – the opportunity to dangle and then withhold information.

'This story is for your ears only,' I said. When she puffed her lips noncommittally, I added, 'Please don't tell Clemence, Mother. This is between you and me. If I cannot trust you, then I cannot continue.'

She squeezed her face into a frown. 'Very well, very well,' she conceded. 'I won't say anything to Clemence, but . . .' She tapped her chest, her fingers drumming lightly on the linen of her chemise – the thin layer of cloth that was the only thing between me and the letter. 'Just remember. I haven't heard the whole story yet.'

Chapter Twenty-four

Kent, June 1349

By my fifth day at Somershill, I'd taken to hiding out at the top of the north-west tower – a part of Somershill that had survived from the original Norman castle built by my ancestors. My grandfather had demolished most of that ancient building to make way for his new house. But, for whatever reason, he had left this tower and section of wall for posterity. Perhaps he had run out of money, or perhaps these ruined ramparts were more than that – serving as a reminder, lest we ever forget our true history. The de Lacys now spoke English to one another. I had even been given an English name, but there had been a time when we had needed these thick walls to protect ourselves from the English. Once upon a time the de Lacys had been French.

I had this tower to myself that day, since nobody else in the household had the time to climb the steps to admire the patch-work of fields and woodland about the village, or to wonder at the misty blue hills of the Weald in the far distance. They were all far too busy. Despite Father's protestations that Somershill and the de Lacys were immune to the Pestilence, there was an unease taking hold. The servants were constantly whispering in corners about a suspicious death in a nearby village. Some said it was nothing more than an ague. Others were convinced it was plague.

In any case, the green shoots of a panic had caused an upsurge of activity in the kitchen. The pigs were slaughtered earlier in the season than usual, and a great number of eels were pulled from the stew pond to be smoked. Extra sacks of wheat were delivered alongside spare barrels of ale and bottles of wine. Even if my father didn't believe in plague, it was clear that the servants of Somershill were preparing for the worst.

I stared down as another cart arrived in the courtyard below, before I turned my eyes towards the road, where I saw my brother Richard riding out towards the forest, followed by his two hunting hounds. He seemed a strangely ephemeral figure, riding off into the distance to enjoy his pastime, while the rest of the household ran about in agitation. It struck me that Richard and I were rather alike in this quality. We were the flotsam and jetsam of the de Lacy family – drifting along without any purpose unless William died.

I followed Richard's progress until he disappeared into the trees and then looked back to the road. From this vantage point I would catch first sight of any messengers who might arrive from the direction of Kintham. After five days of silence from Brother Peter, I was starting to wonder if the man would ever bother to write to me? Had he even gone in search of Sawyer, as he had promised?

I kept a look out, but there was nobody on the road, so I eventually allowed my mind to wander onto different paths. As I stared into the distance, I began to daydream, imagining that William had spoken to Father about my career at the monastery, just as he had promised at our nocturnal heart-to-heart. In an extraordinary turn of the Fates, Father had then agreed that I could leave Kintham and didn't need to take my vows. He had even awarded me a small stipend for fulfilling some role or other about the estate. (The nature of this role was unclear, since my daydream didn't bother with such practicalities.) Not that this lack of income had particularly mattered to me, since I had then married Maud Woodstock, whose own wealth was large enough to support the pair of us. In this imagined union, I was enjoying Maud's company, money and bed, whilst she was enjoying her new status as a minor noblewoman – a leap in rank to which she clearly aspired, given her manners, education and tastes. Father might have previously warned Richard away from such a liaison, on the grounds that Maud Woodstock was only the daughter of a yeoman farmer, but he hadn't minded this union in my case, since I was his third and least important son.

I smiled at this thought for a while, even though it was pure fantasy. A youthful delusion. But, on the other hand, there was always the chance that this dream could become a reality? If I could gain William's support, then anything was possible – particularly if my brother should become Lord Somershill in the next few months, once it was generally accepted that Father wasn't well. My heart flew for a moment, before it sank like a drop weight. How could I hope to win William over, when I had yet to tell him about Agnes?

I was lost in these thoughts, when William himself appeared at the top of the steps.

'So this is where you are,' he said, wiping the sweat from his forehead after the exertion of the steep ascent. It was another uncomfortably humid day – the air still heavy with the early-summer moisture before the arid heat of July and August. 'What are you up to?' he asked me.

'I was just saying some prayers,' I lied.

William smiled at this and pushed the hair from his face, allowing the sunlight to shine through the skin of his ears. For a moment, my older brother didn't seem to be quite as handsome as I had always imagined and for some inexplicable reason this thought suddenly saddened me.

'So you haven't been mooning over Maud Woodstock, then?' he laughed.

'No,' I replied sharply. 'Of course not. I told you before. I'm not in love with her.'

'If you say so.'

'I do.'

He joined me beside the wall. 'Gilbert's been trying to find you,' he said. 'He's been looking everywhere.'

'Why's that?' I asked, feeling instantly nervous. Gilbert had given me a wide berth since our last meeting in the chapel.

My brother shrugged, pulling a flower from a small dog rose that had seeded itself between the old stones. He carelessly rolled the petal between his fingers, released the perfume and then flicked the bruised remains to the floor. 'He's probably on some mission from Father,' he said. 'So, I don't blame you for hiding up here.'

'I'm not hiding,' I said quickly. 'I just like the peace and quiet, that's all.'

'For your prayers?'

'That's right.'

William turned to stare into the distance. 'There's nothing wrong with hiding from Father,' he said. When I didn't answer, he continued, 'When I was a child, I used to come up here to hide from Father myself.'

'You did?'

He inclined his head back to look at me, and once again the sun caught the skin of his ears, as if he were in possession of two small pink wings. 'You see, Little Brother. You weren't the only one who tried to keep out of his way.'

I looked at my feet, not knowing how to answer this.

William cast his eyes back into the distance. 'I liked it up here,' he said. 'I could look down into the village and see all those little people in the distance, scurrying about like ants. Whereas I felt as if I were a giant.' He gave a laugh. 'It made me feel powerful for once.' He paused. 'Can you understand why that was so important to me, Oswald? After Father had made me feel so small and helpless.'

'Yes. I do understand,' I replied. 'And I'm sorry that happened.'

'Oh don't be sorry,' he smiled. 'It's not your fault. But thank you for listening,' he said, before adding, 'It's a rather foolish confession and I've never admitted it to anybody before.' He paused for a moment, before feeling about in the scrip that was hanging over his shoulder, and pulling out a small, grimy object. 'By the way, I found this today,' he said, passing the thing to me. 'I'd forgotten I even had it. But I thought you'd like it back.'

I looked down to see the pewter knight that my father had brought back from London, and then presented to me in front of the family. 'My knight,' I gasped. 'I always thought you threw him into the well?'

William gave an awkward smile. 'I'm sorry, Oswald. That's what I wanted you to think.' He hesitated and then puffed his lips. 'The truth is, I threw a stone down instead, to make you think it was your toy. I wanted to punish you for releasing that foolish dog. But it was very cruel of me,' he added. 'So I wanted to apologise. For this, and for all the other times that Richard and I tormented you as a child.' He heaved the longest of sighs. 'I can't speak for Richard. But I know that I'm ashamed of myself. Whatever Father did to me, I shouldn't have taken out my frustrations on you.' He bowed his head. 'You didn't deserve that treatment, Oswald. You're my brother. A fellow de Lacy, and I just hope you can forgive me?'

This apology came as quite a surprise. It was welcome, of course. But it was a surprise nonetheless. William had never apologised to me for anything, in his whole life. For a moment I was rendered speechless. 'Yes, William,' I said at length, feeling a surprising twinge of affection for my brother. 'I can forgive you.' I paused for a moment. 'But only if you can forgive me?'

William looked up and laughed. 'Why on earth would you need my forgiveness?'

'You'll see.'

And so I told William about Agnes. There and then, as we stood on the ancient, uneven stones of the tower, with the heady scent of the dog rose lacing its way through the air. I couldn't wait any longer to hear news from Brother Peter. It had to be then.

William listened with interest and surprise at first. He was understanding and even a little dismissive, especially when I told him about meeting Agnes in the forest and then making the mistake of chasing her into the river. It wasn't your fault, he argued. Of course you hadn't meant to hurt the girl, so you have no reason to feel guilty. But his lips began to part and face soon drained of colour when I told him about my conversation with Agnes's mother.

'What was the woman's name again?' he asked me.

'Beatrice Wheeler.'

His nose wrinkled and he shook his head. For a moment, he seemed relieved. 'No. I don't know anybody by that name. She must have been lying to you.'

'Wheeler is her married name,' I said. 'You met Beatrice before she wed.' William's face clouded over again, so I added. 'Apparently you were both sixteen. She used to come to the house when her father brought the hounds.'

'Her father?'

'He was our fewterer.'

William stared at me without speaking – his face frozen in horror, before he steadied himself by reaching out for the wall. I could see that my brother remembered Beatrice only too well now. The truth was written all over his features.

'I'm so sorry, William,' I said.

He waved me away, before stumbling towards the steps.

'But William—' I said, chasing after him. 'I would have told you before, but—'

'Just leave me alone Oswald,' he said, pushing me away. 'I don't want to talk to you.'

As William descended the steps, my first impulse was to pursue him – to tell him about my investigation and the fact that I'd identified Sawyer as Agnes's attacker. William had only heard half of the story. But then it was very clear that William didn't want my company right now. I sank down against the wall, feeling dejected. My confession had not lifted my guilt. If anything I felt worse than ever.

I gave a deep sigh, before realising that I was still holding the little knight that my brother had returned to me earlier. I lifted him to my eyes and took a moment to study his tiny face. Now that I had a chance to examine him, I could see that his head was too big and his neck was too long. In fact, he was badly cast in every respect – the sort of common trinket that's churned out by the pewterers of London and sold to pilgrims. This toy hadn't been the special gift from Father that I'd always remembered. Instead it was just some cheap souvenir that he'd picked up at a market stall. I dropped him to the floor, listening as his hollow shell tinkled against the flagstones, not understanding why I had ever cared so much for him.

It was then that Gilbert appeared at the top of the stairs, pulling a frown as soon as he saw my face. 'I told them to look here,' he muttered to himself. 'Lazy churls.'

'Told who?'

'The kitchen boys, of course.'

'What do you want?' I asked, rising to my feet.

'There's somebody here to see you,' he said, looking at me strangely. 'It's a woman.'

'A woman?' I responded with some disappointment. For the briefest of moments I had hoped to hear Brother Peter's name.

'Without doubt,' he grunted. 'And this one's been tupped and no mistake.' He raised an eyebrow. 'Says she wants to speak to you in private.'

I understood his grubby insinuation immediately. 'Who is it?'

'Says her name is Aldith Brewer.'

'Where is she?'

'By the back porch,' he replied. 'Don't worry,' he whispered, trying to nudge me. 'I've kept her out of your mother's way.'

'There was no need,' I replied. 'The child is nothing to do with me.'

I sped down the stone spiral stairs of the tower and ran across the grass towards the back porch, leaving Gilbert to follow in my wake. In the distance, I could see Aldith sitting on the grass, her belly now resting between her legs like a giant bundle of washing. Unfortunately, her presence had already drawn a small crowd of onlookers – a gaggle of servants, all eager to see the heavily pregnant woman who had requested an audience with their young master. They clearly were of the same opinion as Gilbert. That I had fathered her unborn child.

'What are you doing here?' I asked, once I'd helped Aldith to her feet and led her out of their earshot.

'I heard you'd left Kintham and gone back to Somershill,' she replied. 'I needed to speak to you.'

'You've come here all the way from Stonebrook?'

'I'm taking my children to an aunt in Reigate,' she said, before lowering her voice. 'Everybody is trying to leave Stonebrook,' she told me. 'Since plague arrived.' I stepped back from her instinctively. 'Don't worry yourself,' she said. 'None of my family is ailing. You won't catch nothing from me.'

I dusted myself down anyway, as if this would somehow remove the seeds of plague. 'Well, thank you for coming, Aldith,' I said. 'But why did you want to speak to me?'

She paused for a moment. 'I wanted you to know that it's happened again, Brother Oswald.'

'What's happened again?'

She frowned at me. 'Two more women are missing. This time it's Maud Woodstock and Rose Brunham. They left Stonebrook together yesterday afternoon. And they weren't back by this morning.'

'Maud left with Rose Brunham?' I said feeling my stomach roll. 'Are you sure?

'Of course I am.'

'Where were they going?'

'They went to look for herbs in the forest together,' she replied. 'Rose asked Maud to go with her, after Maud said that none of us should walk out on our own.' Aldith wrapped her hands over her belly and shook her head sadly. 'But it was a trap, wasn't it? She's taken Maud to Sawyer, hasn't she?'

I ran my fingers through my hair. 'So Sawyer hasn't been arrested then?'

Aldith looked at me with a quizzical frown. 'Arrested? By who?'

'Brother Peter,' I replied. When she continued to look mystified, I added. 'When I returned here to Somershill, Peter promised to search out Sawyer on my behalf. He was going to take a couple of lay brothers with him from Kintham. They were going to apprehend Sawyer and arrest him.'

She shrugged. 'Don't know anything about that.' She said.

'But Peter promised me,' I repeated.

Aldith folded her arms. 'You should have listened to me, Brother Oswald. We should have hunted down Sawyer with some men from the village. As soon as we found out about Jocelin's bracelet,' she said. 'Instead we left him free to strike again.'

She was right, and I felt chastened. 'Has John Roach looked for them?' I asked, trying to think rationally.

Aldith laughed at this. 'You must be joking. The Cockroach hasn't come out of his house for days. Least of all to look for missing women,' she said. 'Thinks he's going to catch the Plague, doesn't he?' She then hesitated, and looked away. I think she suddenly felt embarrassed. 'I would have looked for Maud myself, Brother Oswald. But I have my children to think about,' she said. She gave a short, awkward sigh. 'And we needed to leave Somershill quickly.'

I placed a hand on her arm, only to hear giggling erupt from the group of servants who were now clustered around the door like a gaggle of goslings. Gilbert was mother goose, stretching out his long neck to get the best view.

'Get back to your work,' I shouted across the grass. 'This is none of your business.' When they didn't react immediately to this command, I shouted again. 'Go on. Before I tell my father that you're all sitting around and doing nothing.'

As they reluctantly wandered back to their chores, we heard Aldith's children in the distance, wailing for their mother.

'I had better go and see to them,' she said, suddenly looking very tired. 'They're hungry and we've still got miles to go.'

'Of course,' I replied. 'But listen. I'll tell the cook to give you some bread and cheese for your journey,' I said. 'Just don't say anything to her about plague in Stonebrook.'

She nodded her thanks. 'I'm sorry to bring you this news, Brother Oswald,' she said. 'I know you're fond of Mistress Woodstock.'

'I admire her courage,' I said quickly. 'That's all.'

Aldith smiled. 'If you say so.'

'I do.'

'So you'll go after Sawyer yourself now, will you?' she asked, fixing her eyes on mine.

'Yes,' I replied. 'Of course I will.'

I searched the house for William, wanting to tell him that I was leaving – but he was nowhere to be seen. Eventually I spotted my brother sitting by the stew pond, where he was staring into the muddy water, steadfastly watching the tangle of eels as they thrashed about in the waters. He looked so sad and reflective that I felt too nervous to disturb him. He was still coming to terms with the truth about Agnes, and I didn't have the heart to bother him.

Instead, I collected some food and ale from the kitchen and then made my way to the stables, where I hoped to find my horse and leave Somershill without being noticed. Unfortunately Richard was there, unsaddling his horse after returning from his latest excursion into the forest. His hounds were flopped across the straw, panting with exhaustion, and there was a sheen of foaming sweat across his horse's neck. Richard also looked weary. His hair was stuck to his skull with perspiration, and his tunic gave off the pungent, spicy stink of sweating armpits. When he saw me looking at his hair, he quickly replaced his bycocket – the light immediately catching the vivid threads of the embroidered peacocks.

I stepped over the dogs and nodded to my brother, before throwing a saddle over my horse and pulling at her reins. As I led her out of the stable, the dogs only moved out of the way when they saw the hooves approaching – reluctantly shuffling to one side so that we could pass.

I had reached the doors when Richard suddenly addressed me. 'Where are you going?' he asked.

I turned back to face my brother, finding myself surprised to hear him speaking. In my five days at Somershill, Richard had yet to address me. I noted that his voice was rather fey and juvenile, not unlike the man himself. 'I'm just going for a ride,' I said. 'I need to get some air.'

'Does Father know about this?' he asked.

I lifted my left foot into the stirrup and then swung my right foot over the saddle. 'Oh yes,' I lied. 'I told him earlier.'

Richard frowned at this. My attempts at nonchalance had only succeeded in making him more suspicious. 'Where did you say you were going?'

'I'm not sure,' I said. 'Just a little way into the forest.' I kicked at my horse. 'See you at supper,' I called out, as I quickly trotted out towards the gate of Somershill, before breaking into a canter and heading for the cover of the forest. I feared that Richard would follow me, so I dismounted to hide in some coppiced chestnut, and sure enough Richard soon appeared, mounted on a fresh horse and clearly in my pursuit. I wondered why he had taken such an interest in my whereabouts and decided that Father must have told him to watch me. Whatever the case, Richard certainly seemed concerned about something. I had rarely seen him this motivated.

I stayed in my hiding place, until I was certain that my brother was not coming back, and then I re-emerged onto the track and set off in the direction of Sawyer's pits. It was my intention to search out Sawyer myself – but I had only got a mile or so along the path before I came to my senses. The last time I'd tried to apprehend this man, he had nearly killed me. The truth was, I couldn't do this alone. Brother Peter had let me down before, but this time he would help me . . . I would insist upon it.

And so I rode for Kintham.

Chapter Twenty-five

I reached Kintham by dusk, only to find that the gates to the monastery were now locked against all visitors, including me. It was Brother Thomas himself, the novice master, who shouted down from the gatehouse to gleefully advise me of this fact. 'You can't come in, Brother Oswald,' he shouted. 'The Abbot won't allow it. You could be carrying plague.'

'I just need to speak to Brother Peter,' I said. 'It's urgent.'

'Peter isn't here,' he replied.

'What do you mean?' I asked, feeling my heartbeat immediately quicken. 'Where is he, then?'

'We don't know,' came the reply. 'Perhaps you can tell us? The man has disappeared.'

'Disappeared?' I stared back for a moment, lost for words. 'How long has he been missing?' I asked, once I'd finally found my tongue.

'Since the day that you left for Somershill,' Thomas replied. 'We wondered if he'd followed you there.' A smile tickled at the edges of his drooping lips. 'We know how fond Peter is of you.'

'He didn't come to Somershill,' I replied. 'I haven't seen Brother Peter since I left Kintham.'

'Then it's a mystery,' said Thomas. 'Now go home, because you can't come in here.'

'But Brother Thomas,' I shouted. 'Please. I need to know more. Did Peter tell anybody where he was going?'

'Not as far as I know.'

'Did he take any of the lay brothers with him?'

'Certainly not.'

'Please,' I begged. 'Let me in. I need to speak to the other brothers. Somebody must know something.'

'We're not letting anybody come in or out,' he replied, as he withdrew from sight. 'It's the Abbot's orders. So go home.'

I trotted away reluctantly, bringing my horse to a halt in a quiet glade, where I gave myself the chance to think. Peter hadn't followed me to Somershill, so he must have gone in search of Sawyer after all – just as he had promised. I felt guilty for having doubted him now, especially as he hadn't returned from this expedition.

I now needed to find Sawyer, if I were to stand any chance of finding my missing tutor or, indeed, of rescuing Maud. Sawyer was undoubtedly behind both of their disappearances – but where to look for the man, other than the one place where we had met previously – his charcoal pits? After all, it was where I had told Peter to go. In all honesty, I felt it was unlikely that Sawyer would still be camped out at these pits, but, in the absence of any other ideas, it was a place to start.

I rode through the night – picking my way with difficulty through the darkness of the forest, until reaching the crossroads near to Sawyer's pits by the following dawn. Remembering how dangerous the man could be (I was still finding scabs in my hair from the wound he had inflicted on the back of my head), I tethered my horse to a tree a few hundred yards away from his camp and then crept towards the pits. I trod softly over the damp forest floor, aiming for the firmer ground and avoiding the nettles, until I reached a vantage point that overlooked Sawyer's hut. I saw immediately that his pits were no longer smouldering – not even with the thin, blue smoke that marks the final stage of the burn. Nor did the air hold the acrid stink of a bonfire this time, so I assumed his pits had not been tended for days.

However, I was still in no rush to enter Sawyer's camp until I knew if the man were there – so I waited behind the trees, hoping to spot him moving about in his long, hooded cloak. I watched for a while, but saw no signs of life. Either the camp was deserted or he was hiding inside his hut – so I crept forward again, passing the piles of seasoned hazel and oak and the blackened pot hanging on its tripod over a long-extinguished fire. When I felt the side of this pot and found it was stone cold, I slowly lifted the lid, only to release a sulphurous cloud from the same rabbit stew that had been cooking at my last visit. It was untouched – the bones and flesh now fermenting in a mouldy froth.

I replaced the lid and then continued to the opening of Sawyer's hut, where I peeked around the rudimentary door to see that the place was empty. I stepped inside to find a makeshift mattress on the floor and a shelf of Sawyer's belongings on one wall. Along this shelf were a selection of different objects, all lined up like a collection of small reliquaries at a shrine. There was a leather purse. A small shoe. A string of beads. A wooden crucifix. A bronze thimble. A belt buckle and a circular shawl pin. Items that I wouldn't have expected to find in the hut of an itinerant charcoal burner. Items that Sawyer must have taken from the missing women.

I stepped outside quickly, needing some fresh air, when I found that my eyes immediately came to rest on a patch of disturbed earth in the distance. I hadn't noticed this at my last visit, so I quickly walked over to investigate. It was a low mound, roughly the length and breadth of a person, and looked very much like a recently dug grave.

My heart thumped, as there was no way of knowing who was beneath this mound of soil, unless I looked. What if it were Peter? What if it were Maud? But who wants to confront the reality of a rotting corpse, especially in the first days after burial? Especially when it could be the body of somebody that you know and love? I might have been practised at dealing with the newly dead of the monastery, but I had never conducted an exhumation.

I closed my eyes for a moment, wiped my face with my hands, and then took the deepest of breaths. I looked around to see if I could find a spade, for this grave had not been dug out by hand. Sure enough, I found the tool tossed away into a nearby bush, still muddy with earth from its recent excavation. And then I set about my grisly task, holding my breath each time I dug out another spade of soil, knowing that the blade would thud against the hardness of a body at any moment.

It did not take long, for this was only a shallow grave. When I first hit an obstacle, I put the spade to one side and then brushed away the earth to uncover a hand. The skin was grey, tinged with purple. The flesh was bloated – swollen like the leather of a sodden glove. The hand belonged to a man, given its size, but that was all I could tell – so I picked the spade up again and dug away more soil, now digging furiously until I reached the face of the corpse.

He had been buried with his jaw falling open, his mouth was now full of soil. His eyes were already sunken into their sockets, and he exuded the full pungent stench of decomposition, but this was still a very welcome sight. The face that I looked upon did not belong to my beloved tutor, Brother Peter. This was Ranulf Sawyer.

I climbed out of the grave and lay down onto the soil for a moment to catch my breath. At first I felt overpowering relief – my feelings of dread turned immediately to joy – before they changed again. I had been convinced that Sawyer was the killer, but how could that be true, now that Sawyer was dead himself? Given the progression of Sawyer's decay – the colour of his skin and the swelling of his flesh, I guessed that he had been dead for a number of days – which meant he could not have taken Maud.

But there was something else that troubled me. This was a Christian grave. Sawyer had been hastily buried, but he had still been placed in the correct east–west orientation, to rise facing the coming of Christ on the Day of Judgment. This burial had to be Peter's work, which meant that my tutor must have come here after all and found Sawyer's body. Which begged the question – where was Peter now, and why had he not returned to the monastery after making this discovery?

I rose to my feet again and forced myself to look down into the grave, knowing that I needed to examine Sawyer's corpse before I refilled this pit with soil. The flies were already buzzing about the hole, drawn to this pit by the smell of decay. I wondered, fleetingly, if it were possible that Sawyer had simply died, and naturally the thought of plague came to mind. I found a long stick and used it to pull back Sawyer's cloak, where the true cause of his death was immediately plain to see. There were no buboes or patches of blackened flesh at the tops of his legs and nestled into his armpits. Instead there was a wound to his upper chest. The clean and deadly mark of a dagger.

I threw soil back onto the body and then found a nearby stream to wash away the smell of death from my skin. As I splashed cold water onto my face, I forced myself to dissect this mystery again. I had been wrong about Sawyer. He wasn't a murderer and a rapist. He was nothing better than a grave robber – taking items of value from dead bodies and giving them to a girl that he admired. And if I had been wrong about Sawyer, then I had also been wrong about Rose as well. If she were not this man's accomplice, then she must have been abducted along with Maud. This time the man had taken two women at once.

I splashed water onto my face once again as if this would shock my senses into action. Who had killed Sawyer and why now? I had to think. Think! I reached down into the stream again, and as my hands found the cold water I had the answer. Sawyer had been murdered to guarantee his silence. After all, the man had been claiming to know the whereabouts of the women's bodies – bodies from which he stole valuable items. And when had this thieving first come to light . . . at the meeting we had held at Maud's house.

I started to pace around Sawyer's camp, walking faster and faster as I tried to corral my thoughts. John Roach had forced his way into that meeting, where he'd learnt about Sawyer and the stolen bracelet. Roach had not only followed me to the edge of the village on his white palfrey, but he'd also followed me into the forest. I'd seen his horse in the distance and then assumed that I'd lost him by hiding in the trees – but perhaps I hadn't after all? I had assumed that it was Sawyer who clubbed me so soundly on the back of my head and left me for dead, but it could just as well have been Roach, for I never saw my attacker's face.

I felt that low sinking feeling in the pit of my stomach. That wave of nausea that descends when a truly unpleasant truth finally reveals itself. I should have suspected John Roach before – for there were so many signs that I'd missed. Roach had made no attempts to look for the missing women of Stonebrook, instead claiming that they had run away to London. He'd tried to frustrate my investigation, and he'd even tried to blame the crimes on me. If all of this evidence were not damning enough, he was a man with a ferocious contempt for the women of Stonebrook – to the extent that he was known to them as the Cockroach.

I ran back to find my horse, swung myself into my saddle and set off. There might be plague in Stonebrook, but that's where I hoped to find John Roach. If he had taken Maud and Rose, then there was a chance that I could still find them both alive.

Chapter Twenty-six

Somershill, November 1370

Mother sat up straight in bed and threw an arm towards the window. 'There's a man out there,' she shouted. 'He's trying to get in.'

I looked up instinctively, though her claim could hardly be true. We were high up in the house, with a sheer drop outside the window. 'There's nobody there, Mother,' I said, after walking over to the window in order to reassure her. 'Stop worrying.'

She wasn't comforted by my words. 'I saw him,' she said, her face pale with terror. 'Look again, Oswald!'

I reluctantly turned back to the window and duly found nothing at my second inspection. The window was free of any intruders, though something did catch my eye in the distance. It was Filomena, riding away from the house, in the direction of Tonbridge. It was late in the afternoon, and she was wearing her fur-lined cloak, which struck me as unusual. I might have left the room to inquire from the servants about her reason for leaving, but Mother soon caught my attention again.

'Is he there?' she said. 'Can you see him?'

'No, Mother,' I said. 'I can't.'

Her face knotted in panic. 'But look, Oswald!' she screamed. 'He's there right now, trying to climb in. He wants to attack me.'

I pulled the drapes across her bedstead on the side closest to the window and then returned to her side, where she clung onto my arm with cold and clammy fingers. I could see that this was a genuine terror. She believed, with full sincerity, that there was an intruder at the window, when there had been nothing there at all. Not even a bird or a shadow to cause this illusion.

I smoothed the hair on her head, and spoke softly, as I used to speak to Hugh, when he'd woken from a nightmare as a small boy. Once awake, Hugh had always been able to recognise the truth – that his sleeping mind had been playing tricks on him. Mother was not able to make this distinction, however, and this was very saddening for me. Suddenly I found myself grieving for the old Mother. The woman who was obstinate and difficult in order to get attention. The woman who told outlandish stories to prompt a reaction. The woman who played one member of the family off against the other, in order to cause mischief. Unfortunately that woman was slipping away in front of my very eyes. Mother genuinely believed that she had seen a man at the window, and I could not persuade her otherwise.

I felt her forehead and found that she was sweating, so I called for the maid to join us from her station outside of the door. I was concerned by Mother's fever and wanted to know if the girl had helped her to the chamber pot recently. The maid informed me that her water was dark and foul-smelling, which meant that she needed to drink more liquids. When I pulled at the skin on the back of Mother's hand, it was wrinkled and dry.

I stepped aside at this point, and let the maid try to feed Mother with a tisane of rosemary and ginger. But Mother soon became aggressive and difficult, and threw the drink to the floor in a fit of frustration, accusing the girl of trying to poison her. I sent for some mead after this, which proved to be the right decision, since the sweetness was comforting and soothed Mother's nerves immediately. Now that she was calmer, I sat beside her and held her hand, while Gilbert and the maid spoke in low tones in the passageway – predicting that Mother was certain to die at any moment.

I leant over to whisper into Mother's ear. 'Can you hear me?' I said.

At first my words met with silence, and I was about to release her hand when she tightened her fingers. 'Yes, Oswald,' she said.

'How do you feel?'

'I'm dying,' she said faintly. 'I know it. But I still have one night left in me. Don't listen to what they're saying.'

'Can you hear them?' I asked, glancing over towards the door to see that it was only slightly ajar. In spite of her grave illness, Mother retained her amazing powers of perception.

'Yes, of course I can,' she said, slipping her hand from mine. 'I haven't lost all use of my senses. I still know when somebody is talking about me.'

I paused for a moment, wondering at this sudden lucidity. 'Can you see anybody at the window now?' I asked cautiously.

'What do you mean?' she snapped. 'How could there be anybody at the window? We're nearly in the roof.' She scraped a thin laugh. 'Goodness me, Oswald,' she said. 'Sometimes your imagination runs wild.'

'Shall I leave you to sleep?' I asked, gratified to see that her contrariness had returned.

'No, no,' she said. 'Soon I will be asleep forever. Don't leave me now. I want you to finish your story,' she said. 'While I still have the energy to listen.' She sighed. 'The Reaper is coming for me tonight, Oswald,' she whispered. 'There's no point in deny- ing it any longer. He's in the courtyard, but soon he'll be at the door.'

'I'm sure that's not true.'

She shook her head. 'I've seen him off before, Oswald. Oh yes. I've hidden from him enough times to know when he's lurking. Each time I had a child, he sat on the end of the bed, leering over me like a scavenger. Sometimes he has sent an ague, other times the sweating sickness. Sometimes the dropsy or a colic. Even a fever or a bloody flux. But each time I've evaded him, and sent him away.' She sniffed away a tear. 'But now he has me in his sights, Oswald. He comes for me tonight. I cannot refuse him again.'

'Shall I fetch the priest, Mother?'

'No, no,' she frowned. 'Not yet.'

'But he should read you the Last Rites,' I said. 'If you think that death is near.'

'But I cannot die yet,' she said, patting her chest, allowing me to hear the folded letter crinkling beneath her chemise.

Our eyes locked for a moment, before I sat down with a sigh. 'Can you remember where we were?' I asked.

'Yes,' she said. 'You suspected that man, the Constable. John Roach.'

'So you were listening, then?' I said.

'Oh yes,' she said. 'Of course I was.'

Chapter Twenty-seven

Kent, June 1349

I galloped into Stonebrook to find the main street deserted. It was so eerie that I reined in my horse to a walk, progressing slowly past rows of silent houses. Occasionally I heard a voice behind a closed door, or saw the odd, fleeting shadow at a window, but my only companions outside were a pack of starving dogs that were squabbling over the carcass of a dead crow – each attempting to grab the limp, bloodied remains of the bird and then disappear into a side alley with their prize. I kicked my horse on, soon arriving at John Roach's house, where a loose cow was greedily attacking a tussock of grass on the verge. I dismounted, shooed the creature away and then thumped at the door.

A short, agitated woman appeared immediately – peering out into the street, as if I might have had a companion with me. When she saw that I was alone, she gave a huff and then waved me inside. 'Come along then. Come along. I've been waiting for you for days.'

I was confused by this welcome. 'I'm Brother Oswald,' I told her. 'A novice from Kintham Abbey. I'm looking for John Roach.'

She gave another huff. 'A novice,' she said, now casting her eyes over my head to see that I was not yet tonsured. 'Oh well,' she sighed. 'You'll have to do, I suppose.' She started to wave again. 'He's in here. So hurry up. Come along.'

I duly stepped into the house and followed her down a thin passageway, until we came to a door at the other end. She stopped here and turned to me. 'You do know how to do it, don't you?' she whispered, putting her hand onto the latch.

'Do what?'

'Hear a last confession, of course,' she said, creasing her brow into a frown. 'That's why you're here, isn't it?'

'Roach is dying?' I said in surprise.

'Yes,' she answered. 'Didn't they tell you? He's very ill. I sent a boy to fetch a priest from the monastery.' She gave a long sigh. 'I'm afraid that my husband has a lot to confess, Brother Oswald. So I hope you know what you're doing?' She opened the door before I could answer. 'Come along,' she said. 'In you go.' When I didn't move, she caught hold of my arm and propelled me over the threshold. 'If you'd taken any longer, then the poor man would be dead.'

The door slammed behind me and I found myself in a small, dark bedchamber with a single window. John Roach was lying on the bed in the corner, with his back to me. His head was bowed forward and his limbs were drawn up into his torso, as if he were a child, curled up and asleep in his crib. There was a foul smell to the air – sickly and overpowering, and I felt the urge to retreat immediately back to the passageway, though I also felt sure that Roach's wife would be waiting there, ready to shove me back inside the room, should I try to leave.

And so I lifted my chemise over my nose and slowly approached the bed, my sense of dread increasing with each step. Daylight flooded through the window, shedding its slanting rays over Roach's stricken body. I could see immediately that he was dying of plague. I had heard the tales of this sickness, but this was the first time that I had seen its true horror in person. Sores bulged at Roach's neck like small, purple orbs. His shock of white hair was stuck to his head in a sweaty mat, and his fingers and the end of his nose were black – as if the man had dipped his face and hands in tar.

I gave a cough that prompted Roach to turn over and open a swollen eye. 'What do you want, de Lacy?' he mumbled.

'I understand that you need to make a last confession,' I replied, cupping my hands over my nose.

'I'm not speaking to you,' he said. 'Go back and get me a real priest.'

'Nobody else is coming,' I replied. 'It's me or nothing.'

He gave a long whine and then closed his eyes again. 'Just give me the sacraments,' he whispered. 'And then piss off.'

I took a small step closer. 'What's the first sin you're going to confess to, Roach?' I asked. 'Murdering Ranulf Sawyer, or taking the women?'

'What?'

'There's no point lying to me,' I said. 'Not now.'

He managed a thin laugh that soon shifted to a cough. 'What are you talking about? You foolish coxcomb.'

I didn't respond to the insult. 'You followed me into the forest, didn't you?' I said instead. 'When I went to speak to Sawyer. You wanted to know what he would tell me.'

Roach groaned. 'What?'

'When Sawyer offered to take me to the dead bodies, you attacked me. Then you went back later to kill him.'

Roach squeezed out a thin laugh. 'Have you lost your senses?'

I could feel my anger rising. 'I know you abducted the women, Roach,' I said. 'I know you're guilty, so just tell me what you've done with Maud Woodstock and Rose Brunham. Don't die with their lives on your conscience as well.'

'How would I know where to find that pair of strumpets?' he said. 'I've been trapped in this room for days?' He waved a blackened finger towards the hall. 'Ask my wife.'

I retreated to the door, lifted the latch and then opened it a fraction. Roach's wife was seated at the other end of the passageway.

'That was quick,' she said nervously. 'Is it all done?'

I ignored this question. 'How long has your husband been ill?' I asked.

She frowned at me. 'Why?'

'I said. How long has he been ill?'

She smarted at my manner. 'John took to his bed four days ago,' she told me. 'As soon as he came down with a stiffness and fever.'

'Are you sure?'

'Yes.'

'And he hasn't left the house during that time?'

She screwed up her nose at this question. 'He's got the Plague, Brother Oswald,' she said. 'Where would he be going?'

I closed the door, and took stock for a moment. I knew she was telling me the truth – which meant that I was wrong . . . Again. Roach couldn't have taken Maud and Rose. He couldn't be the killer I was hunting. I nearly left immediately in disappointment, but then Roach called to me from his bed. 'Want to know what's happened to those whores?' he rasped. 'Then ask that priest.'

'Which priest?'

'The one you keep company with.'

'Brother Peter?' I said. 'What's he got to do with this?'

Roach gave a long, guttural cough, which ended as a thin spittle of blood waved over his chin. He turned to face me. His eyes were bloodshot, eyelids heavy with exhaustion. 'I've seen him,' he said. 'Creeping about behind Maud Woodstock's house. Following her and that other whore out of the village.'

'When was this?'

'Couple of days ago.'

I stood back – puzzled at this news. 'How would you know?' I asked, once I'd gathered my thoughts. 'You haven't left this room.'

He nodded towards the window beside his bed. The shutter was lifted, and the oilcloth pulled back to reveal a short view.

'I've still got my eyes,' he said. 'And I've needed something to look at. Stuck in here on my own.' He waved at the bedroom door. 'That bitch never comes in.' He coughed again. 'Your Brother Peter has been spying on women,' he managed another laugh. 'Lusting after them.'

'That's not true,' I said quickly.

'Believe what you like,' he croaked. 'But I know what I saw.'

I took a moment to peer out of the window to see the gable end of Maud's house. In the distance, I could make out Maud's thin maid Johanna, standing beside the fence and grooming a large white horse. Johanna couldn't have seen my face, but she suddenly looked in my direction. The girl seemed startled and then immediately suspicious, before she scuttled back inside the house – as if she'd known she was being watched.

I turned back to Roach. 'Which path did Maud and Rose take out of the village?'

'Who can say?' he answered. 'I can't see beyond the alley.'

'Take a guess.'

He smiled at me – the corners of his mouth stained with blood. 'You've wasted your time coming here, haven't you?' he rasped – his eyes lighting up with pleasure. 'You little fool. I'm not guilty of anything . . . and I can't tell you anything. Nothing at all.' He laughed again. 'So much for your investigation, eh?' He closed his eyes and curled back into a ball. 'So stop fretting about a pair of worthless whores, and do your proper job,' he whispered. 'Administer the sacrament and let me die in peace.'

I looked down at Roach for a moment. The once tall and strong man, now reduced to this feeble ruin. But the trials of his suffering had done nothing to temper his nature. Despite the tumours and the blackening flesh, he was still the same man inside. He had kept fast to his prejudices. Unable to find empathy, kindness or even the slightest whiff of repentance – not even on his deathbed. In some ways I pitied Roach. But in most ways, I still despised him.

'Come back,' he shouted, as I left the room and strode out of the house. But I didn't turn around — not until I reached the street, where I threw myself down on the verge next to the cow, and quickly breathed in the fresh, sweet air of a summer's day.

It was not a moment before Roach's wife ran out after me. 'You all done in there, are you?' she asked. 'Did he make his last confession?'

'He didn't need to,' I said. 'He wasn't sorry for anything.'

She threw me a sideways glance and then bustled back inside the house, slamming the door as I let out a growl of frustration. Roach's words stung in my ears. He had been right. My investigation was a failure. I was no further forward, despite all of my best efforts. Now Peter, Maud and Rose were missing, and I didn't have a single idea how to find them.

As the cow munched away at the grass about my legs, I took a long swig of ale from my flask and let the sun shine down on my face. It was a trick that Peter had taught me, when I was feeling panicked and hopeless. To stop, close my eyes and turn my face to the sky. Once I had cleared my mind in this way, it occurred to me that I hadn't completely wasted my time in speaking to Roach — the old bastard had been wrong in that respect. Thanks to him, I now knew that Peter had been in Stonebrook, and that he had subsequently followed Maud and Rose out of the village. Peter must have been keeping a watchful eye on the pair, which could only be good news — although it didn't explain why all three of them remained missing. Maud would have returned to Stonebrook by now had she been able. I knew that she would never willingly abandon her ailing father.

I had previously dismissed the idea of searching the forest alone, but now I realised that this was the only option left open to me. But it was such a large forest, with so many different paths. I rose to my feet and walked towards the overhanging jetty of Maud's grand house. Maud's maid Johanna was still at home. She had to know where Maud and Rose were going.

Chapter Twenty-eight

Johanna wouldn't open the door to me at first, despite my banging insistently – so I moved to a window and shouted through the shutters. The girl didn't answer, but I did succeed in rousing Roger Woodstock in his upstairs bedchamber, prompting the old man to groan and bellow in his usual melancholic tones. When my efforts at the front of the house were unsuccessful, I walked around to the garden gate, where, after passing the horse, a collection of chickens and a row of peas, I found myself at the back door. I knocked at first, to no avail, so I then tried to push this door open, only to find that it was locked against me. When I went to kick it in my frustration, the door suddenly opened with Johanna's thin face on the other side.

'Why didn't you answer before?' I said, steadying myself, in the pretence that I hadn't been about to force my way in.

The girl shrank away from me. 'My mistress told me not to speak to anybody. Not if she wasn't at home.'

'But your mistress is missing, Johanna. That rule doesn't apply any more.'

She chewed at her lip, thinking. 'I'm not sure,' she said.

'Look. I just need to ask you a simple question. Do you know where your mistress was going when she went missing?'

She cast her eyes to the floor and refused to speak.

'Come on, Johanna,' I said. 'Think.'

I glared down at the girl, hoping to press her for an answer, when Roger Woodstock began to groan again – although this time the noise was much louder and clearer than ever before. When I listened carefully, I suddenly realised that I could hear a word. He was calling out for help.

I didn't wait for an invitation to enter the house. Instead I pushed past Johanna, ran through the central hall and bolted up the steep wooden staircase to fling the door to his bedchamber open. Inside the room I found that Roger Woodstock had launched himself onto the floor and was attempting to wriggle on his belly towards me. His white chemise had ridden up to reveal a pair of frail, withered legs and a scabby, naked arse.

I knelt down beside him and put my hand on his shoulder. 'What's the matter?' I asked. 'Tell me.'

He turned his head to mine and tried desperately to speak, though nothing materialised apart from a thin spindle of spit. I wiped his chin and then turned to see that Johanna had followed me into the room, her face horror-struck.

'What's going on here?' I asked, rising to my feet again. 'What have you been doing to this man?'

I noted that her hands were trembling. 'Nothing.'

'Have you been neglecting him while your mistress is missing?'

She shook her head vigorously. 'No. Of course not, Brother Oswald. I would never hurt my master.'

'Then why is he calling for help?'

Johanna looked at me blankly.

'I distinctly heard him use that word,' I said.

'Are you sure?' she asked, holding a small hand to her mouth. 'He actually said that word?'

'Yes. I'm certain of it.'

'But my master hasn't spoken in two years,' she said. 'Not since the apoplexy.'

Woodstock groaned again – though unfortunately he had returned to lowing like a cow, and none of his words were now discernible.

I stood back, not knowing what to do next. 'Come on,' I said to Johanna at length. 'Help me to lift him back into bed.'

I managed to turn Woodstock onto his side and loop my hands under his shoulders. Johanna took his shuddering feet and we hauled him back onto the bedstead, though he struggled against us. Once he was laid out, I took a long look at him, but could see no obvious signs of mistreatment. The man was wearing clean clothes. The sheets were dry and there was no smell of urine or faeces about the room. He was fed and clothed at least.

It was then that I noticed a small cup on the table beside the bed, full to the brim with a murky brown liquid. When I lifted this cup to my nose, I found that the contents smelt sharp and vinegary. 'What's this?' I asked.

Johanna looked away.

'What is it?' I asked again, more insistent this time.

'It's something I made myself,' she said quietly. 'To help my master sleep.'

My suspicions were immediately raised. 'What's in it?'

'It's just dandelion root and wine,' she replied. 'Nothing more than that.'

I lifted the cup to my lips and took the smallest of sips, tasting the sourness of the wine, before the bitterness of the dandelion coated my tongue. 'No wonder he's unhappy,' I said. 'Who would want to drink this?'

'But it does him good,' she objected.

'What does he normally have?' I asked.

Johanna looked away again, wary and suspicious. Her hands continued to tremble. 'My mistress buys a tonic of valerian root, mixed with skullcap and lime blossom.'

'She buys it?' I asked. 'Where from?'

'A woman in Winchester,' she whispered. 'She brews her own decoctions.'

I immediately understood why Johanna had been reticent to answer my question. Medicine was the preserve of men – the Benedictines and the physicians – not a field in which a woman should dabble. At least that was the view of most men. In fact, I had often heard Brother Peter describe the women who sold herbal remedies as witches and poisoners, whose so-called cures often did more harm than good. We had dealt with enough poisonings at the infirmary to know the dangers of taking medicines that were brewed up by the ignorant. So many times we had forced a poor unfortunate to drink an infusion of Devil's Bit to induce vomiting, after this person had bought some potion at a country fair, or in the back streets of a local town. But, in all honesty, just as many sufferers had been poisoned following a consultation with a learned physician. Taking herbal remedies was always a risky business, whether they were prescribed by a man who had studied medicine at university, or by a woman who cooked up decoctions in her kitchen.

'Stick to a simple tisane of chamomile or dill,' I advised. 'The man is choleric. You need to decrease his heat and balance his yellow bile.'

Johanna nodded in response, just as Roger Woodstock made another attempt to launch himself from the bedstead, with his hands flailing and his mouth gaping. With a great effort, Johanna and I succeeded in pushing him back against the mattress, where he continued to fight us, until his breathing finally calmed to a shallow rise and fall, and his body relaxed.

After this attack, I sat with the old man for a while to ensure that he was truly settled. As I held his hand he looked at me with a pair of expressive eyes –and for the briefest of moments I thought that he was trying to speak again. His mouth formed an oval. His lips moved tremulously over his teeth. I could see that there was a sane and aware person behind this façade – a person who knew his mind but could not use it to control his body. His face was afflicted with a palsy that had rendered speech impossible, and all that emanated from his mouth after so much effort was another thin line of spittle. Eventually a tear trickled down his cheek as he finally surrendered. Exhausted and defeated, he closed his eyes and allowed his head to fall to one side.

When we were certain that he was truly sleeping, Johanna and I crept out of the room, but not before I'd taken one last look at the man. Roger Woodstock had always enjoyed the reputation of being arrogant, miserly and cruel, but now he was almost pitiable. This was no way for a person to live, no matter their faults or misdeeds. Lying in a bed all day and night, unable to talk, walk or even feed himself.

I turned away. Appalled at the reality of a long and lingering death – for a young man rarely contemplates the end of life, and certainly not in these terms. It is the conceit of youth – that death only happens to other people. If a young man thinks of his death at all, he imagines a valiant defeat in battle, or perhaps even a fight to the bitter end in defence of a dearly beloved wife or child. But he never imagines dying like this. Lying in bed as a frail and powerless old man. Fully aware of the world about him and yet utterly unable to connect with it.

After this experience, I followed Johanna to the kitchen where she ladled a cup of ale for me from the barrel. 'Here, Brother Oswald,' she said, offering me the cup. 'Drink this. I think you need it.'

'Does your master know that Maud is missing?' I asked, taking the cup from her, and quickly downing the ale. 'Is that why he's so upset?'

The girl nodded. 'I had to tell him,' she admitted. 'My master always looks for his daughter. Hoping to see her face, whenever I enter the room.'

'Does he understand what you're saying to him?'

She nodded. 'It's just his body that fails,' she told me. 'Not his mind.' She paused. 'I think he understands everything.'

I put down my cup. We had spent too long discussing Roger Woodstock. It was not my reason for being here. 'Do you know where your mistress was going?' I asked. 'On the day she went missing. It's very important to me that you try to remember.'

Johanna dropped her shoulders and looked away. 'I'm not sure exactly.'

'But you know that she left Stonebrook with Rose Brunham?' I said.

'Yes, well . . .' Johanna hesitated for a moment. 'I know that Rose came to the back door and asked to speak with my mistress.'

'Did you listen to their conversation?'

Johanna shifted from one foot to the other. 'No,' she said. 'I never listen when I shouldn't. The mistress doesn't like it.'

'Just tell me the truth,' I said wearily. 'Did you hear where they were planning to go? Yes or no?'

Once again she hesitated. 'I shouldn't say. The mistress doesn't like me to eavesdrop.'

'God's bones, Johanna! As I said to you earlier. Maud's rules don't apply any more. So just tell me where they were heading. Your mistress will thank you for eavesdropping on this occasion.' When Johanna continued to hesitate, I laid my hand on her twig-like arm. 'Maud will be pleased that you've helped me, Johanna. I can promise you that.'

She began to tremble again. Even though Maud had disappeared, I could see that it was almost impossible for this girl to disobey her mistress's rules. 'They took the north road out of Stonebrook,' she said finally.

'Where were they going?'

Johanna took a deep breath and relaxed. 'To collect the root of the Pestilence wort,' she said.

'Are you sure?'

'Yes. I heard them talking about it. It's said that this plant can ward off plague.'

I couldn't help but sigh at this comment. Having just come from Roach's deathbed, I knew there wasn't a herb on earth that could save a person from this disease. 'When was this?' I asked.

'Around noon. Two days ago.'

'The north road,' I repeated. 'You are absolutely sure about that?'

She nodded her head silently, and I could only hope that she was telling me the truth, because I had no other information to rely upon. 'Did your mistress take a horse?' I asked.

'No,' she answered. 'They didn't plan to go far into the forest. And it's difficult to ride up onto that road from the village. The ridge is steep.'

I placed the cup on the table and rose to leave – but I couldn't go without asking one last question. 'Tell me, Johanna. Have you seen anything of an older priest recently? A man called Brother Peter.'

She stiffened immediately. 'Brother Peter?'

'Yes,' I said brightly, trying to sound as if I were asking an offhand question. 'He's the infirmarer at Kintham Abbey. You may have seen him with me before.'

She hesitated. 'I don't think so.'

I was far from convinced by her answer. 'So you haven't seen Brother Peter near to the house?'

Johanna hesitated again, appearing to consider the question with all the care and consideration of a witness speaking in court. 'No. I haven't seen him,' she said. 'He wasn't here.'

Her answer was too definite. Almost rehearsed. 'Are you sure about that, Johanna?' I asked.

Her trembling resumed. 'I'm not to say.'

'What do you mean?' I asked. 'Has somebody frightened you?'

'He told me not to tell anybody that he was here. He said I would get into trouble.'

'Who told you that?' I asked.

She hesitated again, her face now as white as a cerecloth.

'Was it Brother Peter?' I asked. 'Did he say that to you?'

She nodded lightly, as if not wanting to fully commit herself to this answer. 'I found him outside, near to the back door,' she whispered. 'On the day before my mistress went missing. I knew somebody was there because the chickens kept squawking. So I went outside to look around.' She suddenly gulped. 'When I caught him hiding in the shadows, he grabbed me.'

'Grabbed you?'

'Yes,' she said. 'He pulled me into the alley. Between this house and Master Roach's.' She shuddered, clearly very uncomfortable at this memory. 'He said that I wasn't to tell anybody that he'd been there.'

'And did you tell anybody?'

She shook her head. 'No. I didn't.'

'Not even your mistress?'

'No,' she said, looking up at me earnestly. 'I was scared of him, Brother Oswald. So I didn't say a word to anyone.'

I forced a smile. 'There's no reason to be frightened of Brother Peter,' I assured her. 'He was only watching over the women of this village. To make sure that you're safe.'

'Oh,' she said, as her frown lines deepened. 'Is that what he was doing?'

'Yes,' I replied firmly. 'Of course it was.'

Chapter Twenty-nine

I followed the north road from Stonebrook, up a track that ascended a steep slope to a vast wooded plateau – a part of the forest where my brothers sometimes liked to hunt. These ancient forests were thick with oak and ash trees that had been allowed to grow to maturity. There was no coppicing here. No hazel or chestnut cut down into stunted, knotted stools. In this part of the forest the trees had grown upwards with single trunks, like pillars in a vast crypt. Their branches spread out from the top of these pillars in thickly covered arches, denying light to much of the forest floor below. There was little vegetation beneath these trees as a result. Instead the shadow of the canopy created long, dark corridors that stretched out as far as the eye could see in every direction. This suited the huntsman to perfection. This way he could easily navigate the forest on horseback, whilst getting a clear view of his dogs as they chased down their prey. This forest was not the home of the swineherd, the charcoal burner or the humble woodsman. It was a place reserved for men of nobility, as their boundless, sylvan playground.

I rode along the path slowly, casting my eyes from side to side, hoping to find some sign of Maud and Rose, but the further I travelled, the more despondent I became. The forest was so large, with paths leading off in all directions. And the soil was dry and hard and gave nothing away. In fact, I found no evidence of anybody passing this way, especially not two light-footed women.

I had been riding continuously for many hours without seeing a single sign of humanity, when I decided to dismount beside a trickling stream in a glade of alder. It was here, at last, that my luck finally turned. I spotted a girl in the distance, desperately cupping water from the stream, as if she hadn't been able to drink for many days. I recognised her immediately. It was Rose Brunham – her salmon-pink hair flowing loosely down her back as she leant over the stream to quench her thirst.

I called out to her, but her reaction to me was one of horror. She staggered back from the stream at first and then ran away at speed, disappearing through the trees. I wanted to give chase, but found instead that I couldn't move. The memory of Agnes flashed before my eyes once more. The way that her hands had thrashed as she was pulled beneath the waters. The way that her limp body had flopped in my arms as I dragged her onto the river bank. The way that I had tried to thump the air back into her lungs. And so I watched helplessly as Rose escaped, her bright hair flying wildly behind her, until she was nearly out of sight.

It was only then, as she reached the brow of a hill in the far distance that I finally came to my senses. I couldn't let this girl flee, even though I didn't want to chase her. I needed to know why she and Maud had disappeared from Stonebrook. I needed to know if Maud were still alive. So I quickly mounted my horse again and pursued her through the trees, until I finally cornered her by a patch of brambles.

'Please, Rose. Stop,' I shouted down to her, as she threw herself further and further into this spiny undergrowth. 'I'm not going to hurt you.'

'Get away from me,' she screamed, continuing to push her way through the brambles. Her escape route was tangled and sharp, but at least these plants were not the waters of a swollen river. The worst that Rose could do was to scratch herself badly. I quickly dismounted, hoping that I would be less intimidating on foot – but this only caused her to panic all the more.

'Get away! Get away!' she screeched, throwing herself even further into the tangle. She had that look in her eyes. The same expression that Agnes had worn – a wild, demented fear that drowns out all reason.

'I only want to help you, Rose,' I said. 'What's the matter with you?'

'He sent you, didn't he?' she said, holding her hands in front of her face – her fingers forming bars across a pair of terrified eyes.

'Who?' I asked.

'Brother Peter,' she answered. 'You're with him, aren't you? I know it.'

My heart pounded at hearing Peter's name again. 'What do you mean?' I said, trying not to raise my voice. 'I don't understand.'

She didn't answer. Instead she returned to her crazed scramble, now managing to pull apart the brambles in a last desperate attempt to escape me. I now had no choice but to rush in myself and grasp her by the arm. Rose attempted to fend me off, but it was not a fair fight. I was so much stronger than this young girl, and it was easy for me to drag her out.

Having forced Rose to sit on the ground, I then tried a peace offering. I passed her my flask of ale, which she refused, turning her back to me. When I knelt down beside her and tried to gently touch her arm, she cringed and screamed so loudly that I quickly withdrew.

'I'm not going to hurt you, Rose,' I said. 'I only want to find Maud.'

'You're his friend,' she hissed. 'Aren't you? I've seen you in the village together.'

'Do you mean Brother Peter?' I asked.

'Yes.'

'I am his friend,' I answered. 'So I don't understand why you're so afraid of him.'

She remained silent in response.

'Has he hurt you?' I asked. When she still refused to speak, I added, 'Please, Rose. I am Peter's friend, but I'm not in league with him. You must believe me. I only want to help you. So, please tell me what happened. Tell me where I can find Maud.'

Rose looked at me for a moment, before she dropped her head between her knees and spoke to the earth. 'We were looking for Pestilence wort,' she whispered. 'We needed the freshest roots to protect us from plague.'

'Where did you go?' I asked.

'I don't know,' she replied. 'We took a path I'd never been on before.' She smothered a sudden sob. 'We'd walked for miles and miles finding nothing. But then we saw a cottage between the trees.'

'What sort of cottage?' I asked.

'It was deserted,' she said. 'Without a good roof. We were curious to look inside.' She paused to sniff. 'But we shouldn't have.'

'Why's that?'

She wrapped her arms about her knees and began to rock backwards and forwards. 'I can't tell you,' she whispered.

I put my hand gently onto her shoulder and leant forward to whisper into her ear. 'Please tell me, Rose. I need to know.'

She stiffened at my touch, but didn't shriek this time. 'We were trapped,' she said, her voice still thin and squeaky. 'The door slammed and we couldn't get out again . . . So we pulled at the door. We kept pulling. Trying to get out.' She gave a sob. 'But then it suddenly opened. And it was him on the other side.' She wiped the tears from her eyes. 'We tried to get out, but he stood in the way. He wouldn't let us pass.'

'Do you mean Brother Peter?'

'Yes.'

'Are you sure it was Brother Peter?' I asked, hardly able to believe this story. 'Could it have been somebody else?'

'I know it was him,' she said, stifling another sob. 'He must have followed us there. Through the forest.'

'What did he want?'

'I don't know,' she whispered. 'He just started shouting at us. Ranting and raving.'

'About what?'

Rose looked up at me with anguish, the blood having risen to her face, so that her cheeks were nearly the same shade as her hair. 'I didn't understand any of it,' she said. 'It was just loud words. Cruel things. And I was so frightened.' She broke off again to take a deep breath. 'He tried to grab hold of me,' she said, her eyes now full of tears. 'He took me by the wrist and tried to drag me out of the cottage. But Mistress Maud fought him off, so then he attacked her instead.' Another sob. 'I ran out of the door, Brother Oswald. I wanted to help Maud, but it was too late. There was nothing I could do for her.'

I couldn't speak for a moment, unable to comprehend this story. 'So you ran away?' I asked, finding my voice at last.

'I wanted to get help,' she said. 'But every time I thought that I'd reached the right path, I was somewhere else that I didn't know.' She wiped away a tear. 'Sometimes I was going around and around in circles. For hours. I thought I would never get back to Stonebrook. I thought I was going to die.'

I hesitated, trying to make sense of my wild, conflicting thoughts. 'Do you know where this cottage is?' I said finally.

She shook her head. 'No,' she replied. 'I can't remember the direction I came from.'

'You have to try, Rose,' I said, now letting frustration creep into my voice. 'I need to find this place. Maud could still be there.'

'When I got away from the cottage, I ran so fast that I didn't know what direction I was taking,' she replied. 'And then it was

dark and I was lost. I thought he was going to chase me. I thought
I was going to die.' She started to sob, her whole body trembling
until I offered her the last of the food that I'd taken from the
kitchens at Somershill. The girl was starving – grasping the bread
and cheese from me and devouring it in great mouthfuls.

'Try to remember something about the cottage,' I said softly,
as she began to revive. 'Anything that could help me to find it.'

She raised her eyes to mine. 'Are you going there?' she asked
me.

I nodded. 'Yes. I must.'

'No. You mustn't,' she replied. 'It's too dangerous.'

'Brother Peter wouldn't hurt me,' I said. 'He's been my tutor
for many years.'

She grasped my arm. 'You must believe me,' she said. 'I saw it
in his eyes. He wanted to kill me, and he wanted to kill Mistress
Maud.' She pressed her fingers into my skin. 'If you go there,
then he will kill you as well.'

The words were spoken with conviction, but how could any of
this be true? How could this man – a person whom I had trusted
and loved for most of my life, be the killer that Rose described?
Brother Peter had never behaved this way before. Rose must
have misread his actions, or exaggerated them at least. And I
needed to remember that Peter himself had called this girl a liar.

And yet . . .

And yet I heard a small voice inside my head, desperately calling out for attention – asking me questions that I didn't want to
hear. Why had Agnes been so terrified of priests, unless a priest
had attacked her? Why had Brother Merek disappeared having
just confided in Peter? Why, indeed, had Ranulf Sawyer been
murdered just after I'd sent Peter to find him? And why, why had
Peter repeatedly warned me away from my investigation? I felt
my heart miss a beat and my breath tighten. Had I been blind to
his faults all along . . . No, no. I just couldn't believe it. Despite
all of the evidence building against Peter, my instincts still told

me that he was innocent. I just needed to discover the truth behind his actions. There had to be a reasonable explanation.

I turned back to Rose, and tried again. 'If you can't remember the location of this cottage, then try to describe the surrounding area. Was there anything distinctive nearby? A river perhaps? Or a clearing?'

Rose frowned in concentration. 'There were some rocks,' she replied.

'What type of rocks?'

'They were odd. Full of gaps. Just wide enough for a person to squeeze through.'

This description narrowed my search down a little. There are outcrops of sandstone that rise up from the clay in certain parts of the weald – creating unexpected ridges of rocks in the middle of the forests.

'And you can't remember anything else?'

She creased her brow. 'I know that this sounds foolish,' she said. 'But one of the rocks looked strange. It looked just like . . .' She hesitated.

'Like what?' I asked.

Rose turned her head away from me, seemingly embarrassed. 'It looked like a giant frog, sitting on top of a pedestal. We stopped to look at it, because it made us laugh.' She smiled briefly at the memory, before her face darkened again. 'But then we got trapped in that cottage.'

'So the cottage is near to this rock?'

Rose scratched at her cheek. 'I think so,' she whispered, before another sob escaped. 'But I can't be sure, Brother Oswald. I'm sorry.'

I knew the place Rose was talking about. As a boy, I had heard my older brothers speak about this rock when they returned from their hunting trips. It had sounded so strange and remarkable to my childish imagination, that I had repeatedly begged William and Richard to take me hunting with them. To see something as exciting as a giant stone frog. They had refused, of course – claiming that I would ruin their chances of catching anything with my loud feet and childish, squealing voice; but they had been forced to take me in the end by my father, as he had been driven mad by my whining.

I remembered being so very disappointed when I finally saw the famous frog rock, having imagined a sculpture with all the splendour and detail of the statue of Nebuchadnezzar. Instead of that, this supposed frog was nothing more than a pair of boulders – one resting upon the other and created by chance. Its shape bore a passing resemblance to a frog, but this had been very difficult for a child to appreciate.

I got to my feet. 'Are you going?' Rose asked me.

'Yes,' I replied. 'I need to find Maud.'

'But what will I do?' The tears were forming in her eyes again. 'You can't leave me here. How will I find my way back to Stonebrook?'

'You need to go to Somershill,' I replied. 'Stonebrook is over-run with plague, so you cannot return there.'

'But I don't know anybody in Somershill,' she said.

'Go to the house and ask for Gilbert. Tell him that I've sent you.'

'But how will I find it?' she asked. 'I'll get lost again,' she said.

'Head east with the sun behind you,' I said. 'You'll reach Somershill by nightfall.'

Rose started to tremble. 'But what if Brother Peter is still looking for me?'

'If he wanted to chase you, then he would have caught you by now.' When she looked unconvinced, I added, 'Don't worry. You're safe now.'

She grasped my hand. Her tiny fingers scraping at my sleeve like claws. 'If you find Brother Peter, don't tell him that I told you where to look. Please,' she begged, her eyes wide with fear. 'He mustn't know it was me.'

Chapter Thirty

I continued to the north, finding the forest becoming denser and darker with each mile. The land began to rise and fall in steep valleys that were banked with beech and oak, and lined with dark streams and secretive rivers. There was little sport here, as the hunters preferred the flatter, more open lands that I had left behind – although, ironically, this was the part of the forest where the deer were more likely to be hiding. On more than one occasion, I flushed out a doe and her fawn, feeling relieved as they sprang away into the distance – their summer coats as red as a weasel's. The stags that stayed perfectly still were more menacing – their dark profiles appearing between the leaves as they silently watched my progress. After my conversation with Rose, I felt on guard, keeping one hand on the hilt of my short sword, constantly in fear of what or whom I would meet.

By late afternoon, I had reached the outcrop of sandstone that Rose had described to me. Weathered and grooved by the wind, the rocks were cleft with deep vertical crevices, creating long thin passages that ran back from the rock face and disappeared into the darkness beyond. But there was no derelict cottage nearby. No rock that looked like a frog sitting on top of a pedestal.

I rode along the path that wound its way beside the ridge, often passing beneath an overhang that was coated in moss and lichen.

Birch saplings had found an occasional foothold within the fissures of this rock – sprouting out from the surface like tufts of hair. Despite the strange remoteness of this place, I had the feeling that it was visited by more than the secretive roe deer. This path was kept clear of brambles by the passing of humans, as the long thorny stems had been bent back and broken off at waist height.

I carried on, and soon came to an opening in the rock face that was slightly larger than the other crevices – a gully wide enough for a person to walk along. It was here that I found tangible evidence of human activity at last. There were footprints hardened into the earth here, leading from the entrance and heading off into the dark. And there was something else, calling out to be noticed. A thin skein of scent floating through the air. It was a smell that was unmistakable. Unlike any other on earth.

I dismounted, tied my horse to a tree, and then worked my way along that gully, swishing away at the bluebottles until I turned the corner at the end. At first I could not make sense of the sight that confronted me. I thought it was a pile of rotten debris. A midden heap. But then my eyes focused and suddenly I could see different shapes. A tangle of limbs, one body thrown on top of the other, as if they were carcasses dumped outside a slaughter house.

For a moment, I could not move. I had seen death many times before, but nothing in my history had prepared me for this sight, in all its raw, visceral reality. My first reaction was to turn back and get away as soon as possible, but I couldn't leave yet – not before I'd checked that these corpses were the women I was looking for. And so, with great reluctance, I crept closer, holding my hand over my nose as I looked into the pile to see an array of female bodies, half-dressed in ragged tunics. Their shoes, belts and jewellery were missing – no doubt now located on that shelf in Ranulf Sawyer's hut.

I edged forward again, as far as I dared, needing to see if Maud were among the dead. I couldn't see her face and my relief was palpable, but I did notice a larger body pushed down at the back of the heap. The leg and arm bones of this corpse were thicker and longer than the others and the ribcage was fuller. It was a man. Brother Merek, the missing monk – his body dressed only in its hair shirt – the type routinely worn at the monastery by the most devout brothers. It was strange that Merek's habit had been removed, whereas the dead women were still wearing their tunics, but I guessed that Sawyer had scavenged this garment from Merek's corpse, alongside his other finds. A priest's habit is woven with high-quality wool and would have been worth something when sold.

As I turned away from this horror, I thought again of Agnes, as I often had done in the past few weeks. Her bloodstained, roughly torn tunic. The rubbing and bruising at her wrists and ankles. Her scratched and injured skin. All my feelings of sorrow and remorse flooded back in that moment, before they turned, very quickly, to rage. And it was an almighty, overwhelming rage. I had made a terrible mistake that day. I had unwittingly chased a girl into the river, but I had not been her killer. That man was still at large, and I needed to find him.

I quickly left the gully and rested against the rock face for a while, letting my heartbeat return to its usual speed. There is momentum and energy in anger, but it can also cloud judgment. And I needed a clear head to continue. Once my initial rage had subsided, I then re-mounted my horse and rode along the ridge until arriving at a clearing that was dominated by the strangest sight. It was a rock formation, separated from the rest of the ridge by a few hundred yards, but still formed from the same sandstone. It was a monument formed by nature. One large, strangely shaped boulder rested precariously on top of another, looking something like a giant frog sitting on a pedestal – as if the wind could be credited with sculpting something so specific from a lump of stone. This was the Frog Rock – the place that Rose had described to me. There could be no doubt of that.

I tied my horse to a tree and walked around the rock, hoping to see a cottage nearby which might match Rose's description – but there was nothing. Only scrubby grass surrounded by trees. And then I began to worry that Rose had confused two memories in her state of agitation – the sighting of the Frog Rock and the supposed ambush by Peter. It was possible that I was nowhere near the place where she and Maud had been attacked. I couldn't fend off a brief moment of despair, before I gathered my thoughts again. I couldn't give up now. Maud had to be somewhere nearby.

So I walked the perimeter of this clearing several times until something in the distance caught my eye. Its square proportions meant that it had to be a building and not another natural feature, though the forest had almost completely reclaimed it. I crept closer, seeing a building that had once been a stable, or even a place of habitation – except it was now covered in a thick, dismal blanket of ivy. At first glance it seemed deserted. And yet . . .

And yet, there was a door to the far side. It was made of newly sawn wood, and it was firmly shut. But I could hear voices. Somebody was inside.

Chapter Thirty-one

My first plan was to approach the door and push my way in, until I thought better of the idea. Instead, I waited behind a nearby tree, hoping to identify the voices that were coming from within the cottage. The sounds were muffled at first, but then I could make out the groans of a woman alongside the voice of a man. My heart nearly burst out of my chest as I listened more intently, for the man spoke with the low tones and precise inflection that I knew so well. Even at this late hour, I had still held out some hope that Rose was wrong about Peter. But this was his voice behind the door.

I was deciding my next move, when Peter himself emerged from the cottage, holding a bucket and sniffing the air, as if he were a deer trying to sense the huntsman. Thankfully he didn't see me, as I darted back against the tree just in time to see him lift a wooden locking bar across the door. After this, he headed off into the forest – presumably to fill his bucket from a nearby stream.

With Peter gone, I ran to the door, lifted the locking bar and stepped inside the cottage to find Maud lying on the floor with her back against the far wall. Her hands and feet were bound with rope and her mouth was gagged with a length of cloth. When she saw my face, she whimpered desperately for help, which only caused me to freeze, feeling the blood drain from my head. There could now be no doubt about Peter's intentions.

Maud groaned again and I quickly came to my senses.

'Oswald,' she gasped, as I pulled the cloth away from her mouth. 'Thank the saints. You found me,' she said, kissing my fingers. 'I knew that you would come. I knew that you wouldn't forget me.'

'I didn't know where to look,' I replied. 'But then I found Rose in the forest and she told me what had happened.'

Maud's face darkened for a moment at the mention of Rose's name, before she lifted her bound wrists towards me. 'Please, Oswald,' she said. 'Just cut these ropes before Peter comes back. I need to get out of here.'

I took my short sword from its scabbard and freed her hands quickly, before turning my attention to the rope about her ankles. This was a harder job, as Peter had secured this binding with many twists.

'Come on,' she urged me, starting to panic. 'Be quick. He won't be long.'

I worked my way through the tough fibres, though my progress was hindered by Maud's constant squirming. 'Stay still,' I whispered. 'I can't cut this rope if you keep moving.'

'Please. Hurry,' she replied. 'He'll kill us both if he finds you here.'

I continued to cut at the rope, when a shadow fell across the room. 'Oswald?' came a voice from behind me. I raised my sword and turned around to see Peter silhouetted against the door.

Maud shuffled back to the wall – her legs still bound together – as Peter stepped inside the cottage and closed the door behind him. Suddenly we were in near darkness – the only light coming from the few gaps in the rafters above.

I pointed my sword at my old tutor. 'Keep away,' I said, trying to control the fear in my voice.

Peter calmly placed his bucket onto the floor. 'What are you doing here, Oswald?' he asked me.

'He's come to save me,' said Maud. 'I told you that he'd come.'

Peter laughed at this. 'Nobody could save you, Maud Woodstock.'

I held my ground as Peter stepped towards me. 'What are you doing here, Oswald?' he asked again.

I ignored this question. 'I found the gully, Peter,' I said. 'I've seen the bodies.'

'Oh,' he said with a long and regretful sigh. 'I didn't want that to happen.'

'No wonder you killed Sawyer,' I replied. 'Knowing he could lead people there.'

Peter's forehead creased into a frown, before he started to laugh at me. He actually laughed. 'For Goodness' sake, Oswald,' he said. 'What's got into you? I didn't kill Sawyer. The man was already dead when I reached him. I gave him a Christian burial. Nothing more.' He paused to rub his hands over his face. 'And I shall do the same thing for those poor souls who've been dumped in that gully. Once I've sorted this woman out.' He waved at Maud. 'So, just tie her up again,' he said. 'And stop acting like a fool.'

'No.' I said, turning back to Maud – kneeling down to start cutting again at the ropes about her ankles.

It was not a moment before Peter laid a hand on my shoulder. 'Tie her up, Oswald,' he said. 'Do as I tell you.'

'No,' I said, pushing him away with my elbow before returning my attentions to the rope. 'I will not.'

Peter came at me again. This time his clasp at my shoulder was firm and insistent. I turned to repel him again – thrusting my sword towards him, but he dodged the blade easily before grabbing my wrist. I tried to keep hold of my sword as he tightened his grip, but I was forced to let it fall to the floor.

Maud urged me to fight back, but Peter had retained the strength and agility of his youth, despite years of drinking. After disarming me so easily, he picked up my sword, shoved me through the door and hurled me onto the grass outside. He placed the locking bar across the door, and then strode over to point the tip of my own short sword into my face.

We stared at one another for a moment in silence, but I didn't dare to get to my feet. Peter looked deranged and sweaty, and his hand was shaking violently.

'Not enough brandy in your hunting lodge, then?' I said, nodding at the trembling blade. 'You should have planned that better.'

'This place has nothing to do with me,' he spat. 'How could you even think such a thing?'

I went to answer, when Maud began to kick at the door from the inside of the cottage – her bound feet hammering at the wooden panels like a battering ram. 'Get me out of here, Oswald!' she called. 'Please!'

Peter stepped over to the door and shouted through the wood. 'Get back against the wall. Nobody is coming to save you.'

Maud continued to thump. 'Don't abandon me, Oswald,' she pleaded. 'I know that you came here to save me. I know that you love me.'

Peter looked at me in dismay. 'God's bones, Oswald,' he said. 'Don't tell me that you're in love with this she-devil?' He wiped the sheen of sweat from his forehead with the back of his hand. 'What's the matter with you?'

'Don't believe him,' shouted Maud. 'The man is a liar and a murderer. He wants to kill both of us.'

'Shut up!' Peter shouted, banging at the door with the pommel of my sword. 'I am neither of those things, Oswald,' he replied, turning back to face me. 'Maud Woodstock is the liar here. Not me.'

I rose slowly to my feet, wary of attack. 'I don't believe you, Peter,' I said, stepping forwards, and getting as close to Peter as I dared.

'I don't understand this, Oswald. Why would you doubt me?' he said, his face screwed into a scowl. 'Me? Of all people?'

'Don't listen to him, Oswald!' shouted Maud. 'It's all lies!'

Peter kicked at the door with his heel. 'Be quiet. You whore!'

'It's me who doesn't understand, Peter. How could you do it?' I said, taking another step forward. 'How could you torture and kill those women?'

'Because I didn't do it, Oswald,' he growled. 'That's why.'

'But I found Rose Brunham in the forest,' I said. 'She told me what happened. She told me that you tracked her and Maud to this cottage. That you attacked them.'

'Christ's bones!' he replied, his face now red with anger. 'This is all nonsense. Will you please just listen to me?'

I instinctively stepped back, knowing Peter was at his most dangerous when he was riled. My tutor's passions rose up and down like the pans of a balancing scale – especially when he was missing a drink.

'Come on then, Peter,' I said softly, buying myself some time. 'Tell me about Maud, then. Why should I believe that she's guilty?'

'Do you really want to know, Oswald?' he asked – a pained frown now rippling across his forehead. 'Really?'

'Of course,' I said. 'I want you to convince me. I want to hear your side of the story.'

Peter studied my face for a moment – not sure of my sincerity. Perhaps he had read my mind – knowing that I was planning to feign an interest in his argument. That I was hoping to dupe him into dropping his guard, before I wrestled back my sword. Even so, he wanted me to believe him. I could see that clearly. There was even a tear in his eye.

'I knew there was something wrong,' he began, 'when you told me that Maud Woodstock had been so helpful to your investigation. This didn't sound like the woman I knew of old. That Maud Woodstock would never lift a finger to assist another person, Oswald. Certainly not a group of poor village women.'

Maud shouted again. 'He tried to seduce me, Oswald. That's why he's making up these lies. He came to me with an offer when my father suffered the apoplexy. He said that he'd persuade the Abbot to reduce my rent, if I would share his bed.'

'Shut your mouth,' said Peter. 'I don't want to hear another word from you.'

'Did you try to seduce Maud?' I asked, stepping forward again.

'No. Of course not,' replied Peter. 'I'm a man of God, Oswald. A monk sworn to celibacy. But let me tell you. If I were going to take a woman to my bed, then it certainly wouldn't be this she-devil. A woman who's starving her maid to death and torturing her father.'

'That's nonsense,' hissed Maud. 'How dare you make such accusations?'

'Shut up!' said Peter.

But Maud carried on. Her voice now shrill and desperate. 'You've been to my house, Oswald. You've seen that there's more than enough food for Johanna. You've seen that my father is loved and well cared for.'

I advanced again. 'I'm still not convinced,' I told Peter. 'This sounds like a collection of your old prejudices to me. Where's your evidence that Maud has anything to do with the murders?'

'Very well then,' he replied. 'If it's evidence that you want. Ask yourself this. Why did all the missing women come from the same village?'

'There could be a number of reasons.'

'Maud was picking out the victims, that's why,' replied Peter, rolling his eyes and shaking his head at me. 'She chose the poorest women in Stonebrook. The ones who were easiest to prey upon.'

I could feel my temper rising. 'Are you saying that Maud attacks women in the forest, and then dumps their bodies in a gully?' I made sure to add a laugh to this preposterous claim.

'Of course not, Oswald,' said Peter solemnly. 'She finds them for somebody else.'

I swallowed my laughter. 'What are you talking about?'

Peter dropped the sword for a moment and looked at me with something akin to pity. 'I see that you imagine yourself to be in love with this woman, Oswald. But you must prepare yourself to hear the truth about Maud Woodstock. She lures poor and vulnerable women here.' He waved a hand behind him. 'To this sordid hovel.'

'Why?' I asked. 'Why would she do that?'

'God's bones. Don't be so naive,' he replied. 'She does it to please a man.'

'What man?'

Peter groaned in response to this question. 'Your love is wasted on this woman, Oswald,' he said. 'Can't you see that? She already has a lover. A man who likes to rape and kill.'

'No. That's not true,' I stammered. 'You're lying. Maud would never do something like that. She's been helping me to search for the killer.'

'For the sake of Christ,' he growled. 'She's been keeping her eyes on your investigation. That's the only reason why she's been so helpful.' Peter paused to shake his head. 'If you hadn't let your cock do the thinking, then Sawyer might still be alive.'

I felt my stomach roll again. 'What do you mean?'

'Maud organised that meeting of the village women for you, didn't she?' he asked.

'Well, yes,' I mumbled.

'And then she sat there, listening to what the women told you.'

'Of course she did,' I said. 'We all did.'

'It was then that she heard about Sawyer for the first time. Before that, she had no idea that somebody was scavenging items . . . from the bodies of the women she had helped to murder.'

'Everybody at the meeting heard about Sawyer,' I replied. 'Not just Maud.'

'But the others didn't follow you into the forest on horseback, did they? They haven't even got horses.'

'But—'

'You thought it was John Roach on your tail, didn't you? When you went to see Sawyer.' He waved towards the door again. 'But it wasn't Roach. It was her. Maud Woodstock.'

'No, it wasn't,' I insisted.

'They both ride white palfreys, Oswald.'

I paused to take a breath. 'This is all just invention, Peter,' I maintained, even though my mind couldn't help but dart back to the memory of Johanna grooming a white horse outside Maud's house. 'You cannot absolve yourself by throwing such wild accusations.'

'Maud followed you to the charcoal pits, because she wanted to hear what Sawyer would say to you,' said Peter. 'Sawyer must have caught sight of her, which is why he ran away.'

'But Sawyer attacked me, Brother Peter.'

'No, he didn't, Oswald. It was Maud.'

'Why would she do that?'

'Because she didn't want you to return straight away with a gang of men to find Sawyer. Not before she'd had time to silence him.'

There were elements of this story that were beginning to ring true. Maud must have sensed my resolve waning, as she used this moment to start banging her feet again at the door.

'I don't know what he's talking about, Oswald,' she cried. 'I only know that Peter followed us here, and then he attacked us.'

Peter sighed. His face wearied and grey. 'That's not true, Oswald,' he said. 'Maud led Rose into the forest, don't you see? She was to be their latest victim.'

'No,' I replied. 'Maud and Rose came here looking for Pestilence wort.'

This idea seemed to amuse Peter. 'They didn't need to come this far to find such a common plant,' he said. 'Pestilence wort grows everywhere. Like a weed. You, of all people, should know that.' He paused to sigh. 'Why come to such a remote part of the forest? Unless there was another reason?'

I couldn't deny that this was true. Pestilence wort was a common enough plant, and now that Peter had pointed this out to me, it did seem strange that the pair had walked this far. But this argument was not damning evidence. Not everybody possessed a Benedictine monk's knowledge of wild herbs and plants.

'That doesn't prove anything,' I said, though I wasn't able to completely disguise the doubt in my voice. 'It could have been Rose's idea to come here. Not Maud's.'

'I followed them here from Stonebrook,' said Peter. 'And I tell you this for nothing. It was Maud leading Rose. Not the other way around. It was Maud who suggested that Rose go inside the cottage.'

Maud began to thump at the door again. 'Please Oswald,' she cried. 'Tell me you're not going to believe this story? Tell me that you have more sense than this? You've seen for yourself what this man is capable of. You carried the corpse of Agnes Wheeler back from the forest. You know that she was tied at the ankles and wrists? Just as I am now.' She thumped at the door until the planks shook. 'For the love of Christ, please. Let me out of here!'

I thought back to Agnes. Her limp body. Her wet hair. The scars and the bruises, and I felt my anger return. 'I could never understand why I frightened Agnes so much,' I said. 'I could never understand the bitterness of those words, *Keep away from me, priest*. But now I do. Agnes thought that I was you.'

'And you believe that points the finger at me, do you?' said Peter, wearily shaking his head. 'After all the love and care that I've given you during the last ten years. You still believe that I am capable of such crimes? Have I not proved myself to you, Oswald?'

'You've proven yourself to be a drunkard and a liar,' I said. 'Why not a killer as well?'

This accusation riled him. He strode back to the door of the cottage, lifted the bar and flung open the door, kicking Maud out of the way as he strode inside. She curled herself into a ball – her eyes squinting as the light invaded the chamber again. I followed Peter to find him delving into a dark corner of the cottage as he picked something up from the floor.

'You want to see the truth about this priest, do you?' he said, holding a dirty black garment aloft.

'What's that?' I asked.

'This is Brother Merek's habit, Oswald. Stolen from his dead body.'

I froze – thinking back to Merek's corpse – shoved down the back of the pile and dressed only in his hair shirt.

'Does he wear this?' said Peter, swinging the habit into Maud's face.

'I don't know what you're talking about,' she replied, pressing herself back against the wall to escape Peter's attentions. 'I've never seen that tunic in my life.'

Peter dangled the garment in front of her nose. 'It's easy to lull a woman into a sense of security, isn't it?' he said. 'If she believes that she's talking to a priest.'

'Get away from me,' she spat, which only caused him to push the cloth further into her face.

'I imagine Agnes was easily lured into this cottage by a man of God, wasn't she?' Peter said. 'Or did it amuse you both? To commit your sins in this attire?'

Maud wriggled towards me in desperation. 'Please, Oswald, don't be fooled by this story. I had nothing to do with any of this. This is all lies.'

'Then you won't mind if we wait here to prove it,' said Peter, dropping Merek's habit to the floor.

Maud stopped wriggling. 'What?'

'He'll turn up,' said Peter. 'Sooner or later.'

'Who will turn up?' said Maud. 'What are you talking about?'

'Your lover, of course. The killer.'

Maud cast her eyes to mine. 'Please, Oswald,' she said. 'I don't know what he means. Please. Just get me out of here. I can't bear it any longer.'

Peter put a hand against the wall and leant over Maud. 'Of course he'll turn up. He thinks that there's a girl here waiting for him, doesn't he?'

'This is absurd,' said Maud, shaking her head in disbelief, as Peter found the length of rope that I'd pulled from her wrists. 'Do something, Oswald!' she screamed, trying to pull her hands from Peter's grasp as he went to re-tie her bindings. 'For Christ's sake. Please. Don't let him do this to me again.'

I hung back, paralysed, unable to act as Peter pulled the gag around Maud's mouth, stuffing some of the cloth between her lips.

'And if this man doesn't appear?' I asked.

'He will come, Oswald,' said Peter with conviction. 'Don't worry about that.'

Chapter Thirty-two

Somershill, November 1370

I went to continue my story, but we were interrupted by a sharp knock at the door, before Clemence marched into the room without waiting for me to answer. On seeing our visitor, Mother pulled at my sleeve and whispered. 'Tell her to go away, Oswald,' she said. 'I don't want to talk to her. Not at the moment.'

'What is it, Clemence?' I asked loudly. 'Mother is too tired to receive any more visitors.'

'I'm not here for Mother,' she said, with less umbrage than I might have expected. 'It's you I want to speak to, Oswald,' she said. 'In private.'

Mother bristled at this. If there were anything more likely to annoy her, even on her deathbed, it was the idea of being excluded from a conversation. 'I'm sure that you can speak in front of me,' she said.

'No,' said Clemence. 'This is for Oswald's ears alone.'

My sister folded her arms and glared at me, until I joined her by the door, whereupon she pulled me into the passageway. 'This is not Mother's concern,' she whispered.

'What is it?' I asked, lifting my hood, as it was much colder in this passageway after the warm fug of the bedroom.

Clemence cleared her throat and seemed uncomfortable for once. 'I have something to tell you,' she said. 'About Filomena.'

'What is it?' I asked.

Clemence hesitated again, taking a moment to scratch her nose. It was strange to see her behaving so awkwardly, and it made me feel uneasy. 'We believe that she's run away.'

For a moment I wanted to laugh. 'What?'

'Oh come on, Oswald,' she said. 'You must have realised what's been going on? Between Filomena and Sir John?'

I no longer wanted to laugh. 'You're saying that Filomena has run away with that man?' But then I thought back to the sight of my wife, cantering away across the fields. 'No. That's not true,' I said resolutely, pushing the memory away. 'I don't believe it.'

Clemence flashed her eyes at me. 'Keep your voice down, Oswald. This is a very shameful matter. We don't want the whole house to hear our business.' She drew closer. 'Now you have to listen to me. I've been given this information by Henry himself. I have no reason to disbelieve my own son.'

'So this story is Henry's invention, is it?'

'No. Absolutely not.' Clemence cleared her throat. 'Henry came to me today, after he saw Filomena riding away from the house at dusk. It gave him great pain to relay this story. You know how little he likes to speak. Especially to me.'

I folded my arms. 'He's making it up.'

'Why on earth would he do that?' said Clemence.

I hesitated. 'Because he's in love with Filomena, that's why. He's jealous of her closeness to Sir John.'

My sister rolled her eyes to the heavens. 'Goodness me. So what? So are most of the men in this household. The woman exudes a peculiar attraction to the opposite sex.' Clemence straightened her veil and pursed her lips. 'Personally I cannot understand it. She is a little . . . obvious.'

'What is it, then?' I asked. 'This piece of information that Henry has passed on?'

Clemence lowered her voice, rubbing her hand under the band of her wimple before wiping a thin film of sweat from her brow. 'Henry overheard the pair of them whispering in Filomena's tongue.'

'You mean Venetian?'

'Yes,' she snapped. 'Of course I mean Venetian.' Clemence held up a hand to prevent me from asking the next, inevitable question. 'And before you say anything, Henry has been very well educated. His Latin and Greek allow him to understand many foreign tongues.'

I wanted to laugh. Henry's Latin had been so poor that he'd struggled to read many of the most basic texts at Oxford, and had been forced to quit his studies after a couple of years. The idea that he was listening in to a private conversation between my wife and a house guest – a conversation that had apparently been held in Venetian – was bordering on the ludicrous. However, I decided to play along.

'Well then,' I said. 'Out with it. What did Henry hear?'

Clemence eyed me distrustfully, but decided to continue. 'Henry says that the pair were discussing their plan to elope together. That Filomena would meet Sir John at an inn near Tonbridge. After this they would make their way to Rochester, and then follow Watling Street to Dover.'

'Dover indeed?' I said. 'Goodness me.'

Clemence frowned at my tone. 'You must take this seriously, Oswald. Your wife is absconding with her lover. They intend to escape to Venice together.'

'That is nonsense,' I replied. 'A complete fabrication. Filomena would never leave me. Henry is mistaken.'

Clemence seized my arm. Her expression was pained, desperate even. 'Listen to me, Oswald. It's not just Henry's story that concerns me. I've seen what's been happening between the pair myself. I cannot speak Venetian, and nor have I been listening at doors, but it's still as plain as a pikestaff.'

'I don't know what you mean,' I said.

She huffed in response. 'Of course you do. You spend too long with our mother and not enough time with your wife.'

'That's because Mother is dying.'

'Yes, but that could take ages, Oswald. You know what a tough old goose the woman is. And yet, while you hide yourself away in this room, that clotpole, Sir John, a man whom you invited yourself into this house, has charmed your beautiful wife with his tall tales and amorous attentions.' She shook her head and sighed. 'At least you had the good sense to ask him to leave. Because, if I had to listen to one more tale about monsters who cooled off under the shade of their own giant feet, or creatures that ate their own children because they couldn't be bothered to go hunting, then I would have thrown him out myself.'

She suddenly grasped my hand. 'Filomena has been captivated with his talk of Venice. Can't you see that? She feels sentimental for her old home, and Sir John has played on that. Describing that Gomorrah in fulsome detail every night, and exciting her feelings for the place.' She squeezed her fingers into mine, an act of affection that I had rarely ever received before from my sister. 'Filomena's head has been turned, Oswald. But it's not too late to turn it back. Ride after her now. Tell her to forget about this foolish man and his foolish tales. Tell her to come back to Somershill. She belongs here. Not in Venice.'

'Is this the truth, Clemence?' I asked.

'Of course it is,' she said. 'Why would I lie about something like this?'

'Because you don't like Filomena,' I answered.

She dropped my hand. 'That is nonsense, Oswald. I find her difficult to understand, that's all. And not just because she comes from another country.' Clemence paused to take a breath. 'Her behaviour has always been slightly questionable, in my opinion. The tight-fitting clothes she chooses to wear. And all that ornamentation in her hair. But this is a new low point. This will bring great shame on our family, if you do not go and find her.'

'So that's your true motivation?' I said. 'You're not worried about my marriage. You are just afraid of our reputation.'

'So what if it is?' she answered defiantly. 'What's wrong with wanting to maintain the standing of the de Lacy family? Now, for the sake of your son and my son, and the name of this family, ride out of here and find her.'

I looked away, feeling sick and then angry. How dare Filomena do this to me? Now. When my mother was about to die. 'If she wants to go,' I said. 'Then let her.'

Clemence drew back in surprise. 'You don't mean that, Oswald. It's nothing more than bravado. Of course you want her to stay. You love the foolish woman.'

I hesitated. 'I'll go tomorrow,' I said.

'Tomorrow might be too late. Go now.'

'I can't,' I said. 'I have other matters to attend to this night.'

'What other matters?' snapped Clemence, unable to hide her anger. 'What could possibly be more important than this?' When I didn't answer immediately, she continued. 'Are you too proud to chase after a woman? Is that it?' She puffed her lips with scorn. 'You men and your ridiculous pride. When will you understand that you only hurt yourselves with such stupidity.' She grabbed my hands again. 'Go after her, Oswald. Go now. Before it's too late!'

'I can't,' I insisted, once again pulling my hands away. 'There's something I need to finish. If I don't do this tonight, then I'll never have the chance again.'

Clemence glanced towards the bedroom door. 'I see,' she said. 'Filomena can wait until tomorrow. But Mother can't.'

'You don't understand,' I said.

'You're right,' she replied, as she turned on her heels and marched away. 'I don't understand. I don't understand at all.'

I returned to my station at Mother's deathbed to finish this business, for I knew that we were very close to the end. She looked back at me with tired, sunken eyes, but there was still life in there. Just about.

'I heard you arguing with Clemence,' she whispered. 'Is there something wrong?'

I shook my head. 'No,' I answered. 'There's nothing wrong.'

'Then you will stay and end your story?' she asked, managing to pat the letter that still lay beneath the neckline of her chemise.

'I will.'

'Right to the end?'

'Yes, Mother. Right to the end.'

Chapter Thirty-three

Kent, June 1349

We lay in wait for Maud's accomplice for the rest of the day – Peter watching the door of the cottage like a dog waiting to be fed. During those long hours, we heard nothing from outside, other than the wind through the trees, the ringing calls of the buzzards, and the distant drill of a woodpecker. Inside, the noises were more ordinary – especially the sound of rumbling stomachs. Peter and Maud hadn't eaten for at least two days, and there was no food in this hovel. Every hour or so, Peter removed Maud's gag, so that she could take a drink of water at least – but he always replaced it quickly, because she used each and every one of these opportunities to plead her innocence and beg for release. I kept my eyes from hers – not knowing whether to feel guilty or angry.

The evening eventually bled into night, as the three of us remained seated in our dark refuge, still waiting for this mysterious man to appear. Though it was a summer's night, there was a coolness to the air – a chill that caught at the back of my throat and filled my lungs with its icy breath. I pulled up my hood and fell asleep eventually, but woke suddenly when feeling a kick at my leg. I opened my eyes to find that Maud had wriggled across the floor to lie next to me – her face against mine, our lips nearly meeting. I rubbed my eyes and saw the dawn light creeping into the cottage through the gaps in the rafters above. Outside, the first of the birds were singing – though their chorus was not yet loud enough to drown out Peter's snoring.

'What are you doing?' I whispered, pulling back my hood to see that Maud had managed to loosen the gag from her mouth. It now hung about her neck.

'Oswald,' she whispered. 'Please. Don't give me away. Don't wake Peter.' She looked at me with pleading eyes. 'Just hear me out. Before he wakes.'

I looked back into her face. 'What is there to say?' I asked.

'I want you to know that I don't blame you for any of this,' she whispered. 'Peter has tricked you with his lies.' I went to answer but she moved closer again, and now I could almost feel the vibration of her lips against mine. 'I've been lying awake all night thinking about this.'

'But—'

'I've worked out what happened, Oswald. So please, just listen to me. It was Rose who led me here. Not the other way around.' She paused to sigh. 'I shouldn't have followed the girl this far into the forest. I realise that now. But Rose claimed to know where to find Pestilence wort, and I felt duty-bound to go with her. Especially after the promises that I made to all the women at our meeting.'

'Why would Rose bring you to this cottage?' I asked.

'Because Peter told her to, Oswald,' she whispered. 'That's why. Don't you see?'

'Peter?'

Her breath hot against my skin. 'He gave himself away when he accused me of picking out girls for some lover. He was talking about his own relationship with Rose. Don't you see?'

'Not really.'

'It was Rose's idea that we should look inside this cottage. Not mine. As soon as we opened the door, Peter jumped out on us.'

'Rose told me that she fought Peter off.'

'That's another lie, Oswald,' she whispered. 'The girl disappeared as soon as Peter grabbed me.'

'But Rose seemed very upset when I found her.'

'That's because she's terrified of Peter,' replied Maud. 'He has some sort of hold over the girl. I think he uses Rose to find women from the village. The poor ones. The girls that nobody seems to care about.'

I went to rebut this theory, but stopped short. Peter's condemnation of Rose had always troubled me. He didn't usually pass comment on the villagers, and yet he had repeatedly made the point of calling this girl a liar. And then I remembered Rose's last words to me, when we had parted in the forest. The manner in which she had begged me not to mention her name to Peter.

Maud continued. 'I think the girl has been under his spell for many months.'

'I don't know,' I replied weakly. 'It all just sounds so unbelievable.'

She drew back a little, staring at me with those large blue eyes. Even in this dusty morning light they shone out with the colour of a still, summer's sea. Exquisitely clear and so very, very lovely. 'And yet you can believe the very worst of me?' she whispered. 'You can believe that I was luring girls into the forest for the pleasure of some man?'

I hesitated, not knowing how to answer.

'Where is he, then?' she asked me, her face darkening for a moment. 'This man. This lover, to whom I'm so devoted? Peter has had me locked inside this cottage for at least two days and this man has yet to appear.' She paused, drawing her face near to mine again. 'He's an invention, Oswald,' she whispered. 'A lie. A diversion designed to hide Peter's real purpose in locking me in here.'

'But—'

'You saved my life by coming here to find me,' she said. 'Don't you see, Oswald? Otherwise I would be dead now – my body lying in that gully you've spoken of. Alongside all those other poor women whom Peter has tortured and killed for his own pleasure.' She moved closer again – so near that I could smell the warm, spicy scent of her skin. 'There is no man coming here,' she said. 'There is no mysterious lover.' And then she kissed me – her lips hot and urgent on mine, and all of my uncertainties instantly melted away.

'I'm sorry,' I said, when our kiss finally ended. 'I should have believed you.'

'It's no matter,' she whispered. 'I'm not angry with you, Oswald. Now, please,' she said, a little more insistently. 'Untie my wrists and ankles. Quickly. Before Peter wakes up.'

I rose to my feet slowly, careful not to make any noise, before I pulled out my sword to cut at the rope about her ankles. When I had succeeded in freeing her feet, I helped her to stand, finding that she was stiff and lame after two days of being bound. She was unsteady and she soon lost her balance – falling with enough movement to wake Peter.

He sat up and peered across the room. 'Oswald?' he said, scrambling to his feet when he saw that I'd freed Maud. 'By corpus' bones! What have you done now?'

I was about to answer, when we heard a noise from outside – the sound of hooves approaching the cottage at a canter. I instinctively stopped to listen, giving Peter the opportunity to grab Maud – placing his hand over her mouth while my attention was elsewhere. Though she squealed for my help, I found myself frozen to the spot.

Whoever it was outside, they circled the cottage once and then came to a halt nearby. A few moments of silence followed, before we heard footsteps, loud and confident as they strode towards the door.

Brother Peter glared at me, urging me not to make a sound and give our presence away, but I ignored his warning. Raising my short sword, I crept over to the door and then flung it open to find a familiar face standing at the threshold. The shock of this meeting was mutual.

'What are you doing here?' I asked, dropping my sword a little.

My brother ignored my question. 'Oswald,' he said brightly. 'So this is where you've been hiding, is it? I've been looking for you everywhere. Ever since you disappeared from Somershill.'

'How did you know that I was here?' I felt a sudden rush of blood – beating inside my ear like a baton against a drum.

Again he ignored the question, as a quizzical look crossed his handsome face. His long brown lashes blinked over his almond-shaped eyes. His full lips curled into an arrogant smile. The sun caught the end of his ears as they poked out from his hair. 'We've all been very worried about you,' he said, trying to look over my shoulder into the gloom of the cottage, alerted by the sound of Maud's muffled whining. 'Have you got a woman in there?'

'No.'

'What's that noise then?'

'There's nobody here,' I insisted, though this was impossible to deny when Maud managed to break free of Peter's muzzling hand and scream out loud. Hearing this, William pushed past me and strode into the cottage. I followed him inside to find that Peter now had Maud in a neck hold – the tip of his dagger digging into her throat.

'What's going on?' said William, as his eyes met Maud's. I couldn't help but see the look that passed between them. It only lasted for the briefest of moments, but I will never forget its intensity. I knew then that William was the man we'd been waiting for.

'Do something, William,' Maud gasped, looking at my brother with wild, terrified eyes. 'Help me.'

My brother drew his own short sword from its scabbard then pointed it at Peter. 'Let her go.'

Peter shook his head and pressed the dagger a little harder into Maud's neck, causing her to scream again. 'We know what happens in this place,' he told William. 'We know that this whore brings women here for you.'

William laughed. 'What nonsense is this?'

'You didn't come here to find Oswald,' said Peter. 'You came here to rape and kill.'

'Have you been drinking again, Brother Peter?' William turned to me. 'Make this man see some sense, will you? Before I'm thoroughly insulted.'

The thumping inside my ears had turned to a sharp ringing. I felt dazed and nauseous. 'I found the bodies, William,' I said, my voice a weak mumble.

'What was that?' he said. 'Speak up, Little Brother.'

I took a deep breath. 'I said that I found the bodies, William. I know it's you.'

William only made a short pretence at bafflement, before he dropped the act – striding over to push his face into mine. 'Is that right?' he said.

Peter shouted across the room. 'Take care, Oswald,' he warned. 'He's dangerous.'

'I know it's you,' I whispered, taking a step backwards and feeling the vomit rise in my throat. 'I know what you've done.'

William didn't bother to answer this accusation. Instead he grabbed me, twisting my head into a stranglehold, with his elbow looped beneath my chin. I could hear my brother's breathing. Fast and heavy, as he pushed the tip of his sword into my back, finding a gap between my ribs. Even though I was still holding a weapon, there was nothing I could do to defend myself. William could have killed me with a single jab.

William shouted across the room to Peter. 'Let Maud go.'

'Or what?' replied Peter. 'You would kill your own brother? To save this whore?'

William twisted the sword between my ribs, piercing the surface of my skin. I couldn't help but flinch, which was more than enough cause for Peter to surrender Maud. He would never take any risks with my life. 'She's yours,' he said, hurling Maud across the room. 'Have her.'

William released me in return and I was able to scramble to Peter, whereupon the old monk grasped me in an intense hug. I soon realised that the purpose of Peter's embrace went beyond affection, however. When I broke away from his clasp, I turned around to see that Maud was planting desperate kisses onto William's lips.

Peter sighed. 'I'm so sorry, Oswald,' he whispered. 'I tried to tell you.'

As they parted, Maud threw me a victorious glance and suddenly I felt overwhelmed with a ferocious hatred for the woman. My hand tightened on my sword and I went to attack. 'Not yet,' said Peter, holding me back.

William pulled at Maud. 'Come on,' he said, heading for the door. 'Let's go.'

Maud didn't move. 'No,' she said. 'We can't leave them.'

William thought about this for a moment. 'They can't do us any harm, Maud.'

'But they know everything.'

'So what?' replied William. 'Who would believe their story?'

Once again my brother tried to leave the cottage, but once again Maud refused to move. 'I'm not so sure,' she said. 'They could cause trouble for us, William. I think we need to . . .' She dropped her voice to a whisper, though the nature of her proposal was obvious.

Peter stiffened. 'There are two of us, William,' he said coolly. 'You would find it difficult to kill a pair of men. Especially as we're armed.' Peter brandished his dagger and tipped my elbow, encouraging me to do the same with my own weapon. I tried to keep my sword steady, but my hand trembled like a reed in the wind.

William only laughed at this show of strength. 'What? Am I supposed to be afraid of you? Is that it?'

'It's two against one,' said Peter.

This caused William to laugh again. 'Yes. But you're an old drunk.' He said, before pointing at me. 'And what is Oswald? A milksop, raised by monks.'

'At least I'm not a rapist and a murderer,' I replied.

This riposte instantly killed his amusement. 'You should have kept your nose out of my business, Little Brother,' he growled, as a thin ray of sunlight crept through a gap in the roof and fell upon the bridge of his nose. His eyes were kept in shadow — hidden in their black sockets.

'Agnes was your daughter,' I said. 'A fourteen-year-old girl.'

'It's your fault that girl is dead,' he said, taking another step forward, and finally revealing his eyes to the light. They were wolf's eyes. Cold and predatory. 'You chased her into a river.'

'No,' I said. 'I only made a mistake, William. I was a fool.' I paused. 'But you . . . You raped and killed your own flesh and blood.'

We gazed at one another in silence for a long while, but I knew that my insolence would not go unpunished. Within a moment he had launched himself across the room with the intention of killing me — and he would have suceeded, had Peter not thrown himself between us, pushing William aside.

My brother retaliated immediately, slashing at Peter's arm and inflicting a wound that drew blood. As Peter recoiled, William returned his attentions to me. I tried to defend myself, of course — but I was hardly a match for a man of William's strength and savagery. He soon had me pinned against the wall, about to strike the lethal blow, when Peter came to my salvation once again. Lunging forward in wild desperation, he managed to stab my brother in the thigh, plunging his dagger deep into the flesh.

William screamed out in agony, dropping his sword onto the floor — before he limped away to the other side of the room, where Maud scooped him up in her arms. While she comforted William, Brother Peter quickly grabbed William's weapon from the floor and called upon me to raise my sword again. Our plan was to pounce upon William while he was injured, but we should have known better. It would be much harder to defeat my brother than this.

'Keep away from me,' he snarled, pulling the bloodied dagger from his thigh as we approached. 'Or I'll kill you both.' We retreated immediately, knowing that there is little more dangerous than an injured animal.

Maud pressed a rag against the bleeding wound on William's leg, but he responded by pushing her away. 'Get off me,' he snarled, turning on her with no warning. 'I don't want your help.'

'But—'

He didn't let Maud finish the sentence. 'You stupid whore,' he said, his face twisting with pain as he rubbed at his bleeding leg. 'This is all your fault.'

Maud stiffened at his words, before another emotion took hold. It was an expression that I'd never seen on her face before. In that instant, I saw that she was afraid of my brother.

William continued. 'You brought them here,' he hissed at Maud. 'You led them to me.'

She creased her brow into a frown, and I could see that she was both frightened and bewildered by my brother's sudden turn. 'I didn't mean to do it, William,' she said. 'I swear it.'

'Of course you didn't *mean* it,' he said through clenched teeth, as he continued to wince in pain. 'Just like you didn't *mean* to bring me my own daughter. Just like you didn't *mean* to let her escape before we killed her.'

Maud attempted to stroke William's arm. It was pathetic and desperate to watch. 'I swear to you, William,' she said again. 'I had no idea that Agnes was your daughter. I always thought that she was Ned Wheeler's child. I would never have brought her to you if I'd known.' Her stroking became a frantic pawing, which William only tolerated until Maud tried to kiss him again. At this point he struck her cheek with the back of his hand – delivering a cracking blow, so loud it reverberated about the cottage.

Maud fell to the floor, clutching her hands to her face. 'I'm so sorry, William,' she sobbed. 'I only want to please you. You know that.'

As William stood over her and glowered, I felt an unexpected pang of sympathy for Maud, despite everything. I felt the urge to go to her aid, but Peter held me back. 'It's too late, Oswald,' he whispered. 'You can't help her now.'

William continued, his words to Maud delivered with contempt. 'I think you did know about Agnes,' he said. 'I think you brought her to me on purpose.'

'No,' she whimpered. 'That's not true.'

'That's just the sort of trick you like to play on me, isn't it?' he said. 'Always trying to provoke me. Always trying to gain the advantage.'

Maud threw herself at William's feet. 'No, no. That's not right, William,' she said. 'That's not true. Not a word of it.'

'They're lying to you, William. Can't you see?' she said, suddenly pointing at Peter and me. 'Agnes Wheeler wasn't your daughter,' she said. 'How could she be a de Lacy? You could never have fathered a village runt like that. She was a nothing. A nobody!'

William thought for a moment. This argument obviously appealed to him. Sensing the opportunity to redeem herself, Maud stumbled to her feet. 'We mustn't believe their lies, William,' she said. 'They're trying to cause you pain with this story about Agnes. They're trying to divide us.' When William didn't rebuff her immediately, she began to stroke his arm again. 'Don't let them do this to us, William,' she whispered. 'We always promised that nothing could come between us. That we are the same soul, only in two bodies.' Maud lifted her hand to his cheeks. 'We love each other, William,' she whispered. 'Don't let them part us.'

As William stared into Maud's face, Peter nudged me. Now was our chance. We advanced across the room again, only to find that we had caught William's eye immediately. He looked over Maud's shoulder and fixed me with his gaze – the same look that I'd seen too often as a child. His eyes were glinting with malicious pleasure as he turned to kiss Maud. As I saw their lips meet, I felt a painful stab at my heart, but this was nothing compared to the horror I then experienced. Within a flash my brother had plunged Peter's dagger into the side of Maud's neck – his movement fast and accurate, like the practised blow of a slaughterer.

Maud clasped her hands to the wound and screamed in shock and pain – the blood immediately pumping through her fingers and flooding her gown with its surging flow. 'William?' she rasped, her face twisted in disbelief. 'Why? Why would you do this? I don't understand.'

'I'm not the other half of your soul, Maud,' he said calmly, before he grabbed his lover by the upper arms and threw her into our path.

As my brother limped out of the hut, Peter rushed to Maud's aid, trying to stem the wound at her throat with the cloth of his habit. But I couldn't move. I just couldn't get my feet to obey the instruction.

Peter looked up at me. 'Go after him, Oswald,' he shouted, nodding towards the door. 'Don't let your brother get away.'

I finally came to my senses and ran outside in pursuit of William, only to find that he had already mounted his horse and retreated to a vantage point within the trees. William held one hand to the wound on his leg, and was leaning forward to rest against his horse's neck. I could see that he was still in great pain.

I raced towards him, my hatred and rage now surging. 'You're a monster,' I shouted. 'You'll hang for this.'

He managed to kick at his horse with his good leg and moved beyond my reach. 'Just go back to your monastery, Little Brother,' he called out from a safe distance. 'And keep your mouth shut.'

'No, I won't keep quiet,' I responded. 'You'll pay for what you've done. I'll make sure of that!'

'But who will believe you, Oswald?' He laughed. 'Who will care about a few dead women from a little village? Their lives mean nothing. To nobody.' With those words, he kicked at his horse's flanks again and disappeared into the trees.

I sank to the ground, dropping my head between my knees and sobbing into the soil, as Brother Peter joined me with the news that Maud was dead. He had the good sense to leave me alone for a moment, before he placed a hand softly on my shoulder.

'Come on, Oswald,' he whispered. 'We should leave, before William comes back.'

I looked up into Peter's face. My vision was blurred with tears. 'But what about Maud?' I said. 'And those other bodies? Shouldn't we bury them?'

'No, Oswald,' he replied. 'We need to think of ourselves now.' He pushed the hair from my face. 'The dead can take care of themselves.'

Chapter Thirty-four

Somershill, November 1370

Mother cupped her hands to her face and stared. 'Is this true, Oswald?' she whispered. 'William really did those things? Those terrible things.'

I nodded and took her hand. 'I'm so sorry.'

'Why didn't you tell me about this before?' she whispered. 'When you first came home from the monastery?'

'It was too difficult, Mother. Father, William and Richard had only just died of plague.'

'Did you think I wouldn't believe you?' she said, now close to tears. 'Was that it?'

I shrugged, not knowing how to answer – and so we sat in silence until she spoke again. Her voice now thin and hoarse.

'This doesn't come as a complete shock to me, Oswald,' she whispered. 'Not really.' She beckoned for me to draw nearer. 'There was always a trace of evil in William. I could see it from the moment he was born. But this . . . I never suspected this.' She took my hand and squeezed it in her own. 'I should have taken the whip to him when he was young, Oswald. I should have beaten this cruelty out of him.'

'This is not your fault,' I said. 'It's nobody's fault. William made himself into this monster. Nobody could have stopped him.'

Mother gave a slow, melancholic shake of her head. 'I never understood him, Oswald. You should know that. Though I grew him in my own womb, and fed him at my own table.' She coughed, struggling again to keep back her tears. 'But I never thought that I'd raised a demon.' She waved at the cup beside her bed. 'Just give me a drink,' she said. 'And not from that boiled meadow grass. I'm a human, not a horse. I want wine. Decent wine.'

I refreshed her cup from the decanter of Malmsey that had been placed in the room for my benefit, gently lifting the wine to her lips and letting her take a number of sips, until the wine left a red moustache on her top lip.

The Malmsey was soothing, but it also exhausted her, and I thought she might close her eyes again and try to sleep. But she knew, as well as I did, that this story was not yet over. She forced her eyes to stay open as she slowly patted her breast, tapping at the letter that still remained, as ever, in its place of safety.

'Well, Oswald,' she said. 'Thank you for your honesty. This was not a story that I wanted to hear. But it was right for me to know it, before I die.' She pulled out the letter and waved it, under my nose. 'But you still haven't explained this.'

Chapter Thirty-five

Kent, July 1349

Brother Thomas finally opened the gates of Kintham, once Peter had insisted on speaking to the Abbot. My tutor was blessed with many skills, and the ability to win an argument through a combination of persuasion and threat was his speciality. Peter's contention that a monastery cannot function without its infirmarer when a plague is raging, was sufficient to persuade the Abbot to raise the portcullis. (That and Peter's threat to spread salacious rumours about the Abbot's enthusiasm for Syriac.)

Peter went straight back to work as soon as he had washed and dressed the wound that William had inflicted upon his arm – as if the whole horrific episode had never happened. In fact he refused to talk to me about William and Maud's crimes at all, and made it clear that the subject was closed between us. When I argued that we should write to the Sheriff or even inform the Abbott, Peter lost his temper. William had been right. Nobody would believe our story. And nobody would care about the deaths of a few village girls. Especially not now, when the Plague was wiping out whole villages. Above all we needed to think of our own safety in these coming months, as William was a formidable enemy. We needed to keep our mouths shut and try to return to our life as usual. We could only hope that William would leave us alone.

But I could not return to my usual life so easily. Instead, I lay in bed for many days, my mood swinging between anger and melancholia, as Peter explained away my condition to the other brothers by pretending that I'd been attacked by bandits. He brought me tonics made of dandelion and horehound and even tried to encourage prayer. When I was sad and despairing of human nature, he suggested that I went out for a walk around the gardens, or groom one of the ponies . . . as if this would help? I felt contaminated by association. I had allowed William to befriend me during our time together at Somershill, flattered to have been noticed at last by my older brother. And I had fallen in love with Maud — allowing her beauty and grace to blind me to her true ugliness.

But I could not stay cooped up in my cell forever. Especially not when the monastery had shut itself off from the world and was preparing for plague. Eventually I found respite by returning to my old duties and chores in the infirmary, as there is something calming and restorative about a routine. But my fragile peace was not to last.

I was boiling poppy heads one morning, making a light sedative for the old monk with the amputated leg, when Peter tapped me on the shoulder. 'There's somebody at the gate to see you,' he said.

I turned around, surprised at this news. 'Who's that?'

Peter immediately put a hand over his mouth to deflect the odour of brandy on his breath. I was surprised he smelt so pungent this early in the day, and this caused me to feel nervous immediately. My suspicions were vindicated when I heard Peter's reply. 'It's William,' he told me.

'William?' I echoed. 'My brother William?' Peter nodded. 'What's he doing here?' I said, feeling the blood drain from my face.

'Don't worry,' replied Peter. 'The Abbot won't let him past the gatehouse.' He paused. 'But I've spoken to him myself.'

'What does he want?'

Peter paused again. 'He says that he wants to talk to you, Oswald.'

'Absolutely not.'

Peter cleared his throat. 'I think you should hear what he has to say.'

Our raised voices had drawn the attention of a monk in a nearby bed, so I pulled Peter to one side. 'My brother is a murderer,' I whispered. 'Why would I want to talk to him?'

Peter sighed. 'You won't like me saying this, Oswald,' he replied. 'But it might be best to try to appease him.' He forced a smile. 'And I don't know what other choice we have,' he added. 'Given the circumstances.'

'No,' I repeated. 'I won't do it.'

Peter's smile disappeared. 'Perhaps he wants to ask your forgiveness?'

'I doubt it.' I said. 'It's more likely that he's come here to kill me.'

'He can't harm you, Oswald,' said Peter. 'He'll be one side of the portcullis. And you will stand on the other. I'll wait nearby. Just in case he gets difficult.' When I didn't answer this, he added. 'William would not risk attacking you here, Oswald. There would be too many witnesses.'

I shook my head, still not convinced. 'No. I won't do it,' I said adamantly, turning back to stir the poppies. 'I never want to see him again.'

'You must, Oswald,' insisted Peter, now grasping me by the arm. 'It would look bad if you refused to speak to your own brother.' He leant forward to whisper softly into my ear. It was the tone he had used with me since I had been a boy. The encouraging, soothing voice that persuaded me to overcome an obstacle, or meet a new challenge. 'Please, Oswald,' he said. 'Just see what he wants at the very least. We're in a very difficult situation and it might help us to know William's intentions.' He paused. 'That's all I ask of you.'

Peter walked me to the portcullis and then stepped back a few yards, so that William and I were able to speak in private. A warm breeze was blowing through the tunnel of the gatehouse, sieved through the lattice of the wooden and metal bars.

My brother was an arm's length from me. His lupine eyes staring intently through the grille.

'What do you want?' I said, forcing myself to meet his gaze. Even though there was a portcullis between us, I still felt vulner-able. As if he might poke a sword through one of the gaps and stab me in the chest. I made sure to keep a safe distance.

His face relaxed into an insincere smile. 'I've come to see how my little brother fares during this plague,' he said. 'Is that a crime?'

'Don't lie to me,' I replied. 'You're here to scare me into silence.'

He shrugged in response. 'My leg is better,' he remarked. 'In case you were wondering.'

'You're a rapist and a murderer, William,' I hissed, stepping nearer to the grille. 'I don't care about your leg.'

This prompted him to laugh. 'Oh come on, Oswald. It was hardly a crime. They were just village girls. Little ants.'

'Ants?' The word winded me. 'And you were the giant, I suppose?'

'Yes, that's right,' he replied. 'Well remembered.'

'Just go away,' I said. 'You disgust me.' I foolishly leant forward to utter these words, giving William the opportunity to reach through the grille and grasp my arm.

'Listen to me, Oswald,' he said, pulling me roughly against the bars. I could sense Brother Peter hovering behind me, but he didn't come to my aid as he'd promised. My tutor was deter-mined that I should hear my brother out.

'Get off me,' I spat.

William's teeth were clenched. 'I *am* a giant, don't you see? That's what you need to appreciate.'

'No, you're not,' I replied. 'That's a pathetic delusion. You're just a man, like anyone else.'

'No. I'm a giant,' he repeated. 'But so are you, Oswald de Lacy. We are cut from the same rock.'

'I am nothing like you,' I said. 'Nothing at all.'

He stared at me without blinking. At this close proximity I could see that he was agitated. Crazed even. The whites of his eyes were bloodshot and his hair was wet and sticking to his head. I could smell the sweat on his skin. 'I came here to tell you something,' he said. 'Something that you need to understand. As my brother. As a de Lacy who owes me allegiance.'

With this warning, he released his grip, and though I contemplated running away, I kept my feet rooted to the spot and my eyes fixed upon his face. At some level I wanted to hear what William had to say.

'Go on then,' I mumbled. 'What is it?'

'I'm not like other men, Oswald,' he said without a trace of embarrassment. 'I've known I'm extraordinary since I was nine years old.'

'What do you mean?'

'Something happened to me at that age, Oswald,' he replied. 'Something that changed my life forever.' He paused. 'I've never explained this to anybody else. But I think you will understand. You, more than anybody else.'

'Go on then,' I said.

His eyes suddenly glazed over, as if he wasn't talking to anybody in particular. 'I had climbed the north-west tower at Somershill,' he said, 'and I stood exactly where you and I spoke recently.' He gave a short laugh at this. 'It was the very same spot. As if the Fates had intervened and demanded that we have that conversation.' He paused to push the hair from his forehead.

'It was the usual type of day for me, as a nine-year-old boy. I was hiding from Father because he'd just beaten me again. I was full of shame and resentment. I felt worthless and angry. I even thought about throwing myself over the wall and falling to my death below. In fact, I would have done it, Oswald,' he said. 'I wanted to kill myself.' He paused. 'Does that surprise you?'

I nodded. It did surprise me. I had never imagined that my brother might have contemplated suicide.

'I climbed onto the wall and looked down at the ground below, imagining what death would feel like. Imagining the feeling as my head hit the hard soil and my skull smashed into pieces. But, as I stood there, I suddenly had the urge to look up instead of down. It was as if a voice whispered the idea into my ear and told me to do it. And then, as I looked out across the horizon, another feeling overtook me. It happened so suddenly, Oswald. As if all the powers in the universe were speaking to me at the same time. Instead of feeling small and helpless, I was filled with joy and utter comprehension. Suddenly everything made sense.'

'God's bones, William,' I said. 'What are you talking about?'

My scorn didn't register. His eyes were now glistening, wide open with madness. It was an expression I recognised of old — pulled by penitents at the sight of a holy shrine. A sort of dazed earnestness, as they are overcome with rapture. 'In that moment, I looked up to see the vastness of the world before me, Oswald. I saw its splendour and wonder, stretching out into infinity. But then, when I looked down, I saw the village and all those feeble-minded little people, scuttling here and there. Never looking up from their wretched, meaningless lives, and I knew that I was nothing like them. In that moment I knew that I didn't need to pretend any more. I *was* a giant. The heavens had just told me so. I was a de Lacy, and one day I would be Lord Somershill. Whereas those others . . . they were just insects. Nothing better than maggots.'

I felt stunned. 'I thought you said they were ants?'

He laughed at this. 'No, Oswald. I only used that word for your sakes. To be polite. I know you still suffer from youthful sensitivities.'

'And what about Maud?' I whispered. 'Was she a maggot as well?'

'Yes. Of course she was.'

'She was your lover, William. Your accomplice.'

His face darkened. His jaw jutted forward. Now he looked less like an elated penitent, and more like a backstreet brawler. 'I didn't love Maud Woodstock,' he scoffed. 'She was the worst of them. A grasping, ambitious maggot.' He ran his fingers through his hair. 'All that foolery in the forest was her idea, you know. She was always trying to find ways to please me. It was pathetic.'

'It was rape and murder,' I said. 'Not foolery.' And I don't believe that it was all Maud's idea.'

William grasped the bars of the portcullis with his hands. 'No, Oswald. You're wrong about that. It was her fault. She dreamt up the whole scheme for her own pleasure. I only joined in because I was bored.'

'Maud was your devoted slave, William. She did as you told her.'

'Nonsense. She was an irritation. A pest. Always following me around. Asking when I was going to get rid of my wife and marry her instead.' William laughed contemptuously. 'As if that was ever going to happen.'

'But you allowed Maud to persist in the delusion, didn't you? To believe that you loved her, so that she would carry on bringing women for you. I think you even killed off a string of her suitors.'

'Then you are the one who's deluded,' he replied. 'I didn't kill those men. Maud did. Apparently they weren't good enough for her to marry,' he said, now gripping the bars so tightly that his knuckles were white. 'Maud wanted to kill you as well, you know. I had to talk her out of it. I told her enough times. Keep an eye on Oswald's investigation, but nothing else.'

'I don't believe that.'

'Oh come on,' said William, dropping his hands from the bars. 'Stop being so gullible. The woman was even killing her own father. Slowly poisoning the man so she could watch his suffering.'

'Why would she do that?'

'To punish the man with a slow death, of course. Because of some cruelties that he supposedly perpetrated against her as a child. That's the sort of woman she was.'

I thought back to Roger Woodstock's bedchamber and Johanna's story about the potion Maud had purchased from a woman in Winchester. No wonder the old man was regaining his speech now that Johanna had replaced Maud's decoction with her own. In time he might even make a full recovery?

I had been foolish not to see what was happening. And then another thought came to me. 'Were you poisoning our father as well?' I asked.

William wrinkled his nose. 'What?'

'Is that why he's forgetting names and hiding food?'

'No, no,' said William. 'Don't be so foolish. You're wilfully misunderstanding what I'm saying to you. Why don't you listen for once?' He shook his head in frustration, nearly knocking his forehead against the bars. 'I don't care for Father, but his deterioration is natural. It has nothing to do with me.'

'How can I believe that?'

'Because Father is a de Lacy, Oswald!' he said, leaning his face through a square in the portcullis. His complexion had regained its sheen of sweaty madness. 'His blood flows in our veins. He is our family. And you never turn on your own family, Oswald. Never.'

'What about Agnes?' I said. 'She was your family.'

William drew back into the shadows, and now I could only see his eyes, bloodshot and wild. 'She was not my daughter,' he said. 'You're wrong about that.'

'Yes, she was,' I replied. 'You know it's true.'

'No,' he hissed. 'Agnes Wheeler was just a village girl. A maggot. I couldn't have fathered a girl like that.'

'You're lying to yourself, William,' I said. 'You recognised her mother's name. Your face gave you away.'

William grasped the bars and leant through the small gap to shout at me. 'SHE WAS NOT MY DAUGHTER!'

Our eyes met for a moment, before he pulled back – taking a moment to compose himself. When he reappeared at the bars, his manner was becalmed. His voice unemotional. 'Listen to me, Oswald,' he said. 'I'm going to tell you what will happen now. You will stay at Kintham and you will keep your mouth shut about these women.'

'Or what?'

He ignored this question. 'I expect you to take your vows in the coming months, work hard for a few years and then become Abbot. You will serve your family, and you will serve me, your lord.'

'I will never serve you,' I replied. 'Not ever. I hate you, William. And I will never forget what you've done.'

'Very well then,' he replied solemnly. 'You disappoint me, Oswald. But I feared this would happen.'

He leant down to pick up a box that I hadn't noticed before. It was a small wooden cube, no bigger than a casket for a reliquary.

'This is for you, Oswald,' he said, passing the box through the bars of the portcullis. 'A keepsake from Somershill.'

'I don't want it.'

'But it belongs to you,' he replied, holding the box out until I agreed to take it from him. 'I couldn't keep it.'

His eyes fixed upon mine for one last time. 'Until we meet again, Little Brother,' he called out, as he limped back towards his horse. The dagger wound was still troubling him, as he climbed with some difficulty into the saddle.

'Don't forget,' he shouted, as he turned back to wave at me. 'When the Abbot opens these gates, I'll be your first visitor.' With these words, William kicked at his horse's side and cantered away into the distance.

Brother Peter quickly joined me. 'Was that a threat?' he said nervously. 'It sounded like a threat to me.' I couldn't help but notice that Peter was twitching. 'What did you say to William?' he asked. 'I hope you didn't antagonise him?'

'I didn't promise my silence,' I replied. 'If that's what you mean?'

Peter rolled his eyes and cursed to himself, before pointing at the box. 'What's this, then?' he asked.

'William said it was a gift.'

'What sort of gift?'

'How should I know?' I replied, trying to lift the lid, only for Peter to snatch the box from me.

'Let me look first,' he said.

'Why?'

'In case there's something dangerous inside.'

'Like what?'

Peter didn't answer. Instead he opened the box and pulled out a small object. 'What's this?' he asked me, holding the thing aloft.

I took it from him. It was my pewter knight. My childhood treasure. William must have found him at the top of the north-west tower, after I'd dropped him there. I held the little knight up to the light. His tiny body was still mounted on his horse, but his head was destroyed. Crushed beyond recognition.

Chapter Thirty-six

I suppose there are many reasons why a person will take a life. Sometimes the victims of such violence turned up in the infirmary at Kintham – brought into our care by their friends or relatives, in the vain hope that we could save their lives. (It was rarely possible.) There was the man who'd been stabbed in the chest by his rival in love. Or the woman who'd been beaten about the head by her drunken husband. Or even the old man who'd been robbed and left for dead beside the road. I understood the motives behind these attacks – jealousy, anger, greed. Such reasons were simple and straightforward. They made sense.

But little had made sense about Maud and William until I'd spoken to my brother that day. Only then had I come to truly understand the reason for their crimes. Undoubtedly they had both been born with arrogant, cruel and merciless natures. It also seemed that they had both experienced some ill-treatment at the hands of their fathers as children. But their real misfortune had been to find one another. Like two malefic planets, they had crossed the skies without causing harm until their paths crossed – when together they had created the darkest of conjunctions.

I shared this theory with Peter, but he accused me of being too poetic. Of romanticising their base and squalid depravity with this grand description. To his mind they were just a pair of monsters who gained gratification from inflicting pain upon another person.

They were no better than two rotten apples. Stuck together in a barrel, they had decayed more quickly by touching.

In the end I had to expel all thoughts of their crimes from my mind. It was too disturbing. Too polluting. And so I threw myself back into my work, taking on extra tasks in the infirmary. Even though plague raged outside the walls of Kintham, we continued to be safe inside our refuge. Our patients at the infirmary were only suffering from the usual complaints to trouble a monastery full of old men. A swollen toe. An unexplained ache. A slow digestion.

Little did we know however, that our apparent safety had started to breed a dangerous complacency – particularly when it came to the Abbot. Though Peter begged him to change his mind, the foolish man had ordered new gowns from London. He paid no heed to Peter's warnings that the seeds of plague can hide themselves in the warp and weft of a cloth, no matter how expensive the garment.

In the end Peter gave up. The Abbot was his superior and could do as he liked. And anyway, Peter and I had other fears to trouble us than the threat of plague. The Pestilence would abate eventually, as all plagues do, and then the gates to the monastery would open again. We both knew that William would come for us then. I only had to look at my little pewter knight to know our fate.

Knowing that our days of safety were numbered, I tried to think of ways to solve our problem and ensure that William would not kill us at the first opportunity – coming up with little of any use, until we received a surprise visit. The Abbot might have refused entry to William, but my brother was only the lord of one estate. When Earl Stephen appeared at the gates of Kintham, claiming that he wanted to confess his sins and pray for protection from the Plague, the Abbot had no choice but to raise the portcullis.

The Earl soon proved to be as unpleasant as his reputation suggested. Tall and bombastic, his voice boomed about the silent cloisters and passageways of Kintham like the call of a bittern, as he demanded food, wine, the Abbot's bedchamber and then the forgiveness of his sins (in that order). Given that the Abbot had been ejected from his own quarters, the man was understandably keen for the Earl to leave Kintham as soon as possible – so masses were hastily said in the man's honour, and speeches were given at every opportunity – extolling the Earl's many personal virtues and saintly accomplishments. The Abbot hoped, no doubt, that the Earl would take the hint and leave Kintham at the first opportunity – feeling confident that his soul was now saved – and yet his stay endured. It seemed we were not the only men to understand the advantages of hiding behind these walls.

I was introduced to Earl Stephen briefly, since I was a de Lacy. As a tenant in chief, Earl Stephen held many of the lands in this part of Kent from the King himself, including my father's estate at Somershill. It was through this arrangement that my family paid our allegiance to the crown, providing men from our villages to fight in the King's armies.

I was taken to the Earl's quarters and told to make conversation with the man, though it was difficult for an eighteen-year-old novice to find any common ground with a gnarled and battle-scared veteran of many wars. Thankfully the meeting was short – but it was during my time with the Earl that an idea came to me. A way that I might finally solve our problem with William.

The Earl had arrived at Kintham with a single guard and a single valet, but both of these servants were enjoying some relaxation from their usual duties, as there was little for them to do. The valet was mostly excused from dressing the Earl in his finest clothes each night, since there were no women to impress. The guard had nothing to guard, since the walls of Kintham were thick and the gates were locked. Given this general lack of care and attention, it was easy for me to wander back into the Earl's bedchamber one morning and borrow his seal.

And this was not my only act of appropriation. The same day I had also taken a square of the best parchment, a quill and some ink from the scriptorium without anybody noticing. Once I had a private moment, I assembled my tools and material, and set about my task. It was only as I finished that I realised Peter was looming over my shoulder. It seemed that I could do nothing without his interference.

'What's that?' he asked, pointing to the letter I'd just written.

'Nothing,' I said, trying to push it from his view.

'Why are you hiding it from me, then?' he asked, grasping it from me before I was able to stop him.

He read it aloud.

To William de Lacy,

    I am writing to request that you join me in Rochester, one week from today's date, as a matter of urgency. (Please come no later than ten days from now.) When you arrive in the town, make your presence known at the Angel Inn, near to the East Gate. The innkeeper will send a messenger to inform me that you have arrived, and I will come to visit you there myself. Do not travel to my hall, as I wish to discuss this matter with you in complete secrecy. I will not state the entirety of my business here, but it is enough to say that the matter under discussion will be greatly in your interests.

    The effects of plague have been devastating to our society, but where there is devastation there is also opportunity. I am looking for a select group of men, with whom I can forge a bright new future. A future that takes advantage of these unexpected opportunities. Those estates that have become vacant, thanks to this plague, are now available to families of the right calibre. There are profits to be made, and new land to occupy. I am approaching you before all of my other tenants, so I expect your complete discretion. Please do not acknowledge this letter, nor discuss it with anybody else. Until we meet in Rochester.

    Your Lord, Earl Stephen. Written in haste on the Wednesday following Assumption Day.

I expected Peter to be angry, but instead he handed the letter back to me, before drawing up a seat next to mine. He sat silently for a while, before he finally spoke. 'This is a risky plan,' he said.

I didn't answer.

Peter continued. 'What if William doesn't want to meet the Earl?'

'He'll go,' I said, pointing to the words on the letter and reading them aloud. '*There are profits to be made, and new land to occupy.*' William will not be able to resist such a bait,' I added. 'Also, William would not dare disobey the Earl. The man speaks for the King.' I paused. 'I can guarantee that my brother will be in Rochester within the next ten days.'

Peter swayed his head from side to side, and I could tell that he was still doubtful about my scheme. But, at least he had not screwed up the letter, nor given me a lecture about thieving. He drummed his fingers against his thighs. 'You are relying heavily on chance,' he said. 'That is the flaw in this plan. The chance that William will believe the letter comes from the Earl.'

'Why wouldn't he?' I said, lifting the borrowed seal from my lap, where it had been hiding. 'This belongs to the Earl. Once I've stamped the letter, it will appear completely genuine.'

Peter looked surprised for a moment, and I thought he might chastise me – but this surprise soon altered into something else. I think that he was actually impressed with me at last.

'Very well, Oswald,' he said. 'You've solved one problem. But there are other elements of chance at play here. Let's say that William believes this letter is genuine, how can we be sure that he'll visit a town that's notoriously ravaged with plague?'

'William is arrogant,' I said. 'Conceited enough to believe that the plague won't affect him because he's a nobleman. A de Lacy.'

'And what if it doesn't affect him?' asked Peter. 'What if he doesn't catch the Plague and die?' He paused and fixed me with a stare. 'I'm assuming that is the crux of your plan, isn't it? To lure your brother into a trap and leave the rest to fate?'

I hesitated. 'Do you have any other ideas?'

Peter pulled at the mole on his neck, twisting the flesh between his finger and thumb. 'But what if William is protected from plague somehow? Let's say, for the sake of argument, that his nobility does offer him a shield against the disease.' He paused, holding up his hand to stop me from interrupting. 'If he doesn't die, then William will soon discover that he's been tricked.' He pointed to the letter. 'And then he will guess that you are behind this deception. He will know that you lured him to Rochester, in the hope that he would die.'

'So what?'

Peter drew in a breath and flared his nostrils. 'So what? I'll tell you what. He will be incandescent, and then it will not be long before he comes for us, Oswald.'

'William will come for us anyway,' I replied. 'Don't you see, Brother Peter? Once this plague has abated, we will not have a moment's peace from my brother. As soon as we leave Kintham, we will have to watch our every move, in case William lies in wait. Look at the way he killed Maud. A woman whom he supposedly loved. The man is ruthless. If we do not act now, then we will be prisoners inside this monastery for the rest of our lives.' I paused. 'Either that, or we will be dead.'

Peter looked at me, unblinking. 'You really think William would murder you, his own brother?'

I hesitated. 'He cannot allow either of us to live, Brother Peter. You know that. What if we were to tell our story?' Peter went to answer, but I continued, talking over him. 'Yes, I know that most people would dismiss the tale as preposterous . . . but not everybody. As long as we stay alive, we are a risk to William.' I paused. 'You know the truth. We must kill William, or wait for him to kill us.'

Peter sat down on the bed and allowed his fingers to wander back to the mole at his neck. 'You're right, Oswald. I see that now.' He sighed. 'And you've devised a clever plan.' He puffed the air from his cheeks and seemed to be speaking to himself. 'And we'd get justice for William's victims, wouldn't we? Not to mention the women that we would be protecting from his future attacks. Therefore our acts would not be a sin in God's eyes. It's not as if we would be the murderers ourselves.' I was about to answer, but suddenly he was on his feet, holding out his hand to me. 'Let me help you with this,' he said.

'Oh yes?' I kept my hands on the letter, not fully trusting his sudden enthusiasm.

'How do you intend to deliver this to Somershill?' he asked, ignoring my reticence.

'I'm not sure,' I admitted. I hadn't thought that far ahead.

'Let me organise a messenger,' he suggested. 'It will be easier for me to do.'

I kept my hand pressed about the parchment, feeling wary of Peter's motives. Was he trying to take the letter from me, just so that he could then destroy it? Was he still afraid of provoking my brother? 'William mustn't know that this letter has come from the monastery,' I said. 'Otherwise he might suspect that we're involved.'

Peter nodded. 'Yes. You're right.' He paused. 'In that case, I'll deliver it myself to Somershill, but I'll go in disguise.'

'You'll go yourself?' I said, my unease growing. 'Are you sure about that?'

'I can get in and out of this monastery with greater ease than anybody. And also, I can borrow some livery from the Earl's valet. The man has been in the infirmary with an ague, so I'll insist that he stays in bed for another day. It will give me time to get to and from Somershill without being missed.'

'Somebody might recognise you at Somershill?'

He shook his head. 'I will be a messenger in the livery of the Earl. I'll deliver the letter at the gatehouse and then ride away. Nobody will want to talk to me. Not at times such as these.'

He tried to take the letter from me, but I was still not quite ready to release it from my grasp. 'I don't know if I should involve you in this deception,' I said.

Peter frowned. 'Why's that?'

'It's a plan to lure a man to his death. It is a sin, however we might dress it up as righteous punishment.' I paused. 'And you are a monk. A man of God.'

'So are you,' said Peter. 'A Benedictine. Soon you will take your vows and join our brotherhood, Oswald. Your soul is every bit as important to God as mine.'

I shook my head. 'No,' I said. 'It's not.' I took a deep breath and looked to the shallow vault of the ceiling, unable to make eye contact with Peter. 'I'm not going to take my vows.'

'What?'

'I've had the time to make my decision in the last few weeks. After everything that's happened to us, I cannot continue here.' I paused. 'If I survive this plague then I will leave the monastery.'

'You can't do that.'

'Yes, I can.'

'But where will you go?' he asked. 'What will you do?'

I shrugged. 'I don't know, Brother Peter. I only know that I cannot stay here. I have no calling for this way of life.'

'But that doesn't matter, Oswald,' he said, trying to sound flippant. 'You'll get used to it, in time.'

'I've been here for ten years, Brother Peter. I am still not used to it.' I replied. 'And I never will be.'

Peter began to pace the room. 'I suppose this is your cock talking.' Before I could answer, he continued. 'I've seen it all before, Oswald. A young novice imagines himself in love with a girl, only to throw away his life for a few nights of lust.'

'I was not in love with Maud,' I said.

'But you were,' he replied, turning to point a finger into my face. 'You couldn't see past a pair of beautiful eyes and a shapely figure. You couldn't see that she had the darkest of hearts. So, how in God's name can you trust your own judgment? How in God's name can you be set free into the world?'

I grasped hold of his wrist and pushed his hand away. 'This is not about Maud, Brother Peter. Or any other woman.'

Peter sighed. Perhaps he knew what was coming. 'Then what is it about, Oswald?' he said at length. 'Please explain it to me.'

My throat was swollen and I felt a little off-balance, even though I was seated. 'I have no faith, Peter,' I said, forcing myself to speak the words aloud.

He shrugged. 'Faith comes and goes,' he replied. 'Don't worry about that.'

'I have no faith,' I repeated.

'It really isn't a problem, Oswald. God will speak to you sooner or later.' He put a hand on my shoulder. 'There are plenty of monks at this monastery who lack faith from time to time. I have suffered myself occasionally,' he said with a kind smile. 'Sometimes it completely disappears, but then it always returns.'

'I have no faith, Peter. Do you understand me?' I said. 'I never have had, and I never will.' I rose to my feet, to emphasise my point. 'I am not going to take my vows. And I am not going to become a monk. My mind is fixed on this, and you cannot dissuade me.'

Peter clenched his fists. I think he momentarily considered trying to beat some faith into me, but then retreated from the idea. 'Very well, Oswald,' he said. 'If that's what you want.'

'It is.'

'Though I have no idea what you will do with yourself,' he added. 'There is no role for you back with your family, you know. The de Lacys don't need another spare son. They already have Richard, riding about the forests with nothing to do. Even if our plan works and William dies in Rochester, you will still be surplus to requirements.'

'I don't care,' I said.

He grunted a scornful laugh at this. 'Oh, you will care,' he said. 'When you're left with nothing. You have never been poor, Oswald. You have no idea what it feels like.'

I shrugged and refused to look at him.

'How do you expect to earn a living?' he asked me. 'You will have no land. You will have no profession.'

'I don't care,' I said. 'It doesn't matter how many times you try to convince me. I will not take my vows. I will not join the Benedictines.'

He took a moment to dust down his tunic and compose himself. My confession had come as a shock, but he had borne it well enough. 'You still want to send this letter to William?' he finally asked me.

'Yes.'

He puffed his lips and sighed again. 'Yes, well. It's now more important than ever,' he said resignedly. 'If you are to leave the monastery, then we cannot have you rolling around the country at the mercy of your murderous brother, can we?'

I looked up to catch his eye. Was he being sincere? It wasn't always easy to tell with Peter, but I felt that he was. And so, I folded and sealed my letter and passed it to him. Peter would take it to Somershill that night, and we would wait to hear the news of William's death.

The wait was long. Maybe six weeks. I can't quite remember the exact timings as the Abbey was suffering troubles of its own in the meantime. The Abbot was the first to succumb to plague – thanks, no doubt, to those robes that he had foolishly ordered from London. Once the head of our order had died, there was talk of us all abandoning the Abbey – though many of the brothers continued to argue that we could be saved by praying for forgiveness. But Peter knew this strategy could never work for me. Not after confessing to my absence of faith. No amount of praying could save my soul – so he suggested that we flee the monastery and find somewhere to hide out until the danger had passed.

We had planned our escape and were ready to go. But just as we were about to leave Kintham, a messenger arrived at the gates, delivering a letter from my mother at Somershill. I opened this letter with trepidation, but this was not the news I had hoped to hear. It seemed that my plan to lure William to Rochester had both succeeded and failed.

Chapter Thirty-seven

Somershill, November 1370

Mother opened an eyelid and stared at me without saying a word. The dawn had broken at last, with pale rays peeping through the drapes, and filling the room with a melancholic, wintry light. I had been talking all night, and I was exhausted. All I wanted to do now was sleep, but the house was waking up around me and filling with noise. I could hear the cock crowing, the running feet of the first servants to rise, and the occasional bang and crash from the kitchen, as the cooks prepared for the day ahead.

For a moment, my mind strayed briefly to Filomena, but then I caught my thoughts and dragged them back to the present. Her elopement with Sir John was just too great a problem for me to address, so I deliberately threw it to the back of my mind. There were more pressing issues. By the sound of Mother's deep and laboured breathing, she was about to depart this earth at any moment. But I will admit to feeling liberated instead of sad. Mother had heard my confession and knew the truth. Now I sincerely hoped that she would offer me her forgiveness and return the letter to me. She would have her good death, and I would be free of this burden forever.

I stood up to fill my cup with wine, when she spoke to me at last. For the previous few hours she had simply nodded as I told my story, so it was jolting to hear her voice.

'Oswald,' she whispered. 'Come back over here for a moment.' I returned to her bedside and leant over to listen. I was expecting some soft words of clemency, but that is not what I received.

'What a pack of lies,' she hissed. She was not able to lift her head from the pillow, but she spoke with force, venom even.

'What do you mean?' I asked, stepping back. 'I've told you the truth. All of it.'

She coughed. Rasping and dry. 'Is that the best story you can come up with, Oswald? Did you think I would swallow such a tale, just because I'm feeling unwell?'

'That's the true story,' I said. 'Without a word of a lie.' I drew back. 'And you're not feeling unwell,' I added spitefully. 'You're dying.'

My words kindled an unexpected energy in her – as effectively as if I'd just stuck a spoon of sal ammoniac under her nose. Mother had been provoked, and suddenly found the strength to work her way up the bolster until she was nearly upright.

'You've convinced yourself of this lie, have you?' she said with a scornful flourish.

'It's not a lie. It's what happened.'

She croaked a laugh. 'You are a veritable fraud, aren't you, Oswald de Lacy? All those years, you've been telling everybody that you became Lord Somershill by some extraordinary turn of fate. What nonsense!' She held a hand to her cheek and found the energy to perform a childish parody of me. 'Oh, I didn't want the role, you know. I was going to be a monk, but then suddenly I was a lord. The honour was thrust upon me. And it's been such a terrible burden. To own a thousand acres, a village, a grand house and a stable full of fine horses.' She stopped to make the sharpest, most contemptuous snort. 'Fate indeed! You plotted it all along, didn't you, Oswald? That's what really happened. This was all a deceitful scheme so that you had somewhere to go when you left the monastery. After all, you've just admitted that you didn't care for the church. That you'd lost your faith. It is, perhaps, the only part of your story that I can truly believe.'

'It's all true, Mother. Every part.'

'Says you. But the trouble is, there's nobody to back up your story, is there, Oswald? There is only one person from this tale who remains alive. And that is you.'

I ran my hands through my hair. Despite her great age and closeness to death, I found myself wondering what it would feel like to wrap my hands about her bony neck and squeeze them tightly until she was no longer able to breathe. The moment of madness passed. 'Don't be contrary, Mother. You asked for the truth, and now you don't like it.'

She waved a bony finger at me. 'I know what you did, Oswald. So stop with your lies.' She paused. 'You are responsible for the death of your brothers and father. You wanted all three of them to go to Rochester, knowing they were certain to catch plague there. Knowing their deaths would make you Lord Somershill. You are nothing better than a cuckoo. Pushing the other eggs out of the nest.'

'No, that's not true,' I replied. 'I had to protect myself from William. That was all. I had no idea that my letter would prompt Father and Richard to accompany William to Rochester.'

She hesitated, looking at me with sheer contempt. 'So why did you invite them?' she asked.

'I didn't.'

'Oh yes, you did,' she said, pulling the letter from between her chemise and her chest and thrusting it towards me. 'It's all in here, Oswald. Your father, William and Richard were all invited to Rochester in your bogus letter. So you see. You are proven to be a liar, and here is the evidence. You didn't plan to kill one man. You planned to kill all three!'

I pulled the letter from her hand. The missive that I'd last touched over twenty years previously. The name on the outside was written in my hand – just as I remembered – but when I opened the fold of parchment, I saw immediately that the first line of the letter had been changed. Somebody had washed away the words that I'd written – *'To William de Lacy'* and amended them to read *'To Henry, William and Richard de Lacy'*. I nearly let the letter slip from my hand in shock. No wonder Mother had accused me of plotting their deaths. No wonder she had demanded to know the truth before she died.

I lifted the letter again and forced myself to read on, finding that the rest of my letter remained unchanged. It was all there, as before. The invitation to meet the Earl at the Angel Inn. The request for secrecy. The promise of learning something of advantage. It was just that very small change at the start of the letter that had caused all this trouble. The addition of two names that had altered the whole course of my life. The forger had attempted to copy my style of writing – and indeed, he had made a very good job of it – but he could not hide his deception from me.

'This letter's been altered,' I croaked. 'Brother Peter added Father and Richard's names alongside William's.'

She huffed. 'That's right, Oswald. Blame your crime on somebody else. Claim that you had nothing to do with killing innocent men.'

'But it's true, Mother,' I protested. 'Brother Peter changed my letter so that Father and Richard would also attend the meeting with Earl Stephen. He did it because . . .' I wasn't sure how to end this sentence.

Mother ended it for me. '. . . he was ambitious for you. Is that what you're going to tell me, Oswald? Your beloved Brother Peter acted in your interests, but without your knowledge. Orchestrating the deaths of the men who stood in the path of your advancement?' She closed her eyes and turned her head away from mine. The conversation had exhausted her. 'Shame on you, Oswald. Shame.'

I tried to take her hand, but she pulled it away.

'Just leave me alone,' she said. 'I don't want to look at you.'

'I'm telling you the truth, Mother. You have to believe me.'

She closed her eyes. 'Just take your letter and bring the priest. I want the Last Sacraments. I want to die.'

As the priest arrived, I sat in the solar, clutching the letter, and hardly knowing what to feel. In the end I threw the thin square of parchment into the fire and watched it burn, but felt no release with its destruction. After all, so many of Mother's words had been true. I had never been the accidental lord of Somershill, as I had always claimed. This role had not come to me via the vagaries of fate. The Wheel of Fortune had not rolled in my favour by chance. Instead, I had turned it myself, and made sure that it spun to my advantage.

And yet, I had also told Mother the truth. I had never meant to send my brother Richard and my father to their deaths. I had not written their names on the letter to lure them into the same trap I had laid for William. That part of the scheme had been Peter's, and Peter's alone. But it seemed, whatever I said, Mother would not believe me. We would part in sorrow and without reconciliation. The idea made me feel truly ill.

The morning was a sequence of comings and goings, as members of the family filed in to see my mother before she ended her time on this earth. I watched as Clemence, Henry, Mother's priest, and even our old steward, Gilbert, traipsed their way in and out of her room, each to say their farewells.

It is a strange custom to line up beside the bed of a person who is dying, like members of an audience expecting to watch a play. I hope, when I come to die, that there isn't a trail of well-wishers standing beside my bed, wanting to wave me off as I float away into oblivion. I might feel some requirement to put on a show. To utter some wise words, or make some great pronouncement about the future of the family. Or even to die quickly, now that they have all gathered together, so that I have not inconvenienced them in any way. If I have any choice in this matter, I hope to die quietly, holding a single person's hand and staring out of a window. I do not want this charade.

I had remained outside the room for many hours, when Clemence stepped out to find me. I immediately felt panicked when I looked up into her small face, seeing that her cheeks were stained with tears.

'Is she dead?' I asked.

'Nearly,' said Clemence. 'But she's asking to see you.'

'She is?'

Clemence gave a wearied smile at this. 'You know that you've always been her favourite, Oswald,' she said. 'Of course she wants to see you.'

The room seemed darker than ever before. There was a stillness, a reverence. A peaceful silence. The hurly burly of the morning had passed, and now this chamber was as quiet as a Lady Chapel.

I sat down on the stool beside Mother's bed and looked into her face, noticing immediately that the lines across her forehead had softened and the corners of her mouth were curled into a peaceful smile. She looked younger than she had done for many years – her complexion free of the stresses and strains of her life. I will forever remember her face that way. She was serene and ready for death.

As I watched her, she whispered something unintelligible. At first I thought it was delirium, but then I realised that she was saying my name. I drew my ear close to her mouth, straining to hear what she was saying.

'Oswald,' she said. 'Is that you?' She reached out a hand and took mine. Her skin was cold and hard – her fingers curled like a claw.

'It is, Mother.'

'I don't want to die with bad blood between us.' She paused to gasp for breath. 'But it was very difficult for me to hear your confession. I always suspected there was something wrong with William . . . but no mother should hear such stories about their own child.'

'I'm sorry, Mother,' I said. 'I shouldn't have told you.'

She managed a thin sigh at this. 'You had no choice,' she replied. 'I asked you to do it. I had to hear this story from your own lips, before I could forgive you . . . How else was I to have a good death?' She squeezed my fingers. 'But I took out my anger about William on you,' she whispered. 'I know that Peter added those names. It was in his nature to protect you. And so now I'm asking for your forgiveness.'

'There is nothing to forgive,' I said, lifting her cold fingers to my lips. 'Nothing at all.'

'Good,' she whispered, as I placed her hand back on the sheet. 'Because I have always loved you Oswald,' she said, staring at me, her eyes watery and blurred – studying my face until she was unable to keep her eyelids open any longer. 'Our souls have been weighed, and we part in balance.'

Epilogue

I went to look for Filomena at dawn the next morning, after Mother's body had been prepared for burial. First of all I cornered Henry and demanded to know more about the conversation he claimed to have overheard between Filomena and Sir John. I spared Henry's blushes and didn't bring up the subject of his infatuation with my wife, because I understood what he was suffering. As this story has shown, I had experienced the pain of youthful passions myself. I knew that the agony of hopeless, irrational, unrequited love was an essential part of growing up. In truth, I would recommend the experience to any young person, if only to rid their system of this affliction when they are most able to deal with it. This sort of passion is best suffered in youth. Like the itching pox, its effects worsen with age.

So, once we'd skirted around the reasons why Henry was eavesdropping on my wife's private conversation with Sir John, I was able to ascertain some information about Filomena's disappearance – though Henry's story was far from convincing. Despite Clemence's protestations to the contrary, her son really did not have a good grasp of the Venetian language. If Filomena and Sir John had been planning a tryst in that tongue, then it was impossible to see how Henry could have understood what they were saying. On the other hand, Filomena had taken money, clothes and jewellery with her, and she had not been seen for two nights.

Nor had she attempted to send a letter to explain her absence. There was no doubt that she had deserted me and she had deserted Somershill. We gave the servants to believe that their mistress had been invited to a friend's house in Edenbridge, but I could tell that the whispers and rumours had already started.

With nothing else to go on, I could only rely on Henry's account. He told me that Filomena and Sir John had agreed to meet at an inn near Tonbridge, and then to follow Watling Street to Dover. From Dover they were to start their journey to Venice. Given that they had a two-day start on me, I decided to ride with all haste towards this inn. In the hours since Mother's death, my feelings regarding Filomena's disappearance had ranged from a rage at her betrayal, through to a desperate sadness that I might never see her again. The truth was, I missed my wife desperately. More so than ever. I wanted to find her, and I wanted to bring her home.

I saddled up my horse, ready to ride for Tonbridge, but I was only an hour or so outside the village of Somershill, when I saw a figure riding towards me on the road ahead. It was Filomena. When she saw my face in the distance, she kicked her horse to a canter until she came to a halt beside me.

'I heard the news about your mother,' she said, her breath misting in the air. 'I'm so sorry, Oswald.'

'Where have you been, Filomena?' I asked. 'And why didn't you tell me where you were going?'

She looked away, too embarrassed to answer.

'There were rumours that you'd run away with Sir John,' I said. 'Henry told me that he'd overheard you both talking about Venice?'

Filomena looked up at me, her eyes flashing. 'Did you believe that story?' she asked.

I hesitated. 'No,' I said. 'I didn't believe it.'

She flushed at this. 'But you were coming to find me?'

'Yes,' I said. 'Because I was worried about you.' I paused. 'I wanted you to come home.'

Filomena looked down, letting her fingers run through her horse's mane. 'I stayed at an inn for two nights. But I was on my own, and it had nothing to do with Sir John.' She lifted her dark brown eyes back to mine. 'I just needed to know that you would bother to look for me, Oswald,' she whispered. 'I needed to know that you cared about me.'

'Of course I care for you, Filomena,' I said. 'I love you.'

'But I wasn't sure about that.'

'Why?' I asked. 'Because of Mother?'

She coughed, obviously embarrassed. 'I'm sorry, Oswald. It was childish and unfair. I realise that now. Especially when your mother was so ill.' She took a deep breath, and I knew that she was about to say something that made her highly uncomfortable. 'You see, I thought your mother was play-acting again. After all, she has been mortally ill for the last three winters and has failed to die.' She paused. 'I'm so sorry. I hope you can forgive me? I did not want to cause you more pain at this time.'

I leant over and took one of her hands. 'There's nothing to forgive, Filomena. This is not your fault. It never was.' I paused. 'I allowed my mother to intrude into our lives too often. And then, when she was dying, I had my own, selfish reasons for spending so long at her deathbed. It is my fault you felt ignored and neglected. It is I who should apologise to you.'

She sighed at this. 'I knew what to expect, Oswald,' she replied. 'When we became man and wife, I knew that your mother would always be part of our marriage.'

'But she's gone now, Filomena,' I said, taking a deep breath. 'And we're free.'

My wife gave me a sideways look. She was trying her best to appear disapproving. 'That's not very kind of you, Oswald,' she said. 'You shouldn't speak that way about the dead. Especially your own mother.'

'I didn't mean it cruelly,' I replied. 'But I think you agree?' I paused. 'Don't you?' When she refused to answer this, I added, 'Come home with me Filomena, and let's never argue about this again. I promise you all of my attention. Forever.'

She let her lips twist into one of those lovely, reserved smiles that were so hard to win. 'I don't want too much attention,' she warned me, quickly extinguishing her grin. 'It might become annoying.'

'I promise, most solemnly, not to annoy you.'

She couldn't help but smile again. 'And perhaps we could invite Sir John to come back to Somershill?'

'If you like,' I said through gritted teeth. 'But maybe it might be better to ask him next year?'

My lack of enthusiasm for this idea didn't seem to upset her. 'We could visit Hugh in Oxford, or Sandro in London?'

'Absolutely.'

'I want to pray at St Paul's and I want to walk across London Bridge.'

'We can do whatever we want, Filomena.'

She cocked her head and looked at me. 'Do you love me, Oswald?' she asked.

'Yes, Filomena. You know I do.'

'Really?'

'Forever.'

And so we turned our horses for Somershill.

Author's note

March 2021. *The Good Death* was written during the Covid-19 pandemic of 2020/21, and I must say that it was unnerving at times to be writing a novel about plague against this backdrop. So many families have been affected by this dreadful pandemic, and for some it has been truly tragic. As you would expect, our current experience has given me an even greater appreciation of the horrors endured during the Black Death of 1348-50 – a plague which killed around half of the people in western Europe. If such a horrific mortality rate were not bad enough, the people of the 14th century had no real idea what was causing the disease, nor how to cure it. They had no hospitals, no vaccines and no furlough schemes.

Naturally, fears fermented and suspicions grew, often into wild and, to our modern minds, ridiculous theories. Of course, we now know that the Black Death, or the Bubonic Plague as it is often called, is a bacterial rather than a viral infection. This deadly bacterium lives in the digestive tract of fleas which themselves live on rodents – the infamous rats of plague – and wasn't identified until 1894 by the scientist Alexandre Yersin, hence its name Yersinia Pestis. For many years, rats were held solely responsible for the spreading of plague throughout Europe, but it's now thought that the disease moved with such speed, especially in the winter months, thanks to another vector – via airborne transmission. If you were unlucky enough to inhale flea faeces, or blood droplets from a plague sufferer, then your lungs became infected with the pneumonic form of the Plague. This form quickly spread from person to person simply by coughing or sneezing – rather like flu. Those who contracted the bubonic form (via flea bites that infected the lymphatic system) at least had a slim chance of survival. However, if you caught the pneumonic form, then you died, without question.

There are many brilliantly informative books that delve deeply into the history, the epidemiology and the after-effects of the Black Death. My own favourites are *The Scourging Angel* by Benedict Gummer and *The Black Death* by John Hatcher – a book that first introduced me to the medieval concept of a 'good death'. In our more secular world, it's difficult for us to fully appreciate the importance that medieval people placed on having a 'good death'. For them it was vital to follow the correct religious procedures in the days and hours before death to make sure that they left this earth with their spiritual estate in order – having received the sacraments of confession, communion and anointing. A 'good death' would hasten the passage through Purgatory, and ensure that the gates of Heaven would be open on arrival. In his book, *The Black Death*, John Hatcher tells us that, 'In the later Middle Ages the deathbed was commonly portrayed as a battlefield where the forces of good and evil, mercy and condemnation, fought over the soul of the dying.' I hope to have given some flavour of this battle in my novel.

I've been writing books set in the 14th century for much of the last decade, and I have never failed to find myself intrigued, surprised and entertained by the texts of the medieval age. For a long time I've been fascinated by a book called *The Travels of Sir John Mandeville* – an account of one man's epic journey across Europe, the Middle East, India and China at a time when few left their own parish. The eponymous author of this book is the inspiration for my own character, Sir John.

In 1332, Sir John Mandeville left England to travel the world – returning 34 years later to tell the tale . . . or did he? Was his account a true description of his travels and his own, warped interpretation of the people and places he visited, or was the whole book a work of fiction? His account falls largely into two sections. In the first part, his account gives a recognisable and reasonably sensible description of Egypt, Cyprus, Syria and Jerusalem – acting almost as a guidebook for those who wished to make a pilgrimage to the Holy Land. But the further east Sir John travels, the more bizarre his stories become – as he visits lands that are populated with a host of imaginary savages and monsters. A couple of my own favourite descriptions include the land where people live solely on 'the smell of wild apples'. Or the isle where 'there are people whose ears are so big that they hang down to their knees'. It is easy to now laugh at Sir John's wilder descriptions – but there was a time when his book was widely read across Europe, and his stories were loved and completely believed. If nothing else, it gives us an incredible insight into the medieval mind – its love of the bizarre and its fascination with the 'other'.

Much of my novel *The Good Death* is set inside the world of the medieval monastery. Kintham Abbey is a place of my own imagination, but based on a typical Benedictine monastery of the times – the likes of which would have been commonplace in England until the Reformation, when the monasteries were dissolved on the orders of Henry VIII. The monasteries of the middle ages were incredibly wealthy organisations, holding great swathes of land across England and behaving towards their tenants in much the same way as a feudal lord. In addition to their role as land-lord, the monasteries were also central to many local livelihoods, employing a great number of workers and servants from the villages on their estates. The profits from renting land to farmers was considerable, and allowed the monasteries to support a small body of monks whose life was primarily devoted to prayer and contemplation. The monks themselves were rarely recruited from the highest echelons of society, but neither were they the sons of poor farmers or labourers. They tended, like Oswald, to be members of the minor aristocracy, as the church was seen as a respectable and stable career for a young man of some status. The perfect place for a noble family to deposit a spare son!

Inside these monasteries, the monks lived in accordance with the Rule of St Benedict. Written by Saint Benedict in 530, this rulebook espoused a way of life that centred on obedience, hard work and humility, and was the model for countless monasteries across Europe. Although Oswald finds the rigors of this life difficult to stomach, I should say that the Benedictines enjoyed a more lenient and relaxed regime compared to some of the other, more austere orders such as the Cistercians and the Carthusians. The Benedictines would find ways to circumvent the strictest rules on poverty, possessions and diets, and were known for the generosity of their hospitality. They believed in creating a community spirit within their abbeys and reaching out to the poorest in their parishes – an important function in a society that provided no other safety nets.

I have strived to re-create the world of the 14th century in each of my novels, though it has sometimes been uncomfortable to sit inside the heads of some of my characters, and reflect the prevailing opinions of the time. This has been particularly true with this novel, when the attitude towards women, especially the poorest in society, was sexist at best and repugnant at worst. Whilst, as a writer, it's tempting to return to the past and retrospectively empower women, I wanted to create an accurate portrayal of their lives. That said, I've pushed the influence and the agency of my female characters as far as I've felt possible, given the historical setting. If they sometimes feel too compliant or accepting, then I'm afraid that this is a sign of those times. As Ian Mortimer tells us in his excellent book *The Time Travellers Guide to Medieval England*, 'From birth until widowhood they [women] are living under the control – nominally, at least – of someone else, in most cases a man.'

Acknowledgments

My first thanks, as ever, go to my wonderful editor Nick Sayers and my agent Gordon Wise – for their guidance, feedback, support and friendship. Thank you also to Claiborne Hancock and Jessica Case at Pegasus Books in the US, and to my US agent Deborah Schneider. I am very grateful to work with such a great team! It's been a strange and lonely year in lockdown, so I want to thank my friends – both inside and outside the writing world – for helping me to keep sane during the last twelve months. Being at the end of a telephone line, zoom call or meeting for a socially-distanced walk, has been such an important link back to normality. Thanks as well to my sister Kathy and my Mum for all their encouragement, understanding and patience – particularly when I've been holed away writing, editing or researching for weeks. Lastly, I wanted to express my gratitude to my husband Paul, and adult children Natalie and Adam. Thank you for listening, reading and caring about my books. I am blessed to have your love and support.